JAX

New York Times Bestselling Author

CRISTIN HARBER

CHAPTER ONE

S LAP.

Jax's cheek stung as the eighties rock band hit a power chord and the dance floor went wild. Wedding guests danced, guys lifted their beer bottles as they sang along, and kids screamed through the melee with blinking neon lights. He would've put his hand to his face to calm the sting from the open-palmed hand-slap rejection, but no way would he give Seven that level of satisfaction.

"What?" Seven let her delicious pink lips tip into the slightest hint of a smile. "You've never been rejected before, big boy?"

Maybe he'd had a few too many wedding-reception-themed shots, but that she didn't give him her full smile... He shook his head and considered it a challenge to earn her full, sexy grin. "Was that a no?"

"Most people would think so."

He raised an eyebrow. "Too bad. I thought it was the start of foreplay."

"Not a chance." The tip of Seven's tongue darted out and licked her bottom lip, taunting him with her tongue stud. "I didn't think I had to spell it out."

His deep laugh rumbled as his hand ran behind the dress shirt's loosened collar. "And why's that?"

"You're the type to have been slapped a time or two."

"Never once."

"Really?" An eyebrow with two tiny pink jewels on the end of an unseen barbell piercing lifted. "I call BS."

"Cross my heart." He made a cross as she rolled her eyes.

They would be the oddest pairing in the history of wedding reception hookups—except this one was going nowhere… unless she left with him.

"Never slapped *until me*."

"Until you, sweetheart." And wasn't that the hottest thing that a woman had ever done? Said no with style. Seven was unforgettable in every way he could tell.

For the past two years, they had shared more than a few dirty looks, and for the past two hours, they'd shared liquor, shaken and stirred, poured into shot glasses, and announced with ridiculous names like *Devotion Potion*, *About Thyme*, and *Something Blue*.

Each shot was as brightly colored as Seven. The bold colors were needed, she explained, to combat dark and grumpy people *like him*. Twice, she'd called him a jerkface, and with every jab, he wanted to take her back to his hotel room even more.

When she'd slapped him, it had taken every ounce of restraint not to kiss her until her mind changed. Consent was a thing, and he got it loud and clear, but God, Seven made his chest tight when she got feisty. He was certain her "no" was concrete, but hell if he didn't want to know what lay under her maid-of-honor dress.

Jared Westin slapped Jax on the back. "Am I interrupting?"

Jax grumbled, and Seven snickered her hello. And *poof*—the locked-eye standoff between him and Seven disappeared like forgotten bad dance moves on a wedding reception night gone long.

"Hey, Boss Man." Jax checked his annoyance and decided it was better that Jared thought he was on his best behavior rather than irritating the wedding party. "Just catching up."

"My lady friends deck me, too, *when we catch up*."

Jax's official title could have been Titan Jackass for all the aggravations he'd caused, though most times it was justified. Including now. "No punches were thrown."

Jared tipped back his beer and took a long draw, lifting it away to greet someone a few tables over then turned back to Seven. "Miscategorization. Was it a slap, then? I just saw…" He lifted his arm and swung it out. "The follow-through after impact."

Jax chortled. "Drama llamas."

"Do llamas drink beer?" Boss Man joked.

Jax kept laughing. "Have you been asking your kids for your lines lately?"

"It was a slap." Her coy smile served only to reignite Jax's hope that a "no" today might be a "try again" sometime soon. "As evident by the handprint on that handsome cheek and my deep satisfaction."

"Handsome, huh?" Jared repeated, stroking the beard he'd been growing. "Eye of the beholder."

Jax rolled his eyes. "Some could say the same about—"

"Remember who signs the paychecks."

"Handsome or not"—Seven elbowed Jax's side—"he deserved it."

She lingered, warm and playful, and Jax took a tight breath as Boss Man eyed their dynamic. He'd already been slapped, so what did Jax have to lose? He tossed an arm over her bare shoulder and sensed Seven freeze. His skimming fingers caressed her soft skin as goose bumps prickled. He couldn't wait to try again sometime soon and gave her arm a light squeeze. "You left no handprint, beautiful. No evidence."

"How do you know? You can't see your cheek." She leaned closer, long eyelashes upturned, and the friction of their clothes made a soft swish in the raucous room.

A choked laugh caught in Jared's throat, and amused, he tipped his bottle toward Jax. "But there *was* a witness." Then he took another swig and tipped his head toward Seven. "If you need a guy, I hold up well under cross-examination."

"Good to know," she joked.

Jax fought the urge to fold Seven tighter to his side and mold her to his hip. Her laughter ran the length of her body, staying with him after she stopped.

"On that note..." Seven blew Jax a kiss while her fingernails scraped across the back of his silk shirt, hidden by his suit jacket she'd nuzzled into. Only a few inches separated her lips and his cheek, close enough that he could feel the shadow of heat on his skin. "I have to run. I'll see you if you come back to Iowa sometime."

He dropped his chin and whispered, "Mixed signals, babe."

"Good night, Jared." She extracted herself from Jax's side and turned on the sky-high heel that had first left Jax dazed in church. He'd said a prayer of thanks when he saw her walking down the aisle because she had no idea how much he'd needed to see her, those shoes, and that dress—but mostly her. Now Seven waltzed away as though she knew he couldn't stop staring.

"Don't look so surprised." Jared shook his head, cracking his knuckles against the side of the longneck. "She knows you."

She knows you... For as little as she did, Seven may have known him better than Titan.

A dark cloud coiled in his chest. Accusations of an often-recurring attitude problem echoed in his ears. Gone was the high of toying with Seven, the closeness of touching her, and the adrenaline burst from making her react.

"And your night is about to get worse," Jared warned as Jax caught Sugar, Jared's wife, making a beeline for them.

"I gotta roll also." If he thought some of his teammates were a pain in the ass, this woman had it in for him. He didn't need a liquor-fueled confrontation tonight. "But I'll have my phone on if anything unexpected pops up—"

"Too late." Jared laughed into his beer as Sugar's long stride made record time. "Should've just split."

"*Jax.*" She coolly pursed her red lips together.

And have Jared chew his ass for that? Nope. "Looking nice tonight, Sugar."

The dark-haired, leather-clad façade faded long enough for the ice queen to smile for her compliment. Then Sugar's suspicious, smoky eyes narrowed. "There are more than enough biker bunnies here."

Sugar's social assessment of his behavior was Jax's cue to take cover, and he stepped away, giving no shits how obvious the duck-and-cover was. "There are. Good night."

She stepped forward, on the offensive. "Who would gladly say yes to whatever you offered Seven."

"*Two* witnesses, then." Jared rumbled with sarcasm. "I'll make sure Seven knows."

"Generous of you." With a quick wave, Jax ducked away and kept walking through the eclectic groupings of people.

The straitlaced mixed with the straightedge. All of Sweet Hills' community leaders mingled with 4-H Council leaders, who wore their best overalls and mud-scraped work boots. Then there were Titan Group and Mayhem MC, an odd combination of Ryder and Victoria's social circles, filled with former military, CIA spooks, and gang members of the motorcycle club variety.

Very few occasions—births, weddings, and funerals—could bring this assortment together without needing to call the police. Even the sheriff was on the dance floor, ignoring the outstanding warrants Jax assumed Mayhem had. The motorcycle club had to have a few with their guns and drug runners. Having worked a Titan op a couple years back and turning on national news regularly, Jax didn't believe the club's legitimate business ventures were anything more than a BS front.

He moved to the bar, and the bartender held up a shot glass that Jax regrettably recognized as *Something Blue*. "Never mind." He waved it away. "Water instead."

"No problem."

Jax threw down a tip for the open bar and glanced at the paper embossed with *Victoria and Ryder*. There would be so much hell to give Ryder about this Pinterest explosion. Then Jax cringed that he knew what Pinterest was. He blamed his teammates and the pregnancies over the years.

"Anything else, buddy?" the bartender asked.

"No." Jax held out his water bottle. "Cheers to the day we stop pointing out the obvious. Pretty damn sure I know whose wedding this is."

The obvious surrounded him as the bartender moved on, and Jax *obviously* shouldn't have hit on Seven. Yet, the way she'd slid her arm under his suit coat said she *obviously* didn't mind their flirtations too much. Jax smiled around the top of his water bottle before taking another sip. After she'd slapped him, when they had been close enough to taste and tease, her breath startled for a second, surprised, as though maybe she couldn't believe she'd done that.

Tension had to erupt somehow... and, inhaling slowly, Jax wanted that panting breath next to his ear next time, with her thighs wrapped around—

"Need anything else?" the bartender asked again.

"No." He needed to bail and gulped his water, tugging at the already unbuttoned collar of his shirt. "Thanks, man."

The bartender's good night met his back as he left without so much as a goodbye to his teammates and walked out of the Sweet Hills Community Center.

Farm trucks mixed with minivans and rental cars in the parking lot, and at the front were two rows of Mayhem Harleys, the club's insignia on full display. But more interestingly, Seven was at the end of a row. Her hands were on her hips, and her brightly colored hair matched the *angry* expression on her face. She was pissed, which seemed par for the course. At least he wasn't the only guy there getting a dose of Seven's bitching as she stood behind an MC member leaned over a car.

So a drug deal was going down. *Classy.* At least Seven was pissed about that.

"Should've left with me and screwed." He rolled his eyes at the questionable, illegal activities, turning the other way, not needing to see whatever they were getting into, and wandered until the sidewalk ended.

Behind him, a motorcycle started and revved, and Jax didn't look to see if Seven was on the back of the Harley, going home with a biker. "Have fun."

But he turned as the car Seven and the biker had been leaning against rolled toward the parking lot exit. The driver's window was still down, and Jax froze. The car slowed; the driver's eyes caught his. It'd been years since they had seen one another, and violence long held at bay boiled under his skin.

Jax snarled. He couldn't process words. Hatred couldn't form the vileness needed to justify a breath wasted on the driver.

The car continued its slow drive away, crunching the gravel in the lot until it sped off, and Jax couldn't tear himself away from what—or who— he had just seen.

Deacon Lanes—a ghost from his past, the source of his misery, and a string puller at the CIA.

Why had Seven been talking to the man who had killed Jax's wife?

CHAPTER TWO

THE FAMILIAR ROAR and vibrations of Johnny's Harley should've been comforting as Seven held on to her ex-husband as they flew down the highway. The hog had been a part of their marriage, even their friendship, for as long as she could remember. Seven knew how the motor growled down the asphalt because she had watched him build it by hand, piece by piece, from stripped parts.

The custom front springer and chrome grips to the throwback fenders made the Harley uniquely Johnny—classic but rugged, just like its owner. Sliding on to Johnny's Harley was like slipping on a pair of her favorite jeans.

They slowed as they exited, and Johnny turned his head. "Relax, babe."

"Sorry." She was stiff as a brick on the back of his bike, but then her hiked bridesmaid dress flew from where she had pinned it under her thighs.

As the dress flapped in the wind, she breathed deeply, hoping some of the oxygen would work its way to her angry muscles. She let her mind wander back to Victoria's wedding—to Jax Michaelson. The brooding anti-biker could moonlight as the poster boy for Italian sex gods. Seven blamed his dark hair and matching eyes more than his muscles. At least she was more curious about running her fingers through his hair than along the curves of his cut arms and chest.

Johnny turned his head. "There ya go, babe."

"What?" she yelled, ripping her mind from the absurd fantasy of touching Jax's hair.

"Loosening up, finally."

Ugh. Apparently, thoughts of Jax helped her relax—when he wasn't working her up with obnoxiously rude comments.

She balanced her high heels on the foot pegs as her hair whipped loose from the skullcap. Johnny slowed, leaning onto a side street as she stayed straight. Two turns later, they pulled into the church parking lot where she'd left her car after carting Victoria from the hair salon, in her dress, with makeup and hair done, ready to marry the love of her life, Ryder.

When Seven and Johnny had gotten married, they'd done it at the courthouse, same place they'd gone to drop off their divorce paperwork. There had been no hairdos and no special makeup. Seven couldn't remember what she'd worn to either event but could bet that Johnny had been dressed in his uniform of jeans, a Mayhem MC tee, and his leather cut that proudly displayed his member patch. At the time, she'd thought he looked fine—hot, even. Leathers had worked her up at the time. How times changed.

Johnny killed the motor, and Seven slipped off. She unfastened the skullcap and gave it back to him, not bothering to check out what he was wearing and not caring if he looked good. She leaned over to fluff her hair then stormed as best she could in her high heels toward her car.

"What? No 'thank you'?" Johnny called.

Seven spun, making effective use of the flare at the bottom of her skirt, and evil-eyed him like only she could. They had never had a falling out. They'd never been the couple with big blowup fights who threw bottles at one another or the crazy couple who hollered until the cops showed up. They hadn't made asses of themselves at the MC compound.

They'd simply known they shouldn't be married, so they'd stopped. It was that simple. The elevator didn't go any farther, and they had gotten off the relationship ride. Johnny had kept the apartment, and together, they'd shocked the Mayhem world when she moved into a house and he helped move the boxes of her belongings.

But at the moment, Seven wanted to fight. "I have to go get the kids."

"Fine. I don't want to hear about it later, though."

Unable to wait until she got home, Seven folded the skirt as best she could to calm down, but it didn't look right or stay still, which made everything worse.

"Did you hear me?"

She scrunched the fabric then smoothed it out violently. "I don't want to throw down in God's parking lot. But you *will* hear about it later."

Johnny tossed his leg over the back of his bike, and his boots crunched with every step as he came forward. "Don't even tell me you're mad."

Mad? "You think?" She beelined for her car door, repeating a mantra: "A fight at God's house was seven years bad karma." *Why seven? Why not?* Her name and all... Man, she was pissed and gritted her teeth. With a quick unlock, she pulled the door open.

"Seven," Johnny snapped. "What does your sweet ass have to be mad about? *Nothing.*"

She glanced up at the church steeple. "Sorry, Big Guy." Then she slammed the door shut and spun, her finger up and wagging. "Don't you dare play dumb with me, Jonathan Andrew Miller."

Johnny rolled his eyes. "You're mad about the drugs."

"Am I mad about the drugs? *Of course* I'm mad about the godd*mmm* drugs." She cringed, not wanting to drop the big GD when she'd just told the Big Guy she was sorry.

He shook his head and turned away. "Surprise, surprise."

"Yeah, I'm ten kinds of mad, and you acting like it's some surprising revelation makes me angrier."

"You only care about Bianca and Nolan."

"That's my job in life," she spit back.

"This is why we never had kids. I knew you'd go nuts."

She pleated her skirt between her fingers. This wasn't the time and place to strangle her ex-husband. "Give me strength."

"What are you mumbling?" he asked.

Seven smoothed her skirt of nonexistent wrinkles. "Have you seen me do blow?"

He couldn't say yes because she'd never snorted coke. Drugs weren't her thing. Piercings and hair dye, those could give Seven a high. But not dope.

"Okay, Mother Teresa." Johnny threw his arm out, waving her away.

She stomped over in high heels that threatened to break her ankles. "You don't get to bring up *my kids* and not answer. They saw their mother foam at the mouth, twitch on the floor, vomit—"

"They were too damn young to remember, and you know it."

"Neither one of us will ever know what it's like to watch a mom OD with a pops too stoned to notice. That's trauma, you asshole. No matter how young they were."

His eyes searched the parking lot. "You're wrong, Seven."

She knew the guilt was there. It was for all of them, and everyone had been aware of the risks long before one of their own had OD'd. Bianca and Nolan's dad would be in jail for a long time, and somehow, Seven had ended up with the babies. She'd always raise them as though they were her own. But even before they'd come in to her life, the drug game was all kinds of screwed up when it came to Mayhem.

"Are you a cokehead again?" she asked quietly. "Because I can help."

Johnny's face hardened. "Lay off the pious routine because we're at a church."

She shifted her frustration to the man from earlier. The one in the parking lot who she faulted for everything. Seven didn't know who he was or what he did, but he was a problem. "Back at the reception. Any time I see that man, it's like I'm not supposed to know."

Johnny chuckled as if that was the understatement of the night. "No kidding."

"Why can't I know who he is?" she pressed.

"No one does." He crossed his arms. "You're not supposed to know club business. It's that simple."

"I'm not *no one*." Her voice quieted to a whisper. "Who is he?"

Johnny wouldn't raise his eyes to meet hers, all but confirming what she'd heard a few years ago. There was a mole in Mayhem. What charter did he belong to? Why did he come to their founding charter so often? "Whenever he shows up, things get bad."

Johnny cackled. "Bullshit. They get better."

They had two very different definitions of getting better. "Money does not equate better."

"Equate," he mocked. "I don't know what you're smoking, Seven, but it sure as fuck does."

"You're going to end up just like my father." Disappointment made the night that much colder. "I'm going to go get the kids."

"Just because you're some Mayhem Princess doesn't mean you have a say or a vote," Johnny muttered.

It was her turn to cackle and smirk. "You're not the president, Johnny. The vote's done. Drug days are coming to an end whether you like it or not. It's not the eighties and nineties anymore. Synthetics are made by teenagers in chemistry class. Your profits are cut short, and cartels aren't as powerful as they were. And you know what? I'm good with that, and I don't care what that no-name, bad-news-bearing—"

"*Moneymaker* who can change the hearts and minds—"

"Yeah. Him. I don't care what he brings to the table or says," Seven said, finishing what she'd started. "It was a *vote*. You can't overrule it."

His smile was entirely too slick. "Not yet."

"If you want to be alive to take the gavel…" Seven pushed the tongue stud out of her mouth and toyed with it, wondering how much she should say. "If you're going behind Hawke's back like that, especially open in a parking lot, you won't hold that gavel. You won't stay alive. And I say that as a friend."

Johnny pulled on the skullcap that he had let her wear, letting the straps dangle. "Calm your tits and get your kids, woman. I'll do what's best for the club, and you do what's best for you."

CHAPTER THREE

PILLOWS LINED THE edge of the bed, and every morning, Seven was fooling herself if she thought there was any way that she would get to hear the news amid the tickles and the giggles. It had become their morning tradition. The kids would come in, and they would start their day with smiles and laughter. Those few moments were perfectly summarized by the Life is Good bumper stickers that she collected every time she passed a store.

"Eek!" Seven squealed as Bianca tickled her neck, trying to get to her armpit. "Ow!" She giggled and caught her breath from the tummy dive Nolan had taken. "You two are killing me."

The rumble of the garage door opening stopped Seven as she flipped Nolan over and tickled Bianca. Only one person would dare come over unannounced and use the garage to gain entry except Victoria, and she had left for her honeymoon last night.

"Johnny," Seven yelled. "Why are you awake this early?"

Or maybe he hadn't gone to sleep yet. Seven would kick his ass if he had ridden to her house intoxicated.

Nolan clapped his hands and yelled for Johnny also, scurrying off the bed as Bianca followed in her more reserved way. *So much for getting any news this morning.* Seven grabbed the remote to turn off the TV and heard both kids traipsing down the hall—then they stopped abruptly. A quick worry ran through her. Muffled voices and the sound of the kids running back made Seven sit up. "Johnny?"

"No." The familiar voice matched equally familiar boot steps. "It's Johnny and—"

"Hawke?" Seven swallowed the ball of panic in her throat, wondering why Mayhem's club president was in her house. Had she gone too far with Johnny last night when she had warned him not to go behind Hawke's back? But then Hawke wouldn't be the one to have that discussion.

Bianca and Nolan scurried onto her bed as Johnny and Hawke stood at the mouth of her bedroom, neither with their best attempts at smiles.

Hawke kept his eyes on the ground. "You decent, Seven?"

She eyed the dynamic between the two men. "'Course I am."

"Hi." Her little boy waved to Hawke from a stack of pillows.

He waved back. "Hey, little man."

Nolan liked having men in the house, but Bianca could tell that something wasn't quite right.

"You kids want to go watch TV with me?" Johnny backed toward the hallway.

Her stomach jumped because Johnny was separating her from the kids, but Nolan cheered, leaping from the bed to grab onto Johnny's leg and begging her ex to walk down the hall with the boy riding on his foot. Johnny didn't play well and pried him off, though Nolan still laughed.

Bianca didn't move, and Seven worried the girl had instincts far beyond her years.

"Go on, honey," Seven urged. "Johnny can get you cereal if you want."

Johnny walked back in and held out a hand to help her off the bed, but Bianca did it herself. She fell into line without help. Whether she wanted to or not, Bianca understood that her little feet were supposed to start moving so the grown-ups could talk.

When Bianca was out of the room, Seven looked up at Hawke. "Is everything okay?"

"What do you think?"

Obviously not. It was a quarter past six in the morning, and neither one of those men had likely seen this time of day on purpose for quite some time.

Hawke's light-brown hair bordered on blond, and his beard had been salt-and-pepper-colored for as long as Seven could remember. Hawke was tan and weathered, gruff and to the point. He furrowed his brow, which upped Seven's anxiety, and all she wanted to do was get up and fold laundry—or anything. But that was her OCD tendencies trying to control her behavior. She needed to focus on why Hawke was there and not on her urges to crease, fold, and straighten the chaos out of her life. "You could have called."

He worked his jaw side to side. "Didn't want to."

Which could mean a hundred things. Most likely, it meant he didn't want a record of this conversation.

"Look, I was busting Johnny's balls yesterday." Seven threw her legs over the edge of the bed, smoothing her pajama bottoms. "You know I mean what I say. But I didn't intend any disrespect. Not to you, not to the club." Because Hawke had many years ahead of him as the club president, most likely. No one could predict the future. Nobody could predict accidents, fights, drama, or politics. But he had a solid grip on the founding charter, overseeing the role of all charters.

But his face twisted enough that she knew that wasn't the point of his visit. "I'm not here to get in the middle of your bullshit spats with your old man."

Now didn't seem like the appropriate time to remind Hawke that they weren't together. The not-his-old-lady talk could wait for another day, preferably when she wasn't in her pajamas. "What can I help you with?"

He ran his hand down his beard, stroking it. "The club's getting out of the game."

"I know." She also knew that Johnny was talking to people about how to avoid that. So would it really happen? She wasn't sure.

"Changing distribution isn't a black-and-white decision."

Maybe Hawke knew what Johnny was up to. "Okay."

"Our business partners and friends can't be left hanging. We have to keep our alliances happy."

Friends... Seven hated having a nice word applied to the corrupt DEA and ATF agents as well as the underhanded cops that networked from the waterways and borders across the highways. She had no idea how such a spiderweb of complicity was woven. Mayhem didn't have the organization to oversee payment structures or the connections to work the international agents on border countries.

Friends... But if Hawke didn't figure out how to get *everyone* happy—meaning whoever took over the distribution and therefore Mayhem's network—then the war wouldn't just come from the cartel and the gangs, but also law enforcement who expected paydays and would worry that they'd been cut off.

"You're not telling me anything I'm not aware of." Respectfully, she bit her lip instead of asking him to get to the part about why was he there. "But I don't know anything that might help you." Her skin went cold at the possibility of the visit. "I'm not going to go see my dad."

Her dad would tell her anything Hawke wanted to know. Cullen Blackburn couldn't say no to her, and he'd never had his mind away from the MC entirely, even behind bars.

"No. Not why I'm here."

Relief came quickly. Anything else would be a cakewalk. "Okay, then?"

Hawke paced at the bottom of her bed, and Seven ran her finger along the slim barbell piercing at the bottom of her eyebrow instead of jumping out of bed and folding the blankets over and over until he explained what the MC wanted from her. No need to tip her hand this conversation made her nervous.

He leaned back on her dresser. "Lots of talk how Suarez's folks are less than thrilled with the club vote."

That wasn't news. Mayhem's dissenting votes were pissed and wanted to know how the club would continue to line their fat pockets. *Greedy jerks.*

Maybe the Suarez cartel handled paying off the cops, ATF, and DEA agents that helped Mayhem with distribution, or... *Maybe* she should stop thinking about it. She'd made it twenty-four years of living the Mayhem life without knowing the who and how. If there was a guiding guardian angel who oversaw all cartel-related activities, Seven didn't want to know because she wanted to make it to her twenty-fifth birthday.

Hawke tilted his head. "Seven?"

"I don't know what you're getting at." She smoothed the edges of the sheets, pushing out and up, as his gaze bore down.

"We need another friend. Someone to force a conversation with leaders. Not foot soldiers."

Her fingers splayed on the bedspread. "I can't help you. I know a lot of people. Suarez cartel members? Friends? They're not in my contact list."

"Someone neutral."

"Unless you want Sidney, second-key at The Perky Cup, I'm still useless." Which she hated being. "I'm sorry."

"Victoria knows someone *I* need to know." The intense focus seemed as though he were trying to telepathically pass along his secret, silent plan.

"Oh." Seven reached for her cell phone. "You know she left for her honeymoon. Like, hours ago. But chances are, I know anyone she does." Swiping her screen open, she looked up. "Who am I looking for?"

"Her husband works for a private contracting firm. I believe they have the ability to step in and help negotiate."

"Titan Group?" Seven bit her lip, not wanting to speak out of turn.

Hawke took a step closer. "And judging from their wedding reception last night, you know a few of these guys too."

Her cheeks went hot as she remembered slapping Jax, in public, and storming off. "I have a couple contacts."

"Make a meeting. Feel out the situation."

If her eyes weren't attached to her skull, they might've popped out. "You want me to ask *Titan* to help you *negotiate* drug distribution? With a cartel?" Seven blinked, dumbfounded. "I don't know that that is what they do." She closed her hanging jaw. "I think they do *legal* work. Save people and stuff."

"Actually, I've asked around. I think they do work that needs being done. Simple."

Seven shook her head, not wanting Ryder and any of Titan to know Mayhem's dirty little secrets more than they did. She had spent time with several of the guys years ago and then became friends with a few of them off and on through Victoria and Ryder.

Though her biggest concern wasn't Ryder. It was Jax. The guy was a decent guy except when he was a first-rate prick. When that was the case, he was nothing but a cocky bastard with a bad attitude. All his charm had evaporated in a hot, arrogant Italian second.

Her teeth grated even as her pulse fluttered. The nerve of him, asking what else might be pierced.

Seven drew in a deep breath, hating the way heat crawled up her neck when she recalled how Jax took the tall, dark, and handsome cliché to another level by brooding like a military badass who needed a fucking hug. Someone needed to tell Jax to take his persona down a notch or two. "I'm not that friendly with Titan."

Hawke cast a doubtful glance. Another freaking witness, as Jared would have called it.

"I'd wait for Victoria. She'd be stoked to help."

"Don't wanna wait, Seven."

"If she green-lights this with her thumbs-up, the likelihood of their help will go through the roof."

"Do you really think I'd be up at the ass crack of dawn, coming into your house unannounced, if this wasn't time sensitive as shit?"

Well… "No."

"Get ahold of someone you trust at Titan. Set up a meeting. Make it happen." Hawke didn't wait for her to respond as he walked out but paused at the doorjamb. "If not for you, do it for those kids playing with your old man."

Seven held on to her eye roll with every ounce of respect she could muster. "I'm not his old lady."

Hawke shrugged. "Hard to let an institution die. Johnny might even have been a good pops if he could keep his nose out of the powder bag."

She toyed with her tongue stud. Johnny wasn't snorting coke anymore. She was *almost* positive. "Only if his old lady gave birth to chrome and leather."

A real laugh and smile cracked Hawke's sun-worn face, and he rubbed his chest, letting grease-stained fingers trace the president patch on his leather cut. "I'll be waiting for your call, sweetheart. Don't let the club down."

CHAPTER FOUR

J AX SLAPPED HIS hand on the unfamiliar nightstand, knocking over a bottle of water but not finding his buzzing cell phone where he expected it. He rolled over, rubbing his eyes, and looked around the unfamiliar room.

Iowa, of all places, in an unfamiliar bed, and a wedding was to blame. Weddings were the worst social occasions that he could be forced to attend. Boss Man had given him two options: Show up or plan your funeral. Both needed a suit. Neither would be fun. This one had the benefit of getting laid. But that hadn't happened. "Your own damn fault."

Not much of a difference from a funeral then… Grumbling, Jax buried his head back in the pillow. His phone buzzed again with the text message notification. "Really?"

If they had a job this early after someone from Titan had gotten hitched, they needed hazard pay. Surely, he wasn't the only one who wanted to sleep in. Jax glared at the empty pillow next to him, where a headful of pink hair should've been asleep, and rolled back to grab his phone on the other side of the lamp.

SEVEN: *Are you still in town?*

He closed one eye and read it again, as if that would make the text make any more sense. Was he still in town? Where the hell did she think he went? Jax pinched the bridge of his nose and tossed the phone onto the bed, ignoring her. If she wanted to know, she should have just stayed and found out.

With the pillow to block the sunlight peeking around the drawn shade, Jax burrowed back into bed, pulling the cover over his head.

What was worse? Weddings or churches? The dresses or the—

No, he wasn't going to do this today. Punching the pillow to fluff it, his mind drifted to Seven on the back of the bike. Too bad she hadn't spent the night. If her tongue and her eyebrow were pierced, what else was—

Jax sat up, the pillow falling into his lap. He wasn't going to fantasize about the girl. She was a friend... or something. Either way, they could fuck or they could not. But he wasn't going to let his imagination roam.

Were her nipples pierced?

"Damn it." He rolled his shoulders back, trying to let the thought go, and knowing sleep was a lost cause. Jax reached back over and snagged the phone, swiping the screen open again and staring at her message. "This is all your fault."

JAX: *It's before 8 AM. What the hell do you think?*

SEVEN: *Early flight? I have no idea. Also, chill, Mr. Grumpy Pants.*

JAX: *I was sleeping. Until you texted.*

SEVEN: *Well, now that you're awake, get up and meet me at The Perky Cup.*

His head banged with the dull echo of too many old memories and maybe a few too many drinks. It wasn't quite a hangover because he was too stubborn to admit he ever got one of those. But he didn't feel like getting out of bed.

JAX: *No*

SEVEN: *No one ever taught you manners?*

This coming from a girl who slapped him and hung out with a biker gang?

SEVEN: *Guess not.*

JAX: *It's rude to call out someone's manners.*

SEVEN: *Are you going to meet me at The Perky Cup?*

JAX: *No*

She didn't respond. What the hell did she want to talk about? Apologize for the slap? They'd moved past that when she had wrapped her arm under his suit coat. Talk about their feelings? Not her style, either. Why wasn't she responding? Oh… That was on him, being rude for calling her rude. He grumbled and rewrote his message to make up for his faux pas, rolling his eyes even as he hit Send.

JAX: *No *thank you**

SEVEN: *haha*

JAX: *Now can I go back to sleep?*

SEVEN: *Sure. But one more question?*

JAX: *What's up?*

SEVEN: *Are you a stubborn asshole (a) all the time, (b) some of the time, or (c) most of the time?*

He chuckled. Not all the time, but he kept that to himself.

JAX: *(d) none of the above. I'm sunshine and gumdrops. Haven't you noticed?*

JAX: *And if you're dying to apologize for slapping me, a text message will do.*

SEVEN: *That will never happen, Buster.*

Amused, he tucked the pillow behind him, rereading her text.

JAX: *Who says Buster?*

SEVEN: *Who doesn't know when to say YES? Get your ass to The Perky Cup, *Buster*.*

"You, last night, apparently." But that text he decided not to write.

JAX: *Fine. When?*

SEVEN: *Now would be preferable, but I will give you a few to *politely* say goodbye to whoever your company is. Manners, Jax. They are very important. Be polite.*

SEVEN: *Say things like 'that was fun.' 'You're pretty.' Don't bark or bite her. (Unless she asks…)*

He snort-laughed and could picture her deviously texting him about someone in his bed. Too bad he couldn't picture if Seven had her nips pierced.

JAX: *Jealous?*

SEVEN: *Imagine the biggest eye roll I've ever given you. Now double it.*

He laughed again and lumbered himself out of bed.

JAX: *I'm alone, but I'll see you soon.*

And damned if she didn't make him grin despite how his head pounded.

CHAPTER FIVE

MAIN STREET IN Sweet Hills, Iowa, was like what Jax imagined of an Americana painting come to life. It defined what he had sworn his life to protect the day he joined the Navy and became a SEAL, though it'd been years since he'd felt more than a deadly machine. There'd been a time when small towns and small-business storefronts could stir him, and he could see why Sweet Hills lured his Delta teammate Ryder to call it home with his now-wife, Victoria.

He had seen The Perky Cup as he drove by the day before, and the eclectic storefront matched Seven's personality with a hard-to-miss sign and window decorations.

Jax opened the door, and it jangled with old country-store bells. Inside, the coffee shop was filled with lively decorations and signs, mismatched chairs and tables combined with clashing coffee cups, glasses, and absurd plates and bowls, partnering with seamless effort. He liked it.

Where was Seven sitting? He scanned the tables, and the Sunday crowd fit no set rule. A young couple with a baby sat in their Sunday best next to a guy who Jax was sure was a Mayhem gang member and his old lady. Tables were filled with every spectrum in between, but Jax didn't see Seven.

"Hey, you."

Jax pivoted, surprised to see her behind the counter. "I didn't expect you so fast."

He shoved his hands in his pockets. "You're working?"

Truth was, he had no idea what Seven did for a living. Why hadn't he asked that before? All he knew of her were smiles and attitude, and that had been enough for him. Maybe not enough for her, and that was why he'd gone home alone. But he would've pegged her as… well, hell.

If he'd never spoken to her before and just saw her across the room, Jax would have wagered that Seven would make a terrific art teacher. But knowing the full power of her sass and spark, he could see her as a litigator. Though she would have been fresh out of law school, and he wondered how many law firms in Iowa would hire a magenta-haired, obviously pierced new attorney. But seeing as her best friend was the deputy mayor and her affiliation with Mayhem would likely bring in many clients, maybe she would have been a hot commodity.

He was positive law school hadn't been her calling, especially as she slung a hand towel off her shoulder, mopped the counter, then meticulously folded the towel, avoiding eye contact. "The coffee and crumpets aren't going to make themselves."

Had he embarrassed her by questioning where she worked? *Damn it.* "This place reminds me of you." In addition to the décor, the coffee house smelled like sugar and caffeine. Both were intoxicating, like her—vibrant and exciting. He inspected the pastries and muffins behind the glass then turned back to her at the counter. Even the cash register was colorful.

"How do you like your coffee?" She finally met his gaze when she put her hands over the hand towel, pressing it to the counter, and, maybe nervously, awaited his walk back. "It's on the house."

Coffee normally would sound great, but the flare of the hangover he would never admit to made him hesitate. "How about…" What sounded good when he would rather be asleep? Jax ran a hand over his chin, thinking something cold and with sugar would help the small headache and lack of sleep.

"Or not," she said, studying him. "What's wrong with you?"

"Nothing." *That I plan on sharing, that is.*

"Oh, you feel like crap, don't you?" She turned from the counter toward a blender. "I have a hangover cure."

Jax pulled his poker face on. "I didn't say I have a hangover."

"Oh, you do, Jaxxy, my dear." Playfully, she spun. "I have a killer smoothie that'll cure what ails you, whatever *that* is." Seven paused, casting a quick glance over her shoulder. "But you have to trust me. The color of it alone will be enough to trigger your gag reflex."

"No, *thanks*."

Seven tossed an amused look over her shoulder, challenging him to say no again, but she did seem to pick up on his thanks. "You're most welcome. 'Cause I'm still making it."

Surrendering, he half grinned. "On one condition."

"Sure." But that didn't slow her down any as she scooped powders and poured liquids into the blender. "And what's that?"

"Never say Jaxxy again." He waggled his brows. "Deal?"

The corners of her eyes crinkled. "Deal, so long as you drink the whole thing."

He shook his head, eyeballing the green, goopy mess in the blender. "Really. I'm good."

"This is for me, Jaxxy. I don't want to hear you bitch and moan while I have to talk to you."

The corners of his lips quirked, denying his ability to negotiate. "Sounds selfish, princess."

"You bet your ass, when I have to be." She played with her tongue stud for a second, turned back around, and flipped on the blender. "Since you don't have a hangover, I'll just put this baby on high." She turned the blender on to a louder mode. "Did you say something, Jaxxy? I can't hear you."

Standing with an empty cup in her hand and a blender on high, Seven waited casually. He forced nonchalance as the blender ran out of things to crush and simply whirled and whined. Jax's head throbbed. Really, the girl knew how to torque the hell out of him. Standing there, hand on one hip, glass in the other, torturing him, she was hot as hell. Pinup girl material. Pouty lips and a come-at-me attitude.

"I'll drink the whole thing for you, babe."

Her tongue ran along the seam of her lips as her grin curled. A casual flip of the blender's switch afforded him quiet and sanity. Then Seven poured the concoction into the glass and made a quick cup of coffee. She walked to the end of the counter and called back, "Hey, Sidney? Can you cover the counter for me?"

A guy in an apron came from a side door with a pile of muffins. "Sure thing." He stopped abruptly when he saw Jax, as though it were impossible someone would walk in that he didn't know or expect could be there. "Hello. How are you?"

That question clearly, but silently, sounded like "who are you?" Jax wasn't about to answer when he wasn't sure why he stood there or enjoyed the back-and-forth about the blender. "Hey there, man. I'm fine. Thanks."

Seven popped in between their unspoken conversation. "Thanks, Sid."

"Anytime." But Sid kept a watch on Jax as Seven smoothed her hand over another hand towel, put a straw in the smoothie, and shoved it in Jax's hand. Sidney turned and watched her folding the towel. "You sure you're good?"

"As can be expected given my morning." She took her coffee and walked from behind the counter. "Let's go somewhere more private—start drinking."

"Yeah, sure." Hesitantly, Jax tried a sip of the green smoothie when she wasn't looking. "Hey, this is solid."

Sidney's level of enthusiasm at Jax's revelation was cautiously pleased. "She's a master behind the counter."

"Noted." Jax took another long drink as he followed her, and they passed by the kitchen that smelled like foodie heaven. He wasn't hungover enough that The Perky Cup's kitchen turned his stomach. Not that he was hungover at all…

Seven opened a door and led them into a small office. After he walked in, she shut the door behind them. The lights were low, with a desk lamp already on, and she didn't bother to flip on the overhead light switch.

"That guy Sidney seems protective over you." Jax took in the close quarters of the office. Maybe it was the low light or perhaps the smoothie after all, but being alone with her in the quiet, he felt more settled.

"Sidney knows everyone in town." She set down her coffee on the desk as Jax settled onto a couch.

Seven was younger than him yet seemed years more responsible than anyone who looked her age. "Maybe that's it."

"Maybe you come off as a grumbling jerkface at times. Ever think that over?" The light caught on the tiny pink jewels on her eyebrow, sparkling as she sipped her coffee.

"Part of my charm."

Her quiet laughter floated through the air still permeated by the scent of sugar, but her brow furrowed. "How old are you, Jax?"

"Why?"

"Because, when you sit back and relax, I'd say you're in your thirties, but when you scowl at the world, you don't have an age."

"I'm timeless."

"Ha." She took a much longer sip of her coffee. "No. I mean, you seem like you don't care if you die or not. So age doesn't matter."

"Maybe we're both right."

Seven moved to the office desk. "That's a little sad."

"Story of my life, babe." Jax raised his brows. "You manage this place or something?"

"Or something," she said. "I make a helluva cup of coffee. That's all you need to know."

"Everyone says that."

"But I really do. You should ask Ryder sometime."

Maybe he would ask his Delta teammate more about Seven, though Ryder would likely tell him to back away from her. "You know, I haven't won Titan's Miss Congeniality award." If there'd been an award given out, it would have been "Most Likely to be Called a Dick," and his acceptance speech would've been concise. *Deservedly so. Fuck you very much.*

"You don't need an award, silly. The Perky Cup gives out rocks." She tilted her head to a pile of rocks on the floor he hadn't noticed.

Jax chuckled. "Sounds like my kind of employee incentive."

Who knew Seven would work at a place where employees could throw rocks at each other?

She eased off her chair and grabbed one, tossing it in the air and catching it in the other hand. Close quarters for a game of Stone Jax, but his head already hurt—or it had. But Seven sat back down with her rock. No award for him.

What else had he missed in the office?

Unlike the rest of the coffee shop, the office didn't seem like a place Seven would work. A picture of a woman on the desk caught his attention. The same lady was depicted in a grainy, old photo on the wall, holding a dollar bill. What had to be the same dollar bill was framed below the picture. "Who's the lady? The owner?"

"Her name is Taini." Seven turned to the picture as if she hadn't noticed it before. "She's been having a challenging time the last few years after a stroke."

"Everyone knows everything in this town about each other." Jax stirred the smoothie with his straw. "What kind of name is Taini?"

"It has Native American origins." Seven's eyes narrowed as though he had missed an obvious piece of a puzzle. "What kind of name is Jax?"

"Probably the easiest thing my ma could think to shout when she heard she was having a boy. It stood out on a block of Dons and Johns."

"Your neighborhood was filled with porta-potty kids?"

Her humor made him grin. "Guess so. But that was back in the day. Who cares? This place makes me realize I don't know much about you."

She sucked her cheeks in thought. "I don't think you're always a jerk-face."

"Good to know, princess." He gave her a lingering once-over. "I don't think you're always... I'm coming up blank." Or at the very least, he was having a hard time thinking of an appropriate comparison.

It was too dim to see her blush, but she ducked her chin as though she were. After a second that strung between them for miles, Seven regained her unaffected composure. "I slapped you. I think you can come up with at least one thing."

The memory ran to his groin, and Jax rolled his bottom lip into his mouth, letting go with a slow breath. Her slap hadn't been just a no. It had been a hell no *with style*. She'd rejected his proposition, but he wasn't positive she was rejecting *him*.

"Sweetheart, I *liked* that."

Tension crackled in the few feet between them. The hairs on his skin stood as he waited to see what she would do next, what she would say, and how he would volley it back.

"Don't flirt with me right now," she whispered. "I need a favor." She eased back onto the desk as though she owned the place and crossed her legs.

"Isn't that the best time to flirt?"

Seven rolled her eyes, but she smiled like the devil sipping sweet tea.

"Careful, beautiful."

A thick wave of magenta hair fell over her cheek, obscuring half her face. "Careful or what?"

Her pink fucking hair was ridiculous but artistic, not too serious. She was like splashes of colors sprinkled with surprises—tongue stud, eyebrow jewels, and a name like Seven.

Jax had no idea what to do about that. "You want to have that conversation right now?" He set the smoothie on the ground. "Because if you want to try again, I'll dole out whatever consequences we agree to."

Seven's tiny, unexpected gasp made a shiver of anticipation roll through his muscles. Even if Jax hadn't been trained to pick up on microchanges in human behavior, he would've noticed how her breaths quickened despite her best effort to disguise the natural reaction. Jax wanted to feel her pulse, needed to know how far she would let him push her, how much she would trust him.

"I need"—she let her lids sink shut long enough for him to want her eyes back on him—"to talk to you about Mayhem."

Mayhem. That was like a cold waterfall thrown in his face.

Mayhem Motorcycle Club. *The MC.* He didn't know much about the locals, but he'd learned a decent bit a couple years ago when Victoria had gotten herself caught up in their headache. Plus, they made national news on occasion when members were caught without an alibi for drug trafficking or when a chapter was tangled in a weapons or racketeering investigation. "Should've known. Not my favorite people."

"*Trust me*, if I didn't need your help, we wouldn't be chatting now." Her grimace killed all dirty thoughts that had his blood running hot. "I can't believe I'm even doing this."

"Then don't."

"Thanks, Jax. You're making this so much easier." She crossed her arms and recrossed her legs before pushing away from the desk and moving to the couch. With her came the sweet scent of baked goods.

Jax watched her chew the inside of her cheek and toy with her tongue stud. "Look, this is the deal. Mayhem's club president—his name is Hawke—came to me early this morning. They have decided to get out of a business that is short on profit and long on consequences."

That wasn't anything he'd thought she was going to say. "Wait. What?"

Seven became very still. "Hawke asked me to reach out to Titan. They need a partner dealing with the Suarez Cartel."

Jax couldn't match the woman with the words. Listening to the name of a nefarious drug cartel pass over her lips made Jax feel as if he'd been pushed into the twilight zone. He needed more sleep—or another smoothie—to understand what she was saying.

The eyebrow with the pink jewels lifted accusingly. "*You* have nothing to say?"

"Not really." He blanked. "In what way does Mayhem need Titan?"

A few more seconds of Seven assessing him passed before she apparently decided that it was okay to continue.

"Mayhem has had a long-established relationship with the cartel, and without Hernán Suarez's permission for a peaceful transition, the repercussions are clear. All members of the MC—maybe their families and associates, depending on how pissed Suarez is—will be condemned to death. The cartel likely doesn't want it to end." Seven was casually dropping drug kingpin names and brutal real-life consequences.

Jax blinked, still dumbfounded. "Likely, no."

"Hawke thought Titan Group has the history or the ability to assist in… what might best be called a contract negotiation." Apparently, it was Seven's turn to look lost. "At least, that's what I was told. Who knew there could be such formalities to the process when everyone just wants to kill everyone else at the end, anyway?"

Which summed up Jax's dislike for gangs in general. Everyone would die at the end. "This is some heavy shit, Seven."

"That's why I said to meet me in person."

"Why bring this to me?"

Her gaze dropped. "Let's leave the whys of what Mayhem does out of it. Do you do what they're talking about? Contract negotiation with the scum of the earth?"

"Usually, we're negotiating at the behest of a government. But we do work between organizations that"—Jax extended his hand as if a non-offensive explanation might fall from his fingertips, but none arrived, and she waited in silence for him to continue—"could end up in a bloodbath."

"Right." Seven clearly seemed to understand the stakes.

Her poker face was solid, and that was worth remembering. Jax picked up his smoothie and stirred the concoction with the straw, deciding on the best explanation. The formality was unexpected, and Jax had to give credit where credit was due. Mayhem was trying to avoid chaos in the drug world. Anytime there was a significant shift in the way cartels did business, a bloody fallout followed. "Back to you. Why did Mayhem send you to have this conversation with me?"

"Because they trust Victoria. Victoria trusts Titan. Since she's not available and this is time sensitive…" Seven shrugged. "I'm her best friend, very close to them, and I obviously have a few of my own connections."

He thought back to last night and wondered who all from Mayhem had taken notice of them. "It can't wait, huh?"

She shrugged. "Sometimes I just do what I'm told."

He chuckled and took a long drink of the smoothie. "Call me doubt-ful."

Seriousness shadowed her gaze. "I want this to happen, Jax. For Mayhem to pull out of distribution and drugs, and I would think you'd tell me the truth."

Her sincerity sliced through the room like a razor. "I'll always tell you the truth. I promise."

"Can Titan be a neutral negotiator? Can you make it happen?" She paused. "*For me?*"

Flashbacks from the previous night, including seeing Deacon Lanes in the parking lot, were the only things that kept Jax from reassuring her they could. Deacon was a domestic chaos puppet master. He coordinated the permissions and power struggles between gang leaderships through their government-sanctioned distribution of narcotics. These were the types of deals that funded black ops all over the globe. "How deep are you still in with Mayhem?"

"Still?" Her back straightened. "You sound like you think you know."

Years ago, Jax had first met Seven when Victoria had been abducted. Seven was an intel source on all things Mayhem. But before they'd trusted her word, Titan's IT maverick, Parker Black, had done a background check. The file hadn't been shared with the whole team, but the gist had been.

Seven was the daughter of incarcerated Cullen Blackburn, notorious founder and first president of Mayhem. Sweet Hills authorities had confirmed that she was *friendly* with Mayhem but not *in* the MC life. That was all Jax knew.

"Tell me what I should know," he said.

Seven sighed. "Before my father left my mom, I thought he was the whole world. He let me wear his cut when no one would dare touch it. He had this tough-guy beard. Man, I thought he was so badass. And me?" She laughed sadly, shaking her head. "On the back of his bike, I thought I was coolest."

He didn't want to say much about the man who'd founded Mayhem, but Jax hated how distant she sounded. "Look, if you don't want to—"

She shook her head. Disappointment skewed the soft dreaminess that he expected to see when she told a story. "But I realized he had another lover, another family, and they were more important. They were his reason to wake and sleep. Hell, even to breathe."

Mayhem. "I'm sorry."

"My mom never had a chance and loved him so much." Seven flinched. "My dad banged a lot of pussy, and my mom either turned a blind eye or didn't care. Right or wrong, there was an expectation for what to put up with as an old lady. But it was the MC that finally broke her heart. He loved Mayhem more than us. Mom never totally let go, but she was eventually done."

Jax didn't know what to say, but he could almost relate to her mom's loss in the oddest of ways. The government had broken his heart, but still he served for the greater good, despite what they'd done to his life. Different, though somehow the same.

"When you ask how I'm wrapped up in Mayhem, you should know that I'm theirs," Seven whispered. "They can't get rid of me, and I don't want them to. I can't stand them, and they know that too. I'll forever be their twisted royalty. They call me their princess. They've fucked my life. It's a strange, complicated, fucked-up dichotomy. I struggle with that, and that's cool because that's how family is."

His worries about Deacon Lanes subsided. If anything, he'd learned more about Seven in the past ten minutes than he had in two years. He found that her strength and raw honesty added layers of respect to what he'd already had for her.

She pressed her lips together as stress lines etched across her forehead. "Will you help get Mayhem out of the drug game? Can you bring this to Jared?"

The answer would be an easy yes once he found out how Deacon might be involved. Jax had gone years without telling Jared about his past that a CIA sweep team erased from existence.

CHAPTER SIX

*I*T DEPENDS. BUT that was hard to say, and Jax wanted the truth. Could anyone who worked with Deacon do such a thing? Or should he assume Seven's every word was a lie?

She reached for her coffee, drank a long sip, then eased back onto the couch while he made a cognitive effort not to shatter his smoothie glass. She had no idea what she was asking of him.

"If the answer is no, a simple response works. No need to get growly." Disappointment tightened on her forehead. "It falls in line with *manners*, so I can see how you might be confused. Remember those things we were texting about?"

Jax cleared his throat. There was only one end to this conversation. He had to believe she would tell the truth. "How do you know Deacon Lanes?"

Her honest eyes showed no recollection, and he prayed his instincts were correct.

"Who's that?" she asked.

"He's the big black dude you were talking to in the parking lot last night." Jax focused on keeping his voice even. "Size of a linebacker. Shaved head. Goatee."

Recognition dawned, but the reaction wasn't a pleasant realization. "I didn't know that asswipe's name."

Relief edged into his thoughts. "Does he have anything to do with this?"

"Look, Jax." Seven shifted on the couch, suddenly looking uncomfortable. "You're asking me about club business, and I've been sent here as a messenger with a request."

"Deacon Lanes is a hard limit." Though that was for him, not Titan. Jax was speaking out of turn, which Jared would kick his ass for. "Who is he to you?"

Her face hardened, and it was the first time Jax had ever seen Seven go cold. "I think he's the breeder of bad decisions, but I don't know him. He's involved in Mayhem's business, so that's my personal opinion and nothing that should weigh in on your factor in bringing this to Titan Group."

Spoken like someone who knew the cost of consequences that she couldn't share. Jax had to decide the answer to only one question. Did he trust her? For some reason, *almost*. He trusted few, and that was a lesson taught in a way he couldn't forget. But he would bring the job opportunity back to Jared. "I'll get back to you."

"Thanks." They sat in silence until she picked up the rock again.

"I'm doing it." He tossed up his hands in faux defense. "Don't stone me."

"*You rock*, Jax." She tossed it carefully.

He caught it but hadn't seen the meaning coming. He hadn't been playing before. Yes, he had awards and accommodations for military service. But this was a different gesture, and it struck him as… heartfelt.

"How are you feeling?" she asked.

What a question. Deacon caused instant blood pressure problems, but then she tossed rocks wrapped in happiness.

"The smoothie?" Her gaze dropped to his empty drink. "Miraculous wonder recipe, guaranteed to cure what ails you."

"Right, the smoothie." As if life were that simple… though his headache *was* gone. Jax nodded curtly. "A lot better. Okay. I'll get going."

"Thanks, Jax. This means a lot to me."

"No big deal." Awkwardness hung between them after swinging between flirting and drug cartels. Jax thought about Deacon and his dead wife, and who knew what was on Seven's mind? He didn't know what he was supposed to do now. High-five her? Give her a hug? "Do you ever win the rock?"

She watched him toss it in the air and catch it. "Not really."

Jax reached across the desk and took her hand, wrapping her fingers around the rock in his palm. "You rock also. I'll call you after I talk to Boss Man."

With that, Jax let himself out. He drained the last of his smoothie as he passed the kitchen. Then he filed down the hallway and paused near the counter to drop his smoothie glass in the dirty-dish bin.

Sidney ambled over, quizzically sizing up Jax. "That hangover smoothie is a wonder drug, isn't it?"

Truthfully, he liked that Seven worked with protective people. It made for a good team, something he should remember more often. "You have a recipe that works. Tell the owner to patent that stuff. They'd make a killing."

With a twist of confusion, Sidney chuckled. "All right, bro."

Jax's brow furrowed. "What's that mean?"

"You just left her. But I'll let Seven know."

The Perky Cup was Seven's? She didn't get the awards because she gave them out. He looked around at all the responsibility and success surrounding him then back to Sidney. "Who's the lady in the picture?"

"Who?"

"In the office. The lady with the dollar bill and the other—"

"Oh, Taini?" Sidney nodded, connecting the dots that Jax didn't understand. "That's Seven's mom. You never heard that story?"

Jax shook his head.

"Taini's a sweetheart. She opened this place because she figured that she and Seven would always have a place to sleep and something to eat if things ever got too tough. I think Seven worked every job in Sweet Hills to buy her mom out. While dealing with Johnny. Like a retirement to save her."

"From what?"

"Working to death. Taini had a stroke about the same time Seven and Johnny were through."

"Oh, I thought her mom—"

"She's still kicking. Taini's badass. But she needs a lot of care, and that's on Seven."

Jax ran his hand into his hair. How much responsibility did this woman have? "Why are you telling me all this?"

"Because if that was a social call, you should know who you're dealing with."

"Who am I dealing with?"

Sidney folded his arms and studied Jax. "Someone I'm not sure you deserve."

"Why's that?"

"Because she's a sweet, pierced, hair-dyed *saint*."

Jax's brows arched. "Are you and her…"

Sidney shook his head. "Nah. I'm happily committed to the love of my life and his unending need to troll for news on Twitter."

"Sounds like a happy life."

Sidney motioned toward Seven's office. "Which is what she deserves. Did you want me to mention you liked the smoothie?" he asked, making his scrutiny of Jax's incoming answer clear.

"Nah. I'll tell her myself."

Things he'd learned about Seven—she was a business owner, Mayhem princess, and caretaker of her mother. Did she ever get a rest? And no wonder she'd slapped him. Maybe she wanted to actually sleep.

CHAPTER SEVEN

T HE PASTRY DOUGH was almost at the perfect consistency. Breathing in the sugar-scented air was as relaxing as kneading the giant bowl of scone mix for the batch of Main Street weekend snackers.

Normally, baking was Seven's favorite controllable self-care activity, unlike when she felt urges to fold blankets and linens a specific way. Some people did yoga. Seven contemplated piercings, strayed to a new hair color, and made pastries to relax. Oh, and coffee. She never stopped thinking about coffee. Whoever said that working on the same task for ten thousand hours would make a person an expert might have been right, but she also believed in such thing as status quo, and she didn't want to plateau. Complacency was boring.

"Seven," Sidney called from the front counter. "Phone call."

Her phone had rung a minute ago, but she was elbows deep in dough. One person had called in sick, and Seven and Sidney were slammed, prepping and preparing for the afternoon crowd to hit. "I'll call back. Can you take a message?"

"He said you're not answering your cell and it's important," Sidney called again.

Well, shit. Had that last call been Jax? Seven had set a special ring to alert her if he called, scone-dough hands or not. She rushed over to the wall phone, hands covered in batter, and went to grab the handset but decided to peck the speakerphone with her nose instead then turned to the sink. "Got it, Sidney."

The Perky Cup might have world-class coffee, but they still had a phone system straight out of the 1980s. No one used the landlines except for the vendors, and The Perky Cup's hold button was less than reliable.

"'Kay," Sidney said. "You are now on the phone with the goddess of blueberry scones. You can speak."

Seven froze halfway to the sink and waited for Jax's reaction. On any other call, that would've been funny. But Jax, in all his moody seriousness, likely didn't find it funny. Sidney clicked off, and Seven groaned, ready to apologize. "He didn't know—"

"Good thing you're talking to the god of we're going to do your job," a deeply masculine, non-Jax voice boomed through her kitchen.

Oh, fuck. She lunged for the phone's handset, doughy hands and all. "Well, this is all kinds of awkward."

His grumbly laughter met her ears. "Jared Westin. We've not spoken on the phone before."

"Nope." She resisted the urge to wipe her hands off. It wouldn't have done much good, and she would've still been stuck with buttery, doughy hands plus the shitty benefit of an apron that needed a heavy washing. "I generally keep my goddess-like qualities to myself the first time on the phone."

"Mm-hmm."

"And you probably don't work your god status into normal conversations. Maybe we should start over?" Seven had no idea how to handle a business call with Mr. Titan himself.

He laughed. "You'd be surprised how often I drop that reminder."

Actually, she could see that.

"Now," Jared continued, "you, personally, want Titan Group to do this job. Yes or no?"

He asked in a way that was more of an order than a question, and she almost wanted to snap to attention and salute him instead of saying yes. "Me, personally? Yes. I want Mayhem to stop."

"Mm-hmm. Okay."

"Can you do what people think you can?"

That time, his laughter wasn't grumbly; it was almost amused. Or maybe he found the question comical. "More than that, Seven."

She'd had few interactions with Ryder's boss's boss. But the stories she'd heard were *whoa*. And then there was Sugar, Jared's wife. She wasn't necessarily a fan of Seven's. They'd butted heads, but Seven got the impression that Sugar butted heads with almost everybody at first, and Seven appreciated that apprehensive quality. Sugar seemed very Mayhem-like, protective over her people. "Are you going to do it?"

"I talked to Ryder and Victoria."

Seven's eyes widened. "On their don't-talk-to-us-unless-people-are-dying honeymoon?" Ryder had sworn up and down that, wherever they were going, the place was secluded enough that no one on the face of the earth would ever be able to get ahold of them, lest there was an emergency. The current situation, in Seven's mind, did not constitute an emergency, and the last thing she wanted to do was interrupt her best friend's honeymoon on day one. Did that not make her the worst best friend on earth? Yeah, it kind of did.

"You had a big ask, sweet pea."

Right, right. "And the final decision is…" She bit her lip and clung to the handset, feeling the drying, sticky dough squished between her fingers.

"Then I talked to Jax."

Ugh. No telling how that had gone. "You know you have a thing for drawing out suspense?"

Tick, tock. He laughed. Boss Man was one for theatrics, wasn't he?

"They all agree with you," he finally said. "We'll help. You can let Mayhem know that I'll be in touch."

She opened her mouth to thank him, but the call clicked in her ear as Jared disconnected. Seven dropped the scone-dough-covered phone and spun with her hands in the air, squealing in delight.

CHAPTER EIGHT

THE ROW OF motorcycles in front of the Mayhem compound made Jax uneasy. This entire job wasn't what he was cut out for, given his disdain for gangs in general, even if they went by *club* and had pretty girls that fascinated him as a distractible decoy.

Jax was semi-convinced Jared had assigned him to partner on this project as punishment, and it had nothing to do with sharpening his skills or his ability to establish a working relationship with Seven.

Boss Man wasn't wrong, though. Diplomatic relations weren't his strong suit. Diplomacy with the criminal sect only served to irritate the piss out of him and grate his bad attitude from generally unfriendly to watchfully distrustful.

"You ready, brother?" Jared glanced his way before he dropped his fist against the door.

The setting sun beat down on Jax's back as the faint odor of motor oil and stale beer promised what was in store inside. "Yeah."

Whether he was or not didn't matter since Boss Man had already pounded on Mayhem's door and security cameras had them on lock since the moment they'd pulled into the parking lot.

Mayhem supposedly did custom auto and bike work and some repairs for locals. Jax was sure it was a front, though. Mayhem's reputation for turning out custom stunners had attracted big money normally spent in New York, Los Angeles, and Las Vegas. At least that was what Jax had read. He didn't know or care, mostly because he didn't believe it was their source of income as much as they purported, simply a cover for everything illegal.

Plus, half the auto body shop seemed filled with MC bikes, not moneymaking repairs. There wasn't a row of minivans waiting for oil changes or sedans needing to have dings buffed out. No soccer mom would schedule an appointment there after a drive-by glance of the chain-link fences with barbed wire and skulls marking the entrance.

"A lot of bikes lined up." Jax squinted over his shoulder, counting the Harleys by twos.

He and Jared were supposed to have a two-on-two meeting to discuss a sit-down in Colombia, South America, at the source of the cocaine and Mayhem's money, the home base of Hernán Suarez's cartel. Jax had walked away from the first phone discussion with Mayhem, believing there would be only the four of them on the grounds, not just in the room. Mayhem wasn't playing by the rules. Why wasn't he surprised?

The door opened, and a gruff man mirrored Jared in too many ways. Eerie as hell as Jax took in the guy's dark hair and dark eyes. Jared Gone Wrong had a salt-and-pepper five o'clock shadow and wore his leather vest that the bikers called their "cut" with the Mayhem insignia on the chest. The title of president was stitched high on his right side, and he held his hand out to Jared. "Welcome to Mayhem. Hawke."

"Jared." Boss Man met Hawke's grip. They shook, and Jared stepped aside and gestured toward Jax. "That's Jax."

Jax stepped into the cool shadow of the compound's front entryway and shook Hawke's hand as well, expecting a challenging fight in the grip, but the honest handshake was steadfast. "Nice to meet you."

"Before you're invited in, respectfully, I'd like you to unload your clips and barrels. Don't care if you keep them on you. But the bullets go in the bucket."

Out of the corner of Jax's eye, he caught Jared's jaw flexing.

Boss Man shook his head. "Your house, your rules. I'm always clear, but maybe you didn't understand when we spoke before. There's a lot of bikes out here, and the only ones involved today are me and my guy, you and your guy."

Hawke crossed his arms and took a step back. "There's three others here. And no, I didn't take that away from our conversation. Don't take that as any disrespect. My vice president, my sergeant at arms, and my treasurer. They're here. I want them here. It will go a long way. The rest of them are watching the ball game back in the garage. They have no idea what's happening, and I don't want them to yet. Take that for what it's worth. My head is on a platter if this comes out before it should."

Jared seemed to like Hawke's honesty, and he stepped forward. "We're not unloading."

Hell, they weren't going to make it in the hall. Maybe Jax wouldn't have to worry about dealing with this job. Unarmed and outnumbered in a gang compound? Seems to Jax that they should've brought their own backup. Not that Parker didn't have a tracker on their vehicle and know their exact moves, and there was a team waiting close by if anything went wrong. Still, outnumbered was outnumbered, and this was lesson number one in diplomatic relations: You don't always fucking get what you want.

"Don't shoot anyone." Hawke turned down the dark hall, and they followed as the heavy door slammed and locked behind Jax.

Maybe lesson number one was actually don't make the first demand. Mayhem needed them. Jared could take their contract and money or not. He wasn't hard-pressed.

They wound through the dark hall with the Mayhem insignia on the walls and stale beer and cigarettes staining the air. It reminded Jax of his days in shitty bars after escaping basic training. There'd been no money and lots of stress to blow off. The place stunk like BO, sex, drunken nights, and forgotten memories.

Finally, the hall opened into a main room much larger than Jax expected, filled with pool tables, darts, a foosball table, and a long, fully stocked bar. Draft taps lined the top near a sliding glass door enclosing an outdoor patio the size of a parking lot. Barbecues and metal coolers sat near a raised platform with trash cans and beer kegs strewn at random.

"Through here." Hawke gestured as they cut across the pool table room and came to an ornately carved double wood door. Hawke banged his fist on a giant knocker as he walked past, and they continued through another carved door into a room next to the one Hawke banged on.

Once inside, an adjoining door opened, and three men walked in from the other room. Hawke made quick introductions, explaining who Jax and

Jared were, then ticked off names. Tex was the sergeant at arms, Johnny was vice president, and Ethan was the treasurer.

They took seats at the table, and Hawke eyed his men. His passing glance was a firm reminder that Mayhem was to remain a united front. Interesting to pick up on a slight disagreement in the ranks.

Johnny reacted the most. The other two didn't change their slouch when the VP cleared his throat as though signaling it was time to get down to business.

Hawke scowled at Johnny. "This is how we'd like it to—"

"And I appreciate how you'd like things to go," Jared cut off Hawke. "You gave us intel before we arrived. Distribution plans, financials, potential replacement partners, and the ideal buyouts. I know what you'd like."

Hawke's lips tightened, and Tex shifted to keep Johnny in his peripheral.

No one in Mayhem had to say who their problem child was as Johnny crossed his arms and groused.

Johnny pinched the bridge of his nose. "Maybe *we*—" His glare started with Hawke but ended on Jared—"haven't been briefed on your ideal situation."

Boss Man inched forward, challenging the room.

Hawke ignored Johnny and met Jared's eye. "Our ideal situation is out of the coke game with minimal financial loss and no body count. Does anybody care to amend that?"

Johnny's lip curled. "*Minimal financial loss* is vague as fuck."

"Johnny, shut your goddamn mouth." Tex turned in his chair and shook his head. "It was a club vote. Out of the drug business. The monetary impact at this point doesn't matter worth shit if we're being honest."

"We're just gonna let these assholes watch out for our bottom dollar?"

"Like Tex said, my friend, watch your goddamn mouth and show a little fucking respect for our guests," Hawke growled.

The only one who hadn't weighed in on the money—or at all—was the treasurer, and Jax wondered what the silent guy was thinking. No reaction, and Ethan didn't even seem interested. "What about you? Everybody has an opinion but you."

Ethan's brows went up toward the bandana that tied back his long hair, and he leaned back as though this were the first time he'd been asked. He pulled a pack of smokes from his back pocket then lit a cigarette. Two long drags later, he let the second cloud of smoke curl from his nostrils. "My interests lie in the longevity of my club. Our membership has spoken, leaders have voted, and it's our job to listen to you and protect Mayhem at all costs."

"Spoken like a true politician." But Jax liked what he said because, through all that hot air and cautious wording, Ethan wanted to stop selling drugs and listen to Titan.

"The Suarez cartel has agreed to meet two from Titan and two from Mayhem. That's it. Was supposed to be like this meeting. But now we have a decision." Jared cracked his knuckles. "Who's it going to be? Hawke and who?"

"Me," Johnny answered as though he'd known the question was coming.

Tex's mouth had only half-opened to volunteer, and Ethan eyeballed the two men. Obviously, he wasn't going to volunteer, but there were internal politics at play.

Jared motioned Jax to the door as he stood. "We'll give you a few minutes to hammer out who."

Diplomacy 101 was boring unless a person knew the players and their gossip. Jax followed Jared out of the meeting room as tensions escalated. When the door shut, they both just shook their heads. Neither would say a word aloud—no telling if the place was bugged—but they were in agreement. Mayhem should have had their shit straight before they called in Titan. And Jax wondered if he was paranoid or if it felt as though Johnny had the bead on only one person accompanying Hawke?

The meeting-room door swung open, and Hawke and Tex stood there. "Johnny's your number-two man." Tex pushed by Jared, and Jax didn't bother turning his head when Tex grumbled, "Don't let that greedy motherfucker screw this up."

CHAPTER NINE

SEVEN DECIDED WHEN Victoria first closed on her house that the best part about having a best friend with a cutesy house was that it made for a terrific crash pad to talk about cutesy things. Or when Mayhem life became too dark or heavy with requests she wouldn't touch, she liked to hide at Victoria's place. That same cutesy house could take the edge off of ugly topics. Anything unpleasant was made entirely bearable by Victoria's lemony-yellow wall color and white wainscoting.

She'd made sure that Sidney had more than adequate help this afternoon at work. Extra hands coupled with the miserable weather meant her coffee shop would see less foot traffic. Normally, that was a complaint, but today, it was a great thing. Hawke had laid down the law and demanded that she go to Colombia. Seven couldn't fold enough hand towels at The Perky Cup or blankets at her home to feel in control of that situation.

So she'd done what anyone in her position would do. She'd grabbed her girlfriend Adelia, nabbed an obscene amount of cookies, and banged on her friend's door. Victoria had cleared her schedule for the afternoon and promised to be there when Seven and Adelia arrived, ready to offer no-bullshit advice after Seven had texted four simple words. *I need my passport.*

That had been followed by a slew of texts that summarized how she wanted to strangle Hawke.

"We're here. Anyone home? Life crisis occurring," Seven hollered as she inhaled the rich aroma of coffee. "Is Ryder here too? Ryder! I'm having a moment."

His laughter filtered from the kitchen, and Seven had no idea if that was good or bad. Maybe he shouldn't be involved. The Delta sniper man was no-holds-barred, like his wife. A Victoria-Ryder combo delivering the straight truth might have been more than Seven could stomach as the clock ticked down to boarding an international flight to drug-dealer dreamland.

"I'm up here," Victoria called from upstairs.

"Your husband is laughing at me."

"Lovingly," he added, laughing harder.

"I'm headed to a cartel-infested country. Where's the compassion?" Seven started up the stairs as Adelia chuckled. "Not you too."

"No drama here. Seven is totally handling this fine."

"I don't even want to know how you'll fare." Ryder's Australian accent was deceptively alarmed. "Good luck. Nice knowing you."

Seven laughed to herself as they trudged up the stairs. "What a little Aussie ass."

"Shoot." Victoria shoved the last of her sheets into the linen closet and slammed the door shut. "You got here before I thought you would."

Seven rolled her eyes. "Jeez, things must be worse than I thought they were if you're shoving laundry into a closet before I get here."

"Shut your face, sweetheart. You know it's not like that."

"Liar, liar, pants on fire."

"Okay, fine. But wouldn't this conversation be easier if I didn't have unfolded laundry for Seven to stare at instead of focusing on important things?" She looked at Adelia. "Right? We're here to talk some of this out. Figure out how you're going to stay sane and safe. Just swing by Colombia and come on back. It's a lovely place to visit. A couple nice spas…"

Right. That was what she'd be doing—visiting a spa. Had she been to a spa before? No. Not unless they could dye or pierce her, and then they wouldn't be called a spa.

Adelia walked past both of them and leaned against the wall. "It's ridiculous that Hawke wants you to go down there. You're not Johnny's babysitter."

Victoria headed toward her bedroom. "Are we sure that's the point?"

They moved into the master bedroom, where Seven sprawled in the middle of the king-size bed and Victoria paced at the foot. Adelia crisscrossed her legs in a side chair and pulled a blanket that had been draped over the top around her.

Whether Adelia was cold or not, Seven didn't care. She was just glad that the one folded blanket in the room was now unfolded and wrapped around her friend. Because it hadn't been folded the way Seven would've wanted it, and she wouldn't have cared unless her stress level was at a ten. Today, it was hovering around an eleven, and the entire time they would've been talking, that was all Seven would've thought about.

Victoria stopped and reached for the paper bag that Seven clung to. "What snacks did you bring for brain food?"

"Cookies. I figured the sugar would help."

She dug around then pulled out a peanut butter cookie and took a bite. Then after a buttery, approving sigh, she turned to Adelia. "What's your dad say?"

Tex had adopted Adelia, but he was the father she claimed. Her blood brother, Javier Almeida, even visited them often as if Tex were his relation too. But Tex was currently the talk of Mayhem—not for his family, but because he wasn't accompanying Hawke.

Not all members knew of the trip, but the ones who did weren't sure the current second-in-command was acting his role.

"Not much to me."

Tex didn't talk much, but he conveyed a lot with looks. "Nothing about Johnny? Unrelated to this?"

"Nothing other than the normal bitching that no one should be groomed to run Mayhem since birth."

Seven sighed. "So the norm."

"Yup."

The gossip from a few chatty old ladies had been that Johnny was antsy for the gavel but his face was falling too deep in the white powder. Seven couldn't see one over the other. It was hard to find fault in friends and family.

The treasurer, Ethan, made more sense to her. If someone was going to talk money, it should be the money guy. But if she had to choose between Johnny and Tex, she would choose Tex. Though nobody had asked her.

"Do you think your dad should go?" Seven asked Adelia.

"Over Johnny? Fuck yes. He's one line away from snorting his last brain cell away."

"How am I missing this? And I'm not saying that Tex shouldn't be the one to go. I'm just saying maybe I have blinders on when it comes to him." Not that it would surprise her. "I don't even know if he wants me to babysit Johnny. Hawke hasn't said a word other than 'get on the plane' and 'we have your hotel room booked.'"

Victoria tapped her teeth in thought. "Maybe it's Jax that Hawke wants the ability to tap into."

Adelia giggled. "We should clarify that. Did you mean tap Jax or something more innocent, like converse with Jax?"

Seven groaned. "Could we not talk about *tapping* Jax?"

"God, what is he? One hundred percent full-blooded, hot Italian male?" Adelia fanned herself. "I think it's the hair. Real dark and just long enough to hold on to."

"Oh my God." Seven pulled a pillow over her face. "How about we avoid discussing everything like that? *Please?*"

"I'd tap Jax. Over and over and over—"

"*Adelia!*"

She erupted into a fit of laughter. "And over."

"Would you shut up?" Seven ripped the pillow off her face and sat up. "I do not want to hear that."

"You can't lie and say he's not smoking hot."

Even Seven's best snake eyes were no match for Adelia laughing, and she turned to Victoria, who had rolled her lips together and was trying not to laugh also.

"Come on. You're married. Jax can't be hot. Nobody can be hot but the Australian downstairs."

"Actually, I'm upstairs and searching for something." Ryder walked by with a shit-eating grin on his face. "But yeah, if you were to ask me, I'd say the guy's not bad looking. If you could duct tape his mouth shut. The jackass."

Victoria and Adelia burst out laughing, and Seven groaned for what felt like the thousandth time, dropped back on the bed, and grabbed the pillow to cover her face again. "Can we not talk about Jax? This is supposed to be about Colombia." Carefully, she peeled the pillow from her face and peeked out to see the three of them watching her. "What?"

Ryder shook his head. "Oh, Seven."

Seven's eyes bugged. "What?"

"You have it bad, don't you?"

"Oh, for the love of—" Seven chucked the pillow at Ryder. "I'm here for a very serious conversation."

Ryder caught the pillow and stopped joking. "Okay, very serious conversation. Hawke wants Titan down there. He has hired us for a very pretty penny to stay neutral. It's obvious to the entire world that you and Jax have a"—he tilted his head—"*connection*. Your first loyalty is assumed to be Mayhem. Hawke would never question that. If Titan Group was to ever say or do anything that would endanger the club, you would know first."

Seven's lips parted, but her thoughts hadn't come up with the rebuttal that she was automatically prepared to give. "You think Hawke wants me to screw Jax for information?"

Ryder shrugged. "I don't know the guy."

Seven's eyes dropped to Adelia.

Adelia shook her head. "No way. If he wanted that, he would just say it. And then expect you to slap him."

Seven's gaze went to Victoria then Ryder and back to Victoria. "So then what? I'm not there to keep an eye on Johnny but rather Jax? I don't like the idea of spying on him."

"Then don't," Victoria said.

"But listen to what you just said," Adelia pointed out. "You just chose somebody you don't know above the MC."

"No, I didn't," Seven shot back defensively. "That's a strong accusation." Though all Adelia had done was repeat back what Seven had implied. She rubbed her temples. "Look, Jax is a *friend*. I've always been loyal to my friends."

A few awkward seconds sifted by before Ryder waved goodbye and left with a couple of cookies.

Seven took her own cookie out of the bag. "What's the final decision on Hawke's motives?"

"Who knows?" Victoria volunteered first. "If Hawke asks you any questions that you don't feel comfortable answering, you don't. Nothing that's any different than normal."

"Why does this feel different than normal?"

Adelia's face softened. "Because, sweetie, you two are..." Her voice trailed off as Victoria sat on the edge of the bed. "Opposites. But you have a vibe."

"A vibe?" Seven shook her head. "Nope. That's what Victoria has. The little sex toy fiend."

Victoria laughed. "A connection. Chemistry. The more you deny it to us, the more we're confident you two have that thing. Oh, hey." She reached for her phone on the nearby dresser. "I need Colby Winters's phone number. Do you have it?"

Surprised at the change of topic, Seven shook her head. "No."

"Do you have Javier's?" Adelia asked about her brother.

Seven's forehead pinched. "*What?* No, why would I have his phone number?"

Victoria scrolled on her cell. "How about Roman Hart or Brock Gamble's number? Luke Brenner?"

"No, why would I—Oh, because I have Jax's number."

Neither of them said a word, but both let their wide eyes do the talking.

Victoria scooted next to Seven on the bed. "I think we can drop the Jax part of this conversation, but I wanna say one more thing, and whether it entails him or not, that's your call."

"Is this where you give me the just-say-no-to-drugs conversation, *Mom*? Because I think I'm acing that test."

Victoria locked her arm around Seven's shoulders and hugged. "Remember that best friend necklace we had in eighth grade? And when I lost my side, I swore my life was harder than yours?" She shook her head. "We've had such a rough go sometimes and, through it all, really amazing things have come of it. Bianca and Nolan."

"Don't make me cry." Tears brimmed at the thought of what a hard night that had been and how beautiful it had turned out. Those little babies had had no one, alone with overdosing parents. A mommy who'd died and a father who had given up custody to Seven. She hadn't thought it over when child protective services and a police officer had shown up at her door in the middle of the night with two babies and a bag of ill-fitting clothing.

"Seven, I've never met anyone stronger, and there is nobody that I'd be prouder to call my best friend. *But* the amount of responsibility on your shoulders isn't fair, and sometimes I'm scared that you forget you're a person too."

"I know that," she whispered.

"I have no idea why you can't admit Jax is hot as fuck and you're into him when you easily run a business and support your parents and your adopted kids." Victoria squeezed her again. "I'm terrified that because our youth was taken away, you don't know how to enjoy the life that you have fought for and earned."

"Holy shit, Victoria..." Seven sniffed. "I'll work on having fun. I'll try. I promise."

CHAPTER TEN

BIANCA AND NOLAN ran around the living room, revving their imaginary Harleys with bandanas tied around their hair and Gennita, or Glamma as they called her, calling out directional changes. Seven stared at her small carry-on bag, clothes precisely folded, and resisted the urge to take everything out and start again.

"I can get you a handful of Xanax if you want, sugar pie," Gennita hollered down the hall. "I don't have to see you to know what you're doing."

Seven cringed. *I'm that predictable.* "No, thanks, Glamma."

"Doctors wouldn't prescribe them if there wasn't a reason."

Nothing she hadn't heard a thousand times before. If the worst thing that came from Seven's spikes of anxiety and out-of-control freak-outs were the all-consuming urge to fold clothes, she could handle that. Mostly.

Mind over matter.

That, and she didn't have the extra cash for prescriptions and doctor's appointments for herself. Plus, she had never been keen on the idea of taking pills in the first place. "Doctors prescribed coke once upon a time too."

Gennita changed hats to Glamma. "Lemme hear those throttles."

Bianca and Nolan roared.

"How do those hogs feel? Too tight? Need any adjustments?"

Seven walked into her living room to see both kids turning imaginary handlebars left and right, twisting their knuckles and testing their throttles, with Seven's tools strewn over the carpet. She teased Gennita with a perusing glance then a wink.

"What? We had to make adjustments to our throttle cables." Glamma shined her nails against her jeans, preening in all of her Harley-riding glory. "Can't raise babies to rely on someone else."

"I know, Glamma." She eased over to the woman about her mom's age, dressed in leather pants and a shirt that had "Sentenced to Life Behind Bars" written around motorcycle handle bars screen-printed over her chest. "That's why I trust their Glamma to raise them when I can't."

Gennita dropped her nail-shining routine and softened. "I know, babe."

"Do you want to stay here or at your place tonight?" Seven asked.

"Here." Then she pursed her bright-red lips together as she rethought her answer. "Yeah, here. I don't trust Mack not to bother me all weekend. I told him I have the babies. But if the compound gets rip-roaring tonight, and his drunk a-s-s forgets and comes home? We'll be here."

Seven groaned on her behalf. The guy was a few months post-recovery from pancreatitis. His decision to ignore doctor's orders on lifestyle changes did nothing but piss off Gennita.

"I'll leave pizza money, and it'll be like a vacation."

"No, honey. Don't waste your money because Mack can't handle a sip of water now and then. We're fine on PB and J and raviolis."

The roar of real Harleys arrived outside Seven's house, and tears burned her eyes, threatening her makeup.

"Don't do it," Gennita said in her best Glamma voice. "They're f-i-n-e if you are."

So fucking true. Seven sucked in a breath as a Harley throttled outside, a calling card from Johnny to get a move on.

"Okay, you guys. Remember how I said I had my trip?"

Nolan made a big show of dismounting his bike, but Bianca simply went into her serious mode.

"It's time for me to go, and you have nothing but Glamma time! So. Much. Fun!" She threw her arms around them. "Are you excited?"

"Yeah!" Nolan squeezed Seven's neck, gagging her.

"When will you be back?" Bianca asked for the twentieth time.

"Two days, tops."

"Promise?"

She pulled the little girl into her arms, squishing her next to Nolan. "Swear. I promise. And you can't promise if you don't mean it."

"What if you don't?"

"I will."

"What if you can't?"

"I can." And with every ounce of Seven's being, she wanted to rid drugs from the streets so that little girls and boys never had to have the fear of parents leaving and dying like Bianca did. "But if for some reason I were late—like my flight was delayed—you'd be with Glamma, and you'd know exactly where I was and why."

Bianca blinked but didn't say anything.

Fucking hell. Screw Mayhem; Seven wasn't going anywhere. "Sweetie, I'll stay home."

Bianca's eyes went wide. "What? No! We want to stay with Glamma!"

Seven chuckled. *Denied!* "Oh, okay. Are you sure?"

"Yes! You have to go. Glamma's slumber party is going to be the best. She said so."

"Oh yeah?" Seven mouthed *best* as Gennita laughed, and she threw her arms out to hug her kiddos. "Both of you, c'mere. I love you with my whole heart."

"To infinity and the moon and the stars and the racetrack and the grocery store and the sky and back," Nolan added.

"That's a lot," Bianca explained. "I love you that much too."

Bang, bang.

"Oh, cool your horses," Gennita shouted at the door, shaking her head. "Those men. Let that be a lesson to you both." She scooped the kids from Seven. "We go when we're ready. Not when someone tells us to scoot. Back on those bikes."

They jumped onto their imaginary hogs.

"You ready?"

"As I'll ever be." Seven grabbed her bag and headed toward her ride that would fly her to Jax, Johnny, and cartel country. Maybe Xanax wasn't a bad idea after all with a list like that.

CHAPTER ELEVEN

Bogotá, Distrito Capital
Colombia

THE OLD CITY bustled with sights and sounds that made it seem more like a modern marvel of the political and cultural powerhouse that it was. Flower markets overfilled every corner, boasting the most bountiful and beautiful blossoms in the world, thanks to the ideal humidity and high altitude of the capital city.

Unless someone was searching for the signs on the main streets and parks crowded with children, there were few outward appearances of cartel influence. But not many places in South America had the confluence of power, money, and illegal distribution networks as Bogotá. The city benefited from every ounce of drugs sold in the Western Hemisphere.

It had been years since Jax had walked these deceptive streets. Then, the phrase diplomatic relations weren't a thought. His purpose had been to disrupt weapons distribution networks by any means necessary. They had gone in silently and left a trail of blood and thunder behind. Their mission had been accomplished: massive disruption.

Still, he took the city in with the same predatory filter. Each businessman was assumed to be a cartel employee and blood-hungry. Every window and straightaway potentially housed a sniper nest, and walking next to Jared on the way to the meeting location—a restaurant named after Suarez's wife—Jax heeded the warning of the hairs prickling at the back of his neck. He and Jared were vulnerable with minimal body armor and weapons. The high altitude and low oxygen of Bogotá made each bullet feel as though its weight were quadrupled. Jax would rather be armed like he'd been years before.

"What kind of message does it send to name the restaurant Esmeralda's?" Jared muttered as they made a blind turn.

Jax had wondered that too. "Think she works there?"

Boss Man's hearty chuckle fell easily. "If by work, you mean surveys her people and drinks fine wine, then yes."

The Suarezes had more money than Jax could fathom. Esmeralda's was likely one of many fronts to launder money and host illegal meetings, though Jax had Googled the restaurant and found that it was very well reviewed. After all, who would be ballsy enough to one-star the wife of a cartel king?

The restaurant was ahead, standing out with its opulence in a city that held its own with high-end eateries fueled by the drug profit of Colombia's black-market economy. The reported exports of flowers and coffee couldn't support the surrounding first-world economy. "I think it says we own this city."

"Yup," Jared agreed as they met the doorman.

"Good afternoon, and welcome to Esmeralda's." He opened the massive gold-gilded door with a bow and escorted them into a foyer with pomp and fanfare then dropped his head in silent goodbye as security stepped from the shadows and patted them down, quietly disarming them with none of the doorman's dramatic display.

"Who knew you had this much fun when you went to meetings without us," Jax joked as a hostess appeared on cue.

Jared's bored expression said he had expected the disarmament. Jax had too. But he hadn't guessed there would be a bowing, shuffling, nodding dude at the door.

"Good afternoon," the young woman said. "This way."

The restaurant was eerily quiet, but Jax doubted they were as alone as it seemed. Winters, Cash, and Roman were positioned catty-corner at nearby blocks, and Jax assumed the Suarez cartel and Mayhem each had gunslingers similarly placed. It was the only way any of them would ever agree to the two-person-per-group sit-down.

The hostess batted her long eyelashes as she showed them back to a private room.

"Fancy," Jax muttered.

The walls were carved wood, and velvet drapes hung like tapestries, framing portraits of the beautiful woman who had to be Esmeralda.

"Enjoy." The hostess pushed open a glass door and swept back as Hernán Suarez came forward.

"Jared Westin." Hernán's outstretched hand reached toward Boss Man as he greeted Jax with a nod. "And Jax Michaelson. Pleasure meeting you. I hope you enjoy your evening at one of my prized jewels."

A man trailed Hernán, retreating back to a leather portfolio. Then they greeted Hawke and Johnny, who were already in the private dining room.

For the next twenty minutes, a cadre of servants served drinks and food. Plate after plate accompanied small talk, neither of which Jax gave two fucks about, but Jared bantered as if he had a degree in bullshit. Hernán liked to hear himself talk, and Jax couldn't figure out what he thought about Hawke conversing. Most of the time, the man was silent, but maybe Jax misread Hawke's caution. Johnny, on the other hand, was easy to read and didn't like anyone in the room, including Titan.

Jax had little to do with the wheeling and dealing as Jared eased Hernán and Hawke into the discussion. He listened less for what was said, instead, searching for a reason why Boss Man wanted Jax involved. There had to be more than what was stated: that Jax needed a lesson in diplomacy and to put his past experience with cartels to work.

That was bullshit. Anyone with half a brain could memorize the cartel players and have the same working knowledge that Jax did.

A beautiful woman with long, dark hair and deep, intense eyes glided into the room in a dress that looked more expensive than all of the food combined. She carried an air of sophistication that named her as Hernán's wife before she even said a word. The cartel king stood, greeting her with a kiss on each cheek. Their dynamic was interesting to watch.

Hernán, in no uncertain terms, was a monster. Not necessarily in looks, but in business and in morals. Then again, a cartel king didn't get to the top of the worldwide drug food chain without being a sick, sadistic son of a bitch who made other cartel kings take a step back. And yet the woman who wrapped herself around him as though she were madly in love didn't seem to be put off by that at all. Sometimes money and power were enough. Jax narrowed his eyes as he studied the couple. Or sometimes a couple was one in the same, and he wondered if Hernán and Esmeralda were two peas in a pod.

Hernán introduced her as his queen, and she batted her eyelashes, demurely playing down his attention. Out of the corner of Jax's eye, he saw that Jared was on high alert, and that matched the feeling Jax continued to have about the woman.

"Did you enjoy the food?" Her exotically tinged words curled through the air. But it was the sexy, almost trancelike look she cast upon Hawke and Johnny that made Jax inch to the edge of his seat.

Both men instantly lauded the meal. Jax watched as they talked about how the food melted in their mouths and that the wine had to be rare. Jax wondered if these motorcycle thugs knew what the shit they were talking about or if this was just BS flowing to schmooze with their business partner's wife.

She glided around the table, running her fingertips along Hernán's arm to his shoulder. Then she let her fingers drift along his other arm as she moved to Hawke and Johnny and sat next to Johnny.

Jax ran his tongue along his bottom lip. What would Jared's diplomatic relations do now? Because, by Jax's count, the cartel had just added another player to the negotiation table.

"We appreciate the food, ma'am," Boss Man said to Hernán, notably not her. "But I'd like to get back to business and finish hammering out this deal."

One thing Jax knew about Jared was that he didn't fall for many tricks, and he wasn't going to be lured in by a play between this man and wife. Jared talking to Hernán, complimenting Esmeralda to the cartel king, had nothing to do with her belonging to the husband and everything to do with Boss Man putting Hernán on notice. *I see the bullshit. I see your play.*

Hernán played down Esmeralda's presence at the table. "She's just a woman. Just my wife."

She reached for a corn cake and fed it to Johnny, fingers lingering against his mouth. "Delicious, isn't it? *Arepas.* The simplest foods can be the most pleasurable."

Her sultry voice and the deep V of her dress created a combination that had Johnny literally eating from her hand.

"It is." Johnny's gravelly voice had nothing to do with the food.

She made a production of choosing a new item and did it again. "This is my family's recipe for *aborrajados.*"

Hawke's jaw tensed as Johnny took another bite offered.

"The plantains and cheese melt together." She put it down, offering him a linen napkin but then dabbing at his mouth. "They are my weakness."

Hell, Johnny was *Mayhem's* weakness as he hypnotically agreed with her. He was solidly on Team Esmeralda.

"Now that we've tried the appetizers…" Jared crossed his arms, eying Hernán. "The ground rules were clear. Each party could have two players at the table. I'd like her to go."

Hernán tilted his head. "It's her restaurant."

"That may be true. But it is still hers on the other side of that door." Boss Man tossed his thumb over his shoulder. "Or we're done for the day and can reconvene tomorrow."

"No, no." Esmeralda glided back from Johnny, spreading out her well-manicured hands toward the feast on the table as her jeweled bracelets clinked. "I'm leaving. Enjoy."

"Thank you." Since they had crossed many lines of appropriateness, Johnny's comfort level at a one-on-one goodbye seemed almost benign, but Jax saw the play coming fast.

She bent to her captive audience, perked breasts on display, and leaned close enough to whisper in his ear as her curtain of dark hair shielded the room from her lips.

Jared's fist hit the table, and he stood. "None of that."

"Come now." Hernán leaned back, smirking at Jared. "We boast three five-diamond awards for our customer excellence in addition to the food—"

"Cut the BS and get her out of here." Jared stepped closer to Hernán.

"Or this is done."

Hawke pushed his chair back a few inches, glaring at Johnny, and Johnny shook his head as though siding with Hernán and Esmeralda.

She glided out, coming around to the other side of the table and trailing her fingers along the edge of an empty chair until she came near Jax. She let her fingernails scrape across his elbow. Then she left the room. *What the fuck was that all about?*

The mood in the room had shifted entirely, and tension that had already been uncomfortable was now untrusting and on edge. Jax looked at Jared. "I don't know about you, Boss Man, but I could use a break."

Jared ran a hand over his face and gave a curt nod. "Everyone take two."

Hernán and his associate didn't even turn to one another, and that was all the confirmation Jax needed that Esmeralda was a play. Hernán's associate was nothing more than a straw man stand-in, and he probably knew jack shit about the Suarez cartel business. They'd been doing business with Mayhem for many years, and they likely knew the club's leadership well enough to know that Johnny was the weak link, just like Hawke knew.

Jared could protect them against the bad deal, could help them negotiate good terms, but he couldn't tell them to keep themselves in line, and if Mayhem wanted to fuck up their own situation, that was on them. Boss Man and all of the talent the Titan Group housed couldn't help them with that.

Hawke all but growled at Johnny, and they made their way to a private balcony outside. Jared tilted his head, and Jax stood up, pushing away from the table. They both moved to the corner of the private dining room.

From their vantage point, they could see that Hernán had a smug look on his face as he popped olives in his mouth and appeared at complete ease. The man next to him fiddled with the silverware and barely dared to look at the cartel king. Hawke and Johnny were visibly in a heated discussion, and Jax only shook his head. Both he and Jared knew better than to say anything out loud because there was no telling how the room was wired.

"Fuck this shit." Jared cracked his knuckles and stormed toward the balcony door.

Jax should have let him head out there alone, but he was asshole enough to not want to miss the fireworks, and if Jared was going to tell Johnny to man up, he wanted to see it.

"You mind telling me what you two are bitching about out here?"

Hawke's face said it all, but he didn't utter one word.

"Jesus fucking Christ," Jax muttered.

"Start by telling me what the problem is. Simple. Just spit it out. Johnny?" Jared's ice-cold glare landed on the man causing their headache. "You've got something to say?"

"Yeah. As a matter of fact, I do."

Hawke grumbled, shaking his head, and he turned around, pacing a loop before he returned. "This is not about making money. This was a club vote. This is about shutting it down. What part of this do you not understand?"

"Money talks. We should ask for more of a percentage instead of breaking down the deal. We ask for more money, and everything is justified. We bring it back to the club. If they don't want more money, then we can farm it out. Or we do what we're doing, and we make a better cut. I don't see what the problem is."

"Unbelievable." Jax couldn't contain his amazement. "Is it stupidity or greed?"

Johnny took an aggressive step forward, fists bunching. "Excuse me?"

"Jax is right. What'd she say to you?" Jared asked. "What percentage did she whisper in your ear while she was feeding you corn cakes like she was planning to leave her husband to do nothing but suck your cock?"

"You don't know shit."

"What I do know is you're fucking coked out and"—Jared's eyes narrowed—"selfish as fuck. That's not stupidity. That's greed."

Johnny pulled his right arm back, but before he could make a stupid life-or-death decision, Hawke caught his forearm and whipped him around. "You stupid, dumbass motherfucker. Do you have your face in that candy again?" Hawke grabbed Johnny by his leather cut and pulled him close, studying his face as if he could do a drug test with a hard stare.

Coming up with his own determination, Hawke pushed him away, cursing out his VP.

Boss Man's disappointment registered as a scowl. "You work this out. I'm going back in."

Jax and Jared moved back inside the restaurant, and it would be a lesson in diplomatic relations. Jax would be interested in watching how Boss Man would handle this. Maybe diplomacy was more interesting than Jax had given the subject credit for.

Jared paced as he cracked his knuckles. "I see what you did there."

Hernán didn't say anything. He popped an olive into his mouth and smirked.

"We're going to take a break today. I will contact you when we can sit down again. Sound good?"

"Excellent. I assume that business will continue as normal in the meantime?"

Jax was almost impressed at the cartel leader's play. No, he took that back. He *was* impressed. Hernán had done his research and knew his adversary. He'd gone on the offensive and spiked the play, and it had worked. Hernán's goal had to preserve the production and distribution with the best possible apparatus, and he still had that.

Today was a good day for the Suarez cartel and, technically, a good one for Titan. Jared and Jax were neutral negotiators. They couldn't make Mayhem behave. All he and Jared could do was flag the problem, but they weren't expected to predict the future. In a way, they had made a friend in a dangerous place, which was always handy.

Hawke and Johnny came in from the balcony, and Mayhem's president moved to the cartel king. Hawke extended his hand to Hernán. "I'd like to table this. We're still interested in talking about other distribution options, but for now, status quo remains in effect."

Hernán shook Hawke's hand, and Jax was already walking toward the exit. They would get a phone call when they needed to be brought back in, but he wanted no part in this anymore.

As Jax stalked out of the private dining room, he passed by an alcove where Esmeralda was propped against the wall, shining. Her job as Hernán's number two had been executed flawlessly.

CHAPTER TWELVE

THE LONG DAY in the unknown city had been never-ending, and Jax walked along the busy street in the humid night. He tossed back a beer with Jared and Winters but didn't feel the crowd at his hotel bar.

Maybe the main strip was the problem, so Jax turned off at the corner and took a deep breath as the crowd thinned. Nightlife still existed. Restaurants and bars dotted the blocks as he powered his way through the late night, but he didn't have to deal with work friends or tourists on vacation.

A line of motorcycles parked in front of a no-name bar piqued his interest, and Jax slowed long enough to decide that heading inside was a bad mistake he wanted to make.

Life was easier when he had an enemy to focus on, and whether that was some random motorcycle gang to get in trouble with or sharing a few words with Johnny, Jax was in the mood.

He pushed through the worn wooden door into the neon-lit smoky room and saw more Mayhem than he'd expected. The men wore leather cuts in case anyone needed a primer in who they were, but it was the lone female holding court in the middle of the bar that made Jax slow his angry steps.

More shocking than the amount of Mayhem members, he simply hadn't expected Seven to be in Colombia. She was a grown woman, and if she wanted to travel with her friends and get into MC business, that wasn't his problem. But there she was, a beauty in the sea of ugly, and even if she had been one of a thousand women dressed like his fantasy, he still would have been drawn to the sweetness that danced in her eyes.

Jax walked straight to her, slowing only to give Hawke the respect of a handshake.

Seven had her back pressed against the bar, her elbows leaning on the bartop. She turned her head as he walked up, and the two Mayhem members she was talking to took a walk.

Jax planted in front of her so there was no question who she should be looking at. "Seven."

"Aren't you supposed to be with the rest of the stick-in-the-mud soldiers? Don't you guys debrief or something into the middle of the night and then get shut-eye?"

Tonight she was a tough girl. And angry at that... Titan hadn't come through. Mayhem had screwed up, and Jax couldn't tell if her smirk and tone were because she had a general distrust of the world or only of him. Did she blame him because the meeting had gone so bad so quickly? For whatever reason, she was in a sour mood, similar to him. "I'm not a soldier, sweetheart. I'm a SEAL."

Seven formed her lips into an overexaggerated O then followed it with an accompanying "Oh."

He chuckled, tossing his head back, and turned, leaning against the bar like she did.

Acting annoyed, Seven inched away. "What's so funny?"

"That's not the normal reaction," he said.

"*Of course not.*" She tilted her head and erased the inches she'd put between them without leaving the too-cool-for-school lounge against the bar. "Pray tell, hot shot. What's the normal reaction?"

There were a million things he could tell her about what women did when he said he was a Navy SEAL. But Seven didn't do any of those things. She was impossible to predict, and even when he thought he knew something about her, he was far off base.

Her elbow touched his. The only thing Jax knew about normal reactions was his to her, and he pushed from the bar, wrapping around her chest and caging Seven to the bar with his forearms.

"Normally," Jax said quietly, tilting his lips close to her ear. "If I say that I'm a SEAL, it sets off a chain reaction that can't be seen."

He pulled back enough to hold her eyes, and Seven didn't flinch. "Tell me."

"The reactions I can't see?" Jax eased closer, dropping his voice low. "Fantasies. Wet panties. Needy clits. Tightening, begging pussies." He raked his gaze from her head to her tits as slowly as he could possibly manage, lingering over the outline of her nipples in her T-shirt. "But you wouldn't know anything about that, would you?"

"Not a thing," she whispered.

His chin ducked to her ear, brushing against her skin as the stubble from his chin connected with her neck. "Liar."

She smelled like sweet perfume and addictive flowers, as though she had spent her time shopping in Colombia's flower markets today rather than doing anything with the drug cartel.

A hand clamped down on Jax's shoulder, and he swung around, fist balled, only stopping when Seven snapped the other man's name. *Skull.*

"This guy bothering you?" Skull had crossbones stitched on his leather cut where others had a name, and he snarled as though still looking for a fight.

Seven blew him off. "You need to chill out."

Skull. The names this group had… Jax worked hard not to laugh.

Skull twisted toward Jax. "What's your problem?"

"No problem," Seven reiterated. "He's a friend."

"Doesn't seem like much of a friend," Skull said.

Jax was one drunk biker away from having enough with Mayhem. "Neither do you, jackass. But you don't see me running my mouth."

"Both of you, stop," Seven ordered, pushing her way in between them. "Don't be stupid."

Skull looked down at Seven as though she needed to reaffirm that Jax wasn't bothering her. "You sure?"

"I'm positive," Seven swore and made a cross over her heart. "Don't worry about him. He's like the annoying little brother that just needs attention. Good or bad, I handle Jax how I handle my kids when they misbehave. Similar to how I'm about to handle you. Read me?"

Did Seven just say 'my kids'? He opened his mouth but thought better of it.

Skull sneered but listened like Seven told him to. "You change your opinion on this one, you find me."

But Jax was far past the alpha standoff with the dickhead. Seven had kids? And she said he needed attention? *Nope.* He didn't want attention; he just wanted her.

His eyes narrowed, wondering what else he'd missed about her. Not knowing if her nips were pierced was one thing, but this was like being blindsided. How did somebody have children and a friend not know? ...Because they weren't really friends.

Jax ran a hand over his face. "I gotta go. See you."

Too much spun in his mind, and Skull grumbled behind his back that he shouldn't have walked into a Mayhem bar to start.

"Right." Jax grabbed an abandoned beer bottle and tossed it over his shoulder, listening to it shatter on the ground as he kept walking. It didn't make him feel any better.

Seven's cold laugh carried through the biker crowd. "Bad attention for the win."

Yeah, said the woman who needed just as much attention as he did with her pink hair and piercings.

CHAPTER THIRTEEN

FIFTEEN MINUTES OF Hawke and Tex giving Seven hell was about fifteen more minutes than Seven could handle. At least Skull had wandered off to be with his group of drunks.

She popped another piece of fried sweet dough into her mouth. She had no idea what it was, but once she started, she couldn't stop eating it. "You both realize that you're not my keeper, right?"

"Yeah, but then what fun would we have?" Hawke asked and bumped fists with Tex like they were twelve and not the leaders of Mayhem.

"If I was interested in Jax, I don't need your thumbs-up."

"You're not." Tex snorted then guzzled down the rest of his beer. "Piss poor match."

Hawke nodded. "They go together like bikes and oil slicks."

"Unfinished chrome and a week in the rain."

"You guys are dicks." Seven pointed her finger at Hawke then Tex. "And not dicks in the cool 'I want to hang out with you and grab a beer' kind of way. The kind where you're giving me a headache and I want to get out of here."

"Fine, go, get outta here. You're a buzzkill, anyway."

If Seven hadn't thought that Hawke would get some satisfaction out of her tossing the bird at him, she would have thrown up both middle fingers. But that would've only made him beam. "I'm calling the night. Try not to bring home anything that will give you scabies."

She turned on her heel and left to the sound of the two drunkards ribbing, their poor match comparisons getting worse and worse.

The last thing Seven wanted to do was go to her hotel room, sit there, and think about Jax and his attitude problem and all the ways he had nailed how she might react to him. It had nothing to do with the fact that he was a Navy SEAL and everything to do with him walking up to her in a bar full of bikers and giving no fucks as he wrapped his arms around her and made her melt.

He had to have known what a dominant act like that would do to her inside, and she hated it. Hated him? Yes, *hated him* for reading her so well.

The night was unexpectedly cold and quiet. She slowed in front of a swank hotel. Their clientele would cater to anyone but Mayhem and military rogues, and there wasn't a motorcycle in sight. Only a bellman standing outside even at the late hour and a Mercedes awaiting valet service. She mentally willed there to be a menu of drinks inside in which somebody had put considerable thought. Even if that wasn't the case, this wasn't the kind of place where anyone could toss a beer bottle and let it shatter without security being called.

Seven took a deep breath that was straight out of a meditation chant and changed her path from wherever she was going to straight inside that hotel.

"Good evening, Miss." The bellman graciously opened the door. "Can I help you?"

What was the matter with her life when she smiled merely at manners? "Could you point me to the bar?"

He smiled and nodded with a sweeping directional. "Straight past the registration desk and then make a right. You'll see a grand chandelier before you walk in."

Just what she needed and didn't know—a chandelier. A grand one, at that. "Thank you very much."

"My pleasure."

She glided through the lobby, following his directions. At the sight of the grand chandelier, Seven paused. He wasn't joking. It was maybe the size of an SUV, with glittering, gorgeous crystals that shimmered in pinks and ambers and purples. They stole her breath and instantly relaxed her.

This was precisely how she wanted to end her night, someplace where no one knew who she was and everything seemed soft and beautiful.

Swank music played in the background, a refreshing difference from the dive bar she had been in. Hell, it was a fresh difference from the dive bars she was used to when she spent the night out with Mayhem. Candelabras glittered, and the plush barstools and well-cared-for bartop might have been as old as the one she'd just left, but there was a difference in how the place was maintained. This was where she needed to be to get away from all of that.

The bartender walked over and handed her a menu on a thick cardboard printout that had today's date. It was nothing like she was used to and everything that she was searching for, at least tonight. The drinks had names, and her goal of a liquor concoction that was more of a masterpiece than a drunken old standby awaiting her.

"What do you suggest?"

Two people next to her stood up, pulling her attention from the bartender patiently awaiting her order, and there was Jax. He looked over at the same time but didn't hide his dismay, tossing back his head and laughing.

"Seriously," she muttered and went back to her drink order. "What do you suggest?"

"Smoky Aguardiente."

"What's that?"

"Aguardiente, very Colombian. Anise-flavored, but you might call it firewater, and it's mixed with our house specialty of smoked teas and spices."

"Fancy."

"Is that a yes?"

"Yes." Mostly because Seven refused to look over and needed a distraction. She could tell Jax's attention hadn't left her as the gaping hole of barstools between them remained open.

The bartender made her drink and arrived with the tall, skinny glass, waiting for her to try a sip. "Let me know what you think about the smoked teas."

It would take far more than smoked tea analysis to ignore Jax. She held the well-made concoction to her lips and took a small sip. It was everything she had been looking for and completely unfamiliar. "This is amazing."

The bartender tossed a clean rag over his shoulder. "Thrilled you love it."

Seven didn't have to look at Jax to feel him mocking their conversation silently.

They bantered for another few minutes, and the bartender left. Seven sipped her drink and acted far more preoccupied than she was.

"Hey, you over there." Jax's rough voice raked over her better than any specialty drink could. "I thought I was bad attention for the win."

She fought the urge to ignore him and twisted on her barstool, taking great lengths to cross her legs. "Did you think that I came here looking for you?" Seven arched her pierced brow with as much attitude as she could muster. "Ha."

"Didn't you?"

"Not a chance. I came here to hide."

Jax smirked as though he didn't buy that, and it got under her skin.

"If you don't believe me, I'm blissfully unconcerned." She used her hair as a curtain to block his handsome face then gracefully scooted a barstool farther away and slid her drink over.

Cocky jerk. Did Jax think she was going to troll the streets of a strange country, hoping to run into him? She took another sip, thankful when a small group of businessmen took the empty seats between her and Jax.

The bartender approached with a shot in hand, bypassing the new men, and she glanced up, obviously not finished with her drink. "I didn't order that."

"The gentleman at the end of the bar did."

"Jax?" She rolled her eyes. "Handsome, Italian-looking dude? Dark hair? Looks like he wants to kill everybody?"

"Perfect description." The bartender laughed. "Surly beast."

A beast? Ugh. She wasn't close enough to see his face well in the mirrored bar wall, but Jax was watching her. "Tell him no thanks. You can have it."

"I'm not going to—"

"Then give it to me, and I'll pour it on the floor."

"Can't have that." He took the shot.

"Was it a tasty one, or did he order me something that tasted like death?"

"It was lovely." The bartender winked. "Or I would've let you throw it on the floor."

"What should I send back?"

He laughed. "You two are going to be interesting, aren't you?"

"I don't know yet," Seven said, more to herself than him. "Send him a shot from me. But don't make it look as pretty."

"Would you like him to remember his name after he takes it?"

"Let's not be mean, but a little playful."

"Americans." The bartender chuckled then transitioned into Spanish with the businessmen before making Jax's shot.

Seven watched him offer it to Jax. Jax refused the shot but then took the small glass back from the bartender.

What was he doing?

Jax flung the shot glass down the mahogany bar, past the businessmen, and it came to a slow stop in front of Seven. Her heart jumped, and she would have been lying if she said that wasn't impressive. Seven gave him a slow clap, and he returned with a small nod. Seven picked up the shot, raised the glass, and downed the liquor.

Their bartender tittered. "What are you, a couple in the middle of a fight?"

The businessmen threw down a few bills to pay their tab before getting up from the bar. Empty space stretched between her and Jax again. He stared her way, holding her in place as her heart drummed and her cheeks warmed. *All* of her rushed with a warmth that made her blood race, and far out of her flirting element, Seven tore her eyes away but could tell he didn't stop looking at her.

Jax pushed off his barstool, and the sparkle of anticipation shivered across her skin. Was he leaving? Coming closer? Her breezy breaths seemed too shallow when he stopped short, allowing one barstool between them as he took a seat.

"Scared?" Because she was terrified. Her reaction to him made her almost light-headed, but she was drawn to him despite that fear.

"Man." Jax's head dropped with a chuckle. Then he glanced over. "You don't stop, do you?"

"I should."

"Nah." He moved off the barstool and leaned against her back, resting his arms on the bar. *Caging her.* "Why screw up a good thing?"

He was a sheet of muscle, and he let his chin rest next to her ear as she watched in the mirrored wall.

"Nothing to say?" His scratchy chin burrowed next to her ear, and the dark-whiskered scruff grated her into heaven. "Seven, how much have you had to drink tonight?"

Suddenly, the tingles were gone. "Not much. Why?"

Was he trying to get her drunk? *Tacky!* That didn't seem like his MO, but what did she know? Maybe he liked to get plastered and...

Jax pulled back and spun her around. "Hang on."

Her level of distrust should've been much higher. "*Why?*"

"Because I want to make bad decisions with you, and I want to make sure you're in a good place to agree."

"Meaning you don't want me drunk?"

He winked. "Not at all. What do you say?"

Still, she hesitated. "Why is it a bad decision?" Then she blushed as she waited for him to list a Kama Sutra on steroids or a policy of no strings attached means never talking again.

"Because I always know what I'm getting into, and anytime I'm around you, I don't know, and I don't care." Jax backed up and extended his hand.

She couldn't have slapped him if she'd wanted to. She wasn't a one-night stand kind of girl, and Jax had made it clear at the wedding that he was only a one-night stand kind of guy. Chemistry didn't care what either of them said, and Seven placed her hand in his.

"Why's your name Seven?" He helped her off the barstool and threw down some cash for their tabs.

"I was supposed to be lucky."

Jax grinned. "Lucky number Seven. I like it." He took her by the hand and walked them out. "Come on, beautiful. Get into trouble with me tonight."

CHAPTER FOURTEEN

MAN RUNNING HIS thumb over her knuckles as they moved to the reception desk to the hotel lobby, room keys in hand, with minimal awkwardness.

Even after a night of dive bars and swank hotel bars, Jax smelled fresh and sexy, and she wanted to nuzzle her nose into his collar and breathe deeply. They waited for the elevator, and she decided her first bad decision of the night was to wrap herself around his rock-hard torso and pay a ridiculous amount of attention to his cut muscles.

The elevator dinged, and Jax walked them into the car with her still pressed against his chest, moving until her back met the wall and his cheek was next to hers. "You went from coy to not messing around at Mach speed."

"Do you want me to go to the other side of the elevator and keep my hands by my sides?"

He didn't answer but kept her pinned, only reaching away to press his floor number. Then his forehead touched hers, and he toyed with her hair.

When the elevator slowed, Jax slid both hands into her hair, gluing his eyes to hers. He ran his palms to the back of her skull and gave a careful tug that made her moan and shake.

Then his fingers softened. "Ready?"

She had no idea. "Absolutely."

Jax led them to his room then flicked the lights on. *Whoa.*

"Wow, Jax. This is... swank."

"It's what they had available." He tossed the keycard on the small table in the hallway, and they walked into a sunken living room. To one side was a kitchenette and dining area. To the other was a beautiful bedroom suite. It might've been the nicest hotel room she'd ever stayed in.

Suddenly, nerves bubbled. She didn't know what to do in this kind of place. She was an MC princess, but this was reserved for *real* royalty.

The life she led was simple—middle America, single mom, full-time job. And this was... a fairy tale.

"Why'd you leave your buddies?" Jax asked, pulling her from the unnerving thoughts.

Seven wandered around the living room, letting her fingers trail over the back of a leather couch as she stared out at the skyline of the city fast asleep. "I needed alone time."

"Hmm."

She pivoted, toying with her tongue stud nervously. "Hmm?"

"Alone?" He crossed his thick muscled arms. "You wanted to be alone?"

"I do." She took a breath, trying to be discreet but needing to calm her anxiety more than she needed to save face. "*With you.*"

His jaw flexed. Jax didn't smile, but he reacted in a way that made her stomach flip. Something about how he made her body jump merely by a muscle twitch was intense. Maybe that was because he was very much a man, and she was used to boys. The age difference between them was impossible not to notice. God, she was so out of her league. What was she doing there?

Seven turned back to the window and refused to give away that she didn't have anywhere near the experience he likely did. Sure, she'd dated, and she'd been with Johnny forever. And sometimes piercings seemed like bells and whistles that were far beyond the experiences that Mr. Navy SEAL had had, but never had she thought it possible that a man could look down a bar and make her wet like Jax had done.

She glanced over her shoulder. "What's our first bad decision?"

"Depends." His wicked smile did dangerous things to her insides.

"On?"

"How many do we get?"

She laughed, rolling her eyes. Seven walked one way, Jax the other, and they kept the same distance, circling the room and each other.

He leaned against the glass. "Do you stalk all your prey?"

"I don't know. I don't do things like this." Seven sucked in her cheeks. "Present company excluded."

He didn't respond, and well, hell, so much for honesty. She'd said too much.

"Seven, come here."

Anticipation swirled in her stomach. Her nerves trembled while she stilled, mesmerized by the brilliance of his intensity, overshadowed as though she were a hotel caught in the brilliance of Vegas lights.

He took a smooth step closer, still leaving a mountain of space between them. "Did you change your mind?"

"*No.*"

A sweet flicker of a smile came and went. "Are you nervous?"

Seven flushed. A snarky, defensive protest of the truth was needed, but the words wouldn't come. Jax gently shook his head, holding her gaze like a lion guarding a lamb.

She swallowed the lie before it could be told. "Why would I be nervous?"

His chest expanded on a slow, deep breath. Letting it out just as deliberately, he eased another step closer. "Are you attracted to me, Seven?"

Blood pounded in her chest, lighting a smoldering heat that spread like wildfire, licking its way up her neck. "What's with twenty questions?"

"If our... *bad decisions* are raw and honest, this"—he pointed between them—"could be killer."

A waterfall of reactions cascaded through her senses.

"Or we hold back." Jax's jaw flexed, displeased with the possibility. "We'll have decent sex. Come hard. Earn a round of applause, and walk away without a memorable detail."

"What makes killer sex?"

His eyes narrowed. "Asking for what you want. Getting what you need. Giving because it's good."

"That doesn't sound like any bad decision I've ever heard of."

He tore his shirt over his head. "Come here, Seven."

The air evaporated from the room. Oh God, a shirtless Jax in real life was superior to any passing fantasy. Her nipples beaded as she drank in the visual of his tan skin and dark eyes, gaping as if she'd not seen a half-naked man before. Perfection didn't exist, and Jax was living proof of that with an old scar on his stomach and short, wider ones above his chest. Dark, close-clipped hair colored his pecs, and a smattering of hair led a path down his toned stomach. There were more stories torn, stitched, sliced, and healed into his body than she might ever know.

Seven moved closer as Jax matched her steps.

"I would've gone to you, even if you kept your shirt on."

Inches separated them. "Sometimes it's better to hedge bets."

A reddening laughter broke her enthralled trance. "I'm not sure what to think of that."

"Don't think anything. Just close your eyes."

Seven took a deep breath and obeyed. Jax moved behind her, tucking her hair from one side to the other shoulder, and goosebumps jumped at his touch. She sucked a quick breath, muscles tightening.

"Relax." His fingertips drifted from her shoulders down her arms. The fine hairs on her skin reacted, standing upright in the wake of his touch. "That happened at the wedding."

Eyes still closed, Seven shivered at the memory and loosened under his exploring touch. "I remember."

"Do you like when I touch you?" He traced over her skin until every hair stood erect and her unsteady breaths bordered on quiet pants.

"Yes."

"Simple answer," he teased quietly, now scratching close-clipped nails on her biceps.

Meaning? Raw honesty. Seven could feel the tremor of need build deep in her body, pulsing to her pussy and beading her breasts. "I liked holding on to you. Hiding under your jacket. Your back is..." With her eyes closed, it was like she could feel her fingers playing with his dress shirt at Victoria's wedding. "Muscular."

Jax squeezed her shoulders, massaging back to her arms. "Was that so hard?"

"*Maybe.*"

The warm fullness of his lips connected with hers, and Seven's eyelashes fluttered, so lost in the memory of their time at the wedding she hadn't realized he might kiss her. If there was ever a nerve, a concern, ever a single worry that Jax wasn't a god made to be with, those crazy thoughts disappeared as she wrapped her arms around his powerful neck.

His tongue teased her lips apart, and he took her weight, tipping her head for more. Seven hadn't been kissed like this in her lifetime, and as he teased her, stroking her tongue, testing her lips with nips and licks, she clung to him, moaning for more.

Then he placed a sweet kiss on her lips after the torrid ones. "Hell, this is all a good decision."

Not wanting to let go, she wondered how much of this was fantastic chemistry and how much of this was her needing the attention of a man.

"Don't move." Jax ambled away and returned with an arm full of sheets, kicking pillows to the living room. He turned down a few lights to soften the room.

"What's all this?" she asked, uneasy about how he tossed the sheets but realizing she didn't give a hoot.

"Room to spread out." Jax laid the blankets and sheets on the ground then tossed the pillows to the side next to the couch. He turned around after appraising his work, eyes darkened with arousal and licking his bottom lip.

But her nerves came back. Was this what he did? One-night stands on hotel room floors?

"What's up?"

Wow, he could read her. "Is this your thing? Do you bring girls to hotel rooms to screw on the floor?"

"Do you worry that the way Mayhem treats women has you assuming that you're one of many?"

"You mentioned the tag chasers. Not me."

"I didn't say I checked into ritzy hotels and asked for their honesty."

True. She didn't know how to do this. Have a one-night stand, just sex, and not become attached. She would have to make ground rules up as she went, but—

"Seven, I'll walk you home." He tilted his head. "No worry. Come on, babe."

"*Wait*. I have no idea what I'm doing," she admitted, cringing with her eyes closed. "I don't want to leave. I'd kick my butt a thousand times. It's hard for me to let go sometimes."

He took her cheeks in his hands, and her eyes fluttered open. "So long as you always give me that honesty, this is going to be killer." His thumbs brushed her cheeks. "Your call either way. No harm, no foul."

Would she have ever believed his softness when she needed it most? Seven stepped back, taking a sobering breath, then pulled her shirt over her head and unbuttoned her pants. She thumbed the sides down her hips and triumphed as she kicked them over her heels. It would've been easier to take them off and put her high heels back on, but now, as she stood in her bra and underwear, everything about his stare made her feel empowered.

Approval flared in his eyes. "Is it wrong that I prayed your nipples were pierced?"

"Well..." She bobbed her eyebrows, teasing him. "I have two piercings on my clit too. A small ring and a slender bar."

His lips parted for the moment he took in her revelation. Then Jax tilted his head back. "The power of prayer."

"You're going to hell. You know that?"

"Wouldn't be the first time I've been told."

"So *shocked*."

A playful faux-grimace marred Jax's face, and she wanted to move beyond the sarcasm. Seven unfastened the bra and let it fall then slid down her panties and stepped free. Once again, under his hungry eyes, she stood as he studied, this time only in her heels. She had never felt stronger. Sexier. More like a woman who also happened to be the many other things that she was. Mom. Business owner. Motorcycle mascot at times...

Jax retook her mouth with a deep kiss as he cupped her bottom, squeezing until she groaned. He released the intense hold, and she wanted it again, swaying her butt against his soothing hands.

She drifted into a delirious dreamland where she explored his chest and followed the curves of his muscled arms while he let his tongue and fingers test her body.

"Touch me," she murmured against his lips.

Jax smiled under her next kiss, his hands traveling around her hips to tease her sex. "Getting there."

A delicious eternity passed before silky strokes made Seven pant. She tried not to move her hips and succeeded until his talented fingers played with her clit ring.

"Jax…" Her breaths came heavy, hard. Pleasure reached deep inside her as she had only dreamed possible. He strummed the pads of his fingers against the pierced bar, propelling her toward a blinding pinnacle. This was more than she could do herself and better than she could remember from intercourse.

He dipped his head, and his tongue flicked over her erect nipple, toying with the small bar as he tugged and sucked.

Seven floated in a world of sensations as he played with her sex and breast.

"Arms around me," Jax whispered, switching his mouth to the other breast.

Her heavy arms hung limply over his shoulders as she arched, desperate to keep his wet lips around her nipple. Jax eased back, torturing her as he stopped playing, then lowered them to the ground until he lay on his back with her blanketed across his chest.

"You need to be naked," Seven gasped, rolling away from him.

His hands were on his jeans, and Seven brushed them away, wanting to unclasp his pants faster than he was going. As she kneeled next to his side, she slid him free until his engorged cock lay against his stomach after Jax finished kicking off his pants. She slowed to appreciate the view of a sculpted, scarred warrior.

Looks were fleeting, and she didn't think herself vain or only in search of a hot, toned man. But everything about him, from old scars to his carved muscles, seemed designed to make her eyes wander.

"Fuck, babe. If you're going to look at me like that…" Jax leaned over, grabbed her by the waist, and yanked her to straddle high on his chest. His forearm urged her from behind, propelling her higher, and he tipped his chin forward, pushing her knees above him as she relied on his arms to keep her balance.

"Ohhh!" The uncertainty vanished when his tongue licked her folds and strong lips kissed her pussy. "*Jax…*"

What was he doing? This was too much! Too intimate!

His tongue slid along the vertical bar, and she cried out in a wonderful sensation overload. His hands gripped her sides, controlling the unfamiliar position. Uncertainty battled with how she relished the sparkling fire such closeness created. But what was she supposed to do? Stay still and let her body soar? "Jax?"

The man gave nothing but tongue and kisses, and she fought the quivering urge in her thighs.

He wrapped an arm around her waist, and his chin nuzzled side to side. God, she couldn't breathe. Her body began shaking… no, convulsing. She could combust. She was too inexperienced for this man, and "help" should've come out of her mouth instead of his name.

His firm grip rocked her hips, and Seven whimpered. He groaned, sucking her clit and continuing to shift her as though she were supposed to ride him.

"Okay. Oh God." Her throat had gone dry, and his tongue pulsed in and out of her pussy as she rocked against his lips.

Jax groaned, sucking harder, giving her sweet kisses, and licking until she swayed uncontrollably.

"I'm going to…" Seven panted and moaned, climaxing as the thunder exploded, rippling through her, and she went limp. Jax rolled on top of her, and Seven grabbed his face, awakening again despite the white lightning that still roared. "Holy shit."

His confident grin was so well deserved. Seven curled her fingers into his back, scratching, and he grabbed his pants then pulled out a condom. "You want this?"

She nodded. "Yeah."

"You move when you want to move. You like something, you go with it. You don't, you say it. You're not sure, you can say that too. You want to try more, do less, that works for me. You read me?"

"Yes."

"Good girl." His approving nod meant everything. "I like your piercings, babe."

"I can tell—you might know more to do with them than me."

"Didn't get them to play?" Curiosity touched his voice.

She kissed him back instead of answering, until they were a mixture of gasping breaths and searching hands, with Jax pinning her on top of a mountain of pillows and couch cushions. His erection nudged at her center, and jaw hanging open, Seven would've begged if she'd had the words.

Instead, she watched—he did too, and his thickness eased into her body, stretching inch by inch until he was deep within her. Jax lowered himself, and when their stomachs touched, her clitoris had his weight. Seven squeezed around his cock, and he swore in her ear.

"Tell me what you want," he whispered after his last curse.

Easy. "Everything."

With a soft kiss, he pulled out—nearly to the tip—then thrust into her. Again and again, he rode her deep, hard, driving Seven to dig her nails into his back and pray he wouldn't let go.

"What's everything?" Jax grunted, slowing as though he were making love, taking the plateau he'd built and calming it to a dull roar.

"Please." Seven clawed for more. She dripped for him, and the tease of another orgasm was so close. "Don't stop."

He rolled his hips, and the sinewy muscles corded as she hung on. He worked into her, making use of the angles, thrusting until she forgot who they were, just that they had to come.

Together, legs and arms linked as their lips crashed. A chorus of climactic gasps came in tandem. Jax had thoroughly mastered her world.

He kissed her cheek, nuzzling quietly. "Don't nod off yet. I'm just getting started."

CHAPTER FIFTEEN

HOURS OF SEVEN and sex, and he might be able to die a happy man. Jax rolled over and lay on his back. Seven used his bicep as a pillow. He wasn't entirely sure, but there was a decent chance that she was asleep. He was well-fucked. Better than he'd been for as long as his mind could reach back. He wanted to blame his fascination with her piercings, but that would be the easy way out. She was fun. In many ways.

Fun to flirt with.

Fun to kiss, nibble, lick, and eat.

Fun to screw.

But it was the way that she came, totally and completely letting herself go, giving a raw realness in a way that he didn't know could happen. It was very... Seven-esque, and he dug it.

"You asleep?" He turned, tucking his other arm around her soft waist and sliding his palm over her hipbone.

"Nope. I just can't move."

A quiet rumble of laughter made his chest move. "My job here is done."

"I'd clap, but then..." She lifted her shoulder against him. "The whole moving thing."

"Clap, huh? That'd be a first."

One of her eyes opened. "There's a small chance I don't believe you."

He smirked, taking that moment to pull her naked body on top of his. "There's always the chance I'm wrong."

"You, wrong?" She nodded, sprawled over his torso, and let her chin rest against his. "That I believe a thousand times."

"Good to see pumping you full of orgasms doesn't quiet your attitude."

"Not a chance, big boy. Sorry if that was your grand plan."

"Plans come and go."

She smiled, and her mussed, bright hair hung over her face like a bold frame. "What's the next one?"

Jax ran his hands down her bare back, slowly skimming the beautiful swell of her ass. "Food."

"Oh, that's a good one. But the whole moving thing, remember?" She let her lips tickle against his as she spoke.

If he wasn't starving and she hadn't repeated how she couldn't move half a dozen times, the second time her tongue darted out and teased his lip, he would have flipped her over and started their antics again. But he was starved, and she was… whatever she was.

"A nice place like this? International business travelers?" He rolled her over carefully onto a pillow and stood, noticing that Seven didn't shrink away from how her hungry stare worked over him. "Let's see if their room service is twenty-four hours."

He glanced outside and noticed the sky wasn't the black it had been. A purple hue softened the skyline. He had no idea what time it was. Maybe the hotel even had breakfast open. He grabbed the phone and pressed the button for the front desk.

A moment later, a man answered. "*Buenos dias. Cómo puedo ayudarle?*"

What the hell was the word he was looking for? "*El servicio a la habitación?*"

"*Si.*"

Awesome. "Anything that's *la comida de desayuno.*"

He hung up and turned around to find Seven sitting up, knees pulled up with her arms tucked around them.

"What are we having?"

His grin hitched. "I think I ordered breakfast food. Hungry?"

She slow-clapped. "I'm impressed. Very Navy SEAL of you. Adapt to your surroundings."

Jax rolled his eyes and moved back to the pile of blankets and pillows they'd constructed into their sex den. "I can probably pull it off in Arabic too."

"Ohh, I'm getting hot and bothered all over again."

He curled his fingers, beckoning her to him, and she rolled her eyes.

"C'mere, Seven."

"You get bossy when you're hangry." She crossed her arms over her breasts.

"You've not seen me bossy, lucky." He curled his fingers again, silently calling her to him.

"You've not gotten lucky because of me... *yet*." She moved forward so that she was on all fours, her ass swaying back and forth.

"Oh, yeah? What would you call earlier?"

"It was inevitable." She slinked closer, crawling toward him, sending blood straight to his cock with every inch.

"Yeah—" Jax almost hissed when she burrowed into his naked lap and licked his thigh, dragging her tongue to the sensitive flesh near his groin. "Shit, Seven."

"Relax." She maneuvered his legs so that she kneeled in between them, carefully twisty-stroking his cock and letting the tip of her tongue toy with the thick ridge of his head.

"Not sure if relax is the right word." But his eyes sank shut when her lips closed around his hard-on. His breath stuttered at the wet heat enveloping him, and the smooth slide of the ball stud as her tongue feathered down him was bliss.

A vibrating moan rumbled over him as Seven worked him into her mouth. The crown hit the back of her throat, sliding deeper, and her hands felt as if they were everywhere at once. Twisting. Stroking. Massaging. She worked his shaft and played his scrotum. God, Jax was dizzy as his hips wanted to move. His mind wandered to an infinite blankness where he couldn't experience anything but her wicked mouth sucking him within an inch of his life.

Seven's blow job explored. It was messy with drool and sounds that he would remember. It was perfect, and he was trying not to come, needing this to last forever—or at least until room service arrived. *Fuck.*

Panting, he needed to fill her mouth. "Seven."

She nodded on him, moaning.

Jax thrust up, and she held her mouth down, gagging then massaging, gagging and working his shaft. He didn't want this to end. He gave her short, quick thrusts, and she bobbed her head in time, stacking her hands.

"Oh, shhhh—"

Seven's lips carefully stayed on the sensitive tip of his cock, her tongue and tongue stud sliding along the ridge of his crown as he came.

He collapsed back, landing on a pillow as she pulled away and curled under his arm. He was numb. Just like she'd said earlier, he couldn't move—not after he pulled her to his chest, letting her hair stick to his sweat-dampened skin.

Knock. Knock.

"Damn it." He groaned, not that he wasn't still hungry, but standing would require more effort than he could manage.

"Hang tight." Seven unwrapped from his hold and fashioned the sheet around her like a gown, the end of it trailing behind her as she headed toward the door.

Jax pulled a blanket over his lower half as she opened the door.

Seven laughed. "Wow, you ordered a lot!"

The room service waiter wheeled in their order, glancing his way briefly but catching himself and saying nothing.

Seven smiled with her sex-swollen lips and crazy hair. "Don't mind him."

"I didn't," the man said in a heavy accent, handing her the bill to sign. "As long as he's alive, my boss does not care."

She scrawled on the bill and signed with great flare then smiled as though the devil whispered in her ear. "He almost had the life sucked out of him, but I think he's going to make it."

The guy couldn't hold back his laugh, no matter how much he blushed and tried. Even Jax shook his head and chuckled.

She saw the delivery person out then beelined to the cart of food. "What to start with first?" She searched under lids, oohing and ahhing, then went to the kitchenette to wash up.

Probably a good idea. He lumbered up and headed to the bathroom.

"Whatever. Be back in a minute."

After a quick glance for his boxer briefs, he didn't see them and decided that naked was still the best course of action. A minute later, hands and face washed, he returned to Seven's elaborate picnic on the nearby couch. She'd moved some blankets and pillows, along with the coffee table, and had lost her sheet-gown.

"This might be one of the best ops I've ever worked."

Her eyebrow rose. "This might be one of the best Mayhem headaches I've ever had."

They both stood there, assessing in silence what that might actually mean and wondering if this would happen again. He had no idea. *Too fucking bad.* "Pancakes look good."

"Thought so too." Her flat smile didn't match the chipperness of agreement.

They met on the couch and dug in, devouring food with easy conversation, somehow not awkward even though they weren't clothed.

He was full, sated in many ways. And now, Jax's eyes seemed too heavy to stay awake. Seven yawned, and he eyed the bedroom where they'd stolen the covers. "Now we sleep?"

She popped up like a jack-in-the-box. "I need to get going."

His eyes went wide as he watched her fold all the sheets and extra blankets they'd pulled from the closet, smoothing the corners as if they had to be perfect.

"Are you staying here, or were you going back to…" She gestured to the window, and the city skyline was starting to show the break of dawn.

"You're not going to stay here?" he asked.

"People will worry if I'm not in my bed in the morning. Never know with those guys."

Jax ran his hand over his chin. "Right. I'll walk you—"

Her hand went up as if she were stopping traffic. "*No.* It's okay. I can see myself out."

"Seven…" He tried to get a read on the naked woman folding sheets. "I'm not a caveman. Only a jerk. Okay?"

"Jerk*face*," she joked quietly. "This has nothing to do with you. Everything to do with me. I like to be on my own. Do things my way. Please don't make me insist and pitch a fit, because I will."

Jax studied her, quieting the chivalrous grumble he didn't want to use in protest. "Sure."

Seven finished folding the blankets and dressed as he pulled on his boxer briefs and jeans, watching her tidy the room. He gathered that there was a certain way she did things and the woman liked her independence. Who was he to force his protective nature on her, especially when he wasn't that familiar with it when it appeared?

Finally, she looked around, seemingly pleased. "Okay, then."

He grinned. "Things are to your satisfaction?"

She walked over and pressed her lips to his, melting against him on the couch for a goodbye kiss that could've started everything over again if she'd asked him. Jax pulled back, finger-combing her hair. "We should do this again sometime."

A blushing hue hit her cheeks. "Maybe."

Self-conscious innocence wasn't what he'd expected from her, not after all their shenanigans. "See you around, then."

She kissed him one more time then headed to the door. "Bye, Jax. Thanks for a great night."

The hotel door shut, and he waited, wondering if she would knock and change her mind. It was one thing to want to leave, but walking out alone into a cold, lonely hallway and heading into a foreign city, where they were meeting with a cartel boss, was another.

She didn't. A minute ticked by, and still, her exit didn't sit well with him. He wasn't trying to be a patronizing asshole who got his way, but seriously...

Jax tapped his fingers, waiting for the urge to see her home to dissipate. It didn't. "Fuck it."

He stood, grabbed his shirt and shoes, pulled them on, and looked around the room. He didn't want to stay there without her. His hotel room wasn't far away from hers.

After waiting what he was certain was long enough for her to catch an elevator, Jax left the room, went to the lobby, and asked the doorman which way the beautiful woman with pink went. She wasn't someone people could miss or forget.

A moment later, Jax found himself a half block behind a pink-haired showstopper and walked at enough of a distance that he could get to her if someone hassled her. No one did, and he stayed far away when she walked into a hotel with motorcycles lined nearby.

"Get some sleep, Seven." He should, too, but suddenly, all he could do was think about whether colors had personalities and if bright, bold pink had meaning.

CHAPTER SIXTEEN

THE SILENT CITY began to wake as more cars made their way down the streets and more cafés and corner shops opened. Jax decided to take the scenic route back to his hotel, the one where his team was bunking, and he wondered if they had noticed he didn't come home last night. Hell, he wondered if they cared, because he wasn't sure if he would've noticed if one of them didn't come home.

Any of these streets would lead back to where he needed to go, but he kept his slow pace, each step returning him to his normal numb shell. He didn't want to head inside—in so many ways. He wanted to avoid the claustrophobic confines of his hotel room and not crawl into the overpowering, depressing cave that soured his mind.

Jax didn't hate his teammates. He wasn't sure they knew that, but it wasn't his job to hand out explanations. Truthfully, he respected the hell out of them for their service and sacrifice. Each had talents that were unequaled by few other men and women on Earth, and he needed them, just like the teammates on his SEAL team. But his SEAL team had known the before and the after of who he was long ago, when Jax had a future to look forward to versus a shell of a body used to fight with.

He stepped off the curb—*honk!* He swung toward the car, the screeching tires mixing with the blaring horn as it slid to a stop.

The driver's fist pumped, but Jax was more curious about his lack of fear than concerned. He threw his hand up, waving a non-apologetic apology, and finished crossing the street. The hours he'd spent on the floor with Seven had been vividly alive. Crazy how that feeling didn't last.

He passed a shopkeeper sweeping flower petals before the day started. Carrie would've loved this city with the old buildings, the architecture, and even the crappy stands overflowing with flowers so full they looked fake. Hell, she would've loved them even if they were scarred like him.

It had taken Jax years to realize that he wasn't in love with her ghost. He couldn't love anyone because that would've required feeling anything other than emptiness and anger.

CHAPTER SEVENTEEN

JAX EVENTUALLY STORMED back to his hotel room and slept a few hours before Titan had to make the quick trip to the airport. They were now sitting on a private jet as it taxied down the runway, heading back toward home, and he had every intention of going to sleep. His eyes were heavy, and his mind was too. Why was last night any different than any other time he had spent with a woman?

Jax took a blanket that was left on his seat and covered his face with it after the captain did his spiel on cruising altitude and how many more hours they had left in the flight. Enough time remained to get a good day's worth of sleep. The blanket was ripped off his face, and he squinted one eye open then two as Jared took a seat in the plush leather chair facing him.

"What'd you think?"

Jax rubbed a hand over his face. "Waste of our time. Sorry I asked."

Boss Man shook his head. "It wasn't a waste of our time. Hawke's the real deal. Solid. Guy's got integrity. That Johnny fucker, though. If he hadn't been there…" Jared shook his head again. "I don't know. I should've seen that play coming with Esmeralda."

Jax's jaw fell slightly, and he tried to play it off. He was shocked. There was never an ounce of second-guessing or doubt when it came to Jared. "One of those life-comes-at-ya-fast situations."

Johnny was susceptible, and Tex had tried to warn everybody, but at the end of the day, pulling the negotiations to regroup had been Hawke's decision, and Titan was just a paid contractor—and not one employed to have an opinion. They were compensated no matter what the outcome of the meeting was.

Jared leaned back in his chair, stroking the beard he'd been growing and gazing out the small airplane window. After a moment of uncomfortable, contemplative silence, Jared turned his attention back. "Anyway, everything okay with you?"

His spine straightened, and his jaw tightened. Always defensive at that question for as long as he could remember, Jax consciously reminded himself that it was a perfectly harmless inquiry. "Always."

Jared's eyes narrowed in an assessing way that made Jax possibly want to reconsider his internal mantra that it was a harmless question when people checked on him.

"You know, you get away with being a cocky asshole." Jared ran his fingers into his beard then stroked it back down. "A real dick, if you ask me. But lying to me won't fly, even in dumbass small talk, because I don't ever make small talk without a purpose. Do you read me?"

Jared's outward casual appearance hadn't changed, but the grave seriousness of his tone had, and Jax heard the message. He couldn't bullshit Boss Man. "Yeah. Got it."

Jared stood up, not interested in Jax re-answering the question—and thank fuck because he didn't know how to—then left him to his own thoughts, which might've been worse than having to explain to Boss Man what he thought was wrong.

THERE WAS NOTHING like watching Mayhem board an airplane. No matter where they were coming from or heading to, Seven got a kick out of watching the jeans- and boots-clad men—who wore MC gear because it was their life, not for the fun of a trend—take their seats. Their leather cuts with pins and skulls stitched on got more than a few worried looks. But in Seven's mind, it was better that TSA worry about Mayhem than jump all over some innocent person who *looked* like a terrorist. None of her friends would have their feelings hurt with a few condescending looks.

Their group was called, and en masse, they boarded. When Seven arrived at her seat, Johnny glared back. *Lucky me.*

"Are you always so happy?" She put her backpack in the bin overhead then took a seat. "Or is it just me?"

Johnny shifted toward the man next to him, who was already half asleep against the window. "I'm happy."

"You're five kinds of grump-a-saraus."

"Don't talk to me like I'm Nolan."

She rolled her eyes as she buckled in. "I won't. He's three and light years ahead of you in maturity."

"*That's* mature."

So what if it wasn't? "Get some coffee, and whatever ails you will leave you."

"Wish it were that easy," Johnny grumbled, glancing over her shoulder. Then he reached for a magazine and aimlessly flipped through it.

Seven eased back and casually looked around. Ah, Johnny was having a hard time with Hawke. She could've guessed that. Tension between them had been thick since before they'd boarded to come down to Colombia. After everything she had heard went down at the restaurant, it was no wonder.

"Why are you sunshine and smiles when you look like shit?" Johnny asked.

She twisted in her seat belt. "Like shit, huh? Thanks, asswipe."

"Call it like I see it."

"I don't look like sh—"

"You do." Johnny flipped the pages of his magazine, still not reading.

"Yet another reason I'm glad I didn't stay married to you. Such a sweetheart."

"You stayed for the honesty. Tell me you didn't." He chuckled. "And my c—"

"Don't even." Seven groaned. But Johnny was half-right. She appreciated *the truth,* but nothing else that he might've almost mentioned. "Either way, sometimes you're supposed to lie. Or not bring it up."

"What'd you get into last night?" He closed the magazine and slipped it into the holder on the chair in front of them. "Look at you. Bags under your eyes. You were asleep on your feet earlier."

"Nice of you to notice."

"I keep a note of what's going on."

"I bet," she mumbled. He was right, and she had every intention of going to sleep like the guy against the window as soon as they took off.

"But," Johnny said and left her hanging until she couldn't help but ask.

"But what?"

"Still fucking glowing." He tilted his head. "Haven't seen that look on you in a long time."

Nope. No way was Johnny going to call her out for a post-orgasm glow in the middle of Mayhem while they were stuck on a plane. "You're out of your mind."

"If I didn't know any better…" He leaned close, studying her, and Seven's nerves got the best of her.

She wanted to inch back but didn't want to show her hand. "Back off, buckaroo."

"I'd think you were thrilled we're leaving here with the deal intact."

Seven recoiled, laughing. "Wrong. You do know me, and *wanting the coke business* is impossible. I'd never want that in a million years."

"What problems are you causing now?" Hawke snapped at Johnny from across the aisle.

Instinctively, she wanted to keep the men apart, and her hands went up, but the airplane was taxiing down the runway already.

"Talking to Seven," Johnny said past her. "Not you."

"You two need to chill." She pointed fingers at both. Not many old ladies could get away with that, though she didn't belong to either of them. Then she gave Hawke a long look and turned to Johnny. "Save your drama for when we touch down. I'm going to sleep."

"It's not drama. It was a decision." He grabbed the magazine and flipped pages furiously.

She was going to get no sleep if he was over there on a manic paper-cut endeavor. The flight attendant was two rows ahead of them, pushing a cart. It didn't look like food. Maybe she had more magazines for the international flight. Either way, she was gorgeous and a great distraction that made Johnny and Hawke behave.

As the woman approached, her presence worked like a charm as Seven settled back into her semi-uncomfortable chair. Then listening to Johnny flirt with the woman drove her nuts.

"Ma'am?"

Seven opened her eyes, questioning if she was the *ma'am*. "Yeah?"

"Would you like a blanket or pillow to sleep with?"

Damn it. The last thing she wanted was a stupid blanket that she couldn't stop fussing with.

"She's fine," Johnny said for her, thankfully.

There had been too much craziness in the last two days, and sometimes the folding couldn't be helped. It was a control thing, and nothing had been controllable lately. Seven clung to the armrests. "What he said," she mumbled.

"Are you sure?" The flight attendant pulled out a plastic-wrapped blanket, misreading the dynamic between her and Johnny, her misery, and why she held on to her seat. "If you want it, it's not a problem."

The blanket, folded unevenly and sadly sitting in its plastic wrap of doom, was thrust into her face, and she couldn't look away, couldn't believe how fast she had to take it. Embarrassed by the lack of control, she knew hot tears would fall but still didn't stop. "Thanks."

Seven reached down, found her sunglasses in her purse, and slid them into place. Then she tore the plastic off the blanket, needing far more room than she had, and went about folding the blanket correctly.

And failing.

Then trying again.

And failing.

And again, trying more.

Then, again and again, failing.

Until her last fold. As she studied and smoothed the corner, Johnny took his hands and wrapped them around hers, awkwardly holding her own still in her lap. Together, they sat there, holding hands, holding her in place, as tears slipped free and she concentrated on breathing.

Hawke stood up without saying a word and took the blanket from under their hands. And she was free. It was so stupid. She was trapped and stressed but, thank God, surrounded by people who got her as much as she got them. He walked away and returned empty-handed without mentioning a thing.

CHAPTER EIGHTEEN

HERNÁN SUAREZ CLOSED the handwritten accounting books as his personal financier hovered close by. Classical music played in the background, and the decadent smell of dinner wafted from the kitchen behind the private dining enclosure while he reviewed the day's numbers and had dinner with Esmeralda.

This was their time to connect and his time to inspect the daily tallies from the cartel's various moneymakers, most of which were diversified internationally, with the bulk funneled through the United States.

"All remains good?" Esmeralda asked in English. That was the language of business. When they were in bed, at home, or at the market for a stroll, they always spoke Spanish. But they'd learned to differentiate that part of their life with one single barrier—language.

Hernán wasn't sure what made him more excited. That his wife wanted their fortune to grow because it meant power—not more money, though that was an obvious benefit—or if he liked to see the dark side of her, the devious one. It made his blood run hot and his heart grow. They were partners made to work and to love.

Having perused what he needed to see, Hernán gave a nod and closed the leather-bound portfolio. He ran his hands over his fortune, basking in the decisions they had made over the past few days. "It does, my dear."

Her sweet, sadistic smile could give a heartless man a cold chill as easily as she could spin a siren's song silently around an unnoticing victim. "Excellent."

They didn't want any changes with Mayhem, and she had assured it by planting a seed of doubt and greed. Men could be so simple.

Hernán's perspective and strategy had a businessman's slant. But Esmeralda's… she was much like his father, capable of psychological ruthlessness, and her cold hands reminded him of this even by touch as she put her hand on top of his. "Are we ready for the next course?"

She didn't care about the books as she held his palm down to the pencil-coded bankbooks. Hernán tilted his head over his shoulder as they both lifted their hands, and the financier walked over and removed the leather-bound records.

Hernán stroked Esmeralda's wrist as the next course of their meal was ushered in. "Is there anything you want?"

The question was posed religiously, and whenever she had an answer, which wasn't often, he made it happen. Most times, she made it happen herself. But there was a delicious aspect of providing for her when she didn't need to be cared for. His grip on her forearm tightened, hanging onto her as hard as he could, knowing that no matter how painful the grip might be, it wouldn't break her.

Her bottom lip parted from the top as she clung to the squeeze of pain he offered as a quick gift. When he released, she rubbed the blotchy red mark on her beautiful almond skin, and her lips curled in relaxed pleasure.

"One thing," she whispered, eyes barely focused on him.

"Yes?"

"*La hija.*" Children.

Not business at all. They hadn't had that discussion in some time, and it was the one thing he couldn't give her. Children. But he'd promised if it was something she wanted, it was something she could have. He would find her a way when she was ready.

Esmeralda pushed her long, dark hair over her shoulder and eyed one of the servants, who came over and topped off their wineglasses then scuttled away. She wrapped her fingers around the base of the glass, letting her manicured nails trace up and down the crystal stem as she swirled the expensive vino, lost in thought.

Hernán knew where her mind was but not the dark twists and turns it always took. "You're still worrying about the meeting with Mayhem?"

She tilted her head, not answering with words as much as she did a silent look.

If Mayhem changed the distribution, there was no question that they would lose money, and that was his concern. Hers was more control. She didn't like plays to be initiated outside of their direction, even when they brought better circumstances to their family. It had taken many, many conversations with her before they came to an agreement. It was an agreement, because for as much as he was the head of this organization, she was his wife, his partner, his world. Hernán would give anything to her.

"If Hawke shores up the rift we made with Johnny, then we find a new hole to tear open. That's business, right, *mi vida?*"

Esmeralda picked up her glass and took a long sip. Then they both watched as their plates were traded out for the next course.

"What if they subbed out their distribution?" She picked up her fork and held it over her plate, clearly thinking of various options that Hawke could take while still honoring the agreement between Suarez and Mayhem.

Hernán shook his head, digging in to the feast in front of him. "Never. To be so bold without my explicit permission? Unacceptable."

She speared a piece of meat on her plate, raised it to her mouth, and chewed deliberately. "You trust them too much."

Her words sank in as they feasted on dinner. Interesting that she was positing ideas without solutions. She couldn't see the whole picture, either, and maybe that was the problem.

"Hawke would," she finally assessed. "He's in the MC for *the club*, not for himself. He'd choose the organization's greater good over one of self-satisfaction."

Hernán cut into the Kobe beef, and the bloody meat melted like butter as he thought about what she'd said. For as long as he'd known Hawke, that was true. The man's life was dedicated to his motorcycle club, and that was one of the reasons why he was an excellent distribution partner. The club wanted to make money; so did Hernán. The club wanted to stay protected. So did he. But if the club wanted to get out and there was a vote, then Esmeralda was right. It was Johnny, who even if they had turned, was the weakest link for both of them. "We'll have to find more pressure points than just the one that sat at our table."

Esmeralda nodded. "Something painful to keep our friends in line."

That sounded like his wife, the business partner he knew so well. She loved to work in pain, and that worked with his business acumen. "What do we know…"

"Not enough right now." She stabbed a piece of meat, and as she picked it up and held it before her lips, the rare meat dripped blood onto the plate. "Send Jorge Torres."

Hernán faltered for a moment, not expecting his name to be worked into the conversation. "Why would you suggest him?"

"I have found that he is exceptional at seeing who is expendable and seeing who creates action." She took a long moment to enjoy her beef. "There's a fine line between squeezing the life out of someone that no one will remember and doing so to one person that will ruin the lives of many. He knows how to figure out the difference."

They finished their dinner in silence. Then the server came over and exchanged their main course plates for cheese and fruit. Esmeralda was likely lost in imaginary thoughts of how to do the killing, and he wondered if she was right, if Torres was the right person for the job or if that was too strong of a play.

Hernán plucked a grape from his plate and reached across the table, feeding it to her. Her lips wrapped around his fingers as she took it from him, and everything made sense. The Ying to his Yang, the diabolical to his fanatical. "I'll call him in the morning and send him to the United States."

CHAPTER NINETEEN

"OPEN UP!" SEVEN banged on Johnny's door again after trying the handle. "Damn it, Johnny."

She wasn't sure when was the last time he'd used his lock. Hell, she didn't even know if he had a set of keys to his own place. This time, she hauled off and kicked the door. "Open. Up. Now."

The door across the hallway opened. "Everything okay, Seven?"

She smiled at Mrs. Reed, the woman who turned a blind eye to everything Johnny did and who had made her coffee cake on Sundays when she lived there. "Just want to make sure my ex-hubby isn't dead."

"He was stomping around earlier."

"Good. Thanks, Mrs. Reed."

"Tell your parents that I say hello."

"Will do." Seven smiled as best she could, waited until Mrs. Reed's door shut, then turned around to beat Johnny's door down. His bike was downstairs, and he'd been avoiding her for days. He could've left in a car with someone else, but that didn't feel right. "Johnny, I'm not leaving. I even brought snacks if I had to stay here all day."

The door clicked, and the handle turned. Then it cracked open a few inches.

"Hello in there." She tried to push in but got nowhere.

"You're a persistent pain in my ass." Dark circles and red eyes met her stare. "Go home. I'm alive."

"We need to talk."

"Nothing to talk about, sweet lips."

Seven gave him a big, fake grin. "Good. Then I have to pee. Let me in."

"Jesus, you don't give up."

With both hands, she slapped the door. "Nope. Scoot over." After she pushed through, she waved her hand at the stale air. "Crack a window. It smells like cigarettes and dope in here. Gah."

"Shove it."

"It's almost foggy." Instead of going to the bathroom, she dropped onto the couch. "I didn't have to go."

He rolled his eyes and eased into a recliner. "Of course."

"So how ya been?"

"Fine."

"Johnny..." She assessed him. Bloodshot eyes. Dark circles. Pale skin. Wrinkled clothes. The place needed fresh air, and there were stacks of pizza boxes within arm's length. "Where have you been?"

"Working."

"Where? Doing what?"

"Ease up, Seven. All right?"

She shook her head. "No, sir. If you're going to fall head first into a pile of blow and smoke dope until you can't see straight, I'd at least like you to answer the phone when I call."

"Don't know where it is." He shrugged. "And I didn't hear it ring."

God, she hated when he went on benders. "You shouldn't get like this. You didn't used to, and when you're in business with—"

He perched forward on the edge of the chair. "Club business *isn't* your business."

"Well, talk about taking your drugs away, and you certainly wake up."

Johnny looked away, shaking his head.

"And you seem to find your phone when you need to order pizza." Seven stood up, trying not to fume. She hated when he acted as though she didn't have any investment in Mayhem. Her world was Mayhem. What, since she was a woman, she couldn't talk to him about the empire her father had built? "Call me when you're sober. I like that Johnny. This Johnny is a dick."

"Fat chance."

Seven stormed out as Mrs. Reed opened the door. "Would you like a piece of carrot cake for the little ones?"

It was odd that she would even think about them. "Sure, thank you."

"The nicest man was asking about them. We just chatted and—"

The door opened back up, and Johnny strode out, but as soon as he saw Mrs. Reed, whatever he was about to yell after Seven fell away with an awkward smile. "Hi, Mrs. Reed."

Leave it to Johnny to pull out some charm.

"Hello, dear. Would you like a piece of carrot cake?"

"I have to go. I'm late." After offering a dozen apologies, Seven shuffled away, not willing to stand next to a coked-out Johnny, making small talk with the neighbors as if this were Mayberry.

As soon as Seven got in her car, she turned over the engine and drummed her fingers on the steering wheel. "Screw this."

She didn't have cake and wouldn't have an ex-husband who was going to snort his life away. Seven grabbed her cell phone and called Hawke. The phone rang twice before he picked up. If nothing else, he gave her the respect she deserved, most times, and listened to her thoughts.

"Hey, Hawke, do you have a few minutes?"

"Sorry, Seven, but I was getting ready to call you real quick."

"Why, what's up?"

"Can you make it to Vegas to help sort out our headache?"

If it had anything to do with Mayhem, she was down to help. "Sure. Whenever you need me."

"I'm calling a summit of possible distribution partners. Whether Hernán is on board or not, I'm figuring this out."

Her head dropped back against the headrest. That was terrific news. "What's Johnny have to say?"

"Haven't heard from him in a few days, and honestly? I don't give a fuck. He'll show up or not."

Ah, now it all made sense—why Johnny was on a bender and what had triggered him and his worse-than-normal mood. "He'll be there. He'd never miss anything for the club."

Hawke sighed. "Yeah, that's what I'm afraid of."

ACROSS THE PARKING lot, Jorge Torres spun a pencil between his fingers. He'd parked in a way that allowed him to watch the walk-up apartment complex and also keep an eye on Johnny Miller's window as well as the parking lot.

Jorge had rightly assumed that Mayhem's vice president had locked himself inside his home. He hadn't seen the wife they knew about, women they'd heard about, or anyone besides his blow connection and food delivery.

Fast food was the dinner of champions. He grumbled, staring at the bag of tacos and tacquitos he'd picked up at a drive-through. The smell was almost enticing, but that was perhaps a mind-over-matter situation as he hadn't stopped for a meal in almost a day. Hernán had told him to work and work fast. That Johnny was the weak link, and so there Jorge was, in America, with bad food and no sign of life.

Until the pink-and-blue-haired wild child with leather boots and tight pants had shown up. He'd watched her through binoculars nearly slap down the door. The woman matched the description he had of Johnny's wife. Trouble in paradise. Made sense. Between a woman disrespectful enough to kick the door and Mayhem in chaos with Hernán, Jorge imagined few lived a normal life of love without the complexities that cartel business added.

With few leads, the one small ping of information had come from a neighbor when he'd thrown out random questions about a wife, kids, and a job. Only the kids had seemed to interest the woman. They were most likely staying wherever the wife was.

Jorge tossed the pencil and opened up the bag of food. It'd cooled, but tacos were fine—hot, cold, whatever—when he was starving. He opened the room-temperature taco, shoved it into his mouth, and gagged. "*Mierda!*" He spat into the bag and wiped his mouth with his sleeve.

Why couldn't this have been a job somewhere he liked? New York? New Orleans? But Sweet Hills, Iowa? He spat in the bag again, unable to get the over-processed aftertaste out of his mouth. *I would even take Toronto in the winter. Give me that.* They could make a mean tostado—authentic and fast. Not this *mierda*.

He picked up the phone, dialing the business counterpoint who regularly contracted his services for the Suarez cartel. It rang twice, and when the line picked up without a response, Jorge felt a twinge of relief as he readied to pass the update. "Relay that we have found our negotiating point."

The line went dead. He rolled his window down, held out the bag of food, lit it on fire, and dropped the flaming bag to the parking lot. He pulled out as the wife stayed in her car, talking on the phone. Jorge would find a good position where he could follow her to see where she lived and if there were kids.

Please let there be kids. Children were a much better pressure point. They would get him home faster. Hernán and Esmeralda could work with that, negotiating much better terms on almost anything with kids over an old lady, especially one that slapped doors.

The fruit of the loin of Señor Johnny Miller. Jorge grinned. Esmeralda would use that and get whatever she wanted, and he would have real food sooner than he'd hoped.

CHAPTER TWENTY

THE PERKY CUP'S atmosphere was as buzzed as her espresso. Patrons were busy and talking, sipping and snacking, and posting pictures on social media of muffins and cupcakes. Kiddos played on the train table, and a romance novel book club bantered back and forth in the corner about the boundaries in books lately.

All in all, it was a typical day in Seven's coffee shop, punctuated by the occasional spill and broken mug, crying kid, and the constant jingle-jangle of the front-door bell.

But her mind continued to drift back to Hawke's phone call. *Vegas.*

What was Seven going to do in Vegas? She didn't expect to vacation. Her role was likely part figurehead, part keep-Johnny-in-line, with a dash of give-Hawke-her two-cents-if-he-asked, all while keeping an eye on Titan Group.

Most of Mayhem wanted Titan included, but the idea of outsiders involved was still a concern for some members. They were doing their best to approach this part of club business as business, and in business, there were times that third party... *vendors* were required. At least that was how she'd heard Hawke explain Titan to anyone who balked.

Vegas wasn't her scene, not that she'd ever been. Seven would much rather stick to her precise routine that was mapped out and involved taking care of her priorities: kids, mother, and coffee shop.

Eventually, she was on the list... maybe... or maybe not. Though she could track down a few piercing rock stars and fan-girl them—if there was time.

"Seven!"

She snapped out of her Vegas concerns and ducked her head out of her office, more than glad to have a reason other than Hawke and Vegas to avoid reviewing the latest purchase orders. "What's up?" But she didn't need an answer because Jax stood next to Sidney. It wasn't often Seven was caught off guard, just like it wasn't often that Jax did what she expected. "Hey."

Sidney gaped at them as if he'd been huffing whippets. "I'm good to close if you want to take off early."

"Umm." A dopey grin that made her feel as though she was on a sugar high plastered onto her face, and it took far too much thought to tone down her reaction. "Yeah, sure. Maybe. Jax, what are you doing here?"

"I forgot to mention last time I was here that the smoothie was off the charts." He thumbed to where Sidney stood at his side. "Sidney mentioned this was your place when I said something, and I thought it'd be a good excuse to come back and see you."

Her eyes went as wide as Sidney's. A few customers cast curious glances their way. What most didn't know was Jax didn't live in Iowa! He lived somewhere on the east coast, and she didn't know, because *she lived in Iowa!*

Seven crept closer to the counter. "You could have called." Nervously, she played with her tongue stud. "You *do* call."

He crossed his arms, and every muscle naturally flexed, even those hidden by a casual cotton shirt. The ridges of his shoulders and the definition of his chest magnified as he tried not to laugh, clamping down his chiseled jaw line. "It's infinitely more entertaining to see you figure out how to handle this in person."

He had no idea that he wasn't the only person finding entertainment value at the moment. The normal level of chitchat in The Perky Cup had lowered to the listening level of eavesdropping.

The phone rang, and Sidney groaned as he turned to answer it.

"Let's go back—"

"Seven, hang on a second," Sidney said and went back to his call. "Only if you're sure, because now is *really* not a good time." He paused. "Fine, then. But just so you know, I am *not* happy with you, Gennita."

Oh? Seven's eyebrows arched. "What's going on?"

"Gennita said her old man fell ill. Needs to go get him from the compound." Sidney grumbled under his breath. "She swore up and down he's really sick and it's an emergency. Adelia has the kids for a few, but she has to go to work."

"Not a problem." Gennita grandmothered the hell out of Nolan and Bianca. There wasn't a chance she would push the kids back on Seven at work if her old man was drunk or hungover. "But it looks like you get to cover for me after all." She turned to Jax and had no idea how to handle this. "Come back to my office for a minute?"

He nodded then followed, and Seven shut the door, suddenly very aware that he was next to the threshold, almost pressed against her.

"Maybe I should've called."

The masculine scent of his cologne and the closeness of his body heat made her breaths feel shallow. "You're in *Iowa*."

"When you say it like that…" He winked. "At least a text first."

"That's nuts. You know that?"

"We were done with a job. I was in Dallas-Fort Worth and could go anywhere."

"*Iowa*."

He chuckled. "You want me to get back in a Lyft and go?"

Seven shook her head. "Not really."

"I have to go back to work tomorrow night, and don't read that the wrong way. I didn't fly in to fuck you."

She blinked, having no idea how to take that.

"But I had some time on my hands. Thought I'd stop by."

"*Iowa*."

Jax put his hand on her throat, tilting her head back with the strength of his fingers, and silenced her with his lips. Their firmness made her weak as her pulse pounded in her neck, and she moaned. His fingers flexed for a flash until Jax backed her to the wall and released his hold.

Seven gasped into his kiss, moaning for more when his hot tongue slid between her lips.

"I wanted to kiss you again," he whispered, letting his mouth feather against her cheek before he dropped to her neck and used his teeth.

"God, yes." Her nipples pricked as his words rumbled against her senses. She raked her nails up his back, and Jax left a searing trail of kisses to her collarbone. She pulled back. "Jax—wait."

"Yeah?" She placed her hands on the carved muscles of his chest, flexing her fingers. He pulled her hands off, interlaced their fingers, and pinned them above her head. "I'm waiting."

"I have kids."

He ducked his head close. Him and her, away from the world, in a shadowed room of their faces, their warm breaths, heated from their kisses. "I should've called."

"All these real-life responsibilities. Kids. A business. A thing with my mom. Stuff like that."

He nodded. "You don't have to explain. I'll head out."

"No!" She didn't want him to go but didn't know what to do. "Is Ryder in town? Maybe…"

He shook his head. "Don't worry about it."

"I'd invite you over, but I get it. Kids. Those are scary little people to bachelor guys. Though it's not like I'd tell them who you are, not that you are something, or…" She cringed, not sure what that sounded like to him. "What I mean is that they are around a lot of my friends, many in Mayhem. They're used to friends who are male. Never mind." She laughed awkwardly, making the situation a thousand times more uncomfortable than it had to be.

Jax stepped back. "I didn't think this through. That's on me."

His words hit like a gut shot. Not that she wanted him to meet her kids, but damn, she didn't want him to run from who she really was, and he'd been told in no uncertain terms that she had kids. The guy had flown to Iowa and didn't think about it. He did just want to screw, and his *other* head had led him the entire way there. Why was she surprised—and hurt? "No worries."

But even as she tried to add sunshine into her fib, she heard it fall flat without her permission.

"What I'm trying to say is…" Jax walked back to the small couch in her office and took a seat. "Having an unknown—*houseguest?* Who's a guy.

That's probably a big deal to throw at a woman with kids, and it was screwed up of me not to think it through." He pursed his lips together, having no idea what he was talking about. "That makes me a dick, and that wasn't what I was trying to do." He put his arm over the back of the couch. "I wanted to see you and say hey. I did, so I can bounce."

"Please don't." Seven crossed her office and joined him. "Hang out with us."

"I don't want to cause a problem."

She cackled. "Mayhem showing up at six in the morning and demanding I set a meeting with Titan Group is a problem. Though it's had its benefits," she teased. "If you're down for some serious mac and cheese and dino-chicken-nugget action and then crashing in the guest room, I'd love to hang."

A smile that she hadn't seen before lit his face. Maybe he hadn't expected to be served dino nuggets, or maybe he was amused to be relegated to the guest bedroom. She had no idea, but learning more about Jax was like unwrapping a present that had many complicated layers. When she least expected it, another gift showed up. There it was, and surprise! An unexpected bit of joy came her way.

"Do I get a good-night kiss and tucked in?" he joked.

"I can manage that." Seven stood up and held out her hand. "Hang with us for the night? At Casa de Kiddos?"

He grasped her hand, hoisting himself so their bodies touched. "Just know one thing."

"What's that?"

"Kids shouldn't scare a man away."

Wow... Even as every part of her flew into the air like a dusting of confectioner's sugar, she melted as he headed toward the door.

"Ready?"

How different his childhood had probably been, and for the millionth time, she recommitted to making sure Nolan and Bianca never had the experience she had in which her infamous father saw Seven as an imposition or an asset but never a kid.

CHAPTER TWENTY-ONE

OBSTACLES WERE A part of life. Jax trained for them. He planned courses of action then backup, prepared for them to fail. He was constantly ready to pivot and adjust so that the unexpected never found him waiting.

Right now, he was T-minus five seconds to out of his league and only had a car's drive worth of intelligence gathering.

Adelia hung on the apartment complex porch, waving goodbye to the kids but trying to catch a better eye of who was in Seven's car, and he was transfixed by the three- and almost five- year-old holding Seven's hands as they walked to the car.

The little boy bounced, and his mouth never stopped. He fit his name, and Jax worried the kid never took a breath.

Then there was the little girl. Seven said she was tall for her age and acted much older than she was. She was contemplative and serious on the outside, but really a silly one who craved trust—but only with a select few.

"Nolan and Bianca," he tried their names out loud.

Cute names for cute kids, and watching Seven banter with Nolan painted her in a new light. She was every bit the mom his mother was. Odd how he could pick that out from a couple dozen yards away. Seven's world was her kids, and he respected that more than she would probably ever know.

The back door opened, and the kids crawled in.

"Hi, Mr. Jax!" Nolan shouted as he scampered to the buckles on his car seat. Seven grinned and tugged his car seat straps into place.

Already turned in his seat, Jax waved. "Hey, Nolan. Nice to meet you, buddy."

"Hello." Bianca's greeting was the prim and proper one he'd expected. She was noticeably quieter than she'd been before the car door had opened.

"Hi, Bianca." Jax focused on her. "That's a pretty bow in your hair."

Her eyes lit, but her mouth remained impassive, not allowing a smile to pass. "Thank you."

"It matches your shirt. I really like that." He turned back in his seat, catching her in the rearview mirror as Bianca glanced down.

"I chose it myself," she volunteered, a tiny crack of happiness allowed to cross her face.

Nolan started talking and never stopped as Bianca turned toward the window. Seven had predicted they would do this, and after she checked on Bianca's self-buckled harness, she joined him in the front and turned over the engine. "If I'd known you were coming, I might've cleaned up."

"She would've run around at the last second, putting things in closets," Bianca added, kicking her legs.

Jax laughed. "That's what I do too."

"The little truth-teller." Seven ducked her hand back as she pulled away from Adelia's apartment and squeezed Bianca's leg. "That's a good trait to have."

Five minutes later, they were in Seven's driveway. "Home sweet home."

Her house was cute. The front windows were stained glass, separating her from her neighbors, and her flowerbeds overflowed with colors.

"The flowers are all Victoria's doing." Seven shifted into Park and reached back, unfastening car seats. "Wash hands when we get inside."

A moment later, Jax stood next to her car as the wave of energy blurred past, clambering for the door until she unlocked it.

Jax lagged behind, taking in Seven's personality and style but the house and hearth version—with kids. Her house warmed him from the inside out, and laughter rang from the walls as he followed them in.

"Nolan will give you a tour," Bianca announced. "He knows which light switches turn on all the lights."

That made sense to Jax, and he nodded. "All right."

"*After* everyone washes their hands." Seven walked back down the hall, free of her keys and purse. She held her arms out in welcome. "Make yourself at home."

It'd been a long time since he'd been in a house that was lived in, especially by children. Jax didn't socially hang out with many of his teammates, and his SEAL buddies were like him. They had home bases, and they were furnished with essentials and go bags. Furnishings weren't important. There wasn't much time for art on the walls. The closest he got to homey and comfortable was fake and at safe houses.

This house was lived-in, and he was glad Seven hadn't known he was coming. The place was as clean and neat as one with little kids could safely expect to keep and stay sane.

As he wandered around, he couldn't help but appreciate how they each had added their personality. Drawings and blocks, pillows and blankets, Lincoln Logs and Legos, dolls with all their dresses and multicolored hair.

And the Harley toys. Jax laughed. They were in the life…

Seven's walls were decorated with pictures, art, and occasional references to motorcycle culture. Her vibrant style carried through with leathers and bold colors—turquoise wall here, purple archways there.

He glanced over and saw her leaning against the cutaway to the dining room, watching him take it all in.

"What's going through your mind?" she asked.

"I like this. You three have a cool place."

"It was four. My mom recently moved to a nursing home." Her unreadable face gave nothing away. "But she wasn't in a good place to contribute much, and when she left"—Seven gestured—"I guess nothing changed, either."

Jax sat down on the couch, listening to the kids play in their rooms down the hall. "Do you miss her? Having another adult to help out?"

"She couldn't help before, and her doctor didn't know what made it worse. Old age, I guess. I couldn't take care of her very well for the past couple weeks." She lifted a shoulder. "It's better that way. For her."

"For you?"

Seven crossed the room, joining him on the couch. "No one wants to put their mom in a nursing home, especially now. I'm too young. She's too young. It's just… It sucks."

"I'm sorry."

"What about you?" she asked.

"Family?" He shrugged when the kids sounded as though they were coming out of their rooms.

Seven seemed to have both him and them under observation, and it was a talent to manage without seeming as if she were watching a tennis match. "You weren't magically conceived."

"Ha. No, I wasn't—"

A beep sounded from the kitchen, and Seven popped up. "Don't forget whatever you were about to confess, but mac and cheese waits for no one, not even magically conceived SEALs."

As soon as Seven rushed to the kitchen, Nolan and Bianca arrived. The little boy crawled next to Jax with a Lego plane in hand, while Bianca played with her dolls.

"Want to pway with me?" Nolan shoved the plane into Jax's hand. "Up like this." Then hoisted his arm in the air. "*Up!*"

"Vr-vroom," Jax flew it back and forth and glanced at the kid. *Big fail.*

"Pwanes don't vroom."

Well, the kid knew his shit.

"I'll show you."

Jax landed the plane and moved to the floor as he followed Nolan's lead.

"They can stwart here." He took what was clearly *not* a plane and added wings. Jax wasn't going to point that out even if Nolan took issue with the vrooming. "And go… Vrrrrrrrrrr."

Around the room, he went. Jax followed, and Nolan was dead right. With a couple "Rrrrrrs" and "Annnnnrrrrrsss," Jax had regained trust in the land of block-built toys.

They landed their planes, and Nolan led him toward a box of Legos that rivaled the size of the kid. "Open and out!"

An avalanche of the blocks crashed onto the floor, and Jax jumped as though he were going to get in trouble then laughed at himself. No one else was fazed by the loud cascade. Then Nolan turned into a captain and dictated orders. Jax needed this and that, and before he knew it, his hands were filled with skinny pieces, wide ones, the kind that had angles, and others that attached wheels. And he couldn't see how any of them worked together. But the kid had a vision.

"Put them down." Nolan waved Jax over, as if he had forgotten how to walk, and patted the floor. "On the gwound."

If nothing else, Jax could follow instructions when under command. He lined up the Legos as Nolan set up shop in front of Jax. "Like this?"

"Put that one on thwat side."

"Got it." Jax rearranged, checking with the three-year-old for approval. "What now, captain?"

Nolan glanced up, holding a Lego in each hand, and the kid's happiness doubled down. "Mine and yours gwo like thwis."

For the next five minutes, Jax obeyed every instruction, and they built a tower that connected to an axle with spinning wheels. He latched it on to the flat platform.

"Biwanca, we made it fwr your dollws!"

Jax leaned back, studying the structure that Nolan had created, and saw what the kid had done. It was a swing set—of sorts—but it would work, and it was the right size.

Jax held his hand up. "Nicely done, little man."

Nolan dive-bombed onto Jax as Seven walked in. "Fifteen—minutes." She watched Nolan hugging Jax. "Until dinner."

Shit. Maybe he wasn't supposed to hug the kid? He mouthed silently, "Is this okay?"

Seven nodded, watching quietly. Then Nolan jumped off and spun to her. "Did you see what we bwuilt?"

She smiled one of those proud-mama smiles that made women so beautiful. "Sure did."

Then she winked and went back into the kitchen. Jax scooted back, listening to the oven open and close, Seven's cell phone ring, and a fridge clinking shut. He liked the sound of plates and silverware, drawers opening and closing. "Hey, Seven. Do you want any help?"

"No. I like doing things a certain way."

"Okay. Lemme know if you change your mind."

Jax noticed Bianca watching their conversation as she changed a doll outfit.

Nolan crawled onto the couch and leaned over Jax's shoulder. "We need to make anwther one."

"Good thing you don't need my help," he called back to the kitchen. "My talents are being used elsewhere."

Her laughter rang through the house, and Bianca turned toward the kitchen. A perplexed line drew across Bianca's forehead.

"Why was that funny?" Bianca asked.

What had he said? "It wasn't a joke, funny, ha-ha. It was, well, she was amused. I mean, it made her happy. So she laughed." Was that a good way to explain amusement to a five-year-old? Jax had no idea.

"We make her laugh. Victoria and Ryder do. Glamma. Aunt Delie. Sidney." Bianca tilted her head as though she were wracking her brain to find another source of Seven's laughter.

"I guess I do too," Jax added.

"But you're one of them?" Bianca asked.

"Them?"

"Where's your motorcycle?"

"Oh," he said quietly. "I'm not one of them. I'm a friend, like they are, but I'm not part of their group."

"You're like Sidney?"

Almost... "Exactly."

Bianca's expression defrosted somewhat. "Have you ridden a motorcycle before?"

"There's not much I haven't done, sweetheart."

She put her doll down. "Really?"

Jax flew a Lego into the air. "I've flown up high." Then he dive-bombed it. "And dropped down low." He made waves with the toy. "Dove deep into the water." And then he leaned toward her, gliding it across the floor and flicking it the rest of the distance toward her doll with the bright-green hair. "And I help people when I can."

"How'd you do that?"

"I was in the military."

Nolan ohhhed, and Bianca didn't react. "You shoot people?"

"Um…" Where was Seven when questions like this popped up? "Bad guys."

"How do you know they were bad?"

"I ask questions." Maybe he should've gone to help Seven with dinner even though she'd said no.

"Some people think our parents were bad guys."

Foot in mouth. Fucking hell. "I would not hurt your parents, Bianca."

"They hurt themselves. It's their fault they're gone. Not our fault," Bianca recited.

He shifted on the floor as Nolan pulled on his hair. Jax had no idea what to do with this conversation. Hell, he hadn't known they weren't Seven's biological kids. "I'm sorry, sweetheart. Sometimes it's hard for grown-ups to understand tough stuff like this." He crawled closer to her as Nolan paid no mind but clung to his neck and hung down his back like a cape. "I can't imagine it's easy for you."

Watching him down on his stomach, she crouched down too. "Hi," Bianca said.

"Hey." He smiled. They both put their chins on their hands and propped their elbows on the floor. "I don't have a lot of friends in Sweet Hills. Your mom is my friend—"

"She's everyone's friend."

He could see that. "I could use another. Got any ideas?"

"I could be your friend too," she offered.

"I'd like that."

Bianca's smile beamed. "Okay. I'm going back to my doll."

"Okay. I'll go back to my block-building." Jax pushed onto his hands and knees, letting Nolan stay on his back for a ride to the couch.

The little boy threw his arms in the air. "More! Kweep going!"

Jax turned his head. "More what, buddy?"

"He wants you to give him a ride," Bianca explained.

Then it clicked. Nolan was on his back, and Jax crawling to Bianca had been a *ride. Game on.* "I can do better than that."

Jax held on to Nolan's leg and bounced around the living room to shrieks of laughter ringing out. When he stopped, it wasn't just Nolan laughing. Bianca was too.

"Come on, my new friend. You too."

Hesitantly, she gathered her two dolls—one with green-dyed hair, the other with pink—and set them against the wall. "Can they see?"

"Sure."

As though no one had ever given her a ride before, Bianca beamed and jumped behind Nolan. Both kids bounced on his back, and Jax couldn't remember a time when he'd cared less about what he looked like or had that much fun.

CHAPTER TWENTY-TWO

"DO YOU DO this every night?" Jax was sprawled on the couch, positive he hadn't been so tired in all his life.

Seven laughed. "Do what? Go to work? Pick my kids up? Feed them?"

"They never stop moving."

"True." She folded the kitchen hand towel in that way she did, once then twice. "You just got off a job, though."

He stretched his arm out. "I'm never tired after a job."

She took his hand, and Jax reeled her in. "Sounds like a load of macho crap to me."

"If there was any doubt that I didn't come here to have sex, I can barely move." He laughed. "Kids are hard."

"You've been here for half a day, Mr. Navy SEAL."

"You're a strong woman, Seven, and a really good mom."

She nestled against his chest. "You don't have to say that."

"Those kids, they think you walk on water."

"They didn't have much to compare to."

"Bianca mentioned something about that."

Seven sighed. "It's an ugly story for another time."

He ran his hand up and down her back, yawning. "No worries, babe." He pulled her close. "My mom, she's about as good as they come. I can tell you, you're a good mom."

Seven squeezed him. "I knew you weren't magically conjured into the world."

He closed his eyes, relaxing with her draped over him. Not even a day ago, he'd been halfway around the globe, hunting down a terrorist, and now he was relaxing before bed and...

★   ★   ★

SEVEN BLINKED AS Nolan bounced on her legs, and daylight spilled, urging her awake. The morning had come too soon, and she'd had the best dream. She could even still feel it. Feel him. Jax. His warm breath and sure hands. The scratch of dark scruff on his cheeks.

"Is she alive?" Bianca asked. "Her shoes are on."

Nolan giggled. "She's vwery bouncy."

Jax cleared his throat, shifting underneath her—and that wasn't a dream. Seven's eyes flew open, and she was nose to nose with Bianca.

"She's alive," Bianca announced.

"Is he?" Nolan asked, peering over her shoulder.

Oh God... "Yes," Seven whispered, trying not to panic as she best decided how to handle this monumental parenting fail. "Go to your rooms for a few minutes."

"Why?" Bianca asked, and Nolan bounced on Seven's legs for good measure.

Seven was ninety-nine percent sure that Jax was very much awake and playing dead, as if that was going to help anything.

"His hand is on your private part," Nolan reported as he jumped off the couch.

"*What?*" Seven tried to do a quick summary of her private parts. All were dressed and accounted for, but sleeping-Jax quickly moved his hand off her butt cheek. "Rooms. *Now.*"

Both scampered quickly away, and she dropped her head against his chest. "Feel free to rescind any and all mentions of good mother references." She knocked her head on his hard-muscled chest before pushing up.

Jax opened one eye, trying to suffocate a laugh—or maybe that was what she wanted to do. "Don't play possum with me, Buster."

"There's that Buster again."

She dislodged herself from the warm embraced that had held her all night long, and Jax kicked his jeans-covered legs alongside as he stretched to sit up.

"Don't be too hard on yourself." He hooked an arm over her shoulder.

"I'm not going to tell you it's not a big deal if you think it is or that it could've been worse. It wasn't what we planned."

A wave of awareness ran down her spine. He had said "*we* planned." Did he have any idea what a huge deal it was for someone to take them into account? "Nope. It wasn't."

Jax pulled her close and kissed the top of her head. "But it was the best sleep I've had in a while."

"Same." She rested her chin on his shoulder, falling for him faster than she could recall tumbling into an effortless sleep. "Can you stay for breakfast?"

"Yeah, then I have to head back to prep for Vegas." His body slouched as though reality had interrupted his thoughts. "You'll be there?"

Seven groaned at reality's buzzkill. "Wherever Hawke wants me, yup."

"Can we come back now?" Bianca called from the corner.

"Pwease?" Nolan sang.

"Forget I mentioned Vegas, and when I see you there tomorrow, we'll be at work like it's any other day." He lumbered off the couch, a yawning statute of muscles accented with morning scruff and sexy hair. "Okay, troops. Tell your mama to go back to sleep. Let's find food." Two sets of little feet ran toward the kitchen with excited screams. "You might get Pop-Tarts in bed, but we won't burn the place down." Jax winked then followed the thunder of feet and cabinet doors opening and closing. "Who knows where the coffee is hidden?"

If she had a rock, she would give it to him again and again.

CHAPTER TWENTY-THREE

CHECKING INTO THE hotel was everything Seven had guessed it would be. Same with the airport. From the smoky second she'd walked through the grand tinted doors, she could see why Mayhem liked to do company business in Vegas. The loud, electronic ring of casino games greeted her before the bellhop did. People from all walks of life grouped in every direction, surrounded by gambling and parties. Even the line for check-in had access to the nearby tables.

"They certainly get you as soon as you walk in," Ethan's cigarette-scratched voice said.

Seven turned, moving her suitcase and repositioning her purse to the other shoulder. "When'd you get in?"

"I was on your flight."

"Really?" She'd had too much on her mind to pay attention to her surroundings. "I thought Mayhem arrived earlier."

Other than responding to the few texts from Hawke about where she was supposed to be and what she was supposed to do when she landed, Seven had replayed her time with Jax and how he'd turned into a near-stranger as it was time to leave. His distance had been almost chilling, but she tried to hang on to the fact that he operated much like Ryder, and Seven had seen Ryder go into work mode. Not pleasant, yet knowing vaguely what his job was, she couldn't blame him for compartmentalizing.

"Was on your shuttle too," he added.

"Oh." Mayhem was already there, but she wasn't, and her lips rounded as it made sense. She'd insisted on coming late because of Nolan and Bianca. It wasn't as if Mayhem was going to let her fly into Vegas unescorted. No telling who else was on her plane that she might not have recognized. Their concern wouldn't be the dozens of gang kings coming into town to meet with Mayhem leadership. None would dare hurt her. But unaware criminals of the world might not know who and what she was—the untouchable, Cullen Blackburn's daughter, protected by many decades of favors and history, across many clubs and organizations.

"My own security detail?"

Ethan winked. He might've been the club's treasurer, but he was the roughest financial bean counter she'd ever crossed. "At your service— you're doing okay?"

His eyes dropped to her purse, and she followed his gaze. Inside, there were an obscene amount of origami figurines. It wasn't as if she could do much blanket folding while she was on a plane, and knowing that Jax and Mayhem were heavy on her mind, Seven had grabbed a stack of crisp stock paper on her way out the door. Creasing each piece had given her a small cathartic release even if she'd had to meditate through a moment when the curious woman in the seat beside her had picked one up, asked to keep it, and crushed it when she'd shoved it into her seatback compartment in front of them. Seven had nearly sprouted hives and sweats simultaneously. "I'm fine. Just ready to get started."

With a quick glance around the clamorous lobby, he nodded. "Going to rest until later?"

"No." Seven stepped forward as the line moved. "Hawke has me posted down here, looping him in on who's coming and going before tonight."

"Gotta keep your eyes open this time."

She rolled them instead. "I will when I have to."

"*Next*, please!" called a man from the hotel desk check-in.

Guess she wasn't paying attention. "That's me."

Ethan grumbled toward the man who'd raised his voice. "We hear ya."

"Catch you tonight." She wheeled her suitcase away as Ethan gave a curt wave, but he kept his glare on the front desk, never officially signing off from his Seven-babysitting duty. A Mayhem man's job was never done. Her insides warmed knowing they would always have her back. Stopping in front of the awaiting man, Seven beamed cheerfully, like an antidote to Ethan's death stare. "Hi, checking in. Seven Blackburn."

Poof. The front desk clerk's unfazed expression lit. "You have a gift bag waiting for you."

Oh, brother. "Terrific." Only Victoria would do something sweet but sinister under the guise of being her best friend, especially something that would cause this man to morph from seen-it-all to semi-interested in who received the bag. "I'm sure it's... exciting."

From the look on his face, he'd already peeked inside, and Victoria definitely had not sent a good book to read and relax with by the pool. "One moment." The lightning speed whirl-away-and-back revealed a bag overflowing with tissue paper. "Ms. Blackburn, your *Welcome to Las Vegas Explosion of Fun* bag."

Explosion. Of. Fun. "Thanks." He waited, unmoving, watching the bag, not her. "I'll open it later."

"Oh, hmm." And then his face looked as if his puppy had died.

Really? Really! Was that necessary?

And *another* disappointed sigh.

"Or I can just take a quick..."

He was bright eyes and fun again. *For the love of all that is...* Seven pursed her lips and prayed there was a map of Vegas inside, perhaps tickets to a show. She dug through the tissue paper, which already made her skin crawl as he pretended to go through the motions of not watching as he typed on his keyboard. There was an envelope and—*oh no, Victoria didn't*—Seven clenched the bag shut, cheeks pink.

"Can I have your driver's license?" The clerk peered down like an angel knowing about her bag of dirty fun.

"Yes. Of course." Seven tried to shove the gift bag aside and reach for her wallet, but her purse tipped off the rollaboard suitcase. Origami creations spilled out.

Seven's eyes sank shut, blaming what had to be an industrial-sized, hair-matching, bright-pink bottle of lube for her distracted spill. But the sound of helpful hands scooping up her origami tore her back to reality.

How cool.

These are great.

What a talent.

She dropped down, fishing them back from curious hands. "Thanks. I've got it." The idea of another round of crumpled cardstock coupled with a bag of lube and *more* might be too much to handle at that second. "Thanks so much. Something I've always done."

Flustered but with everything back in her oversized purse so nothing would be crushed, she popped back up to the preening clerk.

"Two cards, I presume?"

"Nope." What else was in the bag? Champagne? Confetti-packaged condoms? Her cheeks heated to a nuclear level of embarrassment. "Just one."

"Really?" The desk clerk took a second too long to ponder why that was, and Seven thought how she might kill Victoria. "However that works best for you."

"*Alone.* I work best alone." Then she plotted Victoria's slow demise, which would happen as soon as she tossed the gift bag in the trash can, where no one else could sneak a quick glance.

THE LIGHTS WERE too bright. The smoke too thick. Vegas wasn't the place he wanted to be, mostly because Jax wanted to be alone. He didn't like the idea of traveling as a motorcycle club drug negotiator. Hell, he didn't like how a gang was called a club, and he didn't like his boss breathing down his neck, telling him to haul ass to Nevada.

But there he was. Jared would be there soon enough. Sugar, his boss's wife, would probably be in tow, and he would be a third wheel. Jax was very uncomfortable when it came down to hanging out with couples. They did their couply crap, and Jax had to put up with it.

He strode into the hotel that had no idea it'd been taken over by a glut of criminals. He almost wanted to tell them, but what did the hotel care? They just wanted money, and it was Vegas. Maybe everyone was a criminal.

But the who's who of cocaine distribution all staying under one roof was interesting.

Bright-pink hair caught the corner of his eye, and he came to a stop.

This was Vegas. He'd passed a hundred girls with hair in a dozen shades of pink. None had brought him to a standstill the way Seven did, and she was across the lobby in a skirt that was short enough to make him want to stare and seemed soft enough to sway with her hips with her every step.

The space between them was immense. People milled. The water in several fountains danced to music as children jumped and tossed coins. But there she was next to Johnny Miller, the asshole who was the sole reason the last deal hadn't gone through and why they'd had to come back out today.

Jax watched them from afar, almost embarrassed at how he stared. They were standing together. Familiar. Friendly. Yet *not*. Very Seven— combative and caring. They weren't flirting, but they were… smiling and comfortable.

A tension built in his shoulders and spread into his back. The dull ache slowed his thoughts and made him feel as if he weighed double his mass, just from a look at something—someone—he *already* had.

He was jealous.

It was absurd to admit, but still, it remained true. At that moment, he wanted to step into Johnny's boots and feel Seven cast her smile on him. The woman was magical.

"Jax." Jared Weston stepped next to him then followed his gaze as Jax reeled himself back to the real world. "What is it with you two?"

"No idea."

"Whatever it is, use it to our advantage. Parker picked up chatter."

If Titan's IT guy had learned anything, it was sure to be gold. "What'd he hear?"

"Hawke is having an informal meeting of the minds. Get invited."

"Sounds like my kind of fun." He smirked at the idea of finagling an invite to hang with Mayhem, but honestly, his blood pumped at the thought that he would be closer to Seven, closer to the smile that she put on his lips and the feeling of how she made the cloud hanging over him part for the sun, even if it was for a few minutes. "I'll be sure to turn a blind eye to everything I see."

THE ONLY THING that made Jax feel normal was the .40 caliber Glock at the small of his back and the snub-nose .38 revolver in his ankle holster. When they had attended the cartel meeting in Colombia, he'd been unarmed and might as well have been naked.

But now with Jared's orders to secure an invitation burning in the back of his brain, Jax tried to figure the best way to do that. Be up front? Or sweet-talk Seven into inviting him along? If it were that easy and Mayhem wanted Titan there, Hawke would've invited him or Jared. So this was on the informal side. Jax needed Seven to bring him, and he needed it to look as though he was there *with* Seven, not *for* work.

That was easy enough. The only question was whether to loop Seven in or not.

It would be a game-time decision, and now was his chance. Jax couldn't say he wasn't excited to see her. His blood ran hotter as he paced across the hotel lobby toward where he'd last seen the wild-haired beauty.

"Hey, you."

Seven's voice caught him by surprise. "How does anyone with neon hair blend in?"

She shrugged. "I don't know. Blame Vegas?"

"Guess so." Jax fell into stride with her. "Where are you going?"

"Hotel bar. What about you? When'd you get in?"

"Little bit ago."

Her shoulder brushed his, and when she wasn't in high heels, it was noticeable how much smaller she was.

She laughed. "What are you looking at?"

"Nothing. I never noticed you'd fit in my pocket."

"Ha!" She tilted her head back, and a tiny silver chain caught his eye. "Have you been drinking?"

"Not yet."

Did everything revolve around drinking with her? The last times he'd seen her had been a wedding reception, a bar, then another bar. Not his thing, but it sounded very MC-like. *Drunk motorcycle motherfuckers.*

They pushed their way through the crowd and into the bar, where there were day drinkers galore. Very Vegas. Some asshole bumped into him, and Jax ground his molars down in an effort not to bump the guy a few dozen feet away. Finally, he and Seven made it to the bar.

"What'd you want, babe?"

She searched over his head. "I don't know? Water?"

Jax grumbled but laughed. "You know there's a perfectly decent place where I don't have to fend fuckers off to get water, right?"

"Are you going to say your hotel room?"

He lifted his eyebrows. "No, I wasn't. But since you're suggesting..."

She laughed. "I wasn't."

"Sounded like a good idea to me."

Seven sidestepped closer as an asshole edged in behind her. "Sorry."

Jax put his arm around her waist. "You're fine." But he glared at the other guy, holding back a fierce *you're fucking not.* "You just want a water? Water and...? What?"

"How about a coke?"

"Okay. We'll do that." He faced the bar and gave himself a solid self-check for thinking all she wanted to do was drink.

Seven lurched away. "Hey—oh. Hey."

Jax spun to see Johnny. *Jesus fucking Christ.* This was not the dude he wanted to see now, and if there was any reason in the world that Seven had been leaning against him and abruptly *wasn't* anymore, he really didn't need that. Jax grated his teeth before he smiled. "What's up, man?"

"Jax," Johnny said as hello.

Seven stood between them, and there was a standoff that he didn't know if she was aware of, but that Jax was now acutely clued in to. If Johnny wanted her, that was going to be his own fucking problem. But at the same time, Jax didn't need to drag her good name through the mud when Mayhem all seemed to think of her as their little sister.

Jax wanted Parker to give him a background on Seven, but that would be awkward to ask for. A personal history on Johnny, maybe not so much.

Either way, he needed to know because his only job right now was securing an invite to the meeting tonight, and that was done one way—by praying upon the spark between him and her.

"When'd you get here?" Johnny inched forward, stepping too close to

Jax for his liking.

"Not long ago." He worked his jaw. "You got a problem?"

Johnny's head shook slowly. "Not if you don't."

"Good. I'd hate for more problems to pop up between us."

Johnny put an arm around Seven. "I didn't realize we had any issues."

Right, because the clusterfuck in South America wasn't soundly put on Johnny's shoulders. But Jax tried to stay chill. Mayhem was a client, just like the DOJ or the CIA. Hell, they were all in bed together, knowing the little he knew about gangs and the far too much he knew about Uncle Sam.

"Excuse me. I'm not your armrest." Seven ducked from under Johnny's shoulder and leaned on the bar.

On top of Johnny screwing up what should've been an easy job, Jax didn't like the dynamic between him and Seven. Familiarity or not, that move right there was like Johnny pissing on a spot he wanted to claim. Seven seemed to be cognizant, and Jax didn't want some alpha-dog brawl over a bone, but fucking hell. "Bogotá didn't go as planned. If this went smoothly, I'd be cool with that."

"If this weekend goes smoothly, it's not because you're here." Johnny smirked, and Jax wanted to punch his face in.

He did one better. He put his arm around Seven. If she dared shove him away, they would get into a fight, and that would make for great sex, preferably against a wall. If she didn't, then sides were drawn, and Johnny had just gotten a big *fuck you.*

Jax's heart punched in his chest, waiting one second, then two. What would she do?

Seven leaned into his side. "You two are giving me a migraine."

Good girl. God damn, good girl. He would make sure there would be many, many good things coming her way for that, even if she had no idea the line he'd just walked and the risk he'd just taken by throwing his arm over her.

The corner of Johnny's eyes pinched, but he didn't respond to her. "I don't know why Titan brought you, anyway."

"Because we needed someone neutral," Seven chided him.

"We?" He shook his head. "All this *we* shit, and it's like—"

"Don't get into it with me here, sweetheart."

"Sweetheart," Johnny tossed back.

Jax noticed the softness leave Seven, but she flipped around and pressed against the bar, leaving him with Johnny.

"Two cokes, please," Seven ordered and was served quickly.

Johnny took an aggressive step forward. His brows furrowed, and the lines under his eyes deepened. "Careful with her."

"Jesus Christ, man. You're the one being a dick."

She turned with the drinks and handed one to Jax.

He took the glass. "Thanks."

Johnny nudged his head. "This guy's an asshole."

Seven sighed. "Is this where I bring out the takes-one-to-know-one argument that we used in sixth grade?" Then her pierced brow arched. "Because I'm ready."

Jax took a sip of his drink and stretched over her head, placing it on the bar.

She curled next to his side, toying with the tip of her straw. "Could you put mine down too?"

He did, and she stepped back to his side, casually resting a hand on his stomach.

The move was casual but intimate. It was a loud message to Johnny, and Jax gave no fucks.

Heat from her palm radiated. The innocent touch bled into his bloodstream. It flooded his mind, heightening his longing to strip her naked and run his hands over her. Not just because she was the sexiest thing he'd touched and tasted in as long as he could remember, but because she was well schooled in the art of shade. That made her fun, smart, and entertaining.

He could go on but wanted to pay attention as her fingers splayed. She dragged the tips of her nails down an inch before letting her hand fall.

Jax swallowed hard. The not-so-innocent clawing had woken up each nerve ending along his abdomen. The undercover move reminded him of the way her fingers threaded into his hair, the way her moans fell without abandon with each thrust into her body.

Whatever Seven and Johnny were bantering back and forth about had nothing to do with him.

"Jax is hanging with me tonight. Deal with it."

Or maybe it did. Jax inhaled, deeply, corralling his thoughts. He didn't need to sport wood in a crowded bar. "What's up?"

Johnny's angry eyes weren't impressed, and Jax ran a possessive hand over Seven's skin.

"I'm down with whatever," he added, realizing that he'd been lost in thoughts of her naked instead of angling for the meet tonight, which was his goal. Mission accomplished.

She peered up at him, lust-darkened eyes wide and wanting the same thing he did—to be alone.

But it didn't feel right pursuing her when there was an ulterior motive. Not that he'd done a damn thing wrong, and his intentions were never going to get him a sainthood.

"I'm out of here." Johnny turned around. "Off to find someone actually drinking at a bar."

"Have fun," Seven called while rolling her eyes.

"What's that between you two?" Jax asked.

Seven reached for her soda. "Where should I begin?"

It was better not to know. "Never mind. You don't have to explain."

Her lips wrapped around the straw, but she didn't drink. He couldn't read her expression, but maybe that wasn't the right thing to say. Hell, he didn't know. "I'll be your piece of meat to ward off unwanted attention."

Her tongue stud slipped out and ran along her lip for a second. Then Seven took a long sip. "Do you care how or why I'm going to use you, sweetheart?"

"Nope." He chuckled, grateful that whatever he'd said to sour her before had disappeared in the busy crowd. And why had he thought it was just him playing a game? It wasn't as though she would be upset because he didn't give her the opportunity to detail her past. That wasn't them. She didn't want that. Neither of them did. "You know what's my favorite thing about you?"

"If you say my ability to ignore male attention, I'm going to be deeply disappointed in your creativity."

He gave a half-smile and a headshake and somehow knew that she didn't do the hair and her various accessories for others or attention. She dug how it turned out.

"Tell me," Seven whispered, but he heard her voice above every loud, crass noise in the place.

"You're no saint." Even if she sometimes sounded like an angel.

Her pink lips pursed into an unexpected smile. "Was it the piercings or the hair that gave me away?"

God… those piercings. All of them. He wanted the one on her tongue against his cock and the bars through her nipples playing in his mouth. He wanted to feel her in so many ways just to see how he could get her to sing.

"Let's get out of here." He put his hands on her sides, slid them slowly to her ass, and squeezed. Having a backside that filled his hands, that he could grip, dig his hands into, made his blood burn hot. That was the kind of ass Jax liked. A woman with curves. One who he could kiss up the backs of her legs, sink his teeth into her cheeks, then kiss his way up her back. "You ready?"

"I'm trying to stay in the lobby, bar—ya know, around—and keep an eye on who's here. For tonight."

"Right. Tonight?"

"I mentioned you were coming. You wanted to come with, I assume?"

He tilted his head to the side. "Yeah. I appreciate the invite."

"It's private. A few folks getting together before the big event tomorrow."

His jaw flexed as he hummed a non-answer. "Are you bringing me?"

"You already knew about tonight?" Her eyes accused him of what they both seemed to know. "Were you hoping that if we hung out last night, maybe you'd get special access to whatever you wanted? Or just an invite to spend the night again?"

He hesitated. The safe play was to deny he knew. She would never know Titan had access to Mayhem's chatter. But there was the right thing to do by *her*. "Last night had nothing to do with this weekend, and I hoped to spend time with you before I knew there was a meetup. *That I want access to.*"

She stared for what felt like decades. "Access and time?"

He shook his head. "Don't be like that."

"Like what?"

"Like you don't know who I am despite whatever roles we're both playing in Vegas."

Seven ran her tongue along her lip. "Give me more than that."

"You want, what? A definition? An agenda? For when? When we're with everyone or when I have you to myself?"

Her face flushed. "Did you have one?"

"If I did?" He brushed the hair off her neck, teasing the back of her hairline with his fingers. No one could see how he knotted the back of her hair around his fingers and pulled softly, but her head tilted back, and her lips parted.

Just as covertly as he'd pulled her hair, he adjusted the top of her sleeve for her and let his hand run down her arm, savoring the shiver bumps that erupted under his touch.

"I don't doubt your dirty mind always has plans."

"The dirtiest."

She came closer, until the way they stood was inexcusable for anything other than heading to bed. The steady beat of his heart quickened, and his mouth watered to kiss her.

"Jax, I—"

"Seven?" The gruff interruption of a man's voice reached through the crowd and ruined the heat building between them.

They both turned to see someone Jax couldn't identify but who was clearly Mayhem as he pushed through the crowd. "You seen Johnny or Hawke lately?"

Seven's quickstep back came with a laugh. "Johnny just left."

"Got it. Thanks, babe." The other man left as quickly as he'd come.

Jax wanted none of the distance Seven had put between them. "Back to our planning?"

"Is that what you want?"

Damn it. Whenever she got an interruption, she went cold. What the fuck did that mean? "Are you as worked up as I am?" He inched forward again.

She glanced away. "You're assuming a lot, my friend."

He put two fingers under her chin and directed her to face him. "Tell me you're not turned on."

"I'm not—"

He shook his head, not removing his hand from her chin. "I get that Johnny's not here so you don't need me to lean against, and you were pulled out of your moment."

"That wasn't like that, and you know it."

"Whatever your reasons are, that's cool. But don't deny that your nipples are hard and your pussy's aching for me."

"*Jax.*" Her eyes went wide. "Why would I admit to that right now?"

He rubbed his thumb over her chin then let go. "Because it's the truth."

Her eyes narrowed. "I would've helped you into that meeting if you'd asked me."

Jax smiled. "I know. Then again, direct requests never work with you."

She held his gaze. "Give me one now."

"Spend the night with me." Easy. It came off his tongue before he thought about what he should say.

Seven closed the distance, and their stomachs touched. Then the crowded bar faded away as she pushed up, hooking her arms around his neck and dragging her lips to his ear. "There was never any doubt where I'd be tonight."

CHAPTER TWENTY-FOUR

JAX'S CONFIDENT GRIP on Seven's hand made her insides melt. She never felt the need to be protected and doted on. But when he took her hand in his, walking her out of the bar and down the busy hotel corridor, the hairs on her arms jumped as if they wanted to reach for him. Her head swam, and she couldn't blame that on a little buzz from the drinks. All she'd had were a few sips of a soda.

Tonight would be a test. Mayhem wouldn't allow a random person in the meetup. She was there, and Jax would be her guest, and he'd be allowed there only if it looked real, personal. And it could. After all, they'd spent the last few years flirting. Seven could live a lifetime in the space of one of their kisses. Even if they were playing a part, she and Jax acted like a couple.

Because, for her, it felt as though they were more than a random hookup, that Jax was more than a guy she shouldn't have slept who was nothing but an attitude. She'd seen the real him lately, and the real man behind the arrogant and defiant persona he showed to the world had brought her breakfast in bed.

That was the scariest part. He didn't do what she expected him to—run away, be the asshole. Then again, he hadn't addressed whatever this was morphing into. They hadn't defined their situations, but this felt leap years beyond a hookup.

Seven should give Jax a thank you and a high five. With the right hum of a kiss or the breeze of his lips, she was sure she would climax, and that was new in her hierarchy of personal priorities. "Where are we going?"

His lust-darkened eyes dropped to her face. "I don't know."

Hawke might have a problem that she'd left her *post*, but he hadn't said she needed to stay put, just keep an ear to the ground and watch out for Johnny. He hadn't said for how long, either. "Sounds good to me."

Jax stopped abruptly. The hungry, powerful stride taking them to somewhere private paused, and she had no idea why.

"What's wrong?"

"Why didn't Johnny give you bigger shit for bringing me tonight?"

Jax was a smart cookie. She didn't have to bring him there, and the truth was, she didn't want to be away from him. There was no reason to bring him at all. But that wasn't what he wanted to know or likely would ever care about. "Some people don't trust you. I'm supposed to keep an eye on you."

"Some people being Johnny."

She nodded.

"Lots of people have you keeping eyes on others."

"True."

"Why would they do that?"

"Because I'm trustworthy, and I do what I do well."

Jax inched closer as people stepped around them. They stood in the center of a hallway, semi-blocking traffic, but he didn't seem to notice how they impeded the flow. "And what is that? Look out for the best interest of Mayhem?" Jax asked slowly.

"Yes."

"If some don't think that I am, why would you tell me at all?"

"Because I know you, and no one knows how much I've shared with you."

His eyes tightened their focus. "What does this MC mean to you?" He looked away but came back, inquisitive, not as judgmental as she would've expected. "They're criminal. Guns. Drugs. Who the hell knows what else?"

Seven bit her lip, not knowing why she couldn't immediately bat away his question. "Because it's my family. Sometimes you hate the people you love and you love the people you hate. You disagree with everything they are, and you do everything you can to change it. Mayhem's in my DNA as much as walking away from them was my destiny."

"Do you know how young you are to say things that are..." Jax shook his head and took her hand, starting them again.

"No, I don't."

He slowed but didn't stop.

"I've been on my own. Then I had to take care of others. My kids? They're not mine... even if they are mine. My dad left us to raise Mayhem, not children, and his first and only true love was the MC, not my mom." Seven stopped. "I don't know how old I am. Unless my best friend reminds me. Because age is just a number I left long ago."

He stopped again, and again, they blocked foot traffic in the busy hall. He didn't say anything, just stared. But not because she was crazy or talked as though she were boastful. She felt more as though he were proud or impressed, and it warmed her heart—and turned her on in a way she didn't expect.

"You have everything under control, don't you?" he finally asked.

Ha, he didn't have a clue. "I wish."

His face brightened. "I want to show you something."

They started walking again. "At least we have a plan."

"A dirty one." He squeezed her hand, and suddenly, they couldn't get there soon enough. "You still game?"

"Absolutely."

"Good." His arm brushed against hers, and every time it did, she thought about when he'd wrapped it around her, how it had felt when they were alone and lost their clothes. It was as if they suddenly breathed different air.

When Jax acted like this, asked questions, it erased the moments when she was certain that before was a one-time explosion of lust and cravings.

"I want to show you something, Seven. In here." Jax veered them off course as if he knew where they were, and they sidestepped the throngs of tourists shuffling the hall until he reached for the unmarked door. He punched a code on a nondescript pad and twisted the knob.

"Where are—"

Jax slapped her hand away as she reached for the light switch. The dim room was open, and on one side, a glass walk overlooked the main casino.

He put his hands on her hips and guided her. "Two-way mirror. They can't see us with the lights down."

Seven's mind rushed. How did he know this? But then, why question anything about Titan and access?

Jax pressed behind her, hands on her hip bones to hold her in place. The pressure of his thick erection, separated by the layers of clothes, made her dizzy with need. Her breath hitched knowing how easily he could inch the frilly skirt up then slide her underwear to the side.

Jax leaned close, letting his warm breath tease the back of her neck. "Seven?"

"Mmhh?"

His fingers gripped tighter, and she arched, melting at the whisk of his slow teases curling along her sensitive skin.

"Are you wet, princess?" Jax nuzzled behind her ear lobe.

"Yes." Her pussy contracted, desperately needing and silently rejoicing because he was so close.

His strong fingers rubbed from her hip bones to her clothing-covered mound and back. "*Are you?*"

When a man made from stone said sweet things... She nodded. "Very."

"Everyone out there wants what you'll have." Jax slid down the front and played with the hem of her skirt.

"*Jax.*" She swayed her backside against him.

His gravely chuckle rumbled against her ear. "Look at them. Wanting..."

She couldn't see their want. Hers had nearly blinded her. Seven nuzzled her cheek against his lips, finding little satisfaction from the lingering kisses that left her biting her lip.

"Keep watching them." He let go of her skirt, rubbing her legs—squeezing then feathering a slight touch—as he worked up, giving a chaotic tornado of sensations. Harsh. Sweet. Easy. Rough. Until his fingers found the edge of her panties. "They're searching." Jax yanked them down her thighs, making her gasp at the quick move and the cool air rushing against her damp skin. "Look at them all, *wanting.*"

"I want. I don't care about them. *You.*"

He stroked her folds, finally putting pressure on her clit piercings, and Seven bucked back against him, moaning for him to never stop. But he did, and the aftereffects of the bar were short-lived, but the piercing on her hood made her pulse. "I can't take this."

"Yes, you can." His fingers gentled back, methodically stroking until her hips swayed and lips begged. Then he teased her clitoris again while kissing the small of her neck.

"Shh—God." She couldn't talk... or think.

Jax dragged his teeth against her skin until sensation overload made her incoherent—he pulled back. "Are you still watching?"

"No," Seven whined.

His fingers slid inside her. "For what you have."

Seven's muscles loosened. Hungry bliss bled into her veins. "Jax..."

He drove into her deep, faster. "God, I missed this tight cunt."

"Please, *please*, be inside me."

"Fucking hell," he muttered as the belt clinked and condom wrapper tore. "Wasn't my plan."

"Screw your plans."

A moment later, sheathed and urging her legs apart, Jax nuzzled the head of his cock against her as she watched the casino floor. He thrust and stole her mind. Again, spearing her with a blessed intrusion of thick heat, Jax's quick breath stayed at her ear as she cried for more, begging for deeper.

Seven couldn't swallow; her eyes couldn't stay open. "Come with me. I need you to."

A strong arm wrapped around her chest, and his low growl made her quiver. He worked like a machine and pistoned like a steamroller—so fluid, she could've floated, and so perfect, Jax made her climb higher and higher.

"Yes, Jax." The orgasm exploded, and Seven pushed back, needing desperately to hold on to something besides the wall. But she clung to it, riding the wave, the climatic high.

He pinned her to the mirror, straining his climax, muttering a thousand indistinguishable words that sent her mind flying as high as her orgasm until she melted into a limp Jax-held mess.

When her eyelashes fluttered open, she zeroed her focus on a woman on the floor who acted as though she'd won big. Nothing that woman had was as good as Jax.

"It's what they all want," Seven whispered. "And we have it."

CHAPTER TWENTY-FIVE

THE SMOKY HOTEL suite had the who's who of the US's most wanted gangs. One quick phone call, and Jax would be rolling in the dough of a dozen reward offers. But Boss Man would kick his ass, and then he would have to deal with Deacon Lanes, who likely had each gang member in his most recent call log, before he was ready. There was something super screwed up when the Feds in one branch of government were in bed with the guys that the Feds in another department were trying to nail.

Seven slipped her hand into the back pocket of his jeans as they walked through the room filled with men hopped up and on edge. It was quite the situation when rival gangs pulled their act together and presented for a meeting like this, which was why it seemed as though only a representative or two from a few of Hawke's top picks were even invited.

Everyone wore their insignias, and their women were plastered on. A few girls that Seven had said were Mayhem pussy, who they trusted, played the role of bartender, server, or whatever else was needed.

For their part and for most of the women, they were dressed like he would expect them to be at a wild night at the Mayhem compound or an ordinary night in Vegas. Short leather skirts, boots that inched high, and tattoos in every direction. Lipsticked and eyelashed women who'd spent years in the sun on the backs of Harleys. Seductresses who'd perfected their stances by running clubs.

There was a lot of testosterone in the room and a lot of drinking. The men thought themselves hardasses, badasses, whether they were or weren't. Seven told him there would be a few other *guests* like him, but he didn't press her as to who they were.

"Beers?" a woman no younger than Seven offered, though she looked years older in how life had treated her.

"Yeah, two'd be good," Jax said.

The server thanked him and greeted Seven then rushed off after Seven pointed at where she wanted to sit. Thankfully, she chose a corner so Jax could keep good tabs on who came and went out the front door.

"Jax." Hawke ambled out of the hallway. A fat joint burned between his thumb and forefinger, and he rolled it slowly between his fingers before offering to him then Seven.

"Hey, man." Jax held his hand up, and Seven gave a quick refusal. "Thanks for the festivities."

"Any friend of Seven's…" Hawke raised the joint as if it were a beer and took a slow hit, finally pulling it back and passing it to another guy walking by. Dark, thick curls of smoke drifted from his mouth before he blew it out. "Relax. Tonight's for friends."

"Eclectic friends." Jax's eyes darted to the black man walking with the Latino man wearing a leather cut.

"Eh, come tomorrow, they'll hate each other again." Hawke lifted a shoulder. "There are a few old guards from around the country that get the weight of leading a club. Some places are a DMZ."

"You're saying I shouldn't be strapped."

Hawke laughed. "Well, how about this? A well-armed *demilitarized zone*."

"I'm not carrying," Seven cut in.

"Honey, that's because you're pretty pussy, and no one would let Cullen Blackburn's daughter be harmed. *No one.*"

She gave a sarcastic bat of her eyelashes.

"There's a princess for you." Hawke laughed again as the joint made its way back to him.

"Two beers." The girl pushed two longnecks into the conversation without entering herself.

"Thanks," they said in unison as Hawke wandered.

Jax took his beer and his woman and headed toward the vantage point he wanted. Easing onto the couch, Seven slipped onto his knee instead of sitting next to him and leaned back, draping her legs over his. They fit in, with her like that, but hell, he didn't care. Mayhem might've gone from the worst gig to best job in the speed of a day.

"Why is it," she purred against his ear, "that you wanted in here to begin with?"

Jax casually drank his beer and positioned her better, running his hand into her hair and bringing her ear to his mouth. "See the players in action. Like a study guide for test day."

"You don't think I could've told you everything you needed to know?"

"I thought you could've told me some." He lined their faces up. "I didn't know how much of the outside world you were schooled in."

"Really?"

He shrugged. "And I didn't know how careful they'd be of you."

Her eyebrow crooked. "Meaning?"

"No one in this room would allow you to get hurt. Not Mayhem. Not the Brotherhood. The Niners. No one."

"I'm just lucky, I guess."

"Don't BS with me, princess."

"Ding, ding. You called it."

Jax chewed on the inside of his cheek, but all the tossing of ideas didn't compute what she meant. "Explain."

"You know my father was a founding member."

He nodded. "Heard something about that."

"Yeah, I bet." She snort-laughed. "I'll bet you've got all kinds of recon on us."

"Surprisingly, not a lot of detail on that."

Seven hummed, almost sounding as though she were taunting him.

"We missed something?" He rubbed his hand up her spine. The short leather top tied around her neck and exposed her back, covering only her front. From her hairline and shoulders straight to her skirt, Seven's skin was exposed. The high-necked, ultra-conservative leather shirt surprised him at first glance—but when she'd turned around, Jax had been floored. He liked both looks—the barely there tease and taunt of hidden curves and then a torturous reminder that her shirt was tied on around her neck. One flick of a knife's blade, and the leather covering would fall away.

"Titan only missed something if they were interested in *me*."

Let him count the ways she had his attention—business, personal, clothed, naked. He could keep going. "Consider me interested."

Seven smiled, but not with her mouth, rather her eyes. They reacted before her lips curled. "Good to know."

Was it possible three boring words could make his dick hard?

Her head tipped closer. "I mentioned my dad's first love was the MC."

Jax nodded.

"He made many friends as he built what became Mayhem, and he didn't care what people looked like, what they rode, who they fucked. He did many favors for many people. They're indebted to me."

"Why?"

She lifted a shoulder. "Maybe because he never was."

CHAPTER TWENTY-SIX

A ND WHY SHE needed to spill family secrets, Seven had no idea. Maybe it was the rhythmic sway of Jax's fingers brushing along her back.

"This is what you need to know." She shifted, wanting to change his attention from her back to the reason he was there. "Your two o'clock. That's who Hawke's betting on."

"And you really think, with all the brass in this room, Hernán Suarez hasn't been tipped off that Mayhem might find a middleman to take up their distribution?"

"Not beforehand. Too much money on the line. Too much of a power struggle that could take place." She looked around. "Now the second that it's decided? It'll get ugly, and they'll know what happened. But part of what Hawke's doing tonight is finding out what the needs are."

"Meaning?"

"If someone doesn't get it? Can't offer what we need? They'll still walk away happy. No one's leaving here unhappy."

"Unless there's no deal," Jax countered.

"Short of Hernán walking in tomorrow, I don't think that will be possible."

Johnny sauntered across the room and eased onto the couch. He had a Mayhem slut puppy and a girl Seven had never seen before under his arms.

"Nothing about that was in any folder, either," Jax said.

"You Navy SEALs should do better research."

"There's a geek who knows how to kill you a thousand different ways that wouldn't be thrilled to hear you say that."

Seven smiled. "I speak geek, so maybe he'd let me die painlessly."

"Do you?" Jax laughed. "What else don't I know about you?"

She tilted her head to the asshole getting ready to let the slut puppy and the unknown suck his cock. Not that there weren't like antics happening around the room, but that was more Johnny sending her a message. "That's my ex."

"Boyfriend?"

"Mm-mm."

Jax's eyes went wide. "Husband?"

She wriggled her shoulders. "And what do I get for such a lovely designation? *Not much.* Other than watching the occasional blow job and knowing when he's into it or about to pass out."

"I don't get this... situation at all."

"We grew up together. We're actually friends. More like brother and sister, if that doesn't sound weird. But obviously *not.*"

Jax side-eyed her. "Obviously..."

"It was assumed we would get married. I was my dad's daughter. He's presumed to take over Mayhem one day. The second we became legal, they pranced us to the courthouse."

Jax rolled his lips together.

"Oh, come on. Nothing to say?"

He burst out laughing. "No."

She pushed his chest. "Bull."

"How romantic?"

Seven leaned close, letting her lips linger near his. "It took me a while to learn about romance."

Jax let his lips touch hers. Amid the chaos and crudeness, the joints and the drinks, his kiss was sweet and real. Sober, even if she tasted the hint of beer. Cool, wet lips, and the tease of his hot tongue pushed past her teeth and toyed with the tongue stud. Seven quietly moaned into the kiss, falling away from this world and the smoky haze to where she could imagine it was just them.

Jax drew back. "Seven?"

"Hm?"

His dark eyes dropped a shade past black. "I'm not romantic."

Cold fucking shower, Jax. "Trust me." How had she spun herself into a situation with him? "You've never given me a chance to be confused about that."

Lines furrowed across his brow.

"But I think we... mesh well." She arched an eyebrow. No need to pretend they didn't have spectacular sex. "And we both have an end game here."

"We do." Though the distance in his voice wasn't convincing.

"I do." She nodded, closing her face to his. "I hate drugs. Hate them so much I'll sit on your lap, across from my ex getting a BJ, and whisper like we're talking sweet nothings."

"You want sweet nothings?"

"You don't do romance. Please don't try something that might kill you while surrounded by a room of men who have likely killed people. The headache that will go into establishing natural causes and all of their alibis?" She shook her head. "You're not worth that much trouble."

"I'm going to start a tally of every time you've screamed my name and show it to you when you say shit like that."

"I don't scream."

"Princess, *you scream.*"

She flushed, and his fingers trailed up her spine.

"Now what?" Jax asked.

Seven let her eyes move around the room. Tex watched her and Jax, not hiding his study of Jax. Tex had never been that protective of her, so his watchful eye meant their back-and-forth was displaying the right show to the room. "I'm not sure, but Mayhem's got an eye on us." She wiggled her bottom and curled into Jax's side.

His hand moved from her back to her side, ducking under the leather shirt and letting his hand run over her abdomen. "Meaning?"

"I'm here because I'm supposed to be, and you're not here to work."

He flexed his fingers into her stomach. "Not at all."

"Tex has got us under his rotation." She ducked her lips to his neck and gave a quick lick, inhaling the faint scent of his cologne and the very familiar, very masculine way Jax naturally smelled. The salty taste of his skin and the earthy, alpha smell that she could close her eyes and imagine was enough to make her hungry for him.

Seven kissed up the tendons in his neck, alternating light brushes of her lips and tongue with sucking carefully. She groaned quietly as he shifted, his hips moving just enough for her to know he liked what she was doing. His possessive hand smoothed over her belly, hidden from the world. Reaching his earlobe, she whispered, "I like how your hand feels."

His jaw flexed against her cheek, and he took a deep breath, expanding his massive chest as she leaned on him.

"I like my lips on you," she continued.

"Good."

"I like that I'm supposed to be playing. But I'm really glad you're into this as much as me."

He groaned. "Yeah. Me too."

It was that time of night, that part in a Mayhem party when nothing really mattered and everyone was blitzed... except them. She didn't really drink, so maybe the beer had gone to her head. The groan was what did her in as Seven twisted on his lap, straddling Jax in her short skirt and boots and wrapping her arms around him.

His erection was hardening under her lap as she moved against him. The room was hazy, and the music's bass thumped low. It wrapped its methodical beat around the smoky air as people who were too loud partied like criminal kings who couldn't be stopped. But the chaos had nothing on her and Jax. In his arms, it was just them.

Jax kissed her, his tongue sweeping into her mouth without a second guess. He wasn't comfortable with anyone there, that she knew, but he was with her... she hoped.

God, if sex could be a kiss...

She melted into him as his tongue teased hers. He stroked her mouth open, each kiss stringing her into a lust-drunk oblivion, where she could feel his hands in places he hadn't touched her yet. Her imagination was as wicked as his tongue, and the hotter and harder he kissed her, the better her vivid daydreams became.

Jax drew back, lingering. Their noses, their cheeks, they still touched. Her breaths came too fast, and her mind spun in a thousand directions—

cold fingers on her shoulder shattered the buzz, and she twisted, licking her lips and glaring at Tex. "Yeah, you need something?"

"Work and play with this one?" Tex asked Jax.

"Seemed like a good idea."

"Are you fucking kidding me, Tex?" Seven shot back.

He didn't answer, eyeing them both. "He's on our side. Don't screw this up, Seven."

"He's not on any side, and since when do you care who I screw?"

Tex rolled his bottom lip into his mouth then ran his hand over his face. "Since it might interfere with club business."

"Do we need to go talk?" Jax offered casually, knowing Tex was high in the Mayhem hierarchy. "You want me to step out? She's pussy. I'm a contractor. She has club history. I"—Jax shook his head, playing his role to a tee—"don't."

Tex mulled the offer, and it was *exactly* what he needed to hear from Jax. Maybe Titan did have good recon on Mayhem.

"Nah." He lifted his beer bottle to them. "Enjoy yourself this evening."

Seven came back to Jax, and he squeezed her ass, pulling her closer.

"You have some info on them," she whispered against his lips.

Jax bit her bottom one. "You bet your sweet ass we do."

She kissed him slowly, playing with her tongue stud, teasing him in the way that seemed to get him to react most. "And I lied to Mayhem. First time in my life."

Jax made a deep sound as she pulled away, flexing his grip on her ass again. "Guess we trust each other?"

"Do we?"

"What's that mean?"

"Navy SEAL. Titan. And... what else? Who are you? Besides a con-tractor and a good lay. You've seen my world. What about yours?"

Jax's muscles tightened. His unreadable face hardened, and the warmth that had radiated from the grip around her somehow cooled without moving. "That's it. All work, no play."

They were playing now, though... "Ever?"

"Never."

"Never ever?"

"Yeah, Seven. Never ever."

"Jeez." She inched back, faking the excuse of drinking her beer. They were hot, cold, hot, and now back to cold.

Jax took that same moment to do the same, draining the whole damn thing.

"I wasn't trying to pry."

"It's fine."

Yikes. Clearly, it wasn't fine.

"Hi there." One of Mayhem's girls appeared the second her ears heard an empty beer bottle touch the table, and she handed Jax a fresh beer.

Gruffly, he nodded as the girl scurried away.

"Forget what I said, Jax, and we'll call it almost-trust." All she wanted was for him to lighten up. "Pseudo-trust." Seven leaned back to his cheek and kissed him. "Come on. I'm sorry. I didn't mean to—"

"Don't worry about it. I just…"

"Don't explain. I'm keeping my own secrets too. Big ones. Big, manly, Mayhem, Titan-sized secrets."

He chuckled.

"Thank the Lord." She threw her arms in the air as if she were praising the gospel at church. Then she clinked her beer bottle against his. "Jax is with me again."

Seven didn't have a big secret, but if it meant lying to bring him back to a better place, then she would. As long as he didn't check up on her badass BS, because if Jax asked anyone, they would say Seven was an open, boring book. "I'm glad you laughed. Let's have a couple drinks and celebrate the almosts in life."

A thousand things seemed to cross his face when she offered that, but he finally took his bottle and knocked it against hers. "To the almosts. To forgetting and moving on."

"Cheers." Her smile was fake because, for a moment, this had *almost* felt real, but it was a job for both of them, and they would forget and move on.

Hell. It wasn't even an almost.

It wasn't even real.

CHAPTER TWENTY-SEVEN

THE GIRL WHO had been refilling Jax's beers reappeared, but this time she had liquor bottles in hand and was flirting. She held up a bottle of vodka and a darker one of bourbon. "White or red?"

"Cute." Seven laughed warily, but liquor wasn't in her plans tonight. "I'm good. Jax?"

"He's thirsty. I know these things." The liquor girl crawled onto the couch next to them, pitching both bottles forward as though she were ready to pour them into his mouth. "Open up, good lookin'."

His body shook with the silent rumble of his laughter, and Seven noticed that he didn't leer and look like so many did when leather-clad beauties crawled toward them with liquor.

"Come on, sweet cakes."

Seven chuckled to herself, not the only one who noticed how he didn't flirt with her.

"What's tall, dark, and handsome's name?"

"Jax." His lack of flirting served only to make her inch forward. "What's yours?"

"What do you want it to be?"

He shook his head. "What the fuck are parents thinking these days? I bet you never find a key chain with your name on it."

Seven choked on a laugh.

"Is he serious?" Her forehead wrinkled in pissed-off confusion. "It's Grace. Or Gracie. Or whatever you want to call me."

His eyebrows arched. "Like '*What Do You Want It To Be*?'"

"Ignore him," Seven recommended.

Grace kneeled back on her heels and rested both bottles on her thighs, pouting. "They say I don't do my job unless I keep the guests happy."

"Trust me. I'm happy." Jax pointed to Seven's hair. "Who can't be happy around this bubble of sunshine? Poof of cotton candy?"

Seven exchanged glances with Grace. "I think I'm his first pink-haired girl."

Jax snorted.

Grace giggled. "I can't tell if he's funny or grumpy."

"Welcome to the club."

The corner of Jax's eyes pinched. "You two think you're cute, don't you?"

"No, no, not with that sourpuss face." Grace inched closer to them on the couch.

"I do," Seven volunteered. "All kinds of cute."

Jax squeezed Seven's side. "You're something."

Ticklish, she moved from his hands but found herself close to his ear. "Come on now, sourpuss. You're here to fit in, aren't you?" Her lips lingered, and she liked the way he smelled clean and masculine in a room packed with liquor and smoke. Seven curled against his hard torso as his hand possessively settled on her naked back.

"Ready now?" Grace tried again. "Seven, tell him my job's to make him happy and drunk."

Seven twisted and pressed her fingers to his chin. "Grace's job is to make you happy—"

"Already told you. You have that covered."

Suddenly scared the night would end and not wanting to feel as strongly as she did for the man who told her he couldn't commit, Seven turned to Grace. "I'll go first. That's the best I can do."

Jax grumbled as Seven tilted her head. Bourbon hit her tongue, overflowing into her mouth, and slipped down her throat. The burn was a wildfire, so sweet and searing that Seven's eyes shut. It overtook her senses and woke her nerves, spiraling to the tips of her fingers and the depth of her pussy.

Drips of liquor slipped to her chin and neck as she closed her mouth and swallowed, and the liquor girl leaned close and licked the bourbon trail from her skin.

Jax tightened his hold, and Seven opened her eyes, locking her bourbon-burned gaze on the handsome man she wanted to be with anywhere. A Mayhem party. Colombia. Iowa. Wherever. The afterburn of a shot always had clarity, and this one told her she was where she needed to be.

Grace angled the bottle. "Your turn, muscles."

He simply opened his mouth, tilting his head back a few degrees, and she poured the liquor down his throat. But Jax didn't close his eyes. He kept his gaze on Seven until he nodded and Grace ended the flow. Then he shut his lips and swallowed.

"No one says no to bourbon." Grace faded away, and Seven didn't care if she stayed or not.

Kissing the corner of Jax's mouth, she followed the trail of his bottom lip, licking along the line, brushing her mouth against his chin and back to the fullness of his kiss. She wrapped an arm around his neck, angling to kiss him better. Her tongue probed against his, hot and wet. He tasted of bourbon and a night that was just getting started—

The crackling sound of a sparkler in the hotel room pulled them apart, and Jax protectively pulled her to his side. Mood effectively killed, though the liquor hadn't gone away because of morons and their pyrotechnics.

She pulled back. "How much longer do we stay?"

Jax eyed the room. "Until we see everything worth seeing."

Seven sighed. That could go on all night, no telling. But, bonus, Grace had left the bourbon bottle on the couch. "Good to know I have my secret weapon."

"What's that, princess?"

She pointed him toward the bottle left for them. "The key to switching your frown upside down is liquor with a little burn and kick."

"Not true. But since it's here…" Jax picked up the bottle, tilted Seven's head back with the tip of his fingers, and poured alcohol into her mouth. Then he did the same for himself. The bourbon coursed down her throat as she savored the buzz. Seven didn't drink often and rarely was it liquor, but perhaps it was time for the "when in Vegas" attitude. She couldn't be safer than surrounded by Mayhem and Titan. No kids. No responsibility.

She opened her eyes, and Jax's eyes were tight at the corners. "What?"

He put the bottle down and roughly dragged a needy hand up until he squeezed the nape of her neck then threaded his fingers into her hair. Jax angled her mouth against his. He was hungry and heavenly, seductive and sensitive, finally leaving her breathless and uncaring who saw how this man could make her pant.

"I needed to check something." His dark eyes were nearly black, and the roughness in his voice nearly scorched her leather skirt away.

"What are you talking about, Jax?"

"It's not the liquor."

Her heart started to race, desperately trying to keep pace with the lust that was steamrolling through her veins. "I'm sorry?"

"I tried the liquor. Then I tried you."

"Jax..." Her whisper sounded whiskey-scratched, and she couldn't breathe for wanting to feel the high of him and her mixed together—words, touches, kisses. Everything.

"You make me feel right."

Seven hooked her other wrist behind his neck, locking her fingers together, and inched forward until she pressed her forehead to his. The longest storm of seconds passed. They didn't blink. The alcohol in her blood could've made her dizzy, but it only made Mayhem and friends fade away. Her pink hair enclosed them in a haven. "Don't look now." She licked her lips. "But..."

"But?"

"You are so romantic."

CHAPTER TWENTY-EIGHT

I F ONE MORE Mayhem party *hostess* made an offer to Jax, he was calling the night short. This hotel suite was like a motorcycle club's version of a 1960s Playboy Club, complete with cigarette girls. Except the offerings included joints in addition to a cigarette or shot. His head swam with more liquor than he'd wanted, but Seven had been right. He would've stood out if he hadn't drunk.

Jax had seen everything there and had mentally made notes of who in Mayhem's leadership favored which other players. They'd reached the point in the night where the party was just a party. "You ready?"

"Finally." Seven had been snuggled into his side, murmuring intel into his ear under the guise of sweet nothings and dirty talk.

Her fingers had worked up and down his sternum, and it had taken more training than he would admit aloud to stay until he was satisfied with his understanding of who and how each player in the room worked.

Seven worked the suite, saying goodbyes, and Jax lifted his chin to Hawke, saying nothing. Tex followed behind Seven and met Jax on the other side of a pool table where the Niners had gathered. "You're good, sweetheart?"

"If I'm with him"—she wrapped a finger around the belt loop of his jeans—"very."

His weathered eyes narrowed, and Jax tried to remember that Tex had a distant, albeit sacred, connection to Titan. Tex had raised Jax's teammate's sister when all had thought she was lost to a horrible world. Adelia's father had saved her, and her brother, Javier, would forever be in Tex's debt. "Adelia and Seven are good friends, aren't they?"

Seven straightened, and her fingers squeezed his side.

Tex's eyes crinkled at the corners. "They are."

"Thank you. For what you did for Javier." Jax tipped his head then took Seven's tense hand and walked her out the door.

The moment they stepped into the hall, the bright lights and clean, cool air ran over them. They were a world away from another life, and all that separated them were a few inches of wood and metal.

"What was that all about?" she asked when they finally reached the elevators.

"He worries about you." Shrugging, Jax beckoned for her to come closer. "I hated being the guy in the room he didn't trust."

"You come here." Seven curled her fingers, mocking his motion as she swayed her hips and leaned against him. "Or not." The elevator arrived, and Seven curled again, rubbing her back to him and wrapping his forearms around her waist as the doors opened. "Shocking that no one trusts you?"

He laughed. "*No one* trusts me. But of all people, they should."

Seven walked into the corner before she turned around, and he slapped the number to her floor before pinning her in the corner.

"Knock, knock."

Jax laughed. "Who's there?"

"Boo."

"Boo who?"

"Boo-hoo? Come on, you big tough SEAL, no crying when the MC guys don't like you."

He cackled and tickled her sides, kissing her neck, not letting her go as she crawled against him.

The elevator doors opened, and she ducked under his arm and escaped but held her arm out, waiting for him.

"You're lucky there could be witnesses." He pulled her close. "Death by tickle. Not nearly the strangest thing that happens in Vegas."

Seven giggled as they turned the hall corner. "Are we drunk?"

"You are. Not me."

"Oh, bull!" She turned to push him, but he grabbed her hand, and Seven spun in the hall as if they were dancing, and her short skirt flared.

"Nice moves." The familiar voice and the applause made Jax spin Seven as he turned to face Boss Man.

With Sugar by Jared's side, Jax couldn't tell if his boss was amused or pissed.

Boss Man crossed his arms. "Guess you got the invite to Mayhem tonight."

Guess their intoxication was that obvious. Knock-knock jokes and dancing in the hall were dead giveaways.

"Do you dance?" Seven asked Jared.

Jax grabbed her arm, needing to reel his tipsy motorcycle princess back to reality.

"He can dance." Sugar's evil grin almost reached her ears. "Do you?" She put her hand over Seven's head, reaching for Jax.

"Depends…"

Sugar howled, spinning around Seven.

This was ten kinds of a bad idea.

"Don't be a stick in the mud."

"I'm not," Jax grumbled.

"Then don't be a dick."

Holy shit, how much had Sugar had to drink? And he'd thought these two women didn't like each other. Maybe it was just him that Sugar didn't like.

But it was Jared that shut Jax up. Boss Man, who'd once killed a room full of enemies locked and loaded on him while he was unarmed, let Seven twirl on his finger with the slightest hint of amusement.

Fucking hell. Jax spun Sugar out—and *that* made Boss Man laugh. Thank God Sugar heard the beat of her own drum and took off dancing around the hall.

For this very moment, Jax was glad he'd spent time with Mayhem's bourbon girl. Between Grace and Seven, he'd survived a room full of questionable people and a cloudy haze of dope, music he didn't like, and business he didn't trust, then semi-danced with Sugar—who hated him.

Seven worked Jared like a ballet bar, and Sugar spun on high heels that Jax was sure doubled as weapons.

"Don't puke." Jared eased Seven to a spinning stop. "Gracefully, though."

"I wouldn't."

"Maybe I was talking to that one." He nodded to his wife.

"Watch yourself, hot stuff." Sugar wriggled away.

Boss Man guided Seven toward Jax, and she leaned against him.

"Not bad, Jax." Sugar laid her head against Jared.

"That was all you."

She preened but then crooked her dark eyebrow. "I still don't like you."

Jax lifted his shoulders, not caring about anything but Seven plastered to his chest. "I don't know, Sugar. Progress? At least you can say it to my face."

She cackled. "Guess so." Sugar crooked her finger at Seven. "She's growing on me."

"On that note"—Jared shook his head—"we gotta go."

Sugar dropped her hand. "Maybe that's why I like you two as a couple."

Jared remained silent, knowing that he'd told Jax to do what it took to get an invite to the meeting tonight and having no idea how much groundwork had already been laid for a friendly arrangement.

Sugar pivoted to her husband on the spiked dagger heel. "You don't think so?"

"I think Jax is off the clock. I give no fucks what he does tonight."

She tossed her dark hair. "I care."

"But you hate us." Seven leaned forward as he tightened his grip on her, making sure she was well anchored to his side.

"I hate"—Sugar pursed her lips—"inconsistency."

They could agree on that, but he wouldn't say it aloud.

Jared chuckled. "This is what I've learned, especially about nights with my favorite people before a job kicks off. You have to relax in whatever way gets the job done so that when it's time to get serious and focus, your mind is sharp."

"Wait, *people*?" Sugar teased.

He chortled. "*Person*. I have one favorite, and that's you, Baby Cakes."

Sugar preened.

"I like his voice." Seven dropped hers low. "It sounds like this. My name is Jared Westin."

They laughed.

"Do you have any more advice for us, Jared Westin?" she asked in the deep faux-baritone.

Boss Man winked. "Take what life dishes you, like two drunk beauties dancing in the hall."

Jax chewed on the inside of his cheek. That was the advice he hated, like there were tragedies he was supposed to handle and keep trucking. "Yeah, yeah. Let's party it up between gang parties."

Seven and Sugar both scowled. Seven pulled her hair under her nose like a pink mustache and said in her Boss Man voice, "You're such a dick."

"Isn't he, though?" Sugar added. "But don't give Jared ideas about mustaches. I'm digging the beard. Goatee? No. Scruff? Yeah. Mustache? Nope."

Seven giggled after the laundry list of facial hair options had been laid out as both she and Jared muttered that they did what they wanted.

"What do you think?" Sugar sidled next to Jax, changing the subject. "Should I trust him?"

"Man, all the true feelings are coming out tonight," he grumbled. "Your hatred of the 'stache and how you won't let me near your stupid-ass trust circle."

Jared failed to keep his jaw from falling open. He didn't stop laughing as he repeated Jax's words, dropping his head back with a belly-laughing, "Damn."

Seven was on Team Sugar and hadn't found the trust circle anywhere near as hilarious as he and Boss Man. She crept closer like Sugar until she edged him back a step. "I'm still figuring that out myself."

"They're turning against you, brother." Jared still hadn't stopped laughing.

"No," he corrected, wrapping an arm around Seven. "This one liked me just fine before that one—"

"It's hard to trust a man who sounds like he's picking you out of a catalog."

Sugar was on fire. Jax had to give her that. "For fuck's sake." But he wouldn't let her win. "This mama liked me just fine before that mama pointed her talons at me. Or how about, this business owner liked me just fine before that business owner said I was inconsistent—and you know what? Straight out of a catalog, Sugar. This beauty liked me before you—who are a beauty too, babe—wondered if she should trust me."

Sugar put her hands on her hips, cocking her head. "That was good... Too good?"

Jax laughed. "Obviously."

Jared pulled Sugar to him. "At least the right woman makes life interesting. That's what I was saying."

"What are you talking about?" Sugar turned to her husband. "You're not the life-advice giver in this family. I am."

Jax was trying to follow both who, he'd figured out by now, had as much to drink as he and Seven had. Not too much... but maybe a little bit too much.

Jared didn't engage Sugar, and that was likely the safest bet. "No joke, Jax. You're off the clock 'til tomorrow. Go have fun."

Sugar walked her fingers up Jared's bicep. "What do you know about fun?"

"I had a leather-clad ballerina spinning circles for me, Baby Cakes. I know a little something."

Sugar rolled her eyes with so much gusto Jax almost threw out an arm to catch her. "Like he never had leather-clad ballerinas in bed before."

Jared's smile cracked. "Go have fun tonight."

"Have fun is code for get naked," Sugar added. "In case you couldn't read between—"

"Got it." Seven's crimson face surprised him. "Thanks for the explanation."

"My job here is done." Sugar whirled around and walked down the hall. "Catch up with me when you're done chatting. I'll be naked in bed." She swayed her hips down the hall, singing to herself. "Maybe I'll keep the shoes on."

Jared's eyes lingered before he swung back to them.

"I'm going this way," Seven said, turning the opposite way. "Maybe I'll keep the boots on."

Hadn't her face just been bright red? What was it with these two? Jax shook his head, sure Boss Man was ready to bid good night, but his face had sobered.

Jax had no idea what was on his mind, but the awkwardness required he say something. "If you're worried I'm not getting in my... *extracurriculars*, I promise, it's covered. Appreciate Titan looking out."

Jared worked his jaw side to side then cracked his knuckles. "Sugar doesn't trust you."

"She's told me. Several times." Jax gestured. "Including tonight."

"Because of Deacon Lanes. Did you know that?"

All the lights in Vegas went out—or it seemed that way. The simple reminder of one name made his cold heart return and any humor that had crept into his body run for cover.

"No. I didn't." And he didn't want to, either. Sugar knew Deacon?

"For the last couple years, she's—"

"*Years?*" As in how long he's been with Titan?

Jared nodded slowly. "Deacon's CIA."

"I know who that motherfucker is."

Boss Man's eyebrows slowly lifted. "You have something to say that I should know about?"

Jax gnashed his molars. All of the bourbon in the Mayhem suite couldn't have numbed Jax enough to pretend he could ever be a good guy, a man capable of love and caring for another human being ever again. He was a trained animal. A warrior. A machine. He didn't make friends. He didn't do anything but operate well with a team when they were in action. And afterward, all he knew how to do was power down.

This bullshit about Jared teaching him to negotiate and diplomatic relations was all crap because Jax didn't care. He wanted to train, shoot, kill to protect the decency and honor of innocents and civilians. He wanted mission goals and targets, but none of this diplomacy BS.

"No." Jax pivoted, surging forward.

"Freeze, asshole."

Jax sucked in a breath and shut his eyes. Jared had said he wasn't on the goddamn clock. But that was a lie. He was always on the clock, and Jax took his orders like he should as his boss marched around.

"What do I need to know about you and Deacon Lanes?"

"Nothing."

"Spill it now."

Pain crept down Jax's neck from the intensity of his jaw clenching his teeth. "It's personal shit."

Jared gave one curt, not-a-chance headshake. "You don't have personal. You have Titan. Or you have nothing."

His arms straightened, and his fists balled. "What do you want from me?"

"Everything."

Jax scoffed, turning down the hall. Seven was almost halfway down. "I've got nothing to give, so good luck."

"Brother, I own you, and if you don't see what that's worth, you're too dangerous to have on my teams."

Surprise made him spin back. "What? Because I won't tell you some stupid part of my history."

Jared squared to him. "Tell me again that it's history, Jax."

Did he say what had happened to Carrie was *stupid*? Guilt roared in his ears with his rushing blood. His body hurt. Then he simply went weak. "Guess I need a new job."

"Wrong answer, dickhead. You stubborn, stupid son of a bitch. You are Titan."

He swallowed over the strangling knot in his throat. He was Titan. Loved it, lived it, even if no one saw it or understood that.

"I know you know that too," Boss Man pushed. "Who's Deacon to you?"

"I wasn't supposed to know who he was, but I wasn't supposed to know what she was, either." There was a reason he never told this story. Reliving hell never got any less awful. "You know I was on a SEAL team. But Carrie was CIA. We were…" He lifted his shoulders then ran a hand over his face. "His cover was blown on an op. *Not hers*. Two men from a cell they'd been watching showed up to confront him. He shot her. Proof she was nothing but an expendable asset and he was whoever he was supposed to be." He braced himself for the memory that haunted him. "I watched her bleed out in the back room of St. Agnes, a church down the street from where we lived."

The silence was uncomfortable. "Never saw you as churchgoing. I'm sorry for—"

"We were just married. Minutes before." Jax cleared his throat. "Deacon didn't turn or look. He drew and shot twice to the side. Got her in the neck and stomach. Took about four minutes for her to bleed out."

Boss Man's face paled.

"I used her veil on the neck wound." Jax licked his bottom lip, chewing it. "Those things have no absorbency. Tried with my jacket and vest around her torso." He rolled both lips into his mouth. "But you know how that goes. Close range, stomach wound. She had no chance."

"They can be hard…"

"Impossible." Jax fought away the memory of red blood at her throat and the dark purple, nearly black, blood spreading from the stomach down. "She couldn't talk, cry. But her eyes were open. Until they weren't."

Jared's hardened face stayed silent, deepening with stress lines from Jax's horrid tale.

"Jax!" Seven called from far down the hall. "Come on."

"How long ago?" Boss Man asked.

"Twelve years. Back when we were both new and green."

Jared's jaw ticked. "Why wasn't it in your file? Family history?"

"The Agency swept it under the rug. No legal record it ever happened, and their sweep team took care of the locals and the scene." He drew a long breath. "The idea that someone can take *someone* from you and it's not supposed to change who you are? I don't think that's possible. But that *experience* made me better in ways. A stronger fighter. Harsher. More prepared for battle."

"Jesus, Jax."

"Nothing I've come across has fazed me since that day. Something came out of it. A hell of a lesson."

Jared stared past his shoulder. "But don't let that one lesson keep you from the sweet, stubborn, over-the-top, brightly colored experience skipping this way. Have a good night, Jax." He paced away but turned. "One more thing."

Seven eased back under his arm, and Jax hung on to her, needing to hold her more than he realized. "What's up?"

"A few years ago, Sugar was abducted by someone I trusted. You've heard the stories. But I read one time that forgiveness can't change the past, only the future. Something to think about."

Forgiving Deacon? Not in this lifetime.

"What are you two chatting about?" Seven asked.

Jared stretched. "Whether I'm going to find Sugar passed out naked in high heels. Good night."

Jax pulled her against his chest. "You feel good to hold on to."

She nuzzled her face against his neck. "I always knew men had serious girl talk when no one was watching."

Quietly, he laughed. She had no idea the depth of the subject they had touched. But what he needed was her smile, to relax and enjoy her, even *his* life and all the opportunities that Jared had said he should be open to. "Thanks, Seven."

She leaned back, letting her bright hair fall off her shoulder. "Are you okay?"

He closed his eyes, wondering what the real answer was. His automatic answer was always yes, but that was never the truth. Until now... "I am."

"I think I am too." Her hair fell over her cheek, and he tucked it behind her ear.

"I lost my buzz, though."

"Same—hey, do you want to see my room?" Flustered, her eyes widened. "Oh, wow. I didn't mean that how it sounded. The view is really gorgeous."

"Standing in a windowless hallway, I can say the same."

All of the sights and shows on the Vegas strip didn't have enough star power to make her feel a tenth as special as Jax could. "There it is again."

"What?"

She cuddled against his chest and tipped her mouth to his ear. "You're sweet and romantic, and I'll keep your little secret."

CHAPTER TWENTY-NINE

THE HOTEL ROOM door clicked shut, and Seven turned to face him. "Welcome to my amazing Vegas suite."

She wasn't kidding. The view of the Vegas strip glowed, but he didn't care. "Looks good."

"You're not even looking around."

"Don't need to." He followed her, taking her hands and pulling her close.

Tension fizzed in the air. Jax would never call Seven nervous. But they were locked in private combat; they'd skirted from flirty to turned on, skated to intense, and parted while he was slammed with an emotional tsunami. She reacted as though she could read him, and as a man who prided himself on an impenetrable wall built high around himself, maybe he was the one unnerved. Either way, he was intoxicated, having nothing to do with alcohol and everything to do with the carefree way she let her laughs fly into the night and the giving way she tried to soothe him, having no idea how he was wounded.

"What was going on back there?" Seven's words were quiet. Her delivery was smooth and sincere enough that it was as if each syllable walked a tight rope and one false move would pop their connection.

"This isn't fragile." He gestured between them. "If you think you might say the wrong thing, the bubble isn't going to pop."

Her long lashes framed deep blue eyes. "I want to know what you talked about."

And Jax knew she would ask. He'd all but asked her to ask again. Talking with Jared made Jax feel more sober, though it wasn't as if remembered pain could negate alcohol in his blood. "We were following up on a job that went bad."

"Bad, how?"

"Someone died. It was a bloody fucking mess." He'd never looked at another bride, never seen another wedding, without an immense amount of pain and misery—except Ryder and Victoria's wedding. Jax ran his hand through his hair, trying to recall the buzzed memories. He'd wanted to see Seven. Before the plane was wheels down in Iowa, he knew he was going to proposition her.

"I'm sorry." She leaned into him, the nurturing side of her taking charge. "What do you need, Jax? To be alone? To be with me?"

That wasn't a characteristic he was typically attracted to in a woman, but maybe it was the pink hair. Seven was a list of things that should never turn him on, but there was only one answer to her question. "Definitely to be with you."

"Good." She nuzzled against him. "Are we still having fun?"

He draped his arms around her. "I am."

Seven kept her cheek against his chest. "You're more subdued."

He laughed silently at the spinning ballerina curled against his chest calling him subdued. "True enough."

Her loose hold squeezed into a careful hug, lingering long after he answered. "We could watch a movie or just go to sleep."

"Hmm." He let her lean against him as his hands slowly ran over her skin. "Do you want to sleep?"

She shook her head then eased back, hooking her hands around his neck and letting him support her. "It's Vegas. We're not supposed to sleep, except I slept most of the day before I saw you."

He slid his palms up along her biceps before skimming down her bare back.

A playfulness in her eyes dared him. It was as though she'd assessed that whatever had happened in the hall was survivable. "If we don't sleep and a movie is out, then what would you rather do?"

He liked how she didn't assume. Or maybe how she wanted him to decide. Her curiosity was a quiet, hopeful hush rushing over him, and that was more arousing than any tag-chasing woman he'd ever met that grabbed his belt and dropped to her knees with hopes of making a memorable impression.

Jax took Seven's smaller hand, smiling that such a brightly dyed woman would have gray finger nail polish, and walked them into her suite. She melted against his side as they made it to the floor-to-ceiling window. The lights below flashed in a blur, reminding him he wasn't sober. But hell if Jared's conversation hadn't cleared his thoughts. "You know what I like?"

"Tell me."

"You."

Seven's grasp on his hand tightened for the flash of a Vegas sign, but she didn't turn from the lights changing and blinking before them. "You know what I like?"

"Let's hear it," he said.

Her study of the neon landscape broke, and she turned. "That I haven't had to be anyone but me, and..." She shrugged.

His eyes narrowed.

"What?" she asked.

"Not for a million dollars do I think you'd act differently for a man."

She laughed. "Exactly. I'm self-filtering."

"What do you mean?"

With a smile and a forget-about-it headshake, she turned back to the window.

"Tell me," he urged.

"You think I should give you reasons to not like me after you just kinda, sorta said you thought I was cool."

Jax tipped his head back and laughed. "Princess, make your list. Thought you knew I give zero fucks what other people think."

She tapped his stomach with her knuckles, chuckling. "Jerkface."

"Try me."

"I have hair better suited for a unicorn." She ticked up one gray fingernail. "I have kids. They're not mine. I don't think it matters, and that's a mind-screw to people. I can't imagine changing my last name. I like the outlaw history that comes with being a Blackburn, and speaking of family, my mother is Native American. Even in this day, people have unsavory opinions." She ticked off more fingers. "I run a business. Not every guy I meet likes that I take on the CEO role, and I work my tail off. If I don't do well, other people don't get paid. And…"

"And?"

"I've always liked older men. I've never been overly impressed with anyone my age, and now, maybe men in their twenties…" Seven sighed. "I wonder if it takes another decade of them asking questions and making mistakes to get to the right answers and adventures worth taking."

He'd wondered what she thought about their age difference. It wasn't much. But if Seven was about the twenty-four or twenty-six he'd guessed, she was on the money with her ten-year reference. "I promise you. My thirty-four years doesn't mean that I have all the right answers—*only* most."

"Ha," she snorted.

He didn't get why anyone wouldn't fight to have such a great girl. "A list like that scares people away?"

"That and I was married for a while. That sort of crimps dating."

He laughed. "Guess so."

"What's your list? On why you're the asshole I thought you were before I got to know you."

Amused to no end, he sucked his cheeks in. "It's shorter but probably worse."

"I'm a motorcycle club princess. You think you're going to tell me something I haven't heard or seen in action before?"

He cocked his head. "Touché." Jax interlocked his fingers with hers. "I'm simple really. Emotionally unavailable and unable to commit to anything longer than a job."

Seven pulled his hand in the air and let her fingers wiggle with his. "Okeydokey, smoky."

"She says patronizingly."

"No. I'm using you for sex." Seven crooked her head to the side. "Didn't I mention that?"

He laughed, again, for what had to be the thousandth time. "But I'm serious, sweetheart. I don't want to hurt you." He couldn't imagine doing that, but he also couldn't imagine... anything that had happened up to that point. Eventually, his normal self would kick in, and the painful memory of his wife's death would resurface. Everything happened for a reason, and if it weren't for how and when Carrie died, Jax wouldn't have become a military machine, capable of anything his Special Forces team needed of him.

Seven's hand fell away, and damn it, explaining he didn't want to hurt her already had.

"Come here." She beckoned him to lean close.

"What?"

"Come on, Jax. All the way."

He obliged. After all, he'd upset her feelings without even meaning to by just warning her they'd have no future together. What if he was wrong? What if he should've kept his damn mouth shut? Because if everything happened for a reason... The vein at his temple pounded, and he bent closer instead of following that wicked, confusing thought trail.

"No one can hurt me, Jax," Seven whispered.

He drew back, surprised.

"Sometimes, something happens to you, and it hurts so bad that no other pain can ever compare."

"*What?*"

"I'm immune to hurt."

Was that why she pierced her body? Dyed her hair? Though that wasn't a pain producer. Perhaps it gave her an adrenaline punch.

"Don't psychoanalyze me," she warned.

"I'm not." They were so much the same it was eerie. "You're talking about your father, right?"

Seven nodded. "It hurt. I'm over it. Maybe it wouldn't be a big deal to others. Maybe if I didn't have to take care of my mom for so long or wasn't so closely tied to what he left us for... But I don't think it's possible to feel hurt like that. Don't worry about hurting me because I'm not sure it's possible to make me feel pain like that again."

Guilt surged in his throat. He should share about Carrie, but he couldn't make the words form on his lips. They choked in his throat, made him want to get sick.

"Wow." Seven stepped away.

His head shot up. "What?"

"I didn't think, out of what I said, that *that* would be what pushed you away."

His face skewed. "It didn't."

"You look ill."

"Look." He scrubbed his face with his hands. "That has nothing to do with you."

"Maybe we should go back to the movie-and-sleep plan."

"Fuck no, Seven." He pulled her close. "You should let me kiss every goddamn inch of you until you can't take another second. *Then* you can sleep."

She didn't say anything.

His throat tightened. With his arm around her bare back and her legs pressed to his, all of him tightened. "I want to slide that skirt down your legs. I want you to untie that top." He smiled. "Because I'll never figure it out."

Seven's chest rose as she took a deep breath and let it out.

"I want to press you against the Vegas lights and lick your pussy until you come."

Her sharp intake of breath was as erotic a sound as he'd ever heard.

"I want to spend the night with you. In you. And I want to stay there until you're ready to fall asleep."

"Holy. Shit." It was so quiet, but the intonation packed the firepower of a bazooka. Seven reached under her hair and somehow unfastened the top that had mesmerized him most of the night. Then she did the same at the base of her spine.

The chaste frontal coverage fell away, and her plump breasts and hard nipples were bared. He closed the space between them, letting his palms drift over her sides and along the waist of her skirt. Seven's warmth radiated, teasing him as he moved his hands to the zipper at her back, dragging it down and loosening her skirt. With an easy tug, he drew it over the curves of her hips then let gravity do his dirty work. The skirt fell as she stood there, statuesque—the most captivating canvas he'd ever stared at. "You're really a work of art."

Her gaze slid to the side, a shy smile tugging on her lips. "I have my flaws."

"Fuck it, who doesn't?" Whatever she might've considered an imperfection, he didn't see and wasn't looking. Jax liked how her hips curved, how she had an ass that he could hold on to. He loved her jewelry and the simple way it highlighted who she was.

Seven turned her blue eyes back to him, dropping her chin but staring up through the mask of feathered eyelashes. "Take off your shirt."

He slipped it off as her gaze flared hungry then worked down his neck and lingered on his chest and abdomen. He had flaws too. Shrapnel scars and ugly, jagged tears on the inside of his forearms were evidence of the night he'd tangled with barbed wire and was days away from the closest medic kit.

"Your pants too." She winked. "I'm not going to be the only one in my undies."

"We're calling those undies?" He arched his brows as he kicked off his shoes and socks, hooking his thumb into his belt, and pausing a distracted second to stare at Seven before unfastening the buckle and sliding his pants free.

Puzzled, she looked down. "What would you call them?"

He sucked his cheeks in. "How about... I don't know. You should just take them off."

Seven laughed, and the sound ran over him, mixing with the confidence she always seemed to show. That, her asking for what she wanted, and the honesty that kept it real were more arousing than how her ass curved or her nipples beaded.

She reached her fingers out playfully. "You do me. I do you."

How was it they were prolonging what they both wanted, *needed*, and it was still so much fun? "Deal. Who goes first?"

"Me!"

He laughed. "All right then, princess."

He was halfway to full mast, and she hadn't touched him yet. No telling what the girl was going to do to him when she put her hands near his cock. Self-control could've been his middle name, but at the moment, Jax was the poster boy for a lack of willpower.

Seven slinked forward, her breasts swaying and her eyes locked on his even as her fingernails teased the top of his boxer briefs. "Ready?"

He rolled his lips together. "Are you?"

Nodding, she let go of the waistband and smoothed her fingers over his groin, stroking his shaft through the cotton.

His head dropped back, and he groaned at how damn good the simple touch was, even with the barrier. He righted himself, giving her warning as best he could with just a look that she was a few strokes away from him not playing so nice and devouring her. "Tease."

"Seems like." Seven bit her lips as she pulled the waistband over his erection. "I shouldn't tease. It's not nice."

His heart thundered. "You're killing me."

"I can't have that." She pushed the cotton drawers over his ass and then them fall along with her widening eyes, gaping at him before her gaze ran a heated path back to meet his stare.

Harder than he should've, Jax pulled her close. Seven's gaze never broke, but her breath hitched. Not in a fearful, worried way, but in the way that made him wish his face was buried in her pussy.

Jax snaked the silk off her hips and pushed down her underwear until Seven only wore the high-heeled, black leather boots. "Now we should go to bed."

"I'm good with that." Seven wrapped her forearms around his neck, backing up to lead him through the suite.

They stepped over gift-wrap tissue paper, and it crinkled as they kicked it closer to the trash can it overflowed from next to a desk. The trash can overflowed with a bright gift bag and more tissue paper. In the untouched room, it was the only sign that anyone had set foot inside. Jax slowed Seven as her body tensed, purposefully ignoring the bright paper. "Is it your birthday or something?"

"Hmm?" She turned, ignoring the obvious even as her olive complexion paled. "No. That's nothing."

With that kind of reaction, it was something. "Oh yeah?"

"A bag full of nothing." Seven grabbed his hand, tugging him toward the bed. "Come on."

"Suspicious, princess." They walked by her unpacked suitcases. "Not big into happy birthdays? I won't sing."

"It's not that. I promise." Seven stared over his shoulder, shifting her gaze to the window, and then her eyes darted to the floor. He'd never seen her avoid eye contact, and she was terrible at it.

Which sucked because with diversion of the eyes came avoidance of the truth, and uncertainty crept into his chest. The idea that she didn't want to share information worthy of a gift was her prerogative. But it bugged the shit out of him.

And *who* had given it to her?

Jax worked his jaw to the side, doing his best impression of chilled out and horny. Good for her. They had no set rules. This was a hookup. He was the one explaining to her they had nothing, but hell if right now didn't feel like a hookup.

Straight as a spike, she stared soberly. "*What?*"

"Nothing."

"Something," Seven shot back. "You're all… stiff. *Not in a good way.*"

"If someone's sending you presents in Vegas"—he lifted a shoulder—"lucky them."

"Oh!" Seven's mouth rounded. "No. Not like that." She slapped her hands over her lips then shook them away. "I'd never sleep around. I don't have time. I can't even imagine. It's a—how do I explain? I must be connected to someone. Like, *get them*. They get me. Flings don't work." She rambled on, talking fast. "Not judging people who do." She gestured to him. "I just can't. Sex should have purpose—" She cringed. "Not that it should for you. I—what I'm saying is I'm not romantically, er, um, *sexually* involved with anyone else." She took a breath, slowing herself down. "I never asked that of you, so my whole verbal explosion there, feel free to ignore except for the relevant parts."

His chest tightened. Goddamn, he was crazy about her. Every word. Every move. Everything. "It's fine."

"It's not."

He nodded. "It is. It's you. I dig you."

"Really?" She crooked her pierced eyebrow at him. "I don't always hold my opinions back."

"One of my favorite things about you."

"No way. I can give you a better list. Scones, coffee, *killer* sex, we laugh…"

"You keep it real."

"That's not fair," she joked.

"What?" he asked.

"Your covert, SEAL, psych-ops tricks to find out about the gift bag."

"Princess, I'm fucking naked. 'Least you have on your boots," he pointed out. "There are things I'd rather do than talk about your trash."

Seven covered her mouth again as she laughed then relented. "It's from Victoria."

Jax rolled his eyes, grabbed Seven's hand, and took the final steps to the bedroom area. "All that for your best friend's gift." He saw a card on top of the dresser, next to the television. The Vegas strip landscape was pictured as the background to a big FIRST TIMERS emblem. He turned to her. "No shit?"

"Guess so. Not my normal jaunt."

Jax swiped the card up as Seven's hand shot out. He held it just out of reach. "I can't read it?"

"This night is so weird." She threw herself back on the bed. "Before I say anything else, I'll just tell you my best friend is a connoisseur of *specialty items*."

Chuckling, he had no idea what she was talking about. "I'll take that as an all clear to open the card."

"Why not…"

It's Vegas! Go wild (as you can for you…). What happens in Vegas, stays in Vegas (but you better dish the deets).

I thought this might be interesting on the off chance that you had another slumber party. Try it. Maybe you'll relax. Have fun and trust me. Him, too.

Love you!
xo, Victoria

A card about him for a bag that ended in the trash? "What'd she get you?"

Seven threw her arms over her face, groaning. "I can't decide if this conversation is going to cause my early death."

What the hell was she talking about? Jax walked back to the trash can and extracted the gift bag. It was heavier than expected. He tossed aside the tissue paper and curled strings. "She put a lot of effort into the wrapping."

"I bet," Seven called.

Jax pulled out a small bottle of cheap champagne adorned with "Vegas First Timer" on the label and wrapper. "Thoughtful…"

"Uh-huh." She still sounded unamused.

He set the bottle aside and dumped the remaining contents onto the desk. Out rolled a pink bottle of lube, Vegas-themed condoms, a second mini bottle of champagne, and tied lengths of bondage rope.

CHAPTER THIRTY

SEVEN WASN'T SURE why Jax wasn't making a sound. When she'd gotten to the bottom of the bag, a flood of *holy shits* and *nuh-uhs* flew from her tongue. There were no gasps or curses to be heard now, and she peeled her arms from her face, peering up as Jax picked up the bag's contents and pivoted.

"I've got questions." He raised the hand holding the lube and rope.

Seven sat up, snickering, and crossed her boots under her butt. "I bet."

"Victoria sent this to you?"

"Mm-hmm."

"Must be a girl thing." Jax let the rope dangle on his finger then raised his chin. "And you threw it away."

"Straight into the trash." She pretended to make a free-throw shot then rolled her eyes. "*What?* No one at Titan airdrops lube, alcohol, and toys as surprise vacation gifts?"

He chuckled. "Not to me, at least."

Seven clucked. "Maybe you need better friends."

"Except you threw it away." He strode forward, unfazed by the gift bag. "Let's get back to why this was in the trash."

Let's not... "Seemed like the best course of action."

Jax crawled onto the bed, dropping her goodies, and eased closer until she tipped backward as he caged her to the bed. "I'm not sure about that, princess."

His weight rested against her naked flesh, and Seven untwisted her legs, wriggling them to his sides. He could've crushed her with his mass, but his powerful body simply covered her from head to toe as his mouth nuzzled her neck.

She'd texted Victoria a one-word message—*Ridiculous*—before trashing it without a second thought, but now a thousand third thoughts had come into play. "I don't know anything about *rope*."

"We're going to talk," he whispered against her ear.

Shivers tore over her skin. "We've been talking."

Jax let his lips have full roam of her neck. "Why"—*kiss, nibble, lick*—"does she want you to relax?"

"She says I don't take time for myself."

He drew back, a questioning eyebrow saying more than he could get away with.

Seven turned her head away, but Jax reached around and rolled them onto their sides. "What are best friends for, I guess?"

"Victoria wants you to use me as though you're headed to the spa for a massage?"

She couldn't keep from laughing. "Apparently. Though I've never heard of a spa where you could be tied up."

"You'd be surprised what's out there," he whispered quietly, tracing his fingers down her side. "If you haven't realized, I enjoy your body." His fingers continued their path from her rib cage down the slope, up to her hips, and over to her thigh. "Whatever it needs to be, however you need to get there, we're making sure you relax tonight."

He flicked her hip bone, gently knocking her back, and slid his hand along the inside of her thigh, over her knee, stopping short of the top of her leather boots.

"That's a good plan," she whispered, stretching as his hand inched higher, massaging her soft skin.

His knuckles brushed over the mound of her sex. Seven had been aroused since she'd met him when the sun was up, and they had flirted their way through the Mayhem meetup. It had been hours.

"Tell me what this feels like?" His knuckles eased down the smooth slope of her skin toward the two piercings. "I've been meaning to ask, why two?"

The heavenly tease of his barely-there stroke stole her words. Seven's insides clenched while Jax took his time grazing the sensitive skin. "One's horizontal, the other vertical. The vertical bar rests on my clit, and the bead ring makes me feel beautiful and—"

"Very." His warm, careful touch explored.

A pulse of ecstasy raced from her clit. Seven gulped a breath.

"I like playing with them." Jax stroked her folds apart. "Relax." He moved close to her side, and his cheek's scruff scratched across her soft belly as her legs fell apart. "Good. Just like that."

"Mm." She rolled her head to the side, basking in pleasure.

His palm cupped her mound, and Jax teased her entry with circles, while his tongue trailed wet kisses to her hip bone.

"You're so good." She arched, running her hands over the swells of her breasts and massaging. Her nipples ached for attention, and she plucked at the tips, playing with the pierced bars with her thumbs and forefingers as Jax slid his thick fingers into her pussy.

Her bottom lifted from the bed as he withdrew. Then Jax lowered his mouth to her clit as he plunged his fingers inside her again.

His tongue flicked the ring on her hood then licked the other piercing, sending cold shivers down her back as his hot lava kiss made her cry for more. "Again. Like that, please."

The kiss became a caress, and he pumped his hand into her. Seven rocked to his rhythm, moaning in bliss.

His kisses trailed down the inside of her thigh. "Grab the bottle."

"What?"

"Pour it all on your tits, princess."

That wasn't what she'd expected him to say, and uncertainty crashed her high. "What?"

"*Listen to me,* sweetheart."

Her heart hammered. "Okay."

"While you're lubing your nipples"—Jax maneuvered to hip level and hooked her thigh behind his neck—"I get to love on this pussy." He dipped forward, teasing her with the tip of his tongue while keeping their gazes connected. "You good with that?"

The quick, light lashes of his kisses whipped her nerves alive. He closed his eyes as though he were savoring her. Seven was transfixed, memorizing the sight of Jax between her legs, with all his sinewy strength wrapped by her leather boot and pliable limbs.

"You good?" he asked again.

"*Yes.*"

He growled, and she shook.

Seven's back arched. "That's so good, Jax."

"I can tell." He chuckled quietly, easing away.

"So don't stop!"

His amusement deepened as his kisses swept side to side, pulling his body on top of hers as he kissed up her stomach to her breasts. Jax tongued the pierced tip while palming her other breast.

"Or..." Seven's head fell to the side. "*That.* Don't stop that."

Her thighs cradled his hips. The firm length of his shaft slid between them as she writhed.

He nipped up her neck. "Let's talk *rope.*"

"Jax." Curiosity and arousal spiraled with surprise. "I..."

His serious face hovered over hers. "Yeah?"

"I don't know the first thing about that."

"Okay." He kissed the corner of her lips, working from one side to the other as though he were listening and not getting back to what had her moaning.

"The lube and condoms got the message across." Seven smacked a kiss onto his lips. "Look how relaxed I am."

Jax threaded a hand into her hair, petting until Seven pulled against his hold. He smiled, stroking her hair then grabbing a tight handful, gripping until Seven moaned, her eyelashes fluttering.

"I think Victoria may know you better than you realize." He released the handful and smoothed his hand over the back of her head as Seven's heavy eyelids fell.

"Victoria has a thing about toys and a message to send."

Jax nuzzled behind her ear as his fingers threaded a tight fistful of hair again. "What message?"

Seven's delirious groan wasn't quiet enough to hide. Breathless, she wanted so much more but couldn't think of what until his grip softened.

"More me time."

"I can concur." He abandoned her hair and deftly rolled off her, lying close on the bed.

"You shouldn't stop playing with me. You're very good."

His thumbs caressed the top of the nipple. "I'm good at a lot of things, princess."

"I know," she murmured, delirious that foreplay with Jax was more than a quick fingerbang before entry. Talking and teasing. She'd learned his gratification was firmly rooted in hers, which wasn't that unexpected. But now that she knew getting off was more of an art form than a feel-good activity to him, Seven wouldn't let anything else surprise her.

"You've never been to Vegas." He held her breast to his mouth and played with the nipple piercing until she squirmed. "You've never been tied up?"

A ripple of arousal cascaded through her body. Giving Jax control could be the ultimate form of relaxation. Or it could be the worst trigger of panic. "That was a metaphorical gift."

He paused. "That wasn't an answer."

A faraway wonder of submission rushed forward, from romance novel fantasy to opportunity with a trustworthy partner. Never having a face to place in a dominant position before, Seven's curiosity had only been diagnostic. Could she use controlled structure to alleviate the feelings of uncontrolled chaos that she felt compelled to fold away?

Right now, that wasn't the reason she would want to explore. "I've never been tied up."

His scrutinizing stare never blinked. "But you've thought about it?"

"Not in the ways you're thinking." She searched his face. "But yes."

"What are you thinking?" He propped onto the pillows beside her.

"That something like that sounds like it could be more than just sex."

"Bondage doesn't mean sex, you're right. Restraint can intensify a connection. It can do many things." Again, his dark eyes searched face, and he didn't touch her no matter how much she mentally willed his mouth and hands back into place.

"It could still my mind," she whispered, admitting more than she wanted to.

"It could," he agreed. "With the right two people."

"We could be the right two people."

The corner of his eyes crinkled, and he licked his bottom lip. "What are you running from?"

"Nothing." She closed her eyes and let her breath drift out before facing him again. "I'm always in charge. Kids need that, but adults? They don't. And even when I was the child, I was the fixer. The doer. The savior. And now, sometimes, I can't turn off the pile of problems around me with... And even in the bed, I'd never say I was the one in charge. But I never stop thinking, 'okay do this, now that. Are we all having a good time?'" She quietly laughed at herself. "Type-A perfectionist, and I'm not running from it. But I never thought there was someone... worthy of sharing that responsibility."

He raised his eyebrows, deadpan. "You know someone?"

"Shut up!" Seven batted his chest, and Jax *finally* put his hands back on her, pulling her closer.

"Hmm." A half-grin barely broke on his rugged face.

"What?" She didn't care if he had a rule about touching during this type of conversation. She pressed her palms to his warm chest, running her hands to his shoulders. "Huh, what?"

"I thought you were just using me for sex, and now I know it."

"Jax!" She pretended to strangle him and followed up with a gentle kiss on his lips.

Jax eased her onto the pillows then stole his hands away. "Let me use it."

"The rope?"

He barely nodded. "Just like you were before. On your back. Your boot over my shoulder."

"And you'll"—her eyes darted—"tie me to the bed?"

"No. Nothing like that." He walked his fingers up her arm and pushed strands of hair off her cheek. "Close your eyes and listen."

Seven's eyes fluttered. "Listening..."

Jax drifted the rough pads of his fingers along her jawline as though she were fragile then scratched his close-trimmed nails down her neck, gliding across her collarbone and rounding over her breast. His electricity stayed after he continued, skimming to her belly. "Let your mind drift."

She floated into a hazy dreamland. The faint alcohol buzz from earlier mixed with the warmth of arousal. "Drifting."

Jax gripped her hip bone. "Good girl."

"I like that, Jax." A tingle of awe branched down her spine. "How you said that."

His agreement rumbled, and both of his hands massaged her legs, first the one closest to him then the leg opposite his side, kneading the muscle to butter. "Bend like this."

He angled the leg opposite him so that her ankle reached toward the edge of the bed, slightly bending to make her knee-high boot form a wide V. "Are you okay?"

"I'm good." Her right leg remained straight, and his hands stayed on her left leg, one hand holding her kneecap and the other at her ankle.

Seven's eyes opened as Jax feathered his hand up her thighs, and she propped onto her elbows. "My boots are hot."

His hand dipped between her legs, stroking her sex. "I don't give a fuck about the boots. They're only a prop to the main attraction, princess." Then he winked. "But a very hot prop."

She laughed quietly and arched at the pressure on her clit. "What now?"

"*Now*, you're not in charge. Lie back." He left her sensitive skin, tracing down her leg, up to her hip bone, over her belly to circle the base of her breast and draw slowly toward the tip.

"Please, Jax," she whispered.

He ignored her nipples, moving to her collarbone and then neck.

Seven huffed and wriggled her hips. She needed his touch but realized that he had his own agenda. Rushing Jax would slow hers down.

His hand threaded into her hair—oh, God, she loved that—and a shaking gasp pulled free as he wrapped her hair around his fist. She willed him to pull it, but he didn't. He simply gathered it into a ponytail.

"I'm going to tie this"—he gave a light tug on her ponytail—"to this."

Then squeezed gently on her ankle. "Thoughts?"

A tidal wave of anticipation rocketed through her. Anxiety. Excitement. Nervousness. Peace. "Please."

The quietest, most gentle smile she'd ever seen touched his eyes before it played on his lips. It stayed for a fraction of that thought, and her heart swelled knowing that one word had made him happy.

"Stay still." That marked the arrival of a wolf. Jax's nostrils flared as he ran the lengths of rope through his hands. His jaw flexed. The tendons in his neck strained when he took a deep breath, and Seven knew he was hungry. But true to Jax fashion, he wouldn't devour her until she climaxed and climaxed and then he made it happen again.

With the rope held in his hand and the bottle of lube and condom placed by his side, Jax asked, "Anything you want to say?"

She blinked, aware of how light she felt, then listened to the silence surround them. "Make this feeling last forever."

"What does it feel like?"

"Like I can fly."

His hands whisked over her like an air kiss. "You'll soar."

Jax eased over to the other side of the bed and gathered hair into a makeshift ponytail. He wrapped the rope around once, twice, and then three times before trailing the end down and pulling it through her hair again, repeating the process and pulling through a second time.

Seven giggled this time as she relaxed, and the now-shorter ends tickled her back. "If Titan doesn't work out, you could be a hairdresser."

"You're going to be so impressed." The playfulness in his voice set her at ease as, again, Jax wrapped the rope around her hair and pulled it through. "That was the last time."

He gave a light tug then a firmer one before dropping his lips to the top of her head. "I like this, princess."

She licked her lip, resisting the rope that he held. "Me too."

"Face your head toward the right." He tucked a pillow under her neck and slid his hands over her straight leg, as though she needed the reminder. "Right leg stays straight." He walked to the base of the bed and grasped her ankle. He folded the rope then wound it over her leather boot, weaving above and below the heel, taking time to make sure the ends were even at the top and bottom with every twist. "Too tight?"

"No." Her pulse raced. "Perfect."

She heard the ends of the rope fall to the bed. Every ounce of self-control was called to keep her head in place until she floated away from worrying about what he was going to do to just feeling his hands caress her legs.

The mattress dipped when he eased next to her, and she smiled, opening her eyes to see him on the other pillow. Her hair and ankle were still tied. Not together. But what the hell, because years' worth of conversation was passing in the quiet while his fingers skimmed her body.

A strand of hair had avoided his ponytail, and he tucked it behind her ear. "If you want to hand over whatever burdens you, I'll take that weight when I'm in control of you."

Invisible weights eased with his every word. "It's yours."

Jax nodded and took the pink bottle of lubricant, and he drizzled a pattern over her chest, watching as it fell from inches above. The cool contact made her shiver.

"Like I asked before, princess. Hands on your chest." His breathing deepened. Satisfaction colored his eyes darker. Jax placed the bottle on the nightstand and leaned over to gather the rope. He deftly corrected her leg's angle and brought the lines together, pulling her ankle and hair.

Jax assessed the tautness and sat back, and Seven tested the connection. Her thighs were spread, and that unexpected vulnerability flashed through her as much as it intensified her arousal.

"The more you move your leg, the more your hair is pulled. The harder I press down on your thighs, the greater the tension."

Her pussy clenched at the immediate thought of him buried deep insider her, thrusting and forcing her thighs apart, hair pulling with every stroke. Seven's breath shook.

He kissed her stomach, wasting no time as he headed to her spread legs. Jax licked her with a satisfied groan, and Seven quivered. Before was heaven, but this was a tornado of expert finesse. His lips surrounded her clit as his fingers entered her.

"Jax." Her hips wriggled, and Seven thrashed her head to the side, unexpectedly catching her foot. The rope pulled as hard as she had pushed, and near-orgasm-level spikes of pain and relief surprised her when she flexed her leg back. "Oh God."

Her sensitive skin clenched against Jax. He never slowed, and his strong tongue stroked, his fingers thrust. Seven arched and angled, squeezing her breasts as a sheen of sweat broke out at the back of her neck.

Arousal like this had never been so consuming, as though she were breathing fire from within. She rocked as he rubbed her clit and spread her legs wider. His fingers drifted to the tight, exposed hole. Her mind screamed *please* as her hips rocked, and her pussy rejoiced in the pulsing heat of his powerful lips and tongue.

"More. Jax, I need you."

She wasn't supposed to call the shots, but she didn't care. Another second without him was too long.

He sat up as she hummed on the edge, and the crinkle of a condom tearing open made her blood boil with lust.

He untied the hair and boot binding then unzipped her boots, slid them off, and stretched her angled leg. "You're good?"

"Yes," she said, hearing her arousal.

"Good." He reached for the ends of the hair tie. Then he took her wrists that had fallen slack from her breasts, formed a column with her forearms, and quickly wrapped the length secure, binding her hands and hair. "Still good?"

"God, yes."

He seated himself between her legs, his hot-steeled tip nudging at her entrance. "Fuck, you're beautiful, Seven."

"I needed this. So much," she whispered, tears in her eyes.

Jax thrust into her as he dropped close to her ear. "Good girl."

Every inch of his thick shaft impaled her, and she prayed that brilliant pain and pressure, the delicious stretching burn and growl and groan in her ear would never end. Her thighs wrapped around his backside.

Jax pistoned into her, giving her nothing but animalistic thrusts and grunts that promised she would never be the same. His kisses mapped her neck. Sweet. Biting. Licking. Loving. Marking. And Seven bucked to meet his stride, wanting to wrap her arms around him, struggling for that hold, gasping at the sting in her scalp, and crying in thanks that he had given her that. She wanted this—to live, to feel, to be needed. This was everything and had been nothing she even knew could exist.

"Please," Seven crooned in his ear with each powerful fuck coming again and again. Her orgasm teetered on the edge of so perfect it would hurt.

"Come with me," Jax's primal growl ordered.

"Yeah," she cried, falling over the edge as he tensed.

His arms wrapped Seven tight, protected from the world as she pulsed around him, grinding for more, rocking her clit against him. Jax strained, deep inside her, nuzzling her neck and panting her name.

Their thundering breaths and pulsing bodies collapsed into loose limbs. He reached up, not moving his face that was buried in her neck, and untied her wrists, loosening the bindings in her hair.

Seven shrugged her hands free so she could drape them over his back in a hug. Together, they stayed a sweat-tangled mix of arms and legs, seesawing heartbeats, and unaimed kisses.

Jax finally rolled off and tucked her close. "What's the verdict?"

She snorted. "Thumbs-up."

"Anything else?"

"I'm..." Seven cuddled to his side. "Really hungry."

He laughed. "It was a workout. Room service?"

There was so much to see and do in life. What else had she missed? "Maybe I should get out more?"

CHAPTER THIRTY-ONE

S EVEN'S STOMACH GRUMBLED, and she slapped her hands over it as Jax propped himself up with a pillow. He moved the empty champagne bottle to the nightstand and hooked his arm around her, pulling her to his chest.

"I can't remember the last time I had food. Day drinking, sex, and champagne are going to give me a hangover if I don't put something in my tummy."

Jax kissed the top of her head. Everything about the night had been mind-bending and sweet. "Get dressed. We'll get some grub." But he rolled on top of her instead of off the bed and kissed her as though he had no intention of going to dinner. "Come on, princess. Let's get you some food."

He bounded off the bed, and she smiled as his tight ass walked away. Jax turned. "Are you coming, or do you plan to starve to death there?"

It had been so long since anyone had taken care of her—if anyone ever had, to be honest—and she was worried that was why her emotions seemed to run so deep with him. But if anything, Seven had always been pragmatic to the point of boring when it came to lust and love. She knew what Jax had said about long-term, and she had no intention of pushing him on it. But they had a connection that was special, and no matter what happened tonight, tomorrow, next week, or next month, Seven knew all the way to her soul that Jax would be someone she would remember when she was old and gray. Or maybe just old; no telling what color her hair would be. "I really like this, Jax. You, I really like you." She shrugged her shoulders and crawled out of bed. "Just want to make sure that you're completely aware of where my head is at."

She almost steeled herself for the inevitable response that she should guard her heart and that he wasn't a made-for-forever kind of guy. But he winked and turned, heading back to where they had undressed, and said, "The feeling is mutual."

She laughed as she trailed him. "Now I know you drank way more champagne than me."

He pulled on his underwear and pants, making a face that would've melted her clothes right off if she had bothered to put them on yet, but he didn't deny that it was the alcohol talking. And that was okay. As long as she was being real with him and herself, everything would be fine.

They quickly dressed and headed out. It took just a moment to head down the hall, call the elevator, and get to the lobby. Jax had his arm around her as they walked across the main hall, and it felt good to be part of a duo. She and Johnny had never had that. They'd never had a spark. They'd always had a "supposed to." They were supposed to date, supposed to be friends, supposed to get married, supposed to go home together.

This was exciting and magnetic. Jax's fingers danced on her shoulder, squeezing, and she leaned into him.

"What are you feeling? There's everything, and it's open twenty-four hours a day. Asian buffet, 1950s diner, takeout pizza place à la New York City, and somewhere in here, I heard there was really good Indian food."

"Oh, that. Indian food."

"All right. Tikka Masala, here we come."

They wandered down one way before he came to an abrupt stop. "This is your first time in Vegas. We're not going to eat at the hotel. Change of plans. I know a great Indian place. Let's go."

They changed direction and were out the front door and under neon lights after a few moments. Jax was excited, and he knew where he was going.

"Slow down a little bit," she said. "The champagne and my equilibrium plus the high heels could be a recipe for disaster if we go too much faster."

"All right, all right," he jokingly complained.

As Seven slowed them down, the conversation wandered from his jobs to her coffee shop then from her mom and kids to his family. She couldn't tell if there was something he was holding back or if he was distracted by the duty of finding her Indian food at midnight in Vegas, but when it came to who he was closest to or the topic of his family, he shifted right back to Nolan and Bianca and her mom. Which was fine because that was her favorite thing to talk about.

"Seven, I hate to break it to you, but we're never gonna get there if you don't go faster."

"*Jax*, I hate to break it to you, but we're going to go to the hospital with a broken ankle if you make me run in these boots."

The look on his face implied a challenge, and before she could register what his thoughts might be, he scooped her into his arms and made his way down the block.

Funny thing about Vegas, nobody seemed to notice or mind that there was a huge, muscly man walking down the block carrying a woman with pink hair, who was wearing a leather skirt and shirt with badass boots. Barely anyone turned a head. But true to Jax's word, they covered significantly more ground at a much faster speed than they had been going even before she'd said they needed to slow down.

Finally, they turned a corner and—

"Motherfucker."

The Indian restaurant had their lights off and a big sign across the front door. *Closed for renovations. Sorry.*

Jax put Seven down, and she buckled over, laughing. He was so upset, and she was so hungry. They were both buzzed, and it was the funniest thing she could possibly have thought about.

"This is funny?"

She laughed even harder, barely able to catch her breath, and he started to laugh too. It wasn't any laugh that she had ever heard before from him, but a deep chuckle that rumbled from his chest. She leaned against him as he draped his arm around her. Tears streamed down her face, and it wasn't nearly as funny as their laughing would insinuate. This had everything to do with the champagne, but it needed to happen.

Finally, they took breaths and pulled it together. "What are we gonna do?" she asked.

"No idea. But I can't let you starve to death. It took a lot of time to find you."

Seven simply squeezed his hand. There wasn't much to say to that. The only other thing she could try to do was describe how her heart had learned jumping jacks since her Jax had arrived.

A small gaggle of people walked by with cake in plastic cups and disposable forks. Now a food truck that sold desserts was something she could totally get into. "Hey, where did you guys get that?"

A drunk guy tripped as he pointed. "We volunteered."

"Like cake sampling? Ohhhh, Jax! I'm a pastry connoisseur." She leaned into him. "Tasting cakes is my calling. This is fate!"

"From Indian food to dessert." He tossed a hand in the air to wave thanks to the group of incoherent cake eaters. "We're off to find her fate. I mean her cake."

"Because I'm starving."

"Let's go." He scooped her back up, and they took off in search of the cake tasting.

One block over, they turned a corner, and Seven pointed. "There! Over there!" A man in a tuxedo stood next to a sign that read FREE CAKE. "Hooray, we're here!"

"Hoorays are reserved for athletic events, babe."

She scoffed. "You've never seen me around free cake."

Laughing, they were ushered in—and stopped, gaping at the sign *above* the one proclaiming free cake.

WELCOME TO THE CHAPEL OF LOVE.

"Ever heard of 'no such thing as a free lunch'?" Jax mumbled.

"I'm sorry?" A tuxedo man stepped forward, confused.

He wasn't the only one, and Jax clarified, "We're only here for the cake."

"Witnesses get cake, champagne, and Jell-O shooters as part of our appreciation for their time. Take as much as you'd like as a memento, or you can get hitched."

Seven's snort-laugh was answer enough, but she tacked on, "I'm just really hungry."

Tuxedo Man eyed them clinging together. "Sure you are. Through the double doors."

Off they went for cake. They walked straight down the hall and ran into an Elvis impersonator. Or was this Prince? Clearly, there was costume confusion.

"Hello, hello! Do we have a happy couple here?" He rolled a sequined hip. "I think you two are the sweetest, albeit most colorful, couple I've seen walk through the door all night. I see a lot of love."

"Actually"—Seven pointed to her eyebrow—"that's my sparkle you've noticed."

"She's hungry." Jax dipped his thumb her way. "Maybe *hangry*. It might be best to step aside."

Their impersonating roadblock didn't move his boots an inch. "Come back tomorrow when you take off the blinders. Keep walking through that door, but first, here are"—he popped behind the desk, his caped sleeves flying behind him, then opened a small refrigerator to reveal a frat party's dream come true—"your Jell-O shooters."

Jax took the first one offered. "This is the size of a mug."

An eye roll worthy of a Vegas stage nearly knocked over the impersonator. "Oh, come on now, my friend. A big, burly man like you needs a shot like that."

"All right." Jax grumble-laughed. "But what's your excuse for her?"

The sequins glimmered and shined as the man studied Seven. "She has to put up with your surliness." He pushed the mug-sized shooter into Seven's hand. "Now keep going. Dum, dum, dee, dum. The wedding chapel waits for no one."

They lingered and watched as another group walked in and Elvis-Prince started the spiel again. Shots were handed out, and he sent them packing also.

"Elvis didn't suggest they should get married," Jax pointed out.

"That's because we're awesome."

"Yeah, we are." He lifted his mug, and they clinked Jell-O shooters then downed the shots.

"Go!" Elvis-Prince popped up again. "It's time for you to move on."

"Jeez." Seven leaned under Jax's arm as they moved into a new room. It looked like a church, which should have been expected, but the exceptions were the Vegas-attired attendees, waitresses with tiny bottles of champagne and straws, a line of couples waiting to tie the knot, and tables with beautifully decorated mini cakes, cupcakes, small pastries, and petit fours.

"This is the best night ever," she whispered, beelining to the closest petit four.

Jax looked down. "You're the easiest date I've ever had."

"*Best*, Jax. Get the terminology right." In another life, maybe she'd been a wedding planner. She popped a petit four in his mouth, and he choked on the unexpected, incoming treat. "Sorry." Seven doubled over, giggling. "Okay, if I don't kill you accidentally, I'm the best date *ever*."

He finished chewing the cookie then swiped a piece of cake from a stand and smashed it into her mouth. "We'll call that even. And the best date ever."

She couldn't stop laughing and wiped it away. "Eww! I just inhaled icing!"

He kissed her, cake and all, and everything slowed. The crunch of other people disappeared. His thumb slid over her cheek, and she loved how he smiled against her lips. Jax smiling when they kissed made her cheeks tingle with pinpricks of happiness.

He pulled back slowly. "You're the best-tasting date too."

Seven blinked, feeling the swell of the room rush back as reality tugged her from the dreamland of sugar and kisses. "Jax…"

"Yeah, babe."

"You're right in front of me, and—I can't stop thinking about you. I just wanted to tell you that."

He hooked an arm around her neck, pulling Seven's sticky cheek to his chest, and she listened as he took a deep breath. "Hell, Seven." His hand stroked her back amid the chapel's chaos. "I always knew you were an adventure. I didn't know where you'd take me. Maybe the best things are the ones that show up without planning—"

"More cake?" A waitress in a sparkly dress held out napkins. "Champagne? Have a seat, please." Then she ushered them into a tiny pew.

The soul-sharing moment was shattered, and Seven peeled away from Jax, instantly missing their intimate conversation. "Yes, please."

The woman reached for a nearby tray with tiny champagne bottles and straws as Jax guided Seven into a row. They were handed more cake and alcohol than they knew what to do with, but the pews came with drink holders and pop-up snack stands.

"Look at this." Seven played with the spring-loaded wedding-bell-shaped cake holders that popped out from the pew in front of them. "Someone thought of everything."

"Cheers, princess." Jax held up his bottle to hers, and they clinked, kissed, ate cake, and kissed again.

Couple after couple were married in front of them, and after the fourth or fifth one, they developed hand signals to covertly decide the over-under of the couple's lifelong likelihood.

A new, glittery waitress appeared with two pink bubbling shot glasses. "Would you two want a sweet-nothings shooter? It matches your hair."

Well, of course they wanted shots that matched her hair.

Jax held his up. "To Vegas."

"Vegas." Seven did the same. "The best weekend ever."

CHAPTER THIRTY-TWO

THE SUNLIGHT MADE noise, and the air conditioner's hum vibrated like a jackhammer. Seven burrowed her face into the cool feather pillow, tugging the comforter over her head as though layers of cotton were enough to shield her from the headache-inducing racket. That plus her grossly sweet dry mouth were swift reminders as to why she didn't enjoy overindulging. *Ugh.* She couldn't even remember how the tail end of the evening had gone.

She pulled at the covers again, tucking them around her pulsing skull, when her fingers caught in her hair. A hair barrette or tie dug into her scalp, pinching, but as she grappled to pull out the culprit, Seven realized it was a headband. She tugged at the tangled mess, threading her fingers into her hair and—froze.

What the heck...

Confusion morphed into panic as the tips of her fingers caressed the headband's netting and flipped the short length down to reveal white tulle. "Oh no."

Seven tore the headband, not caring about how her hair knotted on its spines, then lurched back as she threw the mini wedding veil away.

Her hands shook, and she gasped at the gold band around her left ring finger. "Oh God. Oh no. Oh nooo."

With a quick glance, Seven confirmed that she didn't have any clothes on and that Jax was next to her. Peeling the covers back—*holy shit*—neither did he.

"Are you awake?" Seven hissed loud enough to wake their neighbors.

He didn't budge. She leaned over him and pulled at the edge of the pillow under which his hands were shoved. The left one wore a matching ring.

Seven jumped back to her side of the bed, and the night started to come back in flashes. Cake and champagne, the wedding chapel, and so many people wearing glitter and sequins. "Jax, wake up."

He groaned, mumbled, and rolled face down with a handful of covers. She grabbed them back. "Wake up," she hissed, sitting up in bed and giving him a kick in the leg. "You have got to wake up right now."

"Jesus fucking Christ." He yanked the pillow off his head and rubbed a hand over his stubbled chin. "Stop yelling."

"We have a problem," she snapped.

"Yeah. We're both awake. And hungover."

"Give me your hand." She snatched it before he could move and held up both their ring fingers for his inspection. "A big, big problem."

Jax inched back and propped himself up, forehead creased with deep lines as he blinked awake. "What is that?"

Seven snatched her hand back. "What do you think that is?"

"Um." He scrubbed his eyes. "Can you freak out in a lower volume?"

"I think I'm going to puke. I'm not this irresponsible."

"Aim for the trash can." He fluffed his pillow and lay back down.

Maybe he was the type to panic in silence. She wasn't the type to ever have unforeseen circumstances happen so experience with panic was a new problem instead of her plan A, B, C, D, E…

"Jax, do something!" Because her heart was about to explode out of her chest.

"Will it get you to *please* calm down?"

"Yes," Seven tried in a quieter octave.

"Right." He nodded then reached for the nightstand, picked up the phone, and pressed a button on the dial pad. What did he think? Vegas had divorce attorneys at the concierge desk? It was Vegas. Maybe they did. She had no idea. But either way, he was Titan, and he could fix this.

"Yeah, hello." He paused. "Can I get room service for two? Pancakes, waffles, coffee…" He looked up at her as Seven's jaw fell open. "Do you like eggs? I'm good with scrambled."

"*What?*"

Jax flinched as though she'd made his headache kick his temples then turned back to the phone call. "Scrambled. Actually, make that scrambled with cheese. And if you have any sports drinks, something with electrolytes, we need a couple of those. Some ibuprofen and multivitamins too. And Bloody Marys. That should help." He paused again. "Right, yeah. Oh, I forgot whose room I'm in. Look up Jax Michaelson, and it'll have whatever Vegas package you offer that brings hangover medicine with my breakfast." Another pause. "Titan Group. That's me. Thanks."

He hung up the phone and lay back down as she gaped. "Let me know when they get here. Night, princess."

THE COVERS GRATED against Jax's skin. He could normally sleep through anything, but the revelation was like an earthquake. Every time Seven huffed and puffed, it served as a simple reminder that they'd had far too much to drink last night. But he wasn't upset, nothing like she was. Maybe it was a hangover. Maybe he was hungry. Cake wasn't much of a dinner. Marriage was life-altering, but the non-reaction he was having wasn't what either one of them would have expected.

Or was it?

He grumbled as she groaned, more at doubting his uncertainty than because of the pounding in his head reminding him that he wasn't ten years younger. He couldn't remember a time when he'd had so much to drink that there were parts of the night missing.

"That's not what I meant," Seven snapped.

Why, at this moment, her exasperation made him smile, he had no idea. But it made a small grin crawl onto his face, and he snaked an arm around her bare waist, hooking her to him and eliciting another round of annoyed grumbles. He repositioned on the pillow to face her and was met with a bright-eyed and wild-haired beauty who looked seconds away from figuring out how to conjure fire at the tip of her tongue.

"Jax! This. Is. A. Huge. Problem."

With his arm still around her waist, he chuckled, entertained that he could feel her abdomen muscles punctuate each word.

"I'm not going to do anything with you screeching in my ear," he said quietly.

He got married? He got married. Truth was, he had always been of the mindset that everything happened for a reason. It was the only way he had survived the death of his wife. *His first wife.*

Carrie's life had had meaning. They'd been young, but they had known enough to sign up for a career in which they'd been willing to die. They had each expected their own death, but maybe not the other's. He certainly hadn't expected Carrie's—not by their government, and sure as fuck not before they'd gotten out of the church. It had never occurred to him he wouldn't make it to the honeymoon.

Was there irony that he couldn't remember the ceremony and consummating his marriage with Seven? Or was that a new way to torture himself?

How had he allowed this to happen?

Maybe because it was supposed to happen... Maybe he was still drunk.

"You aren't taking this seriously." The scowl on Seven's face proved she believed he wasn't and that she had no idea what was going through his head.

He'd barely acknowledged to himself how this woman had crawled under his skin and sunk her claws in without even trying. Maybe his subconscious was tired of waiting for him to live again, but this was like going from zero to lightning speed. "Believe me, princess, I am."

"Maybe this is fake. Maybe this doesn't count."

His stomach rolled as a small wave of disappointment surprised him. "Maybe," he said gruffly.

Her eyes shot to him like blue daggers. "Because then we could just leave the rings on the nightstand and pretend none of that happened. Do you see what I'm saying?"

Either way, this was the end of the fucking. Anything moving forward would be tainted and awkward. No dude wanted to get a blow job from someone dying to get his ring off her finger. Yet she hadn't clawed the thing off yet. "Is that what you want, Seven?"

"Of course it is! Obviously, you do, Mr. Ladies Love a SEAL."

That said nothing about her and everything about who she thought he was—which he didn't buy for a second. That slutty SEAL bullshit had been debunked weeks ago, and she was well aware. He gave her a placating smile and pulled his arm back, plumping his pillow. "Tell me when the food is here."

He picked the pillow up, covered his head so he couldn't hear any more grumblings, and wondered for the second time if he was still drunk.

CHAPTER THIRTY-THREE

I F SEVEN COULD have kicked six feet of solid muscle out of bed, Jax would have been naked on the floor. She was learning from this experience that no matter how hard she stared or tried to tap into any mental telepathy she might've ever had, he ignored her screams to get up, and the two-hundred-pound sexy slab of meat hadn't levitated out of bed. His nonchalance was almost too much. Trying his attitude on for size was an exercise in masochism. When she swore to God that she heard him snore, Seven tapped into every yoga and meditation class she'd ever gone to and lied about going to and tried to zen out. If he could be so calm, cool, and collected, she could sure as hell fake it as well as he could. Because there was no way in the entire world that Jax Michaelson was cool with getting married.

Right?

The knock at the door came at the perfect moment before she exploded like a volcano and pounced on him, wanting to shake him until he had some kind of suitable reaction. At least he was a pro at ordering room service. That had never been a quality she knew she wanted in a husband, but she had never sat down and made a list before.

The knock came again, this time harder.

"Coming," she said then bopped the pillow that covered Jax's head. "Food's here. Hope that didn't hurt, honey."

His back shook as though he was laughing, but he didn't get up.

"No worries. I've got this." After she looked around and didn't see any clothing, only that cursed headband with the veil, she pushed the covers onto him and stripped the sheet. She wrapped the white sheet around her like a dress and tucked the train under her arm. "Wedded freaking bliss," she mumbled then stomped toward the door.

Vegas room service had to have seen it all, but still, she tried to smooth down her hair so that her bedhead didn't look like she'd just screwed. She pushed it behind her ears then ran her fingers under her eyes to push away any wayward mascara. There was no telling how she looked other than the presumed hungover and well-bedded. With one last scowling stare at the lump that was Jax, she turned to the door and threw it open, thankful at least for the Bloody Mary. Hopefully, a little hair of the dog would ease her hangover. Afterward, never again would she ever touch a drop of alcohol. Bad, bad, bad decisions happened with that stuff. "Oh!"

"Jesus fucking Christ, Seven, you look like shit," Johnny said.

He didn't look so good himself. One glance said he hadn't been to bed yet. Dark circles under his eyes scored a lack of sleep that was concerning. The whites of his eyes were red, and his gaze jittered. His fingers tapped on his sides, not nervously, but as though he'd been hitting eight balls. This was not the Johnny Miller she needed to see right now. No telling what he'd mixed with the coke; no telling where his head was at. She knew him better than anybody else in the world, and when he went on benders, it could be a bad, spiraling thing. But she wasn't just concerned about Mayhem business and what would happen later on today; she had problems of her own. Johnny, her friend who didn't have the slightest interest in her as a wife or a lover, was not the same person as this Johnny, the dope fiend who didn't see anything in a rational light and became possessive, angry, and irrational of everything. He could see a bird on a tree limb and claim it as his. Then another bird could land next to it, and under the right circumstances, he would see red.

Quickly, she switched the hand that was holding up her sheet so the right fist was between her breasts. "Is everything okay?"

She had no idea where her phone was. If Mayhem was trying to get ahold of her and couldn't reach her by cell, they likely would've tried her hotel room. They had arranged for the suite and paid for it. They knew where she was.

Johnny lifted his chin, his skittering eyes unable to fix on her hair. "What'd you get into last night?"

"None of your business. Why don't I call you when I get dressed if you need something?"

"Looks like someone rammed you across the floor. Hair's all tangled and shit."

"Johnny Gabriel Miller, shut your mouth. I watched you get a blow job last night, and you have no right to talk."

"He here? That Jax motherfucker?"

"I want you to leave. Now. Call me later when you've come down so I can give you hell for being such a prick." She turned and grabbed the door she was propping open, ready to slam it shut, when he grabbed part of the sheet.

Seven reeled around, using both hands to pull it up. "What the hell?" she hissed at him quietly, not needing Jax to hear and come over and cause any more of a problem. "Have you lost your damn mind?"

Johnny's nostrils flared. "Or have you?"

"*What?*"

His eyes narrowed to judging slits, and they dropped to the white-knuckled fists holding up her sheet.

Son of a bitch.

Johnny's smirk was as sarcastic as it was furious. "Never expected this from Miss Responsibility." He snorted. "Or make that *Mrs.* Responsibility."

The wave of nausea rolling through her stomach had nothing to do with having too much to drink last night or the stupid misfortune of having Jell-O shots as a decent portion of what she could remember of her dinner. If there was anybody in the world worthy of marrying, it was Jax. But explaining that to Johnny, particularly in his current state of mind, was a lost cause. For the first time maybe in her entire life, she didn't want to understand, defend, or put up with Johnny. He wasn't the ex-husband that she was friends with. He wasn't the family friend whose indiscretions she had to overlook because they were so close they might as well have been siblings—or lovers, however creepy that was.

Jax was worthy of a defense, but Johnny wasn't worth her breath right now. "I'm so tired of you. But more importantly, he means so much to me that—" She shook her head. "I'll see you later. And only because I have to."

But Johnny was looking over her shoulder, and at that moment, she felt Jax's hands slide around her hips. Without turning from her standoff with Johnny, she looked at him in her peripheral, realizing he'd likely heard what she had to say, but she didn't care.

"Are we all good here, princess?" Jax pulled her closer to his side, dropping a sweet but possessive kiss on top of her bedhead.

"Good luck with her, buddy. I was stuck with her OCD ass and dropped that load like—"

Seven snapped, slapping Johnny across the face. Before her hand pulled back, he coldcocked her. Seven saw stars then collided into Jax.

The next seconds were a blur. Everything moved quickly, but she was certain that Jax picked her up and put her out of the way, shutting the door as he stepped into the hall with Johnny.

Ow! Dang, her mouth hurt, but working her jaw and tasting blood wasn't her concern. She shouldn't have slapped Johnny. He shouldn't have provoked her, either! They were two people who knew the other's most vulnerable buttons to push. Why had he chosen that moment to push something she couldn't control? In front of Jax! Embarrassment had made her reaction that much worse, and Jax, who she was now married to, had no idea. There was so much wrong with this problem!

Seven wanted to see what was going on in the hallway. There were all types of rules when it came to Mayhem, and she was well versed in them as well as their consequences. Still, she could do what she wanted to.

Johnny had hit her, and ex old lady or not, princess or not, there would be fallout. If Jax wanted to whoop Johnny's ass, good for him. But she had words for her ex-husband. At the very least, he was going to see her quickly swelling, fat lip.

She pushed off her butt, wrapped the sheet around her all over again, and reached for the door—

Knock, knock. "Open up, princess." Jax's firm voice was an unexpected relief, and Seven threw open the door.

Both men stood there, Johnny much worse for wear. Jax only wore his jeans that hung low on his hips without the benefit of a belt. But it was his anger that had her attention, and it was clear by his scowl and the veins protruding on his neck that he was holding back.

Seven eyed him, and he gave her an approving nod. She stepped closer to the threshold of the door again, narrowing her gaze at Johnny. "Get off the drugs. Hawke could have your patch and cut, you asshole."

Johnny snarled. "Hawke doesn't give two shits who knocks around old ladies."

"You know that's a lie, and don't you dare forget I'm not *your* old lady."

"Cunt."

Jax let his fist drive an uppercut into Johnny's chin, and her ex's head snapped back. "Johnny, man, say what you have to before my breakfast gets here, or I'll finish this now."

Johnny's nostrils flared, and he worked his jaw. If he weren't high as a kite, Seven knew he would've rebounded. "I didn't mean to say what I said. Or lay a hand on you." His face crossed between stupid and stoned. Then he turned and twitched his way toward the elevator. "Bitch."

Jax scoffed but walked into the hotel room.

"He's a winner," she said softly.

Seven wanted to apologize to Jax for bringing the barrier of sucky, shitty ex-husbands that low. But before she got the words out, he eased her into his arms and farther into the hotel room.

"Damn, Seven, he's a mess."

"You're telling me."

Carefully, he tipped her head back, inspecting her chin and lips. "Sorry I didn't hear it sooner."

Which was a reminder of what Jax did hear: how much she cared for him. But Jax was more interested in possible injuries.

"It's not split," she said.

"Not my standard of acceptable."

"I'm a bloody mess. Exactly how you want to spend the first day of wedded bliss."

His face paled, but then he ran his fingertips along her chin. "I've never had a honeymoon before."

Seven grinned though it hurt. "Bonus. Me, neither."

"I'm going to get some ice. Stay here a sec." Jax brushed her hair off her face, helped refashion her sheet around her chest, and walked with her into the kitchenette. With a quick grab of the bucket and a bag, and still only wearing his sexy jeans, he left the hotel room and made it back in what had to be record time. "Are you still doing okay?"

"Other than a little hungry, a little hungover, I'm okay."

"Room service said they would take about an hour. It's almost been an hour." He moved the ice next to her on the counter then easily lifted her up.

Jax the caretaker was surprisingly quiet and gentle, which she hadn't expected. There was still a lot to learn about him.

"Hang on one more minute." He left for the bedroom area, returning with a pillowcase that he wrapped around the ice bag before gently holding it to her chin. He slowly eased it to her lip. "Think you can handle that?"

"Yeah."

He went to the bathroom and returned with a washcloth. "It's damp. I just want to"—he dabbed at her chin and neck, even her wrist where she'd wiped her lip—"clean away some of this."

"My blood?"

He nodded then tossed the rag toward the bathroom floor as though he didn't want to see it.

Seven leaned against Jax's bare chest, still holding her ice pack. "Thank you."

He carefully removed the ice and held her. Seven took deep breaths that mimicked his and let his heartbeat play her a comforting song while he stroked her hair.

"Hey, Jax."

"Hmm?" He rubbed strands of her hair between his fingers.

"You have a heart."

"Turns out I do, princess."

The quiet rumbles of laughter in his chest and the quickened pace of his methodical heartbeat calmed her, and for a panicked second, she realized she had a fat lip and a punch-throwing, drugged-out ex-husband, yet her OCD tendencies weren't compelling her to act. She didn't want to move from this warm spot against Jax's chest and leave his embrace. She wasn't obligated to fold her concerns into neatly folded issues that were more manageable.

"Let's see." Jax leaned back to inspect her lip again. "I think you're going to live."

Seven had no idea why the funny line seemed to hold so much gravitas as he said it, but her soul squeezed. "You helped me in more ways than you know."

Jax gave her a simple, sweet kiss on the top of her head, resting his chin afterward. "Same."

CHAPTER THIRTY-FOUR

CIVILITY WASN'T A high point of Las Vegas, and that was one of many reasons it wasn't Hernán's favorite place to go.

Esmeralda had her hair tied in a bun and tucked under her large-brimmed hat as they played tourist, walking down the streets with two of their covertly armed bodyguards following closely. The four of them blended in as vacationers among common people.

Periodically, he came out of his castle with his queen. It was interesting, even if it served a business purpose. He liked to walk in crowds to see how cultures behaved, what they wore, what they spent money on. And when his network of spies and friends inside of the tightest of elite circles told him there was a special meeting of North American drug movers and shakers, Hernán desired to be in town at the same time.

Esmeralda did not. Her biggest complaint was the food, but that was one area he did not budge on. When they were in the US, they dined like Americans—and not the type that could afford to eat at Esmeralda's restaurant on the regular. Rather, the kind that would invest every last penny in the white nose candy that made him and his wife so wealthy. That meant, for breakfast, the greasy food would have an aftertaste, and bitter coffee was made tolerable only by additives.

"Are you ready, my dear?" He also used this time to work on his English and on removing as much of the Colombian accent as possible. That was more of a hobby than a necessity, but he so enjoyed it.

Esmeralda, not so much. "*Si.*"

It would be one of those days where he would have to make sure she knew how much he appreciated her. They'd left their expensive suite under the cover of rich disguise and had followed the concierge's list of best, mid-priced establishments for breakfast.

The morning sun warmed his back as they fell into step with milling crowds of tourists and promoters, pickpockets and pros. "Shall I pick one on the list or—"

"I do not care."

Esmerelda would need much attention.

"The closest to the hotel, then." He took her cold hand, unaccustomed to her height in her athletic shoes, and they started down the sidewalk for their breakfast destination. "We'll cross at the first light."

"Hmm."

What would she like to make her feel better? Champagne and caviar? Emeralds were her favorite jewel, mostly because she was named after them and had a room dedicated to her collection like some women showed off their shoes and handbags. Maybe a trip somewhere she wanted to go. Venice? Hadn't she mentioned that recently?

A sweaty, heavyset man in a cotton shirt that belonged *under* a normal shirt bumped into them—elbowing away without a word. Hernán swallowed away his disdain, but Esmeralda dug her fingernails into his hand, sinking her painted claws into his flesh. Sometimes, she needed to expel her unhappiness with pain, and he didn't mind the little bites. It was easier to let the levees be opened when needed lest she be overrun with a sadistic explosion that was far harder to control.

A man in a leather cut pushed past a family of four, almost knocking the mother into the street. The gangs were in Vegas... and that was a Mayhem insignia.

"Hernán." Esmerelda's nails came free as she inched close.

But by the time the man had crossed, Hernán didn't need his wife to point out Johnny Miller as he twitched and jerked across the street, storming and stamping with evident anger.

Hernán's eyes narrowed, and with the tilt of his head, he ordered one of his guards to peel off and follow Johnny. Mayhem's vice president was visibly upset and coming down from what looked like meth.

They crossed with the crowd as the light changed and watched Johnny until Hernán could no longer see him.

"Does that mean what I think?" Esmeralda's hopeful voice meant the breakfast outing wasn't a total lost cause in her mind.

"There are problems in the rank, and their leaders are using the product." Perhaps it was time to run Jorge's report about Johnny's children by his Esmeralda.

They arrived in front of the breakfast recommendation, but Hernán didn't go in yet. If he told her about the possibility of using Johnny's children as a pressure point to keep Mayhem in place, she might want his kids, anyway. Though Hernán could always get her other children if Johnny's didn't work out in negotiations and made a note to have Jorge arrange for options.

"My dear, at the very basic level, what is in our best interest?" She hated games but let him have them at times.

She scoffed then held out her fingernails and checked her manicure. "Mayhem remains in distribution. They keep the status quo."

"Yes." Reminding her of this was needed. "It costs too much time and money to switch distributors. If we had to." He shrugged. "But if we didn't… how could we use Johnny to convince Mayhem to revote?"

"We don't." She dropped her hand. "We torture and kill him then send his body back in pieces. I'll sign the final note that tells them not to try and renegotiate their contract—anything that keeps me from this breakfast again."

"Oh, my beautiful one." Hernán contained his amusement and could've said her response verbatim before she did. "That won't work long-term and teaches no lessons. They might renegotiate again in a few years."

Esmerelda took his hand and kissed it. "Maybe you've forgotten how good I am with body parts in Ziploc bags, *mi alma*."

No containing his laughter that time. "What if, instead, you get a request you've often made and Mayhem will forever behave. A gift for you and non-negotiable terms for them."

Her eyes went wide as her lips sealed. Patience for surprises wasn't her strong suit. But she knew any gift he'd ever given to her was very special and well meaning. "Tell me."

He inched closer and put his hands on her face, rubbing his thumbs over the apples of her cheeks. "Johnny Miller has children."

CHAPTER THIRTY-FIVE

THE HOTEL RESTAURANT buzzed with the chatter of the always-eclectic Vegas lunch crowd, mixing with the clink of forks and knives and the not-too-far-away shuffle of people moving through the busy hotel. Jared had mentioned to Jax that they would meet up to discuss this evening's Mayhem meeting, but when Jax got the text message to join Boss Man for lunch, it caught him off guard. The trip wasn't a vacation, and Jax needed to remember he was there for work.

After checking in with the hostess, Jax was directed to the back room. Jared must have scared the bejesus out of the woman or issued a warning because she simply pointed in the direction he was supposed to go. After he followed the line of tables and turned the corner to a more secluded, slightly quieter side of the restaurant, Jax saw a row of private dining areas with glass doors. Some had curtains that could be shut, some were already drawn, others were wide open, and some were empty. Others were not. At the end, Jared waited against the wall, one boot kicked on top of the other and his arms crossed. He looked as though he were studying his phone, but Jax wasn't stupid and knew that Boss Man had a bead on every person that moved in any direction.

"Hey," he greeted his team leader. "Been here long?"

"Nah." Jared tilted his head, directing Jax into the small room, then shut the door behind them. The drape fell into place and obscured the last of the public views. An opening on each side let Jax see who came by one side and Jared the other, so neither one of them was sitting blind in a box. Jax hadn't asked, but with as many security cameras as there were in the building, along with all of the players and personalities and firepower that walked the halls, he was fairly certain Parker had all of Titan's IT resources working overtime. There were probably eyes on them and everywhere else.

"What's Sugar up to this afternoon?" Jax asked as he leaned back in the plush chair.

Jared chuckled. "Getting her talons worked on—or a manicure, whatever she wants to call it."

Jax laughed, and a knock sounded on the door before their waitress came in.

They took a moment to peruse the menus quickly before deciding on waters, New York strips, loaded baked potatoes, and broccoli. Bread quickly came after that, and it was placed right next to the small device on the table that Jax was familiar with. The contraption made sure that if there were any listening devices in the room, their signals were scrambled. No one could hear what they were saying, though the device wouldn't mess with their phones.

"About last night," Jared started, leaning back in his chair and popping a piece of bread in his mouth. "Give me a rundown of what you learned."

Good thing that Jax could remember everything important about the meeting. It had been a stupid move to drink more than he needed, even if he'd been *off the clock.* Jax focused on the important stuff in regard to work, leaving out the part where he'd gotten drunk and married. "Hawke's pretty levelheaded. He was able to keep rivals civil, converse with people he probably didn't like much, and work the room like a politician. If he spent any extra time with any one group, I'd say he's favoring The Brotherhood. They're both MCs. They have all of their motorcycle shit in common."

"Was that something he was leaning on, motorcycles, or did it seem as though they were talking business?"

"No one was negotiating. Booze, blow jobs, blow. Not a lot of business."

Jared snickered. "Ah, your typical Jax Michaelson social gathering."

"Exactly my type of crew," he groused. Booze, he could handle. Everything else, Jax would rather not. He didn't want to see it; he didn't want to know about it. "But it was more than a comfort level. There was trust there more than familiarity. They had a level of professional respect, and I think it will translate to tonight."

Jared nodded. "Noted. What else you got?"

"One more thing about The Brotherhood. Seven described their president as a robot. So much so, he actually goes by Bot. I think that works in favor of Mayhem handing the distribution off to them because Hawke and Tex don't want any drama. A guy named Robot? That sounds low drama to me."

"Hawke and Tex. Those are the two I'm not gonna worry about." Jared raised his eyebrows. "You saw Johnny, though?"

"About Johnny. That's going to be… a more complicated discussion."

"I excel at simplifying complicated."

At least one of them could. "I've confirmed he's not a fan of Titan."

"Imagine that," Jared grumble–laughed.

Jax recalled the amount of restraint it took not to tear Johnny apart limb by limb, and it might have been one of the hardest tests he'd ever had in his career. Johnny had to make it to the Mayhem meeting tonight—for Titan, for Seven, and for Mayhem. But if it weren't for that, Jax wasn't sure what it would've taken to stop him. The sight of blood trickling down Seven's chin could've been a catalyst for serious injury.

"Johnny unexpectedly came to Seven's hotel room this morning. They exchanged words… She slapped him, and he swung back." Jax wanted to sound unaffected but was failing. "She took a hard knock to the mouth. It tore up the inside of her lip. Those two have history, but not like that. I think she's more shocked than anything else."

Jax was so deep in his own head that he hadn't focused on Jared, but when he did, Jared's viewpoint had always been crystal clear. Right now looked to be no exception, even if they were in business together.

"And?" Boss Man growled.

"I took him in the hall, explained what I thought of that—*with my fists*—until Johnny decided it was time to apologize."

Jared's head moved slightly, agreeing, but his anger had not tempered. "If they have history and she didn't see it coming, what the fuck? You?"

"I don't know. Don't think so. Their past is old. Johnny sat across from her last night getting a blow job. Whatever rules ganglandia has, I don't know. Neither seemed jealous." *Well, maybe Johnny…*

"Then what?"

"He was hopped up and crashing hard."

Jared's eyebrows arched. "Cocaine?"

Jax sucked his bottom lip into his mouth. "I'm no expert, but yeah, maybe coke and something else. He was twitching, jerking. Meth? Dust? I don't know that shit."

Jared mulled in silence. Then their waitress knocked and brought their food. After they had both taken a moment to dig into their steak and potatoes, Jared asked, "How does Hernán not know this? The Irish and the Russian in a room together? The Niners and the Brotherhood? I get that it's one or two members from each and everybody has a financial incentive to behave. But still."

"I don't see how he doesn't know." If he were Hernán, Jax would be there. He would be in the hotel lobby, watching every single person try to betray his negotiated agreements. Hernán wasn't stupid, and his wife was known for many things but not stupidity or sanity. "Seven is confident, though, that Hernán is unaware."

Jared took another sip of water. "I hope to hell she's not naïve."

Jax shrugged. "I think she's idealistic. But I don't think naïve." Idealistic about a motorcycle gang—as if that wasn't a crazy oxymoron.

"What else is going on with you, Jax?" Jared wiped his mouth with his linen napkin and leaned back in his chair.

He ran a hand over his face, hoping the dark circles and lack of sleep weren't showing. "Not much."

Boss Man dropped his chin. "How about that bruise?"

Jax ran his hand along his jawline. "I told you, brawl with Johnny."

"Not that one." Jared's eyes narrowed on his left hand. "*That* one."

Jax looked at the hand from which he'd slipped off his wedding band before he walked in to lunch. Seven had ranted and raged that getting married was an accident, and Jax didn't want his boss to think he was irresponsible. The whole thing was confusing, but Jared asking about his hand unnerved the hell out of Jax.

Jax brought his hand down and looked at his knuckles, red and raw, nothing unexpected from a scuffle. But there was an unexpected bruise on the top of his left ring finger, near the knuckle, that mimicked where his ring had been. "I don't know."

Jared harrumphed, making a disapproving, disbelieving grumble. "Right." He stood up, tossing down his napkin. "Lunch has been taken care of. Leave whenever you're ready, but I have to roll, and I'll meet you tonight. Parker will send you any logistical information you need. I'm going to go find my wife."

Jax tore his eyes away from his hand and stood as well.

"Maybe you should do the same."

Boss Man was the master for a reason. He missed nothing.

CHAPTER THIRTY-SIX

THE HOTEL ROOM suite echoed in silence as Seven lay in the middle of the freshly made bed and tried to contemplate trivial life decisions. Should she change hair colors? Maybe another piercing was a safer adrenaline rush than falling for Jax Michaelson. But no, that was not where her mind wandered. "I'm married."

And now that she'd finished freaking out, the idea that he was hers... Seven smiled. But that freaked her out. How could this have happened? She grabbed her phone off the charger and called Victoria.

"Hey," her best friend answered more gruffly than expected. "Glad you called. I need somebody to talk to who's not going to drive me crazy."

"Are the kids acting up?"

"Oh no. *Ryder* is acting up. Sort of. I may've been in the wrong, but he's overreacting."

"How are my kiddos?"

"Perfect. They're running around outside with him who shall not be named—"

"Your new husband?"

"Yes. Him. And they're angels, like always."

Seven snickered. "I can't believe that sweet, Aussie hottie could possibly be the cause of any headaches."

"That hot Australian is driving me nuts. Bat shit. Absolutely bonkers."

"Really?" Seven crawled up to the top of the bed and shoved the pillows behind her, propping herself up in anticipation of listening to the tales of a honeymoon-gone-wrong story. "You have to be very convincing for me not to take Ryder's side," Seven teased, knowing full well she would never do that. "What gives in the land of lovers? Last time I saw you two, it was all googly love faces and smoochy kisses. I wanted to puke."

"We were newlyweds. I'm pretty sure life has returned to normal. No more nausea for you."

"I was just kidding, and you two were always and will always be cute." She wondered if anyone would ever call her and Jax cute.

"Hope so." She sighed into the phone. "I looked over the first morning of our honeymoon and wondered how did I get so lucky."

Well, hell. Seven laughed at the memory of her morning after. She'd shrieked, nearly fallen out of bed tearing the veil from her hair, and had kicked Jax awake. "That's a dead giveaway that I'm right. It'd be a whole new conversation if you woke up, looked over, and wondered 'what the heck did we do?'"

Victoria scoffed in her ear. "Yeah, how bad would that suck? I bet that happens to people all the time in Vegas."

Seven laughed so hard she choked. "Yep. Bet so."

"Ryder's mad because I let the pizza delivery guy in."

Her brows pinched, and Seven smoothed her hand over the pillow next to her, trying to remove every last wrinkle and crinkle before asking the most obvious question that came to mind. "You ordered pizza?"

"Exactly!" Victoria grumbled.

At that point, Seven knew Victoria was on the verge of admitting that Ryder was right and she was wrong, and at least they would have makeup sex. "You let a delivery guy in who wasn't *your* delivery guy. I think you both have done more questionable things. Not that I'm one to cast judgment," she added as she stared at her wedding band.

"No, he's right," Victoria lamented. "It was probably harmless. But I let somebody into our house when he had no reason to be there. Both of our careers make that a very bad idea, and it could've gone in another direction faster than I was prepared for."

"I get it. But everything was fine."

"The kids were running around earlier, and I was frazzled, and he showed up with his pizzas, insisting that he had the right address. I was insisting that he didn't. I'd been bribing Nolan to eat, and then he started, and I didn't want to leave him alone with food in his mouth. It was storming outside, and so I told the guy to come in while he made his phone call to figure out where the pizza was going to go—"

"Victoria, take a breath. It's okay." Her exasperation sounded as though she had been self-flogging to excess, whether she'd been called out by Ryder or not.

"You just never know what people's intentions are. It was okay this time, but for all I know, that guy was scoping my house out. He could've been some freak that liked kids. It might not have had anything to do with Ryder and me."

"Now you're just getting paranoid, Victoria. It's not like you've had kids for some freak-show pervert to stalk and obsess over. You know?"

Victoria hummed as though she didn't agree but had no defense left to put up. "How about you talk to your super-cute rug rats? They just walked in. I'll put you on speakerphone."

"Seven! Seven! It's Bianca. It's Nolan. Can you hear me? Us? Can you hear us? Me?"

"Hi, guys. I can hear you. What are you doing? Are you having fun?"

They started to talk over each other again with a list of activities that sounded as though Victoria had been offering a day at camp. Arts and crafts. Hide-and-seek. Duck, duck, goose. Something that had to do with glitter.

Seven shuddered.

As much as she loved all things glittery and sparkly, glitter was one of those things that could also be used as a torture device. One sneeze gone wrong, and it was hours of cleaning. She once made the mistake of asking for help with glitter cleanup, and it took about two minutes to realize that all the little hands were making it ten times worse despite their best efforts.

Nolan and Bianca ended their call with a series of competitive I love you's, each determined to say it louder and prouder and mean it more than the other before, apparently, they ended in a hug-and-tickle war that required Victoria to put down the phone, pick them up, count to one, and send everybody to coloring books.

The rumble in the room quieted on the phone line, and Victoria came back. "The coast is now clear again."

"You, Madame Deputy Mayor, sounded very motherly a moment ago. All 'don't make me count' and 'one...'" Seven laughed. "I'm very impressed with that."

"I learned from the best."

"Ahh, I'd say thanks, but sometimes, I don't know if you should say that about me. Speaking of which, how's my mom?"

Victoria grumbled. "First, don't say that about yourself ever again. I've never met anybody more selfless and giving, in general and to these kids, than you. And second, your mom... I don't know anymore, Seven. I think moving your mom to assisted living was the right thing to do, but she seems so much worse than even three or four months ago. I know that's not a conversation you want to have right now." Victoria sighed sadly, and Seven felt the same way on the inside as her best friend continued. "A couple weeks back wasn't that long ago. It's just like something has changed."

Seven hung on to the phone in silence, and Victoria didn't add much. There wasn't much to say. The doctors insisted her mom wasn't suffering, but her quality of life seemed miserable, even if she didn't complain... maybe because she couldn't complain.

"And I got a phone call... from my dad."

Maybe that was one of the reasons why Victoria was in the mood to bicker with Ryder, because her dad could spoil any mood depending on what he had to say and how he said it. There were times when he seemed like a normal, nice person. Those times weren't often.

When Victoria didn't expand on the conversation, Seven's stomach tied in knots. It was a doubly dreadful feeling, given that she was hours over her hangover and raw nausea wasn't a great feeling. "What's the matter?"

"Your dad is... Somehow, Cullen got word sent to my dad while they were in prison. You know how that goes... Your dad's powerful. He can make things happen, and I didn't expect to hear from mine when I answered the phone."

Seven's nausea morphed into anger. The dread that swirled in her stomach snapped into tension, and she closed her fists. "I don't care. I don't want to hear what they talked about. I don't want to know anything." Seven shook her head and could feel blood pounding at her temples. "Tell him to keep my dad far away from my life."

"I'm sorry I said anything."

She let her fingers flare out then relax, trying to shake away the stress of Cullen Blackburn, when Seven caught sight of her left hand. That was a whole new barrel of stress. Why she hadn't taken off the wedding band yet? Jax had when he left to meet his boss.

"Don't worry about it," she grumbled, unsure if she was more aggravated that she wouldn't take off her ring or that her dad had reached out. "Have you ever picked up any legal know-how when helping out on your divorce cases?"

Victoria hummed. "Maybe a little. I'm not sure."

"A little, like about annulments or divorces? Papers involved with that stuff?" Seven held the wedding band in front of her, moving her hand up and down, unable to look away like a cat drawn to a laser beam.

"Well, actually, I think it's all—wait, why?"

She dropped her hand quickly, tucking it under her back as though nothing had happened if she couldn't see it. "No reason."

Victoria sucked a deep breath into the phone. "Holy shit."

Seven rolled her eyes because that was what she would've said. "Heard that before. Don't—"

"Did you get married?" Victoria asked in her most curious, most accusatory voice. "To who? Johnny again?"

"Oh my God, no. Are you insane?"

Victoria gasped. "Holy shit. You married *Jax*."

Seven groaned and slapped the hand that she had hidden over her face. "I blame the rope. This is all your fault."

"Oh my God. I can't—I can't even—oh my God!"

"He really knew what he was doing, and it built so much trust. I trusted him before that anyway, and he's really sweet and romantic to start—"

Wait. Was she defending her marriage?

"Dying. Seven, I'm dying. Right now. I wasn't one hundred percent sure that you two were hooking up. But now you're married? Ryder's going to die too."

Ugh! "Don't you dare tell him."

"I'm texting him now," Victoria said from the far away sound of speakerphone.

"Dammit, Victoria, stop! We're going to fix it! Soon as we can figure out how to get divorced."

There was a long pause, and Victoria's lack of response made Seven sit up. "Why would you do that?" her friend finally asked.

Her face skewed in confusion. "Why wouldn't we? I don't know his middle name. We can't even have a solid foot-stomping, middle-name-calling argument."

"This is the first thing I can think of that you've done because you've wanted to do, not because you've had to do. You married Johnny because you were told to. Cleaned up all the messes your father made because he said so. You fix everything Mayhem asks you to because you feel responsibility for them. You love your kids to death, but you never saw them coming. You didn't plan on taking care of your mother before she had a stroke, and you had no intention to run a coffee shop before then, either. You have major responsibility in your life, and none of it was your decision. I don't know if you realize this, Seven, but you did something pretty huge on your own. Before you try to erase it, I'd try to figure out why. Even if there's alcohol involved." Victoria laughed quietly. "I'm just saying, don't rush, or at the very least, enjoy your honeymoon."

CHAPTER THIRTY-SEVEN

D IPLOMACY HAD NEVER felt more like bodyguard status. Jax stood in the back of the Vegas conference room with Jared as he took in the scene and hoped that Boss Man would never force him through such a bullshit life lesson again. Whether this was punishment or he was actually supposed to learn how to keep his attitude in check, there wasn't much to be said for office work.

At this point, Jax wasn't even sure what was to be said for Seven. He wasn't looking for a relationship. Certain complications came with that kind of responsibility—and it wasn't just her, but Bianca and Nolan too. It was almost more important that he thought about them first. All Seven wanted for those kids was a normal life, and him popping in and out because of her wasn't fair.

But damn, it wasn't fair to run away from all three just because…

Jared cracked his knuckles, and they both trailed behind the assortment of gang—businessmen who had come to their agreement peacefully.

Not that he and Jared didn't want to take out a few of the fuckers. But that was a conversation for another day. For the moment, there was peace in ganglandia for the purpose of financial gain. They filed out of the conference room to where everyone had checked both phones and weapons as though it were normal. And actually, it was. Though Jax hated being around most of these people unarmed.

A stir of conversation grew louder as the group bottlenecked, and a crick of trepidation swept down Jax's back. His senses went on high alert as adrenaline swept through the air, spreading like wildfire, though he didn't know what was wrong.

A quick glance at Jared confirmed he felt the shift also.

"What is it?" Jared mumbled. He took a step left, tilting his head so that Jax went wide and right.

He saw nothing abnormal except for a few terse looks around cell phones while others casually ambled away with fist bumps and chin lifts goodbye.

The group of men parted. Sugar appeared in the middle as they split, and Jax's stomach dropped as he focused on the hard set of her jaw. Her searching gaze locked on to Jared, and she picked up speed. As though they had a silent conversation that sounded alarms, Boss Man rushed ahead and met her halfway. She held a phone outstretched for him as gang members crowded closer. Jax split from the group and pushed through the Niners and the Brotherhood, past Mayhem, then demanded his phone and weapon while keeping an eye on Sugar and Jared.

He had nothing of interest and holstered his sidearm, studying the pack until Seven extracted herself from Mayhem.

Her bright eyes were dead, and her lips had gone ashen as a limp hand reached toward Jax.

"Seven?" Her step faltered, and he surged forward to catch her before she stumbled. "*Seven!*"

She crumbled in his arms as he pulled her close. Jax twisted, looking for a chair and then his boss, wondering what the fuck was happening.

"Seven, get the fuck over here," Johnny snapped.

Hawke's arm flung out and slapped across Johnny's leather cut. It wasn't to hold the VP back but to put up a line that shouldn't be crossed.

"Seven, back here. We've got to talk. Now." Hawke dropped his arm from Johnny's chest, but his authority over the situation remained. He lifted his chin. "No disrespect to you, but we have club business to take care of."

Seven didn't move, and Jax wasn't letting go.

"I'm not going to tell you again," Hawke growled.

She buried her fingers into Jax's flesh, whimpering as though her soul cried. Jax wrapped his arms around her tighter than before. "What the hell is going on?"

Jared and Sugar moved next to Hawke as Ethan and Tex moved next to Johnny, forming a semicircle around Jax and Seven.

"Boss Man, what?"

Seven pressed her forehead against his chest, answering, "He has them."

The shaky shadow of her was hauntingly hollow, and still, he wasn't connecting the dots.

"He, who?" What were they talking about? "The kids?" Jax thought the kids' dad was long gone, in jail because of all this goddamn drug business. Hadn't that been the problem to begin with?

Jared tossed the phone Sugar had rushed in, and Jax caught it one-handed. The screen was open to a message from Parker to Sugar.

Hernán knows about Mayhem's meeting. Victoria was run off the road and handcuffed to the steering wheel. Suarez cartel took both kids. Get in that meeting and tell Jared.

"What the..." Jax knew better than to trust the gangs and their networks. No amount of money and benefits would keep them quiet. Why hurt Seven? He tossed the phone back to Jared. "What are we gonna do?"

Johnny surged forward. "*We* aren't going to do anything, motherfucker."

"Stand down, goddamn it," Hawke barked. "This is your goddamn fault."

Johnny spun toward Hawke. "My goddamn fault? You want to talk about—"

"I would be very careful about what you say in the open," Tex said.

"If you're not Mayhem, get the fuck out of here," Hawke ordered, and the remainder of the Niners started to walk.

But the Brotherhood didn't move. "If we have a problem with Hernán, you know this deal is off the table. That was part of it. The contract conveys. That means all distribution partners, everyone from production to the last distributor that helps somebody sniff it up their nose, is thrilled. Do you read me?" The man with the wretched Brotherhood tattoo across his throat moved toward Hawke. "If you had us come down here, do this song and dance, and it was in bad faith? You will have a war on your hands. And not just from the Brotherhood."

"Get the fuck out of my hotel if you want to speak to me like that," Hawke said, stepping forward. "Hernán is happy when his bank account is happy. You threaten me, I'll bleed you out on the carpet before you can say don't slice open my ink."

Neither man stood down, and Johnny's jitters started to twitch next to Tex, evidence that he hadn't taken a hit of whatever he needed recently. Everyone was armed, and emotions were high. The area was close quarters, and what they needed to do was focus on Seven, Nolan, and Bianca.

"Seven, let's get this worked out," Hawke said with a much lower voice, as though he were trying to cool his own rage, lure her back toward Mayhem, and keep everything good with the Brotherhood.

The phone Sugar had given Jared vibrated, and not missing a beat, Boss Man swiped the screen. His face darkened as he listened, offering only a grunt before he ended the call and turned toward Hawke. "How do you plan on correcting Hernán?"

Hawke barely shook his head, but the tension flexed in his jaw. "We will deal with the business of Mayhem momentarily."

Jared took an aggressive step forward, challenging Hawke. "You think that you can fix this? Titan has been on the sidelines, watching you make mistake after damn mistake. And you don't want to partner with us now? When this is what we do best? *Fools.*"

"They're my kids, and I didn't say no," Seven whispered. "What does Johnny have to do with this?"

"What the fuck does anyone have to do with any of this?" Johnny threw his arms out, twitching his fingers. "If we had left good enough alone, none of this would've happened."

Hawke snarled at Jared. "You obviously know more than we do right now. You could share."

"You're obviously," Sugar snapped, mocking his snarl, "going to play with those kids' lives because you have"—Sugar threw her fingers in the air, making air quotes—"club business. And you don't even know what's up. Is that right?"

"They think Bianca and Nolan are Johnny's blood," Jared explained.

"No," Seven cried, collapsing against Jax.

Johnny let out a string of curse words, spinning in his boots and slamming his fist against the wall. Tex grabbed him back and threw him in line.

"You know whose fault this is?" Johnny paced back and forth, cracking his neck side to side, working his shoulders up and down.

Jax couldn't wait to hear who that asshole was going to blame. Whatever beauties were going to fall out of his tweaking, meth–mouth would have been comedy if it weren't such a serious situation.

"I'm going to shove my hand through your face if you don't shut your mouth," Tex barked.

Johnny snarled and spun, but he didn't stop in front of Tex as he twisted to face Jax. His gaze dropped to Seven. "You."

She balked. "Me?"

"If you had just let them go. But no, you have to take care of the world. You have to have kids to what, fix what was done to you?"

Cold, white fury shook through Jax with such rapid fire that he saw the hotel shake around them. But before he could hold back Seven or funnel his fury to his own fists, Tex swung, and the back of Johnny's skull smacked against the wall. The coke head dropped into a pile of motorcycle leather, cut, and knocked-out tweaker.

Seven's anger and fear vibrated. This was hell; Jax was holding living, breathing pain. He had never experienced her fear, the kind that sliced through muscles and tore at his sanity. He'd never cared in a personal way before. "We'll get them back, princess. I promise."

Nothing would stop him from making this right. Jax turned, holding Seven's hand, and watched Deacon Lanes thunder down the hall.

CHAPTER THIRTY-EIGHT

WITH EVERY STRIDE that Deacon took closer, Jax's blood boiled in his veins, punching at each pulse point and drilling angry memories to the surface. The bastard was the Grim Reaper—pure evil with no remorse for how he got the job done. Jax wouldn't be surprised if he had personally taken Bianca and Nolan.

Though if he did, Jax would steal his last breath.

Deacon's impassive face didn't register that he saw anyone but Hawke. His laser-focused black eyes didn't sweep toward Seven or acknowledge Jax, but he knew the CIA bastard never missed the mark. And that was what they all were to him—targets, tangos, marks, people that he would take out without a moment of hesitation.

The big black man placed himself directly in front of Hawke, squaring off, one tough-ass dude against the next and—

"What are you doing here?" Seven bolted upright, a surprising amount of rigor rushing through the limbs that Jax had just had to support as she pushed him away and charged forward. "Hey, excuse me."

Deacon's head tilted slowly before he twisted his massive frame and towered over her. "Do you mind?"

He was well over six feet, dressed all in black, with a shaved head and a clipped goatee. Even among Mayhem, Deacon stood out as rough, but it was the sinister deadness in his eyes that could make a person's blood run cold. Seven seemed not to notice, or she was all out of fucks to give, because she didn't stand down as he leaned in. "That's how it's going to be? I see you for years. And only when bad news arrives or business picks up through questionable circumstances." Her fingers flared by her hips, and she squeezed them into fists. "Which. Is. It. Now?"

"Do you mind?" Deacon tried again but didn't wait as he turned back to Hawke.

"Yes, I mind." Seven pushed her way in between them as a growl rumbled from Deacon's chest. Hawke's hands came forward protectively.

"Hawke, don't even. That's how this is going to be? Really? My babies are gone! You show up! And nobody is fucking talking to me?" She spun toward Hawke and Tex, jabbing her finger toward them. "You act like I shouldn't ask Jared and Jax for help when you know that they can? I should leave all of you, go call the cops, the FBI, 9-1-1. I have no idea. But we've wasted ten minutes playing some territorial game like my children weren't stolen," she cried before straightening herself and focusing back on Deacon. "Who the hell are you, and what are you going to do about my kids?"

That took serious *cajones,* but she was right to ask, and Jax didn't get Mayhem's rules and protocol. They held Seven up as some sort of legacy while trying to protect her from what they insisted on dragging her back into. She had an established life away from the MC, but he could tell that Mayhem was family. It was possible to love somebody you hated too.

Jax ground his molars. "Yeah, Deacon. Want to share who you are?"

Deacon triangulated his body so that he could face Hawke, Seven, Jax, Sugar, and Jared.

"Ah, finally noticed us, old friend." Jax raised his eyebrow, mocking the small space and the CIA operative's tunnel vision.

"I have no business with Titan right now."

Jared crossed his arms. "Funny." But nothing was the least bit humorous. "Titan has business with Mayhem, and Seven is one of ours, even if she's one of theirs too. She asked you a question, and frankly, asshole, I'm interested in the answer."

Jax wasn't. Jax wanted Deacon as far gone as possible because he was a game player and couldn't be trusted. If Nolan and Bianca got in the way of his end goal, Deacon would make horrific sacrifices for what he thought was best.

"Maybe you should explain if she should trust you with her loved ones." Jax's temper raged but stayed where he caged it. "Because I don't. I care for those three more than your cold heart could ever fake."

Seven let her glance ping-pong from Jared to Hawke to Deacon to Sugar to Tex and then land on him. She slipped back to his side, and her fingers threaded with his, sending her message without saying a word. Titan had her trust, and Seven appreciated what Jax had said. Though *appreciated* was far too underwhelming of an expression.

Deacon chuckled for his benefit but locked his attention on Seven. "I see you successfully made it through half a day with your new bride. Congrats are in order."

Bastard.

Seven's fingers tightened. The air buzzed with a mixture of whispers and violence, with vivid memories that Jax refused to react to. "The difference between you and me? Two kids are missing, and you're trying to bait me." Jax stroked his thumb over Seven's panicking hand as though reassurance could be passed by sheer grip and pressure. "If you have something to share, spit it out. Give it to Hawke; I don't give a fuck. Seven and I'll go for a walk." Jax carefully sucked a breath in, hanging on to the last shreds of his calmness as Deacon smirked. "Otherwise, get lost. We've got the situation under control."

"Like hell you do." Deacon's casual lack of empathy rolled off his tongue. He paced toward Seven, his mouth parting—but he stopped himself, narrowing his inspection on her barely swollen lip. Humor danced across Deacon's features, proof that his sadistic, cruel heart had no shame. His large hands reached for her chin.

Seven slapped his searching touch away. "Don't."

"Then again,"—Deacon backed up a step and leered at Jax—"looks like this bride already got a little blood on her on your watch."

Irrational pain tried to blind him, but he clung to Seven's hand like she had his moments before. "Watch yourself, Deacon. So help me..."

"You can't make it one day as a newlywed without blood, can you, Jax?"

Seven's hand loosened, and confusion marred her voice. "What is he talking about?"

Asshole. His heart pounded as Seven's fingers slipped away, but it was the dead weight of the past that Jax could feel smothering him, weighing him down. That white dress turned red. It had been so heavy when wet, soaked in Carrie's blood.

More of Seven's distant questions echoed far away as Jax fought to focus. He ran a hand over his face. Boss Man said something. Sugar too? *Goddamn it.* Sweat dampened the back of his neck, and the scent of Carrie's perfume, church incense, and blood flooded his memories.

Deacon pointed his fingers as though they were a gun, aimed them at Seven's head, and pretended to shoot. "Bang, bang."

Two words, so quiet among the clatter of sound around him, but it was all Jax heard, all he could see when he lunged.

Years of anguish unleashed as he slammed Deacon to the wall, pressing his fingertips into Deacon's windpipe. Killing the operative wouldn't help Seven, wouldn't bring back Carrie, but it might feel so damn good.

But he would be no better than Deacon. "Damn it!"

Jax let go and spun away. He couldn't kill the bastard, even if everyone in the hall would let it happen. Jax shook his arms out, fighting to dissipate the adrenaline pumping as fast as the memories of hell, the ones that had turned him into the asshole he was today.

With fists still clenched, he swung around. Seven stood like a statue, pale and terrified, unsure who he was other than a stranger. "Seven."

She shied away, uncertain and untrusting. "You're animals. All of you." Another step back bumped her against the wall. "You almost *killed him.*" Then she twisted to Deacon. "And everything gets worse when I see *you.*"

"Chill out," Johnny snapped.

"God, get off the powder already. This isn't Mayhem. I—I don't even know what to do right now."

"*This* is what we're going to do," Jared cut in. "Deacon tells Hawke whatever he needs to and gets the hell out of sight but doesn't leave. Hawke works with Titan. I'm over ego trips and assholes. When it comes to kids, I give no fucks. We're bringing them home. Anyone unclear?"

Agreements were given, not that anyone had much of a choice.

Titan would do what Titan did best—everything. Bianca and Nolan would be okay. That much, he knew. Him and Seven? He needed to talk to her, but they were low priority right now.

Jared focused on Seven. "We'll bring them home."

Jax noticed Boss Man didn't say *safe*, but there was only so much Jared could commit to without a current operational update.

"Thank you. I'm going upstairs," Seven said. "Call me when you need me."

Jax stepped forward. "I'll walk you up."

"No." Her hand went up. "I need to be alone."

Hawke scowled. "Seven—"

"Back off," she snapped. "There aren't threats here, and if I don't get upstairs, I'm going to lose my ever-loving mind. I'd prefer to do that in the privacy of my room."

Mayhem backed down as if that was code for something Titan didn't get. And if she were a Titan client, they would give the victim's mother privacy so long as there wasn't an active threat and they could keep tabs on the hotel and security.

The only difference was that Jax wanted to be with her—almost as much as he wanted to find Bianca and Nolan.

CHAPTER THIRTY-NINE

SEVEN STRUGGLED TO hold her head up high as though she weren't going to come apart at the seams. Thank goodness the babysitting brigade of motorcycle gang members and military operatives knew when it was time to stand down. She didn't go to Las Vegas for the first time in her entire life to unravel, and she wasn't going to stand by and snap in public.

A few minutes of alone time, quiet with her ritual, would calm her mind while professionals took over. Because if she didn't do that, she would melt down and be of no help later.

You're a bad mother. Just like your father. Walking away.

There were other options. She could call the police, FBI, somebody other than the people who surrounded her. But didn't *they* call Titan?

"You doing okay, Seven?" Jax asked.

"Of course. Just leaving."

Abandoning Mayhem. Walking away from her kids. The voice in her head even sounded like her father, and her blood pressure climbed. *One foot in front of the next.* That simple command took more strength than she realized. She needed to get into her room to tell Cullen Blackburn to shut up!

Titan knew what they were doing, and she had to do what would help her to be the best mom possible when Bianca and Nolan came home. If that meant folding stupid blankets, so what?

"Didn't take you for the type to walk away from intel," Deacon said.

"Jesus, dude. Shut the fuck up," Sugar cut in.

"Deacon—" Jax added simultaneously.

Seven pivoted, spiraling out of control. "Are you sadistic? Do you work for them? Or what? Because you're slowing everyone down!"

Behind Deacon, Jax loomed as though he could brawl if she blinked funny. If vibes could kill and rescue, Deacon would be a dead man and she would be home with her babies. How her heart could swell when pure vengeance etched Jax's face, Seven had no clue, but at that moment, she needed him.

"Bye. Again," she said. "I'm going to go call Victoria."

"And we're taking it back into the conference room," Jared said. "Move boots."

"You can't," Deacon said without elaborating.

"Oh, for God's sake," Seven blew out. "And why can't I?"

"She's likely still at the hospital."

"*What?*" Her head shot toward Jax. What had they held back?

A quick look showed he didn't know—Jared or Hawke, either. Seven flew at Deacon, smashing her hands into his chest. "You… you… *asshole!* What happened to her?" Too many things had happened to Victoria. Both her fists slammed into Deacon's chest again. "What happened!"

An arm snaked around her waist, and Jax whispered, "Come on, princess."

Seven clawed the air to fight Deacon still.

His smugness twisted. "She hurt her wrists."

"*Victoria* did?" Seven stopped fighting to get away from Jax, wanting to know what Deacon knew.

"She was fine when they left her handcuffed her to the steering wheel."

"Fine? Nothing about this is fine!" Seven spun and searched Jax then Jared's faces. "How does he know this?"

Hawke stepped forward, his hand on his sidearm. "How, brother? That's some insider info about her children."

Deacon ignored Hawke but eyed Johnny. "Maybe Mayhem shouldn't have messed with the status quo."

"You're laying this at my feet?" Johnny threw up a middle finger.

Deacon lifted his chin. "You had one responsibility. One."

Seven's mind crashed. *Johnny?* "What does he have to do with them?"

"You son of a bitch." Sugar eased closer, her expression dripping acid. "You're calling the shots. Aren't you, Deacon?"

Seven flashbacked to one of the first times she met Sugar and listened to her accuse Mayhem of having a mole working with the feds.

"Oh my God." Seven turned from Deacon to Johnny. "Are you a..."

"A *what?*" Tex demanded as Ethan scowled.

"Spit it out." Hawke changed the direction of his aggression, facing Johnny.

She wasn't talking. No way. Not about guesses and misunderstandings that could get Johnny killed, not when he was high or coming down, making stupid-ass decisions. She hated him, but damn it, he'd been in her life for as long as she could remember. "I need to be by myself."

Hawke's hand rested under his shirt. "Say it, Seven."

Fuck! "Bianca and Nolan. That's the only thing I'm going to say. Do what you need to do." She left, each boot step weighed as much as a lifetime of her burdens, and every inch of space that she put between her and Jax made Seven wish she was wearing her wedding band. A wedding band had always been a cage, but she wanted to spin the ring on her finger and hold on to it as hard as she'd held on to Jax.

It took an eternity to get to the elevator and to her hotel room. Finally, the door clicked shut, and she was alone but no closer to sanity or answers. Maybe Victoria would answer and Deacon was lying. Seven dug out her cell phone from her purse and called. No answer. Then she tried again. No answer. Each time, Seven got her voice mail.

Frustration pounded in her head, and she opened up the slew of ignored text messages from the day, scrolling until she found the only one of importance, from Ryder.

Go find Jax. Trust him.

"Trust Jax." God, she was trying. Her eyes closed. "My husband."

Trust him... How she wished she could remember more of that night. Seven curled the phone to her chest and sank against the door. She'd always thought that if she ever got married again, it would be more traditional, more of what she'd always dreamt of. The fairy tale. A poufy dress with a long veil in a church. Maybe that dream wasn't meant for her. Maybe she was only supposed to marry Jax so she would have a guaranteed abduction rescuer. How about that for fate working her magic?

Knock, knock. "Housekeeping."

Oh, for the love of God. Seven crawled away from the door, barely able to find enough composure to say go away. "No, thank you." But it came out as a whisper filled with tears she hadn't cried. Pushing to her feet, Seven gripped the side of the couch, cleared her throat, and—

A key card clicked in the door before it opened. The cart pushed in before the whistling woman's face showed. "Oh, ma'am. So sorry."

Seven swallowed, unexpectedly grateful to see anyone that didn't wear a leather motorcycle cut or know how to fire a grenade launcher. For a second, life was normal.

"Would you like me to come back later?"

Her tongue stud clicked against her teeth, and she couldn't find the words to send the woman away. Seven had company that didn't kill people, who didn't use drugs, who she didn't know. It was a break from reality. Gesturing, Seven grabbed a folded blanket and moved to the bedroom area, unable to send the housekeeper away. "It's mostly clean..." Everything was exactly how she wanted it. Then her hands started, and she couldn't think of anything else, not the woman emptying the kitchen trash or the guys downstairs.

Smooth, fold. Smooth, fold. Precise and perfect. Over, over, and done.

Again, Seven pulled another blanket out of the closet, smoothing away every possible crinkle and wrinkle until it was impossible for one to exist. A tear slid down her cheek, and she swatted the wetness away.

"No crying." Because what was the purpose of the folding if she couldn't control her mind? Seven bunched the newest blanket into a hideous, skin crawling mess and quickly smoothed it out. Nothing was under control, like the edges of this ratty hotel blanket that wasn't even.

She tried harder, tugging the corners to make the square the right angles as another tear slipped free. "Please don't cry."

Nolan had a blanket just like this. *My babies...* She couldn't stop it, and she buried her face in the softness, sobbing into hysterics. Were they scared? Were they hungry? Cold? Did they ask why? Did they ask for her? Seven hiccupped and clung to the blanket, squeezing it to her breasts as she collapsed on the bed.

She needed Jax. But Nolan and Bianca needed him more. Anything she asked of him—come hold her, hug her, tell her it would be all right— would only slow the process of bringing them home. *Trust Jax.* She trusted Ryder, and he said to. She trusted Jax, and he promised everything would be okay. He would bring her babies home.

"Do you need anything, ma'am?" The quiet compassion of the housekeeper's voice pulled Seven from her cries.

There were so many things she needed, but nothing this nice person could assist with. She shook her head as the shadow of pink hair fell over her tear-stained face. "No."

"Are you sure?"

Seven rolled her lips into her mouth, nodding. "I'm positive. Nothing you can help with."

The woman fished a paper from her uniform pocket and unfolded it for Seven to see. It wasn't a paper. It was a picture of Bianca and Nolan.

The blanket fell from Seven's fingers as she jolted upright. "Wh-who are you?" Her father had taught her to never show fear, and she quickly pulled it together even as anxiety like she'd never faced stood feet away. Seven lifted her chin defiantly. Her eyes turned to slits as her cold terror morphed into disciplined Mayhem royalty. "*Who the fuck are you,* and where are my babies?"

The housekeeping imposter lowered her arm and slid the picture of Seven's children back into her uniform pocket. "I'm just the messenger."

She sealed her molars. "Then tell me the message."

"Senor Hernán Suarez does not approve of the changes to the distribution."

"They have nothing to do with Mayhem. *I* have nothing to do with it, either."

"Señora Suarez cannot have children," the woman added.

Seven licked her bottom lip, sucking it into her mouth to hide the tremble that ran through her at the revelation. Esmeralda Suarez had a reputation for erratic behavior.

"Señor Suarez is more interested in business but has never left her wanting for anything. She wants a family, and if you know much about the

Suarez cartel..."

"They teach lessons," Seven answered. Did Deacon know all this? That it was Mayhem's fault? About Esmeralda wanting kids?

The other woman moved toward the living room area. "Come with me, and you can be with your children. You can care for them."

"*What?*" Seven jerked, trying to understand.

"They always win." A small flash of compassion waved across the woman's face before it went neutral again. "If you want to see the children again, this is your only option. She'll have a caretaker for them. Would you rather do it, or someone else?"

Seven gasped. "They're coming home."

"They aren't, but you can go with me." She reached into the other pocket of her uniform and extracted a notepad and pen that matched the hotel's. "Write a note." The woman tossed them onto the bed. Seven's eyes followed them. Then she turned back to the woman and faced the barrel of a gun. "Your only option."

"What is it supposed to say?" Seven asked incredulously, totally confused.

"That you don't need help. But you're with your kids. That Mayhem is not changing the distribution. And that you'll be in touch." The woman cocked the weapon.

"Why are you doing this?"

"Start writing." She raised the weapon, clearly having no idea how to hold a loaded gun, and that was more dangerous than if she did. "They have my kid. If you don't come with me, I'm going to shoot you."

CHAPTER FORTY

TITAN GROUP POWWOWED privately with headquarters. After one update from Parker, Jared decided that Titan was working this job whether anyone liked it or not and that Deacon was intentionally keeping them in the dark. No one had to convince Jax that Deacon could do such a thing, but Mayhem might be another story.

"Time to go show that CIA pig who's in charge around here." Jared didn't bother knocking as they returned to the conference room where they'd been earlier.

The intense discussions between Deacon, Hawke, Tex, Ethan, and Johnny paused as Tex snapped his mouth shut.

"Time's up," Jared said. "We have a plan, and it involves using your best men not afraid to die."

Hawke's gaze swept to Deacon before he stood. "We haven't decided to work with you on this."

"We *aren't* working with Titan." Deacon pushed out of his chair, also, a united front with Mayhem.

Jesus fucking Christ. Jax would kill Deacon. Those kids weren't pawns in his drug lord game. Whatever power trip he got, courtesy of the crown put on his head by Uncle Sam, needed to be set aside. There was no way Deacon would be responsible for destroying the second... *personal connection* of Jax's because of his sole focus on gangs.

"I have had enough of your shit." Jax strode past Boss Man. "Whatever Deacon's told you, compare it to our list. Then do what the hell you should do."

Hawke nodded as if that was going to matter. Jax would say what they knew. "The kids touched down in Phoenix, Arizona seventeen minutes ago. A woman referred to as Glammah was ditched off the I-10, and she's refusing to talk to authorities. They won't release her. The only thing of note about her is the Mayhem gang insignia tattooed on her. Parker has info from Ryder. The children's personal items were taken from Seven's house. Teddy bears, blankets, pictures. Some clothing. Mostly comfort items. Johnny's apartment was tossed. Nothing looks to be stolen."

The corners of Deacon's eyes twitched.

"What?" Hawke snapped. The MC president wasn't a fool.

Jared growled at Deacon. "We have intel sources that say Esmeralda Suarez can't have kids. Anything to dispute?"

Deacon didn't, and shock tidal waves crossed Mayhem's collective faces.

"If that bitch thinks she has them now…" Hawke's jaw ticked. "What were you saying about Gennita?"

"That Glammah?" Jared asked. "Who is that?"

Johnny shook his head, fists balled. "Deacon, I'm gonna kill you."

Jared's voice boomed louder. "Who is Glammah?"

"Not who. What," Tex said. "*Glamma*. It's the kids' grandma. Sort of. Not by blood, and hell if you tell that old lady she's of age. She calls herself their fucking glam-ma. Mack's old lady, not that you know him."

"They took the kids and ditched the grandma?" Jared asked.

"The *glamma*. A babysitter in leathers, lipstick, and attitude. But, ya know, good with kids and lives across the street from Seven."

Jax turned to Jared. "She wasn't with Victoria when they snatched the kids?" They both turned to Deacon. "Right?"

Deacon nodded. "Just Victoria."

"Why would they grab the grandma and ditch her at the last minute?" Jared asked.

No one from Mayhem answered, and Jax started spitballing ideas. Maybe one would eventually sound right. "She was about to die. Too old to make the trip. Too wild. Too loud. Too protective."

"No, no," Mayhem disagreed.

What were they missing?

"Glamma's good people," Ethan offered. "Has more energy than half of the old ladies I know. Helps Seven so she can open her shop, stays late when she closes. Sings stupid songs about brushing teeth. She's their—"

"Nanny," Johnny said.

"No, dick." Tex shook his head. "Their grandma. *Glamma.*"

Hawke rubbed his temples. "Esmeralda doesn't have kids. No nannies. No *glammas.* If this is a last-minute idea—and they didn't know the kids didn't live at Johnny's—they're not planning."

"Hernán doesn't like that shit." Tex ran his hand over his chin. "They need a nanny."

"Why ditch Gennita?" Hawke asked.

Jared turned as Jax's stomach dropped. "Because they're going after the real deal."

"Makes sense to me," Deacon chuckled. "Einstein."

"Deacon," Jared snapped, "get the fuck out of my discussions. If I need you, I'll call. But get the fuck out."

"I'm gone, assholes."

Jax stepped forward, needing to check on Seven. "Boss?"

"Go," he ordered.

No matter the answer, Jax heard it as he left. He was already running out down the hall.

CHAPTER FORTY-ONE

JORGE'S PHONE RANG as he laid it on the in-room massage table after four days of little work in Sin City. He was so close to escaping without getting his hands dirty. But that was what he did best.

"Go away." He shooed the masseuse toward the bathroom. "But don't go far." Maybe Hernán only wanted another status update.

He answered the phone, knowing that not all of his information had been perfect, but eventually, it had worked out fine, and Esmeralda had the children headed her way. "Hello, Señor."

"Our friend is not listening," Hernán spit into the phone.

Jorge sat up, wrapping the sheet around his waist and knowing that the masseuse was leaving and so was he. He might not have had perfect information on where Johnny Miller's kids lived, but he'd been rushed, and the request had been last minute. There was a difference between Hernán's irritation and when his father's cutthroat viciousness bled into his work. The only other person Jorge knew who was working on Mayhem and remaining status quo was the CIA spook who played all sides and enjoyed Suarez benefits. Jorge had no idea what they were, but no one did business with Hernán without tangling their integrity.

"Your friend at the farm?"

Hernán grunted, making the disappointment linger. "He's not where he should be."

Jorge shook his head. *That dumb motherfucker.* For as smart and savvy as Deacon had been over the years… He respected the unsavory spook as much as a cartel man could respect a bureaucrat who ensured drugs passed safely across the borders.

"I have no use for his services anymore."

That was that. Jorge had work to do. "How soon?"

"He's with them now. If they don't already know about your project, they will soon, and all hell will break loose. Take that opportunity to remove him from the conversation."

Jorge lumbered off the massage table, walked over to the bathroom, and threw open the door. He looked at the masseuse and tossed his thumb over his shoulder. "Get out." Then he walked toward the dresser for a change of clothes before he took a quick shower. "Yes, Señor. I'll let you know when it's done."

DESPITE DEACON'S COVERT measures to remain a ghost, he couldn't be responsible for the people he was with. Jorge had tracked the notable members of the Mayhem MC throughout Las Vegas during his stay, and when he needed to find Deacon, all he did was locate the trackers he had on Mayhem.

Hawke, Tex, Ethan, and Johnny pinged in the same location of the hotel in which they had been staying.

After a quick shower to wash off the massage oil, Jorge redressed and strapped on his custom H & K 9 mm and two nickel-plated throwing knives. The basics would be best to silence a lethal and well-trained CIA agent without any prep work.

If Jorge had his druthers, he would have liked to map out the location, who would be there, and the best ways to kill the guy. But time wasn't on his side. This was one instance in which experience would come in handy.

He filled a syringe with a paralytic, capped it, and slipped it into his pocket. Then he double-checked the subcompact 9 mm tucked under the front of his shirt and the blade holstered against his sock. Jorge wrapped then rewrapped a high-tension length of metal twine in case he had the opportunity for strangulation and put it in his other pocket.

With all bases covered, Jorge moved quickly to scout his location. It took him only minutes to cross the street and bound up the stairs to the floor where Mayhem had converged.

Carefully, he eased out of the stairwell—and backed back in. Several men milled, and the tension was palpable from his view at the far end of the other hallway. *How interesting.* To make a better assessment, he moved to the vending area. No one noticed as men walked in and out of the conference room. His prey was already in a defensive mode.

Jorge didn't know what he had missed. The animosity and hostility among the men was overpowering. Deacon seemed on edge, and Jorge smiled, enjoying the irony.

The Americano was making bad decision after bad decision. Upsetting Hernán then fighting with the people he had chosen over the Suarez cartel. Preoccupation would cloud Deacon's mind and make Jorge's job even easier.

Deacon walked into the middle of the group, slowly postulating from one side to the next. He ended toe to toe with a big Italian–looking guy. Those two were the ones who'd had it out, no doubt. Deacon said what he needed to then peeled off. Jorge watched the back-and-forth, observing the hostility between the two factions. The dark-haired Italian split moments later.

He saw the two men turn the corner from the group and split. The Italian headed for the elevator, and Jorge's prey went toward the stairwell. *How predictable.* The CIA agent wouldn't be trapped in a small box.

He stalked that way, the rush from the anticipation of the kill tickling his veins and hyperfocusing his mind.

Quietly, Jorge slid open the stairwell door and listened for which way Deacon had gone. The agent's steps were barely audible, but with a lock on the sound, Jorge moved in, shuffling silently behind.

It only took seconds to pad quietly behind the man, wait, and walk by casually. Deacon's mind had been elsewhere, and he was a half-second too slow as Jorge's lightning-quick skills let him snap Deacon's neck.

He wished he would have been able to use one of the toys. No paralytic. No strangulation. Not even his favorite gun or knife.

He wasn't worried about Deacon's body being identified because the CIA would send a cleanup team to erase his existence and take care of the security footage for Jorge. Sometimes, offing agents was one of the easiest tasks.

He straightened his shirt, tucking in the back where it had loosened, then continued down the stairs and over to the coffee bar. He ordered himself a drink then sent a signal to his boss that would be read as three simple words.

"It is done."

CHAPTER FORTY-TWO

T HE EMPTY HOTEL suite was like a black hole. It sucked Jax in. There was no escape, and even though he knew Seven was gone, he couldn't fight the feeling that she had just been there.

Bile sloshed in his stomach. Desperate to be analytical and find anything she may have left behind, he knew it was a lost cause when he walked in. "Seven?" Goddamn it, he was too late. "Are you in here?"

The mere seconds it took him to move through the suite and check the bathroom were a waste. The instant he'd thrown open the door, Jax knew she was gone. He could feel it in a desperate, terrifying way.

He saw no signs of a struggle. Seven would fight. No doubt Parker was pulling security footage now, but the cartel could slip her out of the building unseen in any number of ways. He walked to the desk, and his eyes dropped. *A note?*

What the hell was that?

Hi, Jax. I need time to myself and went for a walk. Don't wait up, not sure when I'll be back. I'll check in when I can. xxoo

Fucking hell. What did they do to get her to write that? He reached for his cell phone and called Boss Man, who picked up on the first ring.

"Hey, she left a note—"

Jared cut him off. "Where are you?"

"Where the fuck do you think I am? Seven's room."

"It takes you that long to find a note?"

Jesus Christ. What crawled up Boss Man's ass? It wasn't as if he were dicking around. Maybe he took his sweet time looking around a small room. Maybe he had a hard time with the fact that his girl was gone and every single step tortured him. But he didn't need Jared's damn attitude right now. "Yeah, man. What the hell? Seven left a damn note. Are you interested?"

"Truthfully, Jax, I'm interested in why it took you so long to find a note in a room that's two hundred square feet. Where the fuck was the note?"

"Her desk." Jax wasn't hiding his frustration at all, and that wasn't a great idea after getting into a fight with Deacon earlier. Everybody had an issue with Jax's attitude. But at the moment, he gave no fucks. They wanted him to work faster? Two minutes wasn't going to make a difference when it came to processing the fact that Seven wasn't there and he was losing his shit. "Look, man. Seven. That's the only thing I'm going to think about and worry about."

"Sugar's on her way to you now. I have something I have to figure out, and I will be there in a second. Don't leave that room."

Where the hell did Jared think Jax was going to go? To the strip or to get a beer? Catch a little R and R? A knock sounded on the door, signaling the arrival of his least favorite fan. "She's here," he said, grinding his molars. "I'm not going anywhere, and I'll see you when I see you."

Jax threw the notepad down and stormed to open the door, surprised that Sugar's forceful knock didn't knock the door down. He twisted the door handle, and Sugar pushed through, a leather-clad bulldozer imitating what Jared sounded like but in real life. "Well, hey to you too."

She walked through the room, not acknowledging he was there, then traced the same path to the bedroom and bathroom and came back. She slammed her hands onto her hips. "So?"

So? Well, fuck you, too, Sugar. "Seven left a note. It's total bullshit."

Sugar's eyes narrowed to slits. "Where?"

Jax mocked her one-word snappy tone. "Desk."

After her quick inspection, Sugar shook her head. "Goddamn it. What'd they do to get that written?"

"That's what I would like to know. But everybody is acting like they have an AK shoved up their asshole."

Sugar all but hissed at him, and Jax turned, not wanting to engage with his boss's wife, when the trash can caught his eye. Two crumbled pieces of paper lay in the waste pail, and Jax's heart jumped. He had no idea what Seven's deal with folding was. They hadn't talked about it, but he noticed there was a definite thing there. Crumpled definitely wasn't folded.

He strode over, grabbed the pail, and dumped it onto the desk next to Sugar. Then he flattened the two pieces of notepaper on the desk. Sugar moved next to him, and they stared at the three pieces together.

Nothing. There was nothing there, only two notes on which she had clearly screwed up what they had told her to say before starting over.

Still, the discarded notes struck him as important, but he didn't know how. Something was, though.

Sugar stared at him more than the papers. "Okay, Detective. She gets nervous writing under orders."

There was no way that Seven, the woman who folded *everything*, had crumbled up two pieces of paper and tossed them away. She was neurotic about the way things were folded. "There's something here. I don't know what it is."

"Too bad we can't ask Deacon, isn't it?" Sugar pursed her lips together, antagonizing him with the one name that was like bamboo shoots under his fingernails.

Jax wasn't going to justify the job and ignored her. The wording looked the same...

The door shook with the pounding of a knock. Jared's bad attitude obviously hadn't gone away, and Jax turned to answer the door. Boss Man brushed by him as coldly as Sugar had but didn't do the same sweep. Instead, he sat down on the edge of the couch.

It had taken him longer to get to the room than Jax had expected, but dealing with Mayhem was a pain in the ass.

"Parker reviewed the hotel's security footage, the security cams from neighboring hotels."

"Yeah, and?" Jax asked, sensing the hesitation.

"Seven walked out by herself. What's her note say?"

Damn it to hell. "That she needs time to think and leave her alone."

"I have a bigger problem on my hands right now."

Jax's eyes bugged. "Than Seven going missing? I'm doing everything I can to clear those problems out of the way. What possible problem can you have that doesn't have to do with bringing home those kids and my woman?"

"Deacon Lanes."

Jax roared, throwing his arms out. "Deacon Lanes. Deacon mother-fucking Lanes. Nothing about him has to do with her. We have what we need from him. He doesn't matter anymore. If I never hear his name again, I'd be okay. Everybody's on my ass for years—why do I have an attitude, why don't I play well with others? Deacon. Fucking. Lanes. But now I don't care anymore. Titan's supposed to take care of each other. Right? That's what I've been hearing the entire time I've worked for you. Hell, since before I worked for you. You know our history, and I guess now it's time for you to choose. Who's it going to be? Have I done everything to be Titan loyal and Titan strong? Because I sure have fuck tried. Maybe not with a smile on my face every goddamn time. But I dare you to find a time that I didn't support every man and woman I worked with, push them to be better. So you have a problem with me dealing with Deacon Lanes? Ground me. Take me off the team."

Jared's jaw ticked back and forth. "You're grounded." He turned around and left, not saying another word.

Jax's world came crashing down. He'd never questioned how much Titan had become who he was. He didn't know that he could feel pain until recently. He knew anger lived inside him. But it wasn't until Bianca and Nolan had gone missing that he knew he could fear. Then came this very moment when he realized he had just lost the only way he knew to go get Seven and bring her home.

"What just happened?" he numbly muttered, walking toward the couch, hearing every footstep as it echoed in his ears.

Sugar laughed—and Jax snapped to face her, having forgotten that anybody else was there.

"That's what happens when you murder somebody and don't loop in the boss." Sugar pushed away from the desk, sauntering out of the room, as Jax connected the dots between his raging speech and what he thought he'd just learned.

"Deacon's dead…"

Sugar paused briefly, glancing over her shoulder, then walked out, letting the door slam behind her. Someone had finished the job he'd always fantasized about doing but never did. An odd sense of relief and a smile came over Jax. He wasn't Deacon. He'd never wanted to be the cold-blooded killer that took a life without orders to do so. Avenging personal pain seemed so different than protecting his country and those he believed were innocents. Though still blown away to be feeling *anything* like fear and pain, he was even more confused to feel joy for a brief moment because the devil was dead.

CHAPTER FORTY-THREE

W HAT WAS THAT reaction that had crossed Jax's face? Sugar wanted to assume that the guy was playing her for a fool. But her gut instincts didn't lead her astray often, and rarely did they screech to a halt with a loud *what the fuck* like they had just done.

If he hadn't known Deacon was dead, she would've expected shock. And yeah, there had been some shock. But after Jared had pulled Jax off the job, Sugar wouldn't have expected that doe-eyed, dreamy happiness. It was as though Jax were less angry and more... happy.

Jax and happy were opposite ends of the spectrum, like stilettos and flats or gloss and matte. Jax and happy... It had only lasted for a blink.

Her phone buzzed in the back pocket of her leather pants, and Sugar pulled it out to see a text message from her husband.

JARED: *Keep an eye on him. Stay out of sight.*

Oh, for God's sake. She'd just left Jax with a bit of fanfare. It wasn't as if she could go back in now. She moved to the elevators, rounding the corner with the intention of explaining to Jared in person that she had already left, when she saw Jax stepping out of the hotel room.

"Well, this worked out for me," she mumbled, but he was headed her way. Quickly, she pressed the phone to her ear, and when she saw him, she said, "Okay. Talk to you later. Bye."

Jax held the three pieces of paper in his hand, and Sugar wanted to say something about how he shouldn't have taken any evidence from Seven's room and that Jared was likely talking to Parker about how best to process the notes, but she decided to keep her trap shut. Not the easiest of actions for her, but she was also supposed to stay out of sight. Nothing was working totally as planned. "Where are you headed?"

"You actually care?"

"No, not really." She turned toward the elevator, and they remained in silence.

Jax laughed quietly then walked forward and pressed the button to call the elevator.

"Guess that would help."

He hummed his agreement but then turned. "I get that I'm a dick. Why don't you trust me?"

"I don't trust anybody."

"No, that's bullshit. You're my boss's wife, and you don't trust me. That fucking sucks for me. Particularly today." He turned to face the elevators but then added, "Also, fuck you for that."

Even though Jax wasn't facing her, she tried to keep a straight face. God, she loved his reaction. The elevator arrived and opened, and they filed in, finding themselves alone. He punched the button for the lobby, and she was along for the ride.

"Do you remember when Victoria was abducted—the second time? And Mayhem had her?"

He grunted and lifted his chin, but didn't give any indication that he planned to converse.

"Mayhem knew where the players were when Titan was on a live op. Someone communicated to them."

Jax stepped forward and pressed the Stop Elevator button. "You thought that was me?" He stepped closer to her. "You thought that I was leaking information to a freaking gang?"

"Yeah, the thought crossed my mind."

"In what world would I do something like that?" His disgust at her accusation outlined the veins on his temples. He didn't raise his voice. He simply became a hurricane within himself. "Give me one reason. Now."

Sugar didn't scare. It'd been trained out of her, and any remaining reactions had been numbed away by real-life experiences. But Jax's fury was real and raw. She hesitated, wondering if she should have brought this up after what happened earlier. "Deacon told me. Not in so many words.

But he planted the seed that there was a former CIA operative working with Mayhem. That you were closely entangled with the CIA. It wasn't in your file. I didn't know anything about how you two knew each other. I just knew I was caught off guard and that Titan—my family and friends—they were walking into a death trap."

Jax dropped his head back as though he were staring toward heaven through the ceiling of the elevator. "He's like a stain. Even when I didn't see it, he was there." Jax shook his head and stepped away, walking over to the row of buttons and starting the elevator again.

That was all he was going to say? For the guy that had nearly ripped Deacon's windpipe out in front of everyone and then sort of smiled when he found out the agent was dead, his reaction was again unexpected. "That's all you're going to give me?"

Jax leaned against the wall and looked her way. "Right now, that's all you deserve."

Asshole. Though maybe he was right. She had believed Deacon because, once upon a time, he'd defended her in a situation in which she was uncomfortable. She had been in a power struggle, and Deacon had taken her side. Had Deacon played her?

Damn CIA agents, always playing the long game, and Deacon's had been going on for years, but why? Maybe Jax wasn't as in the wrong as he appeared, and maybe she should've trusted him years before. She'd no reason not to other than what Deacon had said. And the only reason she had trusted him was because he'd defended her in a vulnerable spot. *Damn it.* If she'd been played, had her opinion led Jared astray? *Damn it, again.*

The elevator doors opened to the lobby, and Jax left her wondering what else she'd gotten wrong.

She stayed a few dozen yards behind and watched as Jax moved to the hotel restaurant. Sugar requested a seat where she could see him, but he was not facing her. Jax ordered a water and soup.

They shared a waitress, and the waitress had deep circles under her eyes, clearly having a bad day, with bloodshot eyes and tear-stained cheeks that were powdered poorly.

"Can I take your order?" the waitress asked with a voice that promised

Vegas had chewed her up and spit her out.

Sugar tore her attention away from Jax and felt for the girl. Nothing worse than feeling awful and having to work. They'd all been there. "Sorry about whatever sucks for you today."

The woman gave a weak smile. "Thanks. Just trying to keep my head above water."

Sugar ordered her lunch as she watched Jax get his food, but he barely touched it, sipping his water as he mostly stared at the notes. What did he see there? Or maybe it was wishful thinking.

People came and went, and as Sugar's lunch dragged on, she ordered dessert and coffee and watched Jax study the papers.

Suddenly, he jumped up, grabbing his wallet and throwing down some bills. He borrowed a pen from the table across from him, wrote a note on a napkin, then took his pieces of paper and split.

What had just happened? Sugar knew she had to keep an eye on him but needed to pay her bill, so she likely did the same thing he had. She fished a pen out of her purse and wrote "room charge" along with her name and room number. Then she stood, preparing to chase him down, when she heard a sob and turned to see the waitress dropping into the chair that Jax had just vacated.

Sugar faltered and didn't know which way to go. Follow Jax or see what he had said that made the woman cry?

Honestly, she wondered if he had written something awful to the poor girl. Sugar would kill him herself. Deciding she could track him down in a minute, she stomped over to the waitress. "What happened?"

The waitress sniffed. "That guy. He left this and…" She didn't finish her thoughts. "There really are good people out there, aren't there?"

Sugar took the napkin and read it.

I didn't mean to overhear you talking with your coworker. Keep the change. It'll be okay one day.

— From the guy that has to believe that and is maybe starting to figure that out today

Sugar didn't ask what Jax had given the waitress, but between the woman's tears and the wads of hundreds sticking out between her clenched fingers, she realized he had helped the waitress when he thought nobody was looking.

Sugar headed toward the hotel lobby, pulling her cell phone out to text Jared.

SUGAR: *I think you've made a mistake.*

CHAPTER FORTY-FOUR

JARED TOSSED HIS cell phone on the table and rubbed his sternum. If Sugar thought he was headed in the wrong direction, she wasn't going to like the conversation he'd just had with Parker. But flying blind wasn't an option. Intelligence was what they lived and died by. It was a working assumption that he knew Titan's every move, anyway.

Jared hadn't shared with any of Mayhem that Deacon was dead. How the CIA had found out, he had no idea, and the only reason he'd been tipped off was because Beth, who worked for both Titan and CIA, made fast work of getting on the phone.

Tex knocked with his Mayhem-ring-covered knuckles. "Deep in thought, brother."

Jared leaned back in his chair and popped his knuckles, shifting his scrutiny from Tex to Hawke then down the line of remaining Mayhem members until he ended on Ethan, who was the easiest barometer of the truth. "Waiting for intel."

Parker's name popped up on his cell, and he answered as he stepped away from the table. "Hang on a minute."

"No problem," Parker said.

Once Jared moved back to the small conference area where he'd installed a device to jam signal interception, he gave Parker the go-ahead to continue on their secure connection.

"I've tapped the feed to Jax's phone and hotel room and Seven's. Any incoming or outgoing call will register on your phone. He won't hear if you pick up. Disconnect whenever you feel like it."

"Got it. How's Victoria doing?"

"To put it in the most mild of terms," Parker said, "she's pissed. I'll keep an eye out if Ryder loses sight of her, because the woman is on a warpath."

"I bet. What about her injuries?"

"Mostly superficial. They thought her wrists were broken, but they were dislocated after she forced her hands out of the handcuffs. There'll be some scarring."

Jared cocked his eyebrows. "That bad?"

"Yeah, Ryder said she's a mangled mess. The cuffs were on secure before she got loose."

What strength and pain that must have taken. But hell hath no fury like a woman whose best friend's babies had been stolen out of her back seat.

"Anything else I need to know?" Jared asked. Parker paused, and his lack of immediate response made Jared uncomfortable. "Spit it out. I don't have all goddamn day."

"I don't know the details of what's going on. And I wouldn't have said this was conversation-worthy except for the fact that we're tapping Jax's phone."

Jared pinched the bridge of his nose. "Whatever it is, if it has to do with Jax, I'm interested."

"I'm getting the few details that Gennita Johnson, the kids' *glamma*, has shared with the Phoenix authorities. She hasn't discussed Mayhem, barely touched on where Seven was, and not mentioned what she's doing. But she's talked about Jax like the kids thought he was a superhero."

How much didn't Jared know about Jax? He hadn't known about the Deacon-Jax connection, never expected Jax to marry Seven, and now they were getting information from a third party about kids who thought his man was their savior. "All right, good to know. I'll figure out what to do with that." Jared hung up, more confused than before the phone call.

An unfamiliar beep came from his phone, and Jared realized that must be Jax making a phone call. He pressed the green button on the screen and put his cell back against his ear to listen.

"Hey, Ryder. It's Jax."

"Oh, hey, Jax, hey."

"Yeah, last person you'd expect to be calling. I know. Victoria is doing better?"

Ryder chuckled quietly. "Relatively speaking. She's not bleeding all over the place anymore. Not threatening doctors to patch her up and let her loose. So, yeah, mate. Better."

Jared laughed along with Jax as he listened to their call.

"I've got a question for you," Jax continued. "Does Leyva mean anything to you?"

"No, not off the top of my head. I could ask Victoria, but I finally talked her into pain meds, and everything she's talking about sounds like unicorns and making video game gun noises."

"Leyva," Jax repeated.

"Why? What is that?"

"I don't know. You know Seven better than me—"

"But I guess that's changing. I heard congratulations are in order. Might even make us brothers from another mother, my friend."

Sounding uncomfortable, Jax changed the subject back to what he needed. "But real quick. Have you ever seen her crumble up a piece of paper?"

Ryder cackled. "Seven? That'd be a hell no."

"What if she did?"

"Trust me." Ryder snorted. "If you haven't realized this yet, you soon will. Things have to be folded. A certain way. But not crumbled up. Never."

"Ryder, man. What if I told you she left two pieces of paper crumbled up?" His voice was gravely serious, and Ryder's chuckling stopped.

"Jax, she wouldn't. Why did you ask me about Leyva?"

Jax paused for a long time. For so long, Jared pulled the phone away to see if the line was still live. It was.

"She's missing. The security footage looks like she left for a walk after leaving a note that said she was too stressed to sit in the room and wait. That she had to go think. But in the trash can, there were two balled-up notes where she started on the same thing but threw it out."

"No. No way. Seven wouldn't do that."

"She would have folded them up, right?"

"Yeah," Ryder agreed. "Or leave it flat. I'll ask Victoria about Leyva. She wrote it on the note?"

Jax let out a long breath into the phone. "Last week after breakfast, Bianca showed me a way to leave *secret messages*." He laughed sadly. "You draw a picture. Decide you don't like it. Cross it out. But when crossing out, you write your code word then scribble lightly over it."

Ryder asked what Jared was thinking. "Bianca can write codes?"

"No, it was letters and numbers and gibberish. You're missing the point. Seven knows how to spell, asshole. It says Leyva, but I have no idea what that means."

Ryder hummed in thought. "You need to talk to Boss Man."

Jax paused. "Yeah, good idea. I should've thought of that."

Jared dropped his head back, feeling like shit that one of his guys had actionable information and he'd driven him away with it. Jax had literally yelled at Jared to trust him, and Jared hadn't.

Jared called Parker, who answered on the first ring. "What do you know about Leyva?"

"Off the top of my head? Nothing. It's a vacation place in Colombia. Give me a couple seconds. Cross-referencing." Parker whistled. "Check that. Leyva is a known cartel vacation locale…" Parker's keyboard clacked. "There's a military stronghold…"

"I need more, Parker. Give me a reason Seven is leaving breadcrumbs."

"I know. I heard. Okay… This is what you're looking for. Leyva was the name given by locals to a compound and estate owned by Hernán and Esmeralda. It's also a military instillation and a proving ground for his militia trainees."

"Jesus fucking Christ." Jared cracked his knuckles. "The cartel has a training ground? What else you have on them? An armory? Commissary?"

"Actually, according to the notes that I'm reading here—yeah, almost, they do."

"Of course, they do," he grumbled.

"It's like the home base of a third-world army. A well-financed, highly-armed, well-trained militia. Two levels, with an inner guard and recruited ground forces."

"How big of a ground force are we talking?"

"Big, Boss Man," Parker muttered. "Like the kind of job we do when partnered with a government unit. We're going to need bodies."

"Fucking hell." Jared pinched the bridge of his nose. "Route in all the assholes."

"Titan and Delta are already in route. Their contracts were put on hold. Brock and I have mapped out supplier hookups for what we couldn't bring with us." Parker made a tapping noise. "We're assuming Seven and the kids are headed to Leyva instead of Bogotá?"

"Yeah."

"I'll get on the horn for midflight re-routing."

Jared's mind was going a hundred miles a minute. It had been a long time since he'd pulled something off like this. But it had been just as long since they had been potentially outnumbered like this without working directly with a government. He didn't have time to get that kind of approval, and to be honest, he likely wouldn't get that kind of approval, especially now that Deacon had turned up dead.

"Parker, what I meant by the assholes was we need more reinforcements. Ping ACES. Tell them their team needs to haul ass from Abu Dhabi. Whatever they can get their greedy spec op hands on; I want them on a different continent. Now."

If the situation hadn't been so serious, Jared would've enjoyed seeing Parker's face. In the last six, eight years, Jared hadn't asked Parker to comingle ACES with any other team.

Parker cleared his throat. "Roger that, Boss Man. Pinging the assholes now."

CHAPTER FORTY-FIVE

SEVEN'S HOTEL SUITE was empty and dark without her. Jax had used his key card to access her room. On his phone, trying to figure out what to do next, he was nothing more than a pit of unease.

Internet searches had done no good when he searched Leyva, other than revealing a general tourist spot in Colombia. The more he thought about what it meant, the more he became convinced that it wasn't a generic place but that it held specific meaning, and Seven knew it too.

Jax had a few contacts spread throughout the world that he could call and ask anything of, and they wouldn't ask any questions. His phone buzzed with a text message.

JARED: *Get back to the conference room. Let's talk.*

Had Jax ever met someone who had been fired from Titan before? Was *let's talk* Jared's code for *adios*?

JAX: *Sure thing. Give me 20.*

No reason to rush and get canned.

He dropped his head back, wanting to think more about Seven and the kids than himself, when the blinking light on the room phone caught his attention. Jax leaned over and grabbed the phone off the nightstand and pressed the message button.

"You have one unheard message." He followed the prompts to play and listened.

"Ms. Blackburn. This is Ingrid from Wayside East Nursing Home. We've been trying to contact you on your cell phone as well as your emergency backup, Victoria Hall. It's imperative that someone call us back immediately. It's a medical emergency having to do with your mother. I'm sorry that we tracked you down at your hotel. You know how these things are; small towns know things. But it's important. We're not sure who else to call at this point. Thank you. Please call."

Jax wrote down the number and hung the phone up. What the hell was he supposed to do with that? Quickly, he called Ryder. No answer. Then he shot him a text message and watched… waited. No reply. Victoria wasn't available, obviously, and Jax didn't know what else to do. He dialed the phone number. "Err, hello. Is Ingrid available, please?"

"One second, please," a receptionist said.

Elevator music came on interspersed with commercials for the nursing home's robust senior activities.

"This is Ingrid. Can I help you, please?"

Jax scrunched his face and ran his hand over his forehead. "Hi, I'm calling on behalf of Seven Blackburn. You left a message for her, but she can't come to the phone."

"It's an emergency," the woman said with such immediate disdain that Jax snapped out of his didn't–know–what–to–do funk. "I've been trying to reach her for a couple of hours now. And Victoria. She's the deputy mayor, and nobody can get ahold of her."

If this lady only knew. "They're tied up at the moment with an emergency also. Is there something I can help you with?"

"And who are you?"

"Jax Michaelson."

"Jax, in relation to Seven and Taini, *who are you?*"

Taini was Seven's mother. Jax connected the dots to the conversation about the unwell woman at the coffee shop and how Seven had been taking care of her mom. But besides that, was this an interrogation or a medical emergency? He should've said that he was Seven with a bad cold and scratchy throat. "I'm her husband."

A moment of deafening silence hung on the line before Ingrid likely picked her jaw off the floor. "*Of course you are*, Mr. Michaelson."

What was that supposed to mean? "Just Jax. Jax."

"*Jax*, Taini had a seizure. She likely had another stroke as well. The stroke probably occurred sometime last week, maybe two weeks ago. It was minor, and maybe even the trigger to the change in Taini's behavior."

Jax should act as though he knew Taini or knew anything about what had gone on in Seven's life for more than the past few days since they'd gotten married. "Uh-uh." He had no idea what he was supposed to contribute to this conversation. What did this woman want from him? "Was there a problem after the seizure?"

Ingrid harrumphed into the phone. "Generally, when something of that magnitude happens, people rush to their loved ones. Would Seven like to rush to her loved one?"

"She would like to, but—"

"Yes, *I see.*"

The snooty bitch. She didn't *see* anything. "Do you?"

"Of course." Her condescension poured through the line. "I'm sure someone will stop by when they have free time—"

"Listen up, lady, Seven would rush as fast as her gorgeous goddamn legs could get her there. But she cannot right now."

"People forget about their loved ones when they drop them here. I see this a lot."

"If Seven could've answered the phone, she would have. If Victoria, the *deputy mayor*, could've answered her phone, she would have also. You do whatever it takes to keep Taini alive, happy, healthy, and upbeat until I get there, Seven gets there, Victoria gets there, anybody she knows gets there. Do you get me?"

"Well, um, yes—"

"And if you ever so much as speak to my wife with that haughty attitude, you'll be looking for a job. I don't care if I have to replace you myself. *Now*, tell me what *I* can do to make Taini's situation easier. What do you need? Money? Medicine? An insurance card?"

"Um... no. I believe I misinterpreted the situation. I'm, well, I apologize."

"I'm sure." Jax took a deep breath, trying to chill out. "If there is something that might help Taini, please tell me, and I might be able to make it available."

"A friend, even socially or casually, who could come over. To just sit with her. I think she would appreciate that. She hasn't been with us long, and... I think that it would help."

Jax squeezed his eyes shut, not having a clue what to do. Short of calling through the Sweet Hills telephone book, he didn't know anybody other than Victoria and Ryder—that wasn't true, actually. "Okay, thanks very much." He hung up then quickly Googled the phone number for The Perky Cup.

The phone rang twice before Sidney answered. "It's a happy day at The Perky Cup. What do you need?"

"Sidney, it's Jax. I need a favor."

"Oh, okay. Is everything o—"

"Not at all, Sid. Can you help me?" He sent up a quick prayer that Sidney would listen and not ask a thousand questions, because Jax was at the end of his rope.

"Yes."

Sidney didn't say a word after that. Jax could've kissed the guy. "Would Taini recognize your face?"

"Taini as in Seven's mom?"

"Yes, do you know another Taini?"

"No, but yes, she would recognize me." Then not another word.

God, Jax loved Sidney. "Can you leave work and have someone cover for you?"

"Nobody else is here. June left early, and Peter called in."

Again, Sidney for the win. His information was concise and done. Not great intel, but still, Jax could work with that. "I need you to get everybody out of the coffee shop and close up. Don't need to sweep the floors. Don't have to wrap the muffins or dump the coffee. Just kick their asses out and lock the door behind you."

"Jax, I'm sure this is probably cool with Seven, but I'd like to talk to her first. This is our biggest moneymaking day of the week, and we need the money. So..."

"Whatever revenue you expected for today, I will make up the difference personally and double it. Are you okay with that? Because Seven can't come to the phone right now, and I need you to trust me." He ground his teeth. "In lieu of not trusting me, which nobody in this goddamn world seems to do, I'll wire you cash. Just shut down and go see Taini. Seven can't be there. Victoria can't be there. Ryder can't be there. And Taini is alone after she had a seizure, and I don't know who the fuck else to call. Where do you want the money wired?"

"Hang on." The phone muffled, but in the background, Jax heard, "Sorry, everyone, we're closing early. You have to go." More rustling. "Okay, I'm back. I don't need money wired. What nursing home is she at?"

Jax dropped back on the bed and ran his hand into his hair, feeling as though he were running a small job with untrained operatives that had just worked out well. He filled Sidney in with all the information available, hung up, and went to go find Boss Man so he could be fired.

CHAPTER FORTY-SIX

WITH HIS HEAD held high and his shoulders back, Jax knocked on the closed conference room door then let himself in to a room full of bikers, Sugar, and Jared. It wasn't often that a boulder of tension lodged in his chest, but it was there now. Part of that was frustration that he couldn't do as much as he wanted to help Seven with the team, and part of that was disappointment.

Boss Man stood up. "Hey, I've been taking calls out here." Then he brushed past Jax and moved to the small conference room next to where they were.

Jax turned on his heel and followed. He should be happy it wasn't a public flogging. They'd all had verbal ass-kickings by Jared—Jax more than others. But he would be flat out lying if he said his ego wanted to get canned with a live studio audience.

Closing the door behind him, he turned around and said, "Look, no hard feelings. I'll head out. That's the way these things go sometimes." Then again, if Jared thought he had murdered Deacon, maybe volunteering to leave the city wasn't the best thing to do.

Boss Man paced the length of the small room with one arm across his chest and the other one propped under his chin until he squared to Jax. "When I don't know a situation, I send out for reports. Parker pulls intel, siphons data. I'll ask you guys for recon. The team will get what we need. But if I don't know, I'll *ask*. And"—Jared straightened his arms—"when I'm wrong, I need to own that shit. Say that I'm wrong. I'm not perfect, and I don't expect you to be."

He stopped, and Jax let the *I'm not perfect* sink in.

Jared ran his hand over his beard, shaking his head reflectively. "The way I came at you earlier today? I had assumptions, and that's on me. I'm sorry. Even if I still have questions, I owe you more than I gave you."

Jax stared, overwhelmed.

"When it comes to standing by my men, I see loyalty like I do consistency. Like I do the truth. There are very rare exceptions when that shit's not black and white." He dropped his hand from his beard. "And you? You're consistent. You call it like you see it. Not even one to talk shit behind someone's back. You give no fucks. Just say it to their faces. No one questions where they stand with you."

"True."

"I need to figure out what happened to Deacon, but if you say you didn't kill him, you didn't kill him."

His jaw tightened as he tried to ignore the flicker of hope his job wasn't lost. "I didn't."

"If you say you want Titan to be loyal and you'll be loyal to Titan, consider it done."

Jax nodded.

Jared took a step closer. "If you want back on this job, Jax, I need you with us, man. I didn't follow my own standard operating procedure, and there are consequences for that failure. But I hope that it doesn't mean I'm a man down. Stay on, would ya?"

Of course Jared Westin could apologize like a badass pro. There's nothing the guy couldn't do like a boss. "I don't want to leave Titan. Ever."

"Good." Jared threw out his hand, and Jax shook it.

"One more thing," Boss Man said. "In the process of pulling my head out of my asshole, I heard that you figured out the situation with the notes. We decoded Leyva and you saved us from a bloodbath."

His brows arched. "Yeah?"

"If we'd tracked Seven there anyway and gone in blind? We'd be fucked. I called in extra hands. Mayhem's dropping in. Whole new approach. Appreciate you looking out."

Maybe that was why Ryder wasn't answering his phone, and Jax wasn't going to get upset that Titan likely tapped into his phone to learn what he knew. "No prob."

"You good?"

"All's good with me as long as Johnny Miller isn't involved."

Jared smirked as he nodded his agreement. "Why don't you go in with me and tell them you're back? I think Johnny will particularly like that little bomb that he's staying home."

Jax followed Jared out of the small room, feeling one hundred percent different than he'd thought he would when he walked in. As they entered the main conference room, Hawke stood up as Jared acknowledged him and Sugar watched intently.

He cast an eye to Jared. "As most of you know, Boss Man called in all of our teams and asked for men from Mayhem. Except for…" Jax turned to face Johnny. "You. You're staying home. I don't trust you. And you cause more problems than you've helped since the day I met you. You hurt my wife. And you put her kids in danger. Your ass is staying home."

CHAPTER FORTY-SEVEN

THE INS AND outs of the rescue operation were catalogued in Jax's brain, but his mind was on Seven. He heard every word that Boss Man and Brock shared in his earpiece.

This was the primary residence for Hernán and Esmeralda Suarez and the main place of business for the Suarez cartel. A larger presence of Suarez militiamen was located on and near this property than anywhere else on earth. There were two classes within the militia: the trained militants and the hand-picked inner guard recruited from special ops teams across South and Central America.

This op was the largest offensive maneuver on a drug cartel that Jax had ever taken part in with the Titan Group. It included the Titan and Delta teams, plus there was an additional team that Jax had only heard about in passing and still didn't know the actual name of. They only went by ACES.

ACES knew Parker well, but who didn't know Parker? From what Jax could tell, the team was based out of Titan's Abu Dhabi offices. There was also a large contingency from Mayhem. They were mostly gunners. Many were veterans. All were loyal to bringing Seven and her kids—*their kids*, they called them—home and willing to take command from Titan, no questions asked.

"You ever heard of ACES?" Locke asked no one in particular as they sat in the belly of the Black Hawk, hovering low and fast toward their drop zone.

"Nope," Bishop said. "I heard Roman mention the asses a couple times."

"Beth and Caterina talk about the asses," Locke added. "I just assumed they were talking about Jax."

The team laughed. He even laughed.

"We're a whole team of assholes," a female voice cracked from the third Black Hawk.

Jax had a feeling they didn't have a clue of the total expanse of Titan Group, and short of tapping into Boss Man's brain, no one ever would.

"Focus," Jared barked. "All teams. All assholes."

Jax smiled but needed to concentrate. Titan worked with many organizations on operations of all scale, but the large ones took the most strategic and tactical breadth. There was a hand-to-hand combat and assault offensive and snipers nested in trees like birds ready to pick off tangos. Jax and most of Titan, Delta, and ACES were sitting in the bellies of stealth copters, ready to be fast rope-dropped over the tall brick walls of the Suarez compound outside of Leyva. Mayhem and some key Titan Group players had stationed themselves in tactical positions earlier.

"ETA is a minute-thirty," Parker called through their headsets. "Calling time at the thirty, then the twenty, ten to countdown."

Jax worked through the final checklist before they got the kids and his woman. Adrenaline pumped, and his mind hyperfocused. He could picture the maps, where Colby Winters would detonate charges, the blueprints, and assumptions of where the kids would be and how they would be guarded.

Best case and most likely scenario was that Hernán and Esmeralda would be swiftly evacuated by the inner guard. Worst case was that Esmeralda had taken to the kids and would fight to stay with them. Psych-ops reported she was likely a sociopath and children were likely a hobby. That was about the only good thing Titan had going for them.

"Sixty seconds," Parker said in his com piece then continued the countdown as promised.

The three helos would drop men simultaneously.

"Inbound, you are… ten, nine"—the hatch to the helicopter opened—"four, three, two, and—*go*."

One after the other, his team jumped and rolled to where the black night met the ground. Titan would hit the main house, and ACES would subdue the inner guard's housing. Delta would do the same for the foot soldiers and slow the outpouring of what would arrive when the alarms blasted, with the help of Mayhem, who would then serve as backup for Titan's main team.

There were motion sensors, dogs, thermal imaging, and guards that they didn't have a bead on ahead of time.

The sniper and spotter teams worked in tandem, subduing obvious threats now that all teams were on-site. Alarm systems disabled. Guards taken out. Tangos were sighted, and shots called.

The unexpected voices of ACES flowed with smooth familiarity with Parker, Brock, and Jared, while Mayhem's communication was less practiced but still as familiar.

Bishop and Locke broke right. Winters stayed dead ahead of Jax with the detonator trigger in hand. Best they could tell, getting through any door at the Suarez complex would require significant explosive effort.

Jax and Nicola ran with their close-range assault rifles as his backup. She fanned left and high against the brick of the house then spun around and dropped to her knee, barrel up and finger on the trigger.

Lights that hadn't been shot out flooded the expansive, manicured yard as Jax saw Sugar taking a position similar to Bishop, Locke, and Nicola.

Now that Jax had teammates accounted for, he stayed on the pivot, keeping Winters covered as he stayed at the door. Having attached the explosive charge, Winters backed up and positioned back-to-back with Jax. "Detonation in—"

"We've got vehicles," ACES called. "Moving fast. *Snipers.*"

"Got them in sight," Ryder said. "Shit. Freaking MRAP."

"I've got the Lone Ranger," called Cash.

Winters motioned to Jax. "We gotta get in there."

He agreed. "They get close, I'll keep them out."

An MRAP exploded in the near-distance, lighting up the sky. "Two more."

Target practice on those armored vehicles was nearly impossible. The shot had to go up and under, exploding into the engine.

"Detonating—three, two, one." The front door blew off the Suarez house. "Here we go."

There were six of them, but two more MRAPs held an untold amount of manpower.

"They're coming straight for the main residence," Cash reported.

"Winters." Jax slung his rifle down. "Throw me something."

Bishop hustled over, nabbing a block of explosives from Winters too. "It's come down to a game of chicken." He held it up as the headlight of the MRAP became visible. "Cheers."

Jax had to smile, maybe feeling as though his team were also his guys for the first time. "Let's go."

They ran as the MRAPs came straight for them, stopping long enough to light the fuses, then rushed toward the war vehicles.

Jax and Bishop pulled sharp in opposite directions as the MRAPs came forward. They threw their charges.

Jax sprinted and dove, covering his head, rolling hard as the two blasts shook the ground—the MRAPs crashed in fiery accidents, mangled against one another.

"Go, go," Ryder said. "We'll clean up behind you."

Jax hit his feet, and Bishop was by his side three strides later, knocking gloves against his. "That was badass."

CHAPTER FORTY-EIGHT

THE LIGHTS WERE out, and the power had been killed. Jax kept his night-vision goggles on as Bishop signaled they were inside.

"First floor, secure," Winters responded.

"West wing, clear," Sugar said.

"Nicola? Locke? Status update now," Brock demanded.

A rustling noise crackled through Nicola's mic piece. "Working on it—second floor, east wing, third door down after the sitting room. I see the two packages."

See? Are they safe? Alive? What does that mean?

"Nicola?" Brock followed up.

"I'm going to need a minute. By myself, please," she quietly whispered.

"*What?*" Jax hustled to the closest set of stairs in the giant residence.

"Who has eyes on Nic? Now, goddamn it," Jared ordered. "Cash? Roman? Ryder? Any snipers?"

No response, and Jax's panic surged.

"My name is Nicola, and I know your mommy," Nicola said in a sing-song voice so sweet it made Jax run up the stairs faster. "I'm going to bring you home. But the first thing we're going to do is play a game. Want to?"

No response, but they had to be alive...

"Don't move, chickadee and chickadude. Like a statue—no. Don't move."

"I know how to hold this," Bianca said.

Jax faltered. *This?*

"Nic," Jared calmly said. "Sing a song if they're armed."

"Before I bring you home to Glamma and Victoria, can I sing you my little boy's favorite song? It's *Twinkle, Twinkle.*"

The earpiece was eerily quiet; Jax had never heard it like that before. No one was muted, but everyone was silent.

"It goes twinkle, twinkle—"

"Are you a good guy or a bad guy?" Nolan asked.

"They all lie," Bianca said.

"*Don't* move, honey." Nicola drew in a quick breath. "I'm good. So very good. And I promise you, from the bottom of my heart, that I'm telling you the truth, and I know your mommy wants you to put that gun down. Would you do that for me?"

"*Ohfff.* Hi, Nolan, thank you for the hug. You're very strong, but I need you to stand behind me. Bianca, move your fingers, baby. Like this."

"No, thank you," faintly came through the earpiece, and Jax died inside.

Nicola tried again. "I promise it's okay. I'll trade you my cell phone for that, and you can call anyone. They'll tell you to trust me."

"She knows Glwamma and Vwictorwia," Nolan said. "I'm hungrwry."

Jax reached the threshold of the third door and held his breath as he peeked around the corner. Nolan hugged onto Nicola's back. She had one arm outstretched to Bianca while she firmly held the little boy in place against her back and body armor. Bianca cradled a handgun haphazardly in both hands. All his faith was placed solidly in Nicola's hands. His teammate could get them through this. He had to believe that like he'd never trusted Titan before.

His heart raced. He covered his mouth and whispered into his mic piece, "Say my name. You know me."

"Jax is my friend."

Nicola trusted him, no hesitation. Jax held his breath, praying as he inched closer to the edge of the door, catching a glimpse of the squirming boy who Nicola desperately tried to keep pinned.

"He is?" Nolan's excited voice wrapped around him.

"He's here and wants to see you. Freeze like a statue so I can take that from you."

"Okay," Bianca said.

Relief rolled through Jax that Bianca had stopped fighting. But until that weapon was out of her hands, uncertainty still had him hanging by a thread.

"You're now a statue," Nicola said. "Do. Not. Move. A muscle or a finger."

"Can I breathe?"

"Yes."

"Can I blink?"

"Yes, sweetheart. One second. Your brother gets a game, too, and I have to move, Bianca. So don't be surprised if I'm moving a tiny bit. Okay?"

"Okay."

"What a good statue."

"Nolan, your part of the game is to lie on the floor like a piece of paper, and I'm going to cover you with my hat and my coat—"

"Nicola..." Jared's only warning came, and Jax knew that she would ignore it and he wouldn't say it again.

She slipped off her body armor and covered him. "Okay, you're still a statue. Don't move a muscle. No fingers, no toes."

Jax watched Nicola cross the fifteen feet, and it felt like an eternity until she had the gun in her hand. "Any other weapons on you, my little statue?"

"No."

He moved into the room, taking his face covering off. "Hey, you two."

Both kids did exactly what he and Nicola had feared. Nolan jumped up and down, waving his arms, and ran, launching into Jax's outstretched his arms, while Bianca rushed, her arms crossed to her chest, hands clasped under her chin, and burrowed for hugs. If that little girl had had a gun in her hand when he'd walked in, no safety and set to semi-auto, there was no telling the damage she would've done to her brother and herself. Jax caught sight of Nicola leaning against a wall, shaking her head as though she were catching her breath and maybe reliving the hell of the last few minutes.

He squeezed them even tighter. "I heard you went on an adventure."

"It wasn't very fun," Bianca reported.

He chuckled. "I know, kiddo. Now let's go get your mom."

"But"—Nolan's bottom lip quivered—"I thought they sent her away."

Jax dropped to his knee as a firefight broke out in his earpiece and out the window.

Nolan threw his hand wide. "Thwre were *bad* guys with guns—"

"We're going to talk about guns later," Jax interrupted.

"And thwey were like thwis and thwat." He chopped his hands. "And Victwria said *lots* of bad words."

"A lot," Bianca added with a tiny scowl.

"Then Glamma—"

"No sign of Seven," Winters said in his earpiece.

"Hey, my little team. Where's your mama? Do you know where she stays?"

"She has to leave every night." Bianca leaned against him, and Jax put an arm around her waist.

"In a rocket humvee."

The kid knew his vehicle, and Jax's stomach dropped at the thought of Seven in a MRAP. The chance that Suarez militia would bring her on-site during a hostile takeover was slim. They didn't know who was there, even if a safe assumption could be made about the kids. But a man like Hernán Suarez had many enemies.

"Checking the MRAPs," Sugar said as though she were discussing mail call and not a body search.

Nicola walked out of the room, her gaze meeting his. "You want to go or stay?"

Jax needed to find Seven like he needed to take another breath. "You met my friend Nicola. Do you want to hang out with her while I go get your mom?"

Neither said anything as they turned to study her. Bianca grabbed on to his forearm, and Nolan leaned against his chest as, warily, they watched her drop to her knees also.

He gave them a squeeze that he prayed conveyed his faith in Nicola. "You know what my favorite thing about Nic is?"

Bianca turned. "What?"

"She's like a machine. You can tell her something in English, and it comes out another language. Watch." He tapped his head. "I want a cheeseburger."

"*Ich will einen cheeseburger*," Nicola offered.

"German?" he asked.

"Yup. Good guess."

Jax hugged the kids close. "How about... I love ice cream?"

"Somebody's hungry." Nicola came closer with her most disarming grin. "*Eu amo sorvete*. Portuguese this time. You want to try, Bianca?"

She shook her head.

"Nolan?"

"Say... My shoes smell. Eww, eww, eww!" Nolan jumped and danced, sticking up his feet.

"*Mój zapach buty*. Eww, eww, eww!" Nicola scrunched up a silly face, waving her hand. "Polish. But next time I'll try for Pig Latin. Much more fun."

Both kids fell apart in giggles.

Jax gave them one last squeeze. "Go with Nic. I'm going to get your mom, okay?"

Nolan waited for Bianca's reaction. Then the little girl took a step forward. "I'm sorry I picked up that gun."

Nicola signaled for them to go. "Thank you for listening when I asked you. Let's go get Jax a cheeseburger and ice cream. You, too, if you want."

"I'm coming in for your back up," Winters added.

"Same," Sugar said. "Seven wasn't in the vehicles. But, Jax, I left you someone tied to a tire axle if you'd like a Suarez bitch ready to cry uncle."

"See you two soon." Then Jax hustled out the way he'd come, mentally slipping back on his warrior mask.

CHAPTER FORTY-NINE

T HE GREAT LAWN was littered with bodies and three smoking MRAPs as he approached the back tire of the second militarized vehicle. Gunfire buzzed in Jax's earpiece as smoke billowed from the blazing MRAPs. He stood over the Suarez militant with the tactical gun palmed and his trigger finger itching for a pull.

His heart pounded, and sweat coated his back. Licking his lips, Jax prayed for strength. "Do you understand English?"

The bound man shrank against the tire. "Y-yes-s."

"Good." He tugged his face mask back then ran the muzzle of his weapon along the man's jaw. "Of all the assholes you didn't want to see, I'm the one that will give you nightmares."

The bastard bared his teeth, hissing at the gun in his face.

Jax pistol-whipped him. "Those kids? They're very special to me."

Again, the man's mouth opened, but this time he simply held up his hand and pointed at the gun. "Think hard. I don't kill for sport, and I don't care if you take another breath. I give zero fucks. But the woman who was taking care of those children?" Jax dropped his hand and inched his weapon forward again. "Her, I care about. You have a simple decision. Tell the truth and live. Where is she?"

The man hesitated, and Jax shook his head. "That was your warning. Next, I'll shoot ankle, knee, gut shot. I've seen how they bleed so purple, it looks black. Interested?" He aimed for the man's ankle. "Where is she?"

"The militia quarters—" Then he buried his face in tied arms, preparing for death, anyway.

"I gave you my word." He ran toward the barracks to the sound of the man sobbing and thanking him.

"ACES," Jared barked in his earpiece. "Target is on-site. Find her. Jax, you can get there on foot. Follow the way the MRAPS came."

"Roger that." He recalled the satellite maps and was already hauling ass.

The acrid smoke burned the night air as Jax covered as much of the gravel road as he could.

"Hold your fire! ACES, confirm targets visually or under direct assault only."

Jax rounded a bend and saw one-story buildings surrounded by a flood of people.

"Report. What's the situation?" Jared demanded of the change in the operational directives.

"Freaking chaos." Jax didn't recognize the voice. "Civilian captives released. Scattering like ants out a flooded hill. Young, old. Kids. Women."

A tsunami of people rolled in every direction. How many prisoners did the Suarez cartel have captive?

"First priority remains the same," the ACES commanding officer ordered. "Eyes stay on the pivot. Report on back side and jungle line?"

"They're being pushed in all directions," another unfamiliar voice reported. "Diversions and body shields—"

"I have eyes on the target, eyes on the target!"

"Who's that? Where?" Jax rushed through the chaos that the Suarez militia had created. Half the people didn't know who to trust or which way to go, but ACES could manage that. "*Where?*"

The faces were indistinguishable. Some people were dressed in rags, while others had been obviously forced into military garb and held weapons awkwardly. Jax took a defensive position and scanned the perimeter, unable to find Seven in the churn of people.

"Give me your location and her direction," Parker said calmly. "I'll lock a bead on her."

Jax's heart thundered in his ears as the two men volleyed intel back-and-forth regarding one of the women who had fled toward the jungle. A civilian might've assumed the jungle was safe. But that only took into account the threat of man with his weapons and military maneuvering.

Fleeing into the jungle was unlike escaping into the woods at a park. A jungle tree canopy would block the light from the moon and the stars, and most wildlife inhabitants survived by the eat-or-be-eaten code.

Seven was fierce, but she had no idea what she had walked into.

"Jax," Parker said. "I'll ping her coordinates to you. Find her, and I'll get you an extraction locale."

Like there was any other option. He was coming for his woman.

EVERYWHERE LOOKED THE same as Seven stumbled to the ground. The thick vined plants tangling around her feet were just as black as the sky was above her. No matter which way Seven turned, she smacked into thorned bushes or trees that were wider than the expanse of her arms. Her eyes never adjusted to the dark; she couldn't see anything anymore. What was the point of running away when she didn't know if she was getting any closer to a neighboring village or town where someone could help?

Her lungs screamed with pain from pushing past any athletic ability she had and from panting against tiny bugs and spiderwebs.

Seven wrapped her elbow across her face as a mask even as she worked to suck in as much air as possible. She hadn't been able to catch her breath while in Columbia, and today was even worse. But she didn't care because she had to get help for her children.

Tears welled in her eyes as she took in the magnitude of the situation.

"Seven!" Jax's voice sifted through the hot, humid air, and maybe she had been bitten by something venomous.

Hallucinations had to be one of the signs that she was losing her mind or had been poisoned by some stupid jungle insect.

"Seven, stop moving. I'm coming for you."

She laughed as delirium strangled her common sense. This was what it was going to be like when her mind finally gave up—delusions about Jax riding in to the jungle to save her. She should've guessed.

The crunch of leaves and branches startled her, and the cold prickle of sweat cascaded down her back and arms. She had nothing to fight off whatever animal may have sniffed her out, sweating and crying.

"C'mere, princess, I'm here." The snaps of twigs and the crumble of plants underneath steps came so close she was sure that if she held out her hand, she could touch its source. What she wouldn't do to have Jax with her now. "Target acquired."

He wrapped his arms around her, pulling her tight to his chest and dropping his mouth to her sweaty forehead. "Found you. I promised you everything would be okay."

"Oh God. It's not." Seven sobbed. "Bianca and Nolan." Her arms shook then her body with the full force of terror. But if he was there, maybe there were more resources to save the kids? "Jax, please tell me you're real. Please."

"Real." He slowly released her.

"My babies," Seven whispered, trying to make sense of what was true and what wasn't a dream.

"Titan has them. They're fine. Anxious to see you."

"God, thank you." Relief found its footing and overtook her. Light on her feet, as if she could breathe fire and float on angel wings all at once, she leapt back against Jax and hugged him. "Thank you, thank you, thank you. I owe you forever."

He chuckled. "That's what husbands are for."

Seven kissed him on the cheek and would kiss him head to toe if she wasn't foul and they weren't in the middle of the jungle, likely being hunted by the men who had kept her captive.

"We need to get moving again. I have a rendezvous point for a helicopter pickup. But it's not close, and we have to hustle." He gave her shoulder a squeeze. "Are you good to start hustling?"

Seven took a deep breath in the dark night. Tears dried on her cheeks as the man she was crazy about held on to her. "I'm so good I might be able to fly if I tried."

"YOU KNOW, YOU'RE my hero." The darkness was all surrounding, and Seven could no longer make out his face.

"One person's hero is another person's nothing to lose. My job well done happens to mean extreme circumstances have occurred. But, Seven, don't make me out to be something I'm not."

His words were everything with a far more evocative texture than she had ever heard before. "You don't have to be perfect to be a hero. You know that, right?"

At his urging, they began moving again, faster than the leisurely pace he'd let her take before. They had all the time in the world, at least until they found the abandoned field medic station and their rescue helicopter came in the next twelve hours. Jax could speedwalk her through the jungle all he wanted, but he couldn't outrun a conversation.

"Where did you grow up?" she asked.

He grumbled. "Is this the point in our walk where we start the twenty questions? Is this where you want to pick me apart and figure out what's wrong? What could be fixed?"

Seven planted both of her feet firmly in the squishy jungle ground, yanked her hand back from his, and, unable to see his face clearly, twisted in his general direction. "What the hell crawled up your ass? I'm the one that's dead tired and not used to jungle walks, *thank you very much*. If anybody wants to get in a snippy-pants mood, I call dibs. Not you."

"Keep moving, Seven. We don't have time for this."

"Then we didn't have time for you to push your lips against mine a few minutes ago. I'm not moving. If you're going to be a dick anytime I ask you a simple question, I'm gonna be a bitch. See how that works? It's the whole yin and yang thing. Like a teeter-totter."

"Then I'll throw you over my shoulder and get there faster, anyway." Jax took a step closer, his hand jutting out as though he might follow through on his threat.

"So help me God, big boy. I'll never forgive you if my feet leave the ground, and it's a simple freaking question. Where are you from? Who are your parents? Are they alive? What's the deal with not wanting to share personal information? Because that's *weird*."

Jax muttered and snagged her hand but didn't start walking. "They're alive. They live in Jersey. Everybody's Italian and eats sausage and peppers on Sunday." He started walking, and Seven relented, falling into stride next to him. "I played in the river with my friends when we were kids. Football was king. Still is in that town. It was a perfectly normal childhood. Nothing to talk about."

"Ever been in love?" she asked.

"*Really, Seven?*"

"I want to know who you are. I'm not some nutso chick that's going to go into a jealous rage in the middle of the goddamn Colombian jungle. I have a compulsion with folding when I wish I could control chaos." She grumbled because this moment was pretty much the definition of chaos. "I've never been in love. I thought I loved Johnny. I didn't really know what it was because I grew up with everybody telling me that I was supposed to love him and that we were supposed to date and that we were supposed to get married. It was like a checklist—" She tripped over a branch and stumbled then limped for a step but refused to issue a complaint. "He grew up as one of my best friends, and if I had had a brother, he would've been it. And I understand that's very weird to say because obviously we got married. It was more like he was the boy next door. Essentially, it was an arranged marriage. I never dated anyone else in high school, and when I turned eighteen, we got married."

"Jeez, that sucks."

"No, it doesn't suck if you don't know what you might be missing. I care about him. I want good things for him—"

"The cokehead who hit you."

"You've never made a mistake before?"

"That's not a—never mind."

"When I was sixteen years old, he gave me butterflies."

"At least it wasn't the clap."

"*Jax.* I'm trying to explain that he's always been a very attractive person, and I didn't think anything of it. It was what I knew. Normal. We did the prom thing. Johnny was the first boy I kissed, lost my virginity to, and the same person I ended up marrying. It seemed like that was how it was supposed to go."

Jax helped her down a small embankment, and she heard water splash around his feet. "Back up." He shuffled them up the hill and moved in a different direction. "When did you know you wanted something different?"

Seven groaned into the jungle humidity. "I'll tell you if you promise not to judge me."

Jax lifted her over a downed tree. "Maybe. Hang on. Duck for a minute." They crawled through thick branches, and he helped her through the last ones. "You know I'm not going to judge you."

He held her still as though she had to acknowledge that he meant what he said. "I know."

"Careful over here."

Footing wasn't easy, but it was better than baring her soul. Still, she wanted Jax to know about her, regardless of how uncomfortable sharing made her. "It wasn't when I knew he was sleeping around. But when I realized my dreams and fantasies revolved around things I'd never have with him, I started to change. More importantly, I knew it was happening, and *why* I was changing scared me. In how addictive it felt. Like a compulsion." Which she already had and couldn't stomach explaining.

Jax stopped and turned to her. "Like what?"

Nervously, she fidgeted, unable to see where she could pace but wanting to move. Maybe she'd said too much. Maybe he'd picked up on the OCD and thought she wanted to talk about that. "I don't know. Stupid stuff."

"How did you change?"

"The first time I dyed my hair an outrageous color, it was a rush. And then the piercings. It's not the high from the pain that excites me. I like the rush of planning, the nerves of not knowing, the thrill of seeing something that some say shouldn't be there. It's the closest thing I can find to butterflies, and I wanted to keep chasing it."

"Why would I judge you for that?"

"I didn't work on my marriage."

"You were eighteen years old."

"How old were you when you joined the Navy?" she asked.

"Eighteen."

"And you're always a SEAL."

"That's different, and you know it."

Seven agreed but could still make the argument against herself. "I'd been through the ugliness of my parents' split and couldn't handle that one decision trapping me for the next fifty, sixty, however many more years of my life."

"I get that."

"I didn't want to be like my dad. He ran out on my mom. Or maybe, it was that I didn't want to be like my mom, who finally gave up on my dad. I don't know... My father fucked around on my mom a ton, and perhaps that's why I didn't bat an eyelash when getting married didn't stop Johnny from sleeping with whoever he wanted to. But you know what the weirdest thing is?"

Jax put his hands on her biceps and gave a soft squeeze. "Tell me."

"It didn't feel real. The marriage, wedding rings. I had this fairytale wedding in my head. And I know the wedding ceremony doesn't make the marriage, but I wanted this very traditional wedding with a giant wedding gown and veil, bridesmaids, and groomsmen. I fantasized about a church with an organist and people throwing birdseed or blowing bubbles as we ran out."

Jax grumbled.

It wasn't everyone's ideal day, but it was hers. "You know what else?"

"Hmm?" The cold, rough edge of his disinterest barely registered because she'd tried to share her dream with Johnny time and time again, and his responses had run along the lines of "better luck next time" to "sounds like a waste of money."

"I couldn't see Johnny's face. It was never him." Seven shook her head. "No matter how hard I tried, I couldn't put him in my dreams."

Jax squeezed her arms and let out a deep sigh. He finally said, "You would look beautiful in a big white dress."

"Thanks." That was more than she'd ever gotten before, and Seven squeezed her eyes shut, wanting to be closer to him than their layers of clothes would allow. She leaned nearer and held on to him, refusing to be overwhelmed by history.

Jax stroked her hair. "I was in love before."

Seven tilted her head back.

"I was a couple years younger than you. Man, and I was naïve. Green as fuck. Her name was Carrie, and she worked for the Agency as an operational analyst. Essentially, an intel grunt. She would take info from ops and digest it. Sometimes, that meant fieldwork, but mostly, she was behind a computer. The whole thing is classified, actually. What I'm about to tell you doesn't even exist. But…" His body tensed, and Seven thought he might never continue. "I married her."

Having no idea what to do, she stayed wrapped around Jax because those last three words sounded like they hurt him to say. If nothing else, Seven wanted to simply touch him, tell him without a sound that she wished he never hurt.

"Carrie wore a white dress. Sounds like you might've liked it. A long veil too. Her hair was long and… up. There were these pins. They shimmered and held the veil in place."

Seven couldn't tell if pain or anger made Jax's voice gravelly. She inched back, wanting to ask if he was okay, needing to see his face, but the jungle night was dark to the point of blindness. It was cruel not to be able to see his eyes, his cheeks, those lips that she wanted to kiss when his pain shook the wilderness. "You don't have to continue."

"I should tell you." His ragged, broken sigh shattered her heart. "There was a small room at the back of the church. Music still played. We didn't even have a chance to laugh over the stupid way one of her bridesmaids kept sneezing during the ceremony and how the priest kept glaring. We never got to talk."

"Jax, what happened?"

His clothes rustled as he pulled back, rubbing his chest. "*What happened?*" Jax's hurt bottomed out in a deadness that sent chills down Seven's skin. "Deacon Lanes happened."

Oh—They were both employed by the CIA. Did they have an affair? Or—

"Their cover was blown for a job, and Deacon's identity was in question while we were at the church. Him and her at the same location. They walked into the room seconds after we shut the door, and Deacon didn't even look—"

What happened? Seven would never ask, but hell…

"He said, 'she means nothing,' shot her in the head, and kept his cover."

"What!" Seven's heart broke for Jax. The idea of a loved one killed in action was unbearable, but to witness it? And after getting married? Seven didn't know how Jax was still standing.

She also understood the rage she'd witnessed in Las Vegas. What had seemed like a snap, out-of-control decision to attack and nearly kill Deacon now didn't seem vicious enough.

How was Deacon still alive? She had no idea. She would never ask why Jax hadn't murdered the man who'd murdered his wife. They were raised in different ways. But his self-control, the dedication he had to his cause and country, and the fact that he placed what he did and what he was doing for Nolan, Bianca, and her so high had elevated him to sainthood.

"I've been angry and hateful since that day." He wrapped his arms around her. "Time heals wounds, but, Seven, I have to thank you too."

She jolted back in his arms. "Me?"

Jax didn't let her go anywhere. "Yeah, princess, you. Because I go through the motions and do a hell of a job, but I couldn't feel a damn thing." He inched her close until his breath tickled her face. "Until I felt my heart beat when I woke up married, next to you."

Seven had no doubt how deeply she'd fallen in love with him, but she had no idea how to focus her mind around the gravity of that realization.

"Not too much farther and not much left to say. Let's get in and get some shut-eye." He slid his hands down her arms and found her grip. With a squeeze, Jax signaled that it was time, and into the darkness they went.

CHAPTER FIFTY

S EVEN WAS HOME and safe after an exhausting trek through the jungle delivered her to a helicopter which materialized out of nowhere then whisked her away.

The bright morning held the promise of a return to normal. Nolan and Bianca were in their beds, and Jax had held her all night long until he had to go, giving her a quick update on her mom.

Sleepy and exhausted, she had only a few minutes to say goodbye before he rushed off to Titan-land, and now she replayed their conversation with a smile.

"Your mom got sick while we were out of town."

Seven had been abducted. Interesting how he'd chosen to word that.

"She's doing much better now, and Sidney went to be with her as often as he could."

Jax had explained that the reason her mom had been sick was because she'd had a seizure, which had stolen her breath until he'd explained that Taini now took the proper medication to combat that.

Then he'd also explained the reason her mom's rapid health decline over the past few weeks. She'd been pissed it took a stroke to find the problem, but her therapy and activities had been adjusted.

Jax had dealt with everything, all in the course of a couple days, while rescuing her and the kids. So he was a superhero. Then off he'd gone to save the world again.

The moment Glamma was able to take Nolan and Bianca, Seven called Adelia and made plans to hustle over to the nursing home as soon as visiting hours were available.

And now Seven waited outside Adelia's apartment. She ran her hands in semicircles along the steering wheel, replaying the last few days of insanity. Somehow, she was supposed to act as though life were normal again.

But it was normal. Normal had turned out to be one of the most relative words she'd ever thought about, and now she had to figure out how to coexist with that realization. Her normal was Sweet Hills and Mayhem.

But now she knew that somewhere in the world, there was a normal of cartel slavery and abductions as part of business dealings. That was their normal—both the evil, inhumane excuses for people who made those decisions day in and out as well as the people who lived until they died under the consequences of others' choices.

Yet she was back in Sweet Hills, where everything was old normal. Bianca and Nolan woke up at the crack of dawn, like normal. Just hours before, she'd tucked them into their beds after jet-setting back from South America and caravanning home under the watchful eye of a security detail.

Then they had Cheerios for breakfast. Like normal...

Seven had awoken alone after Jax tucked her into bed, promising all would be okay and she should sleep. Her hand still reached for him when she opened her eyes, but he was gone. At work, in another state or country... That had been Victoria and Ryder's normal for the past few years. It seemed easy enough from the outside looking in, but Seven had been wrong.

"Hey!" Adelia broke Seven's thoughts as she dove into the car.

"Hi."

"I'm so happy to see you." She hugged Seven. "Are you good?"

"I'm good. My muscles are a little sore from—"

Adelia's eyes rounded. "Crazy sex with the hot Italian."

Seven flashed her a side-eye. "No!"

"Liar."

"From walking for miles in a freaking jungle, thank you very much." Then, hot cheeked, she quietly whispered, "Though there might have been time spent with a certain man."

"Mm-hm." Adelia buckled her seatbelt. "Victoria's told me all about the *Welcome to Vegas* gift package she arranged for."

"What!" *Ugh.* Her face flashed hot. "No idea—"

"Champagne and lube?" Adelia giggled. "That's what a best friend is for."

Seven's cheeks flamed a whole notch hotter. "Holy shit! Is nothing sacred?"

"No. Spit it out."

"We're *not* having that conversation."

Laughing harder, Adelia bounced her eyebrows. "Victoria would dish."

"Well, the deputy mayor can do whatever she deems appropriate." Seven looked down her nose and rolled her eyes with a smile. Then she put the car into drive and pulled out. They followed the familiar small-town streets toward where her mother's nursing home was. Adelia fiddled with the radio and switched from station to station.

"Sweet Hills feels so quiet," Seven said.

"What do you mean?"

Hmm. What *did* she mean? "Some places in the world are in upheaval, and we're flipping the radio stations. Forty-eight hours ago, I was trudging through a jungle after Special Forces saved my children. There should be parades and confetti on the streets, headlines on the top of the *Sweet Hills Sentinel,* but no one knows."

"You haven't shared."

"Some things are so monumental it seems the universe should know." Seven turned and accelerated down the main thoroughfare.

"I know you got married and haven't mentioned it." Adelia tucked a leg under the other on her seat. "Why don't we start there?"

Her fingers tensed around the steering wheel even as her heart fluttered. She was *Mrs. Seven Michaelson.* Or would she keep her last name like with Johnny? What was she thinking about? Vegas weddings were a problem to fix, even if the sex was mind-blowing and the man was one of a kind. "We were drunk."

"Not something I hear you say very often."

"It was a mistake, and I barely remember anything." Which wasn't true, and every time she closed her eyes, more memories fought through to permanently embed themselves in her memory. "I didn't mention it because it's not news."

Adelia sighed. "I can't believe the pre-Vegas discussion about a possible crush has morphed into a post-Vegas discussion about your nuptials."

"And impending divorce."

Adelia pouted. "Really? I did not see that coming."

Seven clicked on her turn signal then eased into the parking lot of the nursing home. "But you saw me getting married to Jax?" She rolled her eyes. "Come on. Give me a little credit for being the most responsible person you know."

Adelia harrumphed.

"People make drunken mistakes, and obviously, I wasn't exempt, as surprising as that is to both of us." She forced a laugh. "Which is why God made divorce attorneys—*ohh*." Seven cocked her eyebrow as she parked and stared at Adelia. "You're my divorce hookup."

Lenora Appleton was a prominent attorney in Sweet Hills. She was the first phone call when Mayhem needed legal counsel or a quick bail out of jail, and behind closed doors of Sweet Hills society, she was also Tex's old lady, making her the pseudo-stepmom to Adelia. Even if Adelia's dad wasn't with Lenora, Seven could've asked, and Lenora would have discreetly processed what was needed for a quickie divorce. "Can you call her after we see my mom?"

Adelia pushed her bottom lip out. "Do I have to be part of ruining this fairy tale?"

Seven groaned. "Have your own. Plus, Jax and I can still do whatever he and I… *do*. We just don't need to be bound by a legal contract."

"For a woman who nearly crawled out of her skin when Ryder and Victoria got together, I cannot believe you're poo-pooing this."

"My wedding day can't involve Jell-O shooters."

Adelia let her eyebrow creep up. "Maybe your wedding day was supposed to teach you to loosen up a bit, darlin'."

"Right, and maybe I'm going to magically learn a better way to cope with my anxiety than my ridiculous compulsions when I pop in to see my mom. Same likelihood of life-changing epiphanies." Seven shouldn't complain. Her OCD was minor and far more manageable compared to what it could be. But when ideas got planted in her head, they were hard to let go. "Tell Lenora it's important. I'd like to have whatever I need for Jax to sign by the time he gets off of his assignment."

Adelia's heartbreaking frown could've been for both of them. "If that's what you think is best."

What was best and what was responsible were on opposite sides of Iowa. "I do."

She shifted into Park, and a motorcycle a few parking spaces over caught her eye. Narrowing her gaze, Seven looked to see who she recognized, and Adelia followed her stare.

"Who is that?"

"I don't know." Seven turned off her car and pocketed the keys in her purse. They didn't know everybody who rode a Harley in Sweet Hills. But more often than not, they did, and it wasn't normal to see one there.

"Let's go," Adelia said. "Maybe there's a hot biker for me to flirt with after I talk to your mama."

Seven laughed. "Maybe." Adelia's outlook on love and relationships vastly differed from Seven's, which was surprising since they'd had vaguely familiar upbringings. Adelia's had been far more traumatic. Both of their dads were criminal pieces of shit, or rather, Adelia's biological father was. Tex was a rock star in Seven's book. But he hadn't come along until Adelia was a teenager.

They got out and walked toward the check-in, pausing when they passed the Harley.

Adelia ambled closer. "What the... Who is that?"

Seven shrugged. "I don't care. So long as it's not Johnny, if they're here to visit my mom, I'm sure she's good with company."

Loud voices marred the normally serene foyer of the nursing home as they walked in, and the hairs on the back of Seven's neck spiked. "What do you think that's about?"

"Old folks gone wild?"

They picked up the pace, rounding the corner. And there stood Cullen Blackburn.

"Motherfucker," Adelia whispered.

Seven choked on air. Why was her father there? Adelia's hand found Seven's and gave it a quick squeeze but didn't let go.

Why wasn't he in prison? "What are you doing here?"

Her dad sauntered forward with a bastard's grin and mischievous eyes. "My little girl."

"Don't call me that." She'd rather they were on a first-name basis—or a no-contact one. "You're not allowed here."

"That's what they say." His forehead furrowed as his scrutiny became a visible inspection. "You are..."

Adelia squeezed her fingers around Seven's hand again, offering more reassurance.

"Colorful," he finally added.

Seven wasn't sure if Adelia had ever met her dad in person. She couldn't recall the last time she had seen him. Sentencing when his lawyer had trotted her out for sympathy points, maybe. But he had years left before he could even hope to be paroled. How many years had it been? Six? Maybe, she didn't know. "I *am* colorful."

"You look good, Lucky. Grown up a lot."

Lucky. Her stomach churned, and Seven fought the nausea that came with his nickname, bad memories, and childhood panic attacks. "Don't call me that."

He reached out as though he were going to touch her chin.

"Don't touch—"

Adelia stepped in front of Seven. "Like hell."

Her dad smirked. "And who is this Latin beauty? Holding hands, defending her?" He inched his obtrusive hand back. "Did my lucky girl turn into a dyke?"

Seven's molars ground, and a headache pulsed at her temples. Engaging with Cullen Blackburn was an exercise in stupidity, but so was avoiding his behavior. "Find your respect for the MC. This is Tex's daughter." Still holding onto Adelia's hand, Seven squeezed back. "I've got him. Will you go to my mom? Make sure she's okay?"

"Sure thing." Adelia took off for Taini, and the added benefit of sending her back to Mom's room was Adelia was like a soldier. Who knew why

Seven's dad was there? But if all hell broke loose, Adelia could hold her own protecting Taini while they flagged Mayhem for backup.

Cullen cackled once she was gone. But they were not alone. The nursing home staff, including orderlies, lingered close. Her dad must've been quite the problem.

"Just you and me, kid, like old times."

Nothing would ever be like old times. "Did you break out of prison?"

His greedy grin curled onto his whisker-covered cheeks. "You don't think very highly of your pops, huh?"

"Go back to whatever hole you came from."

"Guess that's a no."

She sneered. "If they won't let you back into federal lockup, find a new hole."

He sucked his cheeks and tilted his head. "There'd be a lot of people pissed off if they heard you talking to me like that, Lucky."

Inside, she seethed, but Seven contained the gut-tearing scream. "Stop calling me Lucky."

He pulled a pack of smokes from his back pocket, tapped out a cigarette, and stuck it behind his ear. "I dunno what Mayhem and Suarez have gotten themselves into, but there are many people unhappy with decisions lately." He pocketed the box as Seven's blood ran cold. "But it worked out well for me. You got me sprung."

She couldn't swallow past the knot in her throat. The feds had let him out? What? The CIA—"Do you know Deacon Lanes?"

His eyebrows bounced. "Doesn't matter who I know, just what I'm supposed to do."

"Stay away from us. The club. Go back."

"And just when I thought it'd be a good time to work on our family relations."

It was the CIA and Deacon. They had done this. The government really was working against Hawke and wanted Mayhem to control the US cocaine distribution, and there was nothing she could do.

Mayhem was ruining her world. Johnny was coked out, speedballing meth, coming down, getting high. Her children lived in fear of people around them dropping dead from overdoses, asking if she was alive after she fell asleep on the couch with her shoes on. Jax and Titan had risked their lives to change the trajectory of the MC, and now Uncle Sam was a goddamned puppet master, pulling strings that she didn't know how to compete with. "Go away. I never want to see you again. Stay away from Mayhem."

"We both know that's never going to happen."

She didn't care, didn't have the right to say anything she thought. But it was time, and she had to make a stand. "Take off your cut."

"From *my* motorcycle club?" her dad mocked.

"I'll tell them you're working with the feds."

His face went from sarcastic to sadistic, and her dad took bold steps closer until he towered over her. "Lucky, they won't believe you, and then I will kill you." He took another step. "After those two beautiful children—"

"Get out!"

He laughed, taking a step back, and winked. "Always the Mayhem princess. It's in your blood, defending your own until the bloody end."

Seven realized more staff had gathered as though she might need help. Or maybe for Sweet Hills gossip. She'd worked so hard to remove herself from association with Cullen and build a new reputation for her and her mom. "You need to leave."

"Then we'll have this conversation elsewhere." He nodded goodbye to onlookers. "I'll see you at your house on Landover."

He knew where she lived... Numbly, Seven rushed past the check-in desk as the Harley roared out of the parking lot.

CHAPTER FIFTY-ONE

S EVEN HELD A mug of coffee between her hands as she paced the length of her kitchen table, watching her father make origami creations out of her mail pile.

He might think that he was cool under pressure, but she knew better. As far back as she could remember, he would make pyramids and buildings out of the junk mail when he was nervous. Cullen would fidget with whatever crisp paper was at his disposal.

It had driven her mother silly. That was how they had always been able to tell when times were tough or Mayhem business was toeing the edge of a brutal decision, from the number of accordion-shaped pieces of paper stacked around the house and pinned down by beer bottles and lighters. No doubt Cullen's time in lockup had only expanded his origami talents— though he'd always gotten in a piss whenever she called it that, saying that was a girly word, that he was just folding shit.

Either way, she knew he wasn't as confident as he seemed.

"You have me alone. What do you want to say here that you couldn't possibly say there?" Seven backed against the wall, inhaling the scent of coffee to keep her calm. She leaned against the wall as though it were just a casual conversation and not one that she'd thought she had years to plan for.

He tossed his papers aside, and Seven gripped her coffee mug as the mess went in every direction, no order to how it landed. Even though he took time to stack and crease the papers, when they landed zigzag, on top of one another, the mess was like fingernails down a chalkboard to her. She wrenched her eyes back to her dad, and he pushed his chair onto the back two legs.

"You know? You disappoint me."

Her arms dropped a few inches, but she stopped their freefall, pulling the coffee mug against her chest. He could not bait her. He could not shock her. That needed to be the day's mantra. Seven painted on a fuck-you smile like it was war paint. "The feeling's mutual, *Dad*."

"I wonder if Johnny feels the same." He crashed down on all four legs of the chair to punctuate his thoughts.

"The only thing Johnny cares about right now is blow. So I'm sure it's fine. Is that what you came here to talk about? My ex? Your ex?"

"Sure, Lucky. Family. Loyalty. Where's your loyalty, kid? Your pop shows up out of the clink after six years, and that's how you act?" He raised a cocky eyebrow. "Sounds to me like you have too many masters."

Her heart beat faster, hating that even behind bars he was able to get information about her. "So long as my master isn't you, I'm doing all right in life. If that's what you had to say, just go to the compound. We'll be polite with each other if I'm there. I won't get in your way. Whatever it is that you're here to do, I think they're smarter than you are."

Her dad shook his head, chuckling as though Seven were mistaken. "You still listen to me. Otherwise, we wouldn't be here, talking. You serve foolish masters and don't even know. But this is where your loyalty should be. Always with me. Not with your coffee shop. Not with those new bloods, who think they know better about my club."

Seven's heart jumped as he called it his club. It hadn't been his in a long time, and even though Mayhem had him on a pedestal, Cullen Blackburn was old news and no longer president. He was too dangerous and wanted things the club didn't need. It wasn't the intention of how he had set it up to begin with. That was what she could recall from when she was little—the great stories about why Mayhem had come to be. The talks about brotherhood and about bikes. The belief in Harleys as a lifestyle, the power of the open road. Not what they had become—greed and corruption and power.

The front door opened as the terrifyingly beautiful sound of Nolan and Bianca ran inside followed by Glamma trailing them. "Get a clean shirt. Next time, I'll find a smock first."

The temperature of the room plummeted to subzero, and Seven jumped in front of her dad as he stood. "Don't you dare go over there," she hissed.

"You want me to miss a chance to see my grandbabies—two other *things* that you're a slave to."

Tunnel vision was in full effect, and her hands itched to push him away, force him out of their world, away from what she loved best. "Don't go back there."

"At least you don't have a man who's your master too. Maybe that is the one benefit of Johnny choosing the powder over you."

"Oh—oh!" Gennita stepped into the kitchen behind Seven, and she had not heard the older woman even coming.

Masters and loyalty. The kids had been kidnapped. Her dad. There was so much in the tornado of chaos happening right now that Seven wanted to scream, and she hadn't even heard someone coming near—even though Gennita was as safe as one could be. Seven needed to clean up her life, control things more... better. She turned around, eyes imploring Gennita to get the kids out of the house.

"We'll be going. Right now." She backed out of the room, smart enough not to turn her back on Cullen Blackburn, and called to Bianca and Nolan that they were leaving that second, new shirts or not.

The door slammed shut, and Seven turned back to her dad.

Those babies, Nolan and Bianca, those were who she was supposed to be loyal to. That was who she was supposed to protect from horrible, life-sucking decisions and people like her dad and their dad. She was supposed to be their mother, their protector. "Get out." Cullen didn't move. "Get. Out!"

It was all she could say. Over and over and over until she saw his boots moving then heard the door close and his Harley roar away.

The sun was out, but her world was squeezing down. The walls inched in closer as the ceiling dropped, and the floor held her feet with every step, making walking an effort. Breaths were harder to take as she cleaned up her father's pile, first trying to smooth out the papers and fold them the way they should be then failing and shoving them in the trash can, where they mocked her, calling to her, making her skin crawl.

"Holy shit. This is too much," she whispered as her cell phone rang. Unable to catch her breath, Seven glanced at the screen. Adelia. She could handle Seven's mother fine.

Seven scooped every piece of paper that her father had folded out of the trash and brought them to her sink then lit a match and watched them burn. The black smoke was stronger than she'd expected, and the fire alarm beeped in her hallway, making her head pound as the alarm screamed. "Shit." She ran to the couch and grabbed a pillow, knocking over the blankets as she moved to fan the fire alarm.

Finally, the siren stopped. She was panting, not from effort or exertion, but from the mental toll that this exasperation had taken on her. The blankets were on the floor, and she wanted to pick them up immediately, but she forced herself to go to the kitchen, wash the ashes down her sink, and scrub them away.

This was too much. Tears burned her eyelids, and she had to force herself to slap off the water faucet. It felt as though Seven were drowning as the water dripped to a stop.

She turned, unable to look at each drop, and rushed to the living room to pick up the blankets, folding them as precisely as she could, when her phone rang again. Shoot, she didn't have time to talk to Adelia.

She didn't have time for any of this!

After the last blanket was folded and everything was stacked the way it needed to be, she walked over and picked up her phone, fingers shaking, and saw the text message.

JAX: *Hey. I wanted to say hi. I won't be able to talk for a few days. If you're around now, that'd be cool.*

She swiped the message open as though she were going to type something, but she had no idea what as overwhelmed tears spilled.

Her dad's words about loyalty and serving too many masters circled in her head as chaos erupted like a volcano, poisoning her thoughts. All she could see was Bianca and Nolan's faces and how she had failed them. Her crushed heart hadn't dared even ask them how scared they had been when they were taken.

There was only one thing that she could be responsible for. It wasn't herself. It was her kids. Seven threw the phone onto the couch, and her tears refused to stop until she walked away, leaving Jax's message on the couch. With her dad's voice in her head, Seven kept walking out the front door to Gennita's house to be with her kids.

CHAPTER FIFTY-TWO

A LOUD KNOCK rapped on the door, and Seven knew it was Jax without looking through the peephole.

"It's been five days, princess." *Bang, bang, bang.*

She wouldn't be stupid enough to ask five days since what. Lenora had let Seven know five days ago that Jax had been served with divorce papers. All he had to do was sign. Same with her, though she hadn't signed, either. They sat, ready with a pen, on the counter for the right moment.

"Sidney said you weren't at work, and Gennita dished. You're home."

Seven scowled at the door. Jax was making phone calls? "Coming." She opened the door. "People are going to talk if you start making calls like that."

He brushed by her. "Let 'em talk."

"Easy for you to say. You don't live here." And he hadn't had to do decades' worth of reputation repair, thanks to dear old dad. There were still people talking about the stunt her father had pulled at the nursing home. She'd had to apologize to the staff there, and the stink about town that had started was almost more than she could handle.

Her dad was out of prison. Years early. It made her sick. At any minute, the bastard could show up and point a motor-oil-stained finger, questioning her fitness as a mother, her loyalty, her drive. She would be ready next time. Her defenses would be up. Cullen Blackburn wouldn't ruin her life again.

Except that was all she could think about.

"Seven," Jax said, standing in front of her. "I don't want a divorce. Are you listening?"

"No." She walked to the kitchen. Honesty was the best policy, at least when she had a clue what was going on in her head. Since she had come back from Colombia and crashed into her dad, it seemed as though that wasn't as often as it should be.

"What are you going to do? Move to Iowa? Get a job at the bank?" She shrugged then reached for the paperwork and pen. Now was as good of a time as any. She'd been waiting for the perfect time, but maybe it didn't exist. They could both sign her copy, and Lenora could file today and be done with it. Seven could pretend the last few weeks of her life were a dream. "The only thing I need to do is raise Nolan and Bianca so that they can have a normal life. It's the right thing to do."

His lips twisted. "The right thing?"

How could doing the right thing feel so wrong? Seven held on to the pen, paralyzed and terrified. The right decision was in front of her. There was no logical reason they should be married.

"You haven't signed? I'm surprised."

"I've been busy," she said.

"Then sign already." Tension ticked at the corners of Jax's eyes. "If that's what you want to do."

What she wanted and needed were polar opposites, and damn him, she didn't want to cry. "You don't have to be an asshole."

"I *am* an asshole, Seven. If there's one thing you've known about me for years, it's that I'm—" He crossed his arms and worked his jaw back and forth in silence. "What'd you call me? I'm a *jerkface*. Right?" He smirked. "Cute, by the way."

He wasn't an asshole or a jerkface. He was… Jax. And he was being that way to prove her point—that she knew him better than most who maybe thought that was true.

There was a right way and a wrong way, and she had spent her entire life trying to get away from the wrong way of doing things.

"Hell. Put the pen down."

"I can't." She squeezed her eyes shut, ignoring the small urge to listen. Tension wrecked her. The chaos and her need to organize it were driving her to the point that simple right and wrong, black and white were an upside-down gray mess.

"Princess, give me the pen." Jax pushed away from the wall and rounded the table, dropping down so they were face-to-face.

Her right arm ached from the intense force with which she held the pen, and dropping the pen seemed wrong, but handing it to him—hell, he had to sign, anyway.

Trust Jax.

He trusted her. She jolted like a rusty robot and thrust her hand to his. He clasped both hands around hers. "Don't sign that."

"We don't even remember getting married."

"That's bullshit. Maybe a few details are fuzzy. But stop fighting it and tell me you don't remember that night."

"I don't," she lied. Every night, dreams came to her. True or not, she became more confused about fiction and reality.

Jax stood up, tugging her hand. "On your feet."

Gently, the brooding man pushed back the chair and gave another tug until she stood. Jax removed the pen from her loose grip and placed it next to the paper then gathered both her hands in his. Seven let her eyes drift shut as she rested her chin on his sternum.

"There was Elvis in sequins," he said quietly. "Desserts that you were *way* too excited about."

She quietly laughed then placed her cheek against his heart. "We should blame the bakers for this mess."

His chest rumbled, and he played with her hair. "Do you remember giving the over-under on whether couples would last?"

No… "*Yes!*" They'd agreed most wouldn't make it past the end of the year. Jax had said a few of the couples wouldn't make it past the end of the month. But she bit her tongue at that realization, eyes wide open, because it was *Seven* who'd said she bet they would last forever.

Heat hit her cheeks, but it wasn't embarrassment. She had pushed that first domino, causing the chain of reactions to where they stood now.

"We can't get married." Jax picked up her hand. "No engagement ring. There's been no proposal."

She rolled her eyes then took the last bite of her cake between her fingers and pushed it to his lips, giggling as he finished the bite then licked the last of the icing.

"I don't need a ring. I don't want anything."

"You're crazy, Seven."

"For you. So. Very. True."

He pulled her close and kissed her. "Tell me what you want."

"Simple." She wrapped her arms around his neck. "Just you. Jax."

"That sounded a helluva lot like a proposal, princess. Better be careful. Otherwise, I'll take you up on that."

"I forgot about the part where this was my idea." Seven pulled away, convinced this was the perfect time to rearrange her laundry. When he took her by the elbow, she grimaced. "Now's as good of a time as ever to tell you that I have a... nervous tic."

He let go of her elbow, reached for the counter, and tossed a hand towel her way. "Fold it all you want. If it makes you feel better, I don't care."

"It's more like a compulsion at times."

"Do you want to talk about that now instead of divorcing me?" he asked.

She smoothed the towel on the table. "I'd rather not discuss either."

"Your plan was to never pick up the phone again?" Jax smiled. "Seems very un-Seven-like."

"Similar to marrying someone in Vegas. It goes hand in hand." Methodically folding the towel was so simple. "I didn't think about how or why we were married. I only tried to fix what wasn't planned. Look, I have to focus on my kids. That's it. Not me. Not you. *Them.*"

Jax pulled away abruptly. "Sorry to drop a rainbow bomb on all your self-sacrifice, but your belief in smiles and sunshine is supposed to surpass all of my grumblings. Your hair is pink for God's sakes. It's a happy freakin' color because you're a true believer in this stuff. Don't shy away from me now because something didn't go as planned. That's life, and you roll with it."

"You're not supposed to roll with marriage."

He closed in on her. "You are if you love the guy."

The world stopped spinning. Seven stopped breathing. Jax's piercing eyes glared, and his hard-set jaw clenched as though he challenged her to say anything but the truth she had been denying.

There weren't enough ways to tell him how grateful she was to him for bringing her kids home, how much they idolized him, and how desperately she needed him. She couldn't begin to count the times she'd smiled by herself, knowing she loved him.

How many masters do you serve? Seven squeezed her eyes shut, unable to get her father out of her head. Nolan had had nightmares every night since he'd come home, and Bianca was even more wary of the world than she had been before the kidnapping.

"I have to focus on them. Not me." Seven reached for the pen, and— Jax grabbed it and threw it across the room. "What the—?"

"Do you know what scares me?" he asked.

She was shaken by the somberness in his tone and how he'd launched the pen away. "Nothing scares you."

He laughed hollowly and stared out the dining room window before moving to the living room. Seven followed, and Jax put his hands on her shoulders, guiding her to the couch, but didn't join her. Instead, he paced the area rug for what felt like hours as he battled whatever his internal demon was.

"Are you okay?" But really, what was the answer? She was asking for a divorce from a marriage she was scared of wanting.

Jax stopped and pulled an ottoman in front of her then sat so they were eye to eye. "You think I'm not terrified to lose you?" He shook his head and pinched the bridge of his nose. "I never thought about the future outside of my SEAL team, and Carrie probably never thought about hers outside the Agency. But you? Seven…"

Seven's stomach turned, not in jealousy but from the unknown and distant sadness she couldn't pinpoint. She hated the idea that he'd been hurt and that she'd called him out on a pain she couldn't comprehend.

Jax dropped his hand. "Until I crashed into you? I thought I knew what sharing my life with another person was about, and I didn't know that part was incomplete until I met you—*and* your dynamic duo."

"Jax, stop." Why did he have to say things like that? "There are so many parts of me that you don't know or even like."

"Like what?"

Cullen Blackburn was too complicated a discussion. "Mayhem."

Jax cackled. "You have no idea what I think about Mayhem. You haven't asked, and my opinion is evolving."

She rubbed her temples. "Why are you—"

Fighting for me?

So perfect?

Stronger than me?

The list could go on, when it seemed like she was drowning. "Just... why?"

"You're *my wife*, Seven. That has to count for something."

Her heart shredded into a thousand bleeding ribbons of love she had to deny. There were so many real-life implications of their carelessness; the worst of which was her falling for him when she had no way to break free from the invisible chains she'd bound herself in. "Please stop talking."

His heart broke in front of her, and she shattered on the inside, turning to stone on the outside.

"What a sad fucking joke." Jax's crestfallen face hardened as he walked out. The door slammed behind him, and Seven knew it would be the last time she talked to him.

CHAPTER FIFTY-THREE

THE LIGHTS IN the small office at the back of The Perky Cup were low, and the air smelled like blueberry muffins freshly topped with crystallized sugar. Seven spun a plate littered with scone crumbs and finished her final bite. No matter how many times she went over the bank account statements for the month, there was one day that she just couldn't figure out.

This month had a day with astronomical sales. Sidney had more than sold out. But that was the problem—he had *more* than sold out. It was impossible for him to have made as much money on baked goods and coffee as he had. There wasn't enough flour and sugar in all The Perky Cup storage containers to make that many consumables, and on top of that, he had been short-staffed.

She'd gone through the credit card transactions so many times, she had a headache, and everything matched up. There were no weird charges, which left only cash. Which there was a lot of.

She stood up and stuck her head out the door. "Sidney, can you come back here one more time?"

She stared at the list of everything he said he'd sold and what the bank statement reported for deposits. "I hate to beat a dead horse. Again. But there's no way we sold this much. I'm not sure how you have forgotten making and selling an extra"—she hummed as she calculated in her head—"five hundred pastry items in a day, but if this is some sort of charity or you feel bad about what happened and you're trying to..." She let her voice trail off because she had no idea what to say. He didn't have that kind of extra money lying around. "Sidney, what is going on?"

The bells on the front door jingled, and Sidney turned. "I'm going to go make more mystery money. Try not to freak out when you see it at the bank."

Seven went back to her desk, still confused. She could just roll with it, or perhaps she was hyperfocused on a nonissue to avoid thinking about Jax.

Life lesson number… Oh well, she'd lost count by now. Another life lesson learned in very short order: Mental pain was physically anguishing. It had been far too long since she'd seen or talked to Jax, and heartbreak was a real thing. The stars in the sky had lost their diamond shimmer, colors had gone to gray, and maybe she would even look better as a brunette or a blonde.

The door pushed open, and Adelia popped in. "What the hell? I call, and I text, and no answer." She threw her hands out. "Feeling a little neglected, just so you know."

"You're not the only one I'm ignoring if it makes you feel any better."

Adelia's beautiful dark eyes narrowed. "Oh, sweetheart. I know. That's why I'm here. We're going to talk."

Seven shut her accounting book and pushed her calculator away, giving up on the day. Pretty much giving up on everything at that moment except for sulking. She leaned back in her chair, not wanting to hear what Adelia had to say. Seven's dad had been right. Her mind was focused in too many different directions, and she needed to focus only on one thing—her kids, because she screwed up when she tried to do too much else. They wouldn't have been in danger, they never would have been abducted, if she had just stuck to watching them and earning a living. No Mayhem and no falling in love.

"Oh God, you're going to cry. You're worse than I thought," Adelia snipped. "We need to talk about Jax."

Her desk phone rang, and Seven rolled her eyes, not wanting to talk to a vendor, but that was the only thing she was doing because it correlated to providing for her children. "Hang on." She picked up the phone. "This is Seven Blackburn."

"You are alive," Victoria said. "Put me on speakerphone. I want to hear Adelia also."

"*That's right, beautiful.*" Adelia smirked at Seven. "This is an intervention."

Seven rolled her eyes toward Adelia and groaned. "You guys, you're insane. I've been busy."

Adelia put her hands on her hips and inched closer to the desk. "Victoria gave her supportive 'everybody has their own issues to work through' speech before you went to Vegas. Now it's my turn, and my speech is called 'pull your head out of your ass.'"

"Co-sign!" Victoria said from speakerphone, giving her agreement.

"You don't even know what happened. You have no idea what I think or what I'm focused on."

"Wrong," Adelia said. "You're forgetting that Victoria's a private investigator. Whether or not her hands are in casts doesn't matter. The girl's a first-class snoop. We're going to tell you what we know and what we've decided. Then we're going to help you extract that pretty pink head from your derrière."

Seven couldn't handle this conversation. "Or you can leave because I have some banking issues to work through."

Victoria burst out laughing, and Adelia grinned. "We should just hop to it, then. Seems like the crowd's already warmed up."

Curious, she crossed her arms and decided to listen. "Go on."

"Do you know what Sweet Hills does best?" Victoria asked.

"Yeah." Seven laughed as well, noting the irony. "They get in other people's business."

"Victoria talked to Gennita. Glammas don't miss anything, honey. And when Cullen was dropping his *loyalty* speech, your neighbor picked up every single, arrogant, awful word." Adelia's smile softened. "You can't just dedicate your life to those kids as an excuse to shelter yourself. You can't make everything perfect for them because of what they went through, and even if you could, it won't make up for what you went through."

"Plus," Victoria added, "you'll miss out on the best things."

A knot formed in Seven's throat. "*They* are the best things."

"No, honey," Adelia said. "Love is. Family is. Stop suffering to make them happy. Otherwise, you've become Taini, and they've become

Mayhem. I don't know what your father is in this metaphor other than your internal self-suffering, but you're creating sacrifice to avoid pain."

Seven tried to swallow. She wanted to defend secluding herself away from the world but couldn't.

"Have you talked to Jax lately?" Victoria asked.

Seven shook her head.

"She shook her head," Adelia said for the benefit of Victoria. Then she raised her eyebrows and put her hands on the desk, leaning close to Seven. "We know."

"Of course you do," Seven mumbled.

"Now for the audio presentation." Adelia grabbed her purse. "There's something you need to hear, and you can thank Victoria for harassing her poor husband."

"Eh, he can take it," Victoria said.

"And you can thank Jax," Adelia continued, "for having an attitude bad enough that Titan tapped his phone lines." She pressed the play icon on her cell phone, and Jax's voice flooded the room. Seven wanted to cry simply from hearing the sound of his voice, but the three of them listened as he put Ingrid in place for suggesting Seven didn't want to come to the nursing home and then paid Sydney to close down the bakery. Jax took care of the costs so the coffee shop wouldn't suffer and made sure her mom would have a trusted face, and he did it all with a few phone calls never meant for her to hear.

"Now that's a Titan man," Victoria whispered.

Seven sat back in her chair, and it wasn't until Adelia handed her a tissue that she realized the tears were streaming down her cheeks.

"Oh God, I've made a terrible mistake."

CHAPTER FIFTY-FOUR

THE SCENT OF gun oil permeated the air as Jax finished cleaning his .38 caliber revolver and reassembled it. He checked the grip and appreciated how the solid weight had remained dependable throughout his life. It would fire in anything. Sand. Dirt. He trusted that gun and could recall the first time he picked it up. That cold metal still felt the same some twenty years later.

As Jax was sighting the gun, Winters walked into the storage locker, and Jax dropped it down. "Hey, man. Wanna go over to the range?"

There had been a subtle change in the last few weeks since the Vegas conversation with Jared, and Jax didn't think Jared had said anything to the team or that his own attitude had changed. Still, there had been a shift in perspective after news had quietly gotten out about his background and how he'd almost lost those he most cared for.

Or did lose. But Seven was still breathing, and they were still married so he didn't know what to think.

"I was on my way up to ask you the same thing, but Brock caught me. He wants to talk to you and said to head over his way."

Jax nodded, unsure what that was about, but he stored his weapon in a locker and washed his hands then made his way to where he knew Brock was working.

After a quick knock, Jax walked into a smaller conference room and saw the pile of papers surrounded by multiple cups of coffee that kept his boss going.

"Winters said you were looking for me."

"Actually, we're playing a game of messenger. Head on down to the war room."

Jax pursed his lips together and thought better of asking Brock why when there were four empty cups of caffeine and two weeks' worth of paperwork in front of him. "Will do."

After a few twists and turns through Titan security, including a retina scan, a thumbprint, then a swipe of his ID badge, Jax reached the other side of headquarters and walked into the war room.

Rather, walked into an empty room.

No signs of life. No cups of coffee. No sign of Boss Man's bulldog. Jax decided to take a seat and give Jared or Parker a minute to show up before texting Brock and—

The door opened with Seven clinging to its handle.

"Seven." He hit his feet as his heart jumped. "I had no idea you were here."

"I was." She pointed toward the hall. "But I went to the bathroom. Now here you are."

Seven crept into the war room but still hadn't let go of the door handle, and Jax wanted to take her in his arms and just hang on, but the last time he'd seen her... Not a great moment. She had trapped him in here with her divorce papers and excuses. *Sucks...*

Even still, he'd never needed to kiss a woman as badly as he did at that moment. "Do you want to come in?"

Nodding, she finally let go, and the door drifted shut. The click echoed around them. She didn't move to a chair, instead hovering in the open space. He watched intently, trying to figure out why she was at Titan headquarters. "Everything okay?"

"Yes."

"I give up, Seven. Just tell me why you're here."

She squeezed her eyes tight and dropped her chin, and with that painful look, his soul fell too. The day of divorce papers. *Damn it.*

"Jax, I don't know if you can ever forgive me."

He didn't want to hear a speech; he didn't want to hear any of this.

"But..." Her voice cracked.

"But..." he repeated and reached for a defense of mock and retaliation. It wasn't there. He couldn't be an asshole, couldn't hurt her because he wished he had her as his wife.

Flinching, she waited for the verbal punch, but it never landed, and she met his eyes. "I don't know if… you can forgive me. I made a mistake, and I'm sorry. I hurt you, us. And I probably will never be able to get that back." Tears spilled down her cheeks as he tried to make sense of what she was saying. "If you could ever forgive me—"

His brow furrowed as he replayed her words. The woman didn't take his calls or texts. "Stop." He swooped forward and pulled her soft body into his arms, exhaling with his smile buried against her hair. "Stop apologizing."

"It needs to be said." She sniffled. "I screwed up. I saw one thing that wasn't even there when it was just you wanting to be with me the whole time."

He squeezed her tight and rested his chin on top of her head. "A couple weeks ago, a great man who I thought never made mistakes showed me it's possible to have a filter over your eyes and not know it."

"What's that have to do with me?" Seven asked.

"Adelia and Victoria told me that your dad's back and how he got in your face, in your head."

Seven dropped her eyes as though she were hiding. "I can't believe they did that."

"I'm glad they did. It helped me understand more about you—and me. I had to forgive myself, princess."

"Why?"

"I couldn't save Carrie. I'm not God. It couldn't be done. But I had to forgive myself."

Seven inched back and tilted her face up. "That's different. I should've known better."

"Believe it or not, beautiful, I knew I wasn't God."

"I know my dad and the things he does. I should've seen it and changed courses. He'll never go away." She bit her lip. "He'll try again."

"Lean on me."

"You don't know what you're asking. That's a lot to say. I-I'm too much." She looked heartbroken and even disgusted. Jax didn't know if it was because of her family, her background, the things she couldn't control, or the decision she had made, but it did nothing except reaffirm everything he felt for her. "More than anything, I needed you to know how sorry I was."

He took a step back and ran his hands over her biceps, smoothing up and down. "You think you're too much?"

She snickered. "Yes, I think I'm too much."

"You are—for someone else. Those people? They aren't our people. And not the person you're supposed to be with, princess."

Her eyes rounded as though she were having a revelation.

"Seven." He let go of an arm and touched her chin. "*I'm* too much."

She laughed quietly. "No, you're not."

"There are many people who'd disagree with you on that. Trust me." He brushed her hair off her face and smoothed it behind her ears. "Come here, princess, I have something to tell you."

She inched closer. "What?"

"I love you, Seven."

"When I first met you, I had no idea that I'd get to say *I love you too*."

EPILOGUE

"GIVE ME MY bag!" Bianca threw a fistful of leftover birdseed at Nolan. "How are we supposed to win if he doesn't gimme my bag?"

"Oh yeah." Adelia pointed at Bianca. "She has a point. If you don't hustle, you're going to lose—"

"Adelia!" Gennita tried to stop the impending disaster before it crashed, but it was too late.

Bianca's bottom lip began to quiver. All the sugar from the cake had gone straight to her blood, and Seven's kids were in the process of losing their ever-loving minds.

Nolan spun around in a circle, his bag and Bianca's in each hand, filling them with air.

"Nolan." Seven scooped him up as Jax went in for the crier. "You're going to puke. Stop spinning."

Jax sat next to Seven as she settled back into her chair. With Bianca now on his knee and Nolan thankfully not spinning, he fixed the fuchsia bow in the little girl's hair. "You know what, buttercup?"

Bianca sniffled. "What?"

"I hid every ring."

She brightened, tears instantly gone. "Where?"

"Get your brother, and I'll tell you where the one no one will find is."

Bianca hopped off, hugging Nolan and dragging him back to Jax. "We're ready."

"Under the bubble refill station."

Her eyes went wide. "*Under it?*"

"Yes." He leaned down. "That's top secret. Tell no one and get it without being seen. *Go.*"

Both kids snuck into the crowd, and Seven laughed. "How very Titan of you."

Jax leaned close, stealing a kiss but letting it linger as she sighed. "Oh!"

He slid her onto his lap. "Where are you? Somewhere in here…"

"Stop it." She pulled the skirt from under her, readjusting. "Better?"

"Better when I take this dress off of you," he teased. "But until then…" He dropped a kiss on her shoulder, and they looked over as Adelia gagged.

"You know I'm still here, right?"

"You could always go hunt for plastic rings with the kids," Jax said. "I hid a few hundred all over the place. You're bound to get one somehow."

"You're lucky I love that guy." Adelia eyed Seven and pointed at Jax. "And that he looks good in a tux. Because he's toeing the line of getting slapped."

Jax chuckled. "Worked out well for me last time I was slapped at a wedding."

"Actually, it didn't." Seven turned, shaking her head. "You were denied."

"I played the long game, princess, and got married."

"Twice," Adelia pointed out.

And this one knocked every hope and dream off the wedding wish list, all the way up to the organ music and big poufy dress.

"I get two honeymoons," Jax added. "Bonus."

Though this one wouldn't involve a hangover or cartel but rather an all-inclusive resort and pampering.

Colin walked up with Victoria and Ryder. She was tucked under her husband's arm as she and Colin tried to jam two plastic puzzle pieces together. One was a heart, and the other a key.

Ryder just shook his head then eyed Seven. "These games were all your idea?"

"Absolutely. I wanted to make sure everyone talked to each other." Seven had even made signs for the church that said there was no such thing as sides; anyone could sit anywhere. But when she had seen how much fun Jax had putting the kid games together, it was a natural fit to add adult icebreaker games as well.

Ryder winked at his wife. "She's going to sulk all night long that I didn't unlock her heart."

"My key is heartless," Colin added.

"*You're* heartless." Ryder craned his neck. "I gave my heart to Hawke, and look at the guy"—they all followed Ryder's nod—"making out in the corner with someone half his age. I'd like to think I had something to do with that."

"Ugh, things I never wanted to see! Hawke getting his groove on." Victoria's face pinched. Then she turned to Seven and Jax. "You guys good?"

Seven beamed. "In heaven."

"Good. Because I want to dance so I won't sulk." Victoria pulled Ryder up as he groaned.

"She's using me for my moves."

"Well, I'm not good." Adelia pouted, holding up her partnerless puzzle piece. "And I've looked everywhere."

Colin flipped his key in the air. "Didn't ask me, either, V. The non-married crowd is feeling excluded."

Victoria playfully huffed as Ryder came behind her and wrapped his arms around her waist. "Oh, for goodness sake, you two. Did you even try your puzzle pieces together?"

Colin laughed at the oblivious mistake, holding his out to Adelia. "Now you're blowing us both off."

Adelia feigned disillusioned agreement, not paying attention as she pushed the key toward Colin. "They can't help it if—" Her head snapped toward the connected heart-and-key puzzle then up. "*Colin!* You had the key to my heart the whole time!"

Victoria's mouth fell open—even Ryder seemed surprised, raising a hand. "I brought him over. I claim this couple, too."

Seven leaned against Jax. "Aw, I even heard them click."

"That's not a couple. It's a game."

"It's whatever happens." Ryder snuggled close to Victoria as Adelia threw her arms around Colin. "Let's go, love."

It was as though Seven saw hearts bubbling above the forming connection. She took Ryder's cue, turning to her husband as Jax ran a hand down the intricate buttons on the back of her wedding dress.

"Come on, princess. Time to dance again."

Seven pursed her lips because Jax *never* wanted to dance. Even he could see that there was a moment unfolding. "So that's how it's done."

"What?" he asked.

She pulled her heavy dress up as she slid off his lap. "A meet-cute at a wedding that doesn't involve a slap."

"Hardy-har." He winked. "Let's see you shake your booty, babe." Then he followed Ryder and Victoria.

Seven fluffed out her princess skirt, catching sight of a linen napkin that either Ryder or Victoria had accidentally knocked onto the floor, out of her reach. It was barricaded by chairs and next to Colin and Adelia, who were still very much in their moment.

Seven's pulse tripped, and she wanted to look away but couldn't.

"Seven?" Jax made a face. "What's the holdup?"

He hadn't a clue about that stupid napkin mocking her, and as her blood pressure climbed, Seven watched Jax lift his hand and wait. The muscle-filled tuxedo didn't hurt, but it was the stoic man, silently promising he would always be there when she needed that helped her take that next breath. "Coming."

Seven swished toward the dance floor, holding up the layers of white tulle, silk, and lace.

Jax took a step forward. "Mrs. Michaelson?"

Her fingers took his, and over his shoulder, she saw Nolan and Bianca *Michaelson*, who he'd adopted, dancing and spinning. They were a family in every sense, but just like the day she'd signed the paperwork to change all their last names, he reminded her what she'd told him. A name was only a name.

He was simply *Jax.*

Then he reminded her they were already a family, and not because of blood, paperwork, or fluffy dresses but brought together by love, blended by choice, and dreaming toward the future together.

Seven glided into his arms, glowing with happiness. The big dresses didn't hurt. Bianca was proof of that as she jumped and fluffed hers not too far away.

"What's that look for?" Jax asked.

"In case you didn't know"—Seven pushed onto her tiptoes for another wedding-day kiss—"I will never stop falling in love with you."

ABOUT THE AUTHOR

Cristin Harber is a *New York Times* and *USA Today* bestselling romance author. She writes sexy romantic suspense, military romance, new adult, and contemporary romance. Readers voted her onto Amazon's Top Picks for Debut Romance Authors 2013, and her debut Titan series was both a #1 romantic suspense and #1 military romance bestseller.

Connect with Cristin at Cristin@CristinHarber.com or join her newsletter! Text TITAN to 66866.

The Titan Series:
Book 1: Winters Heat
Book 1.5: Sweet Girl
Book 2: Garrison's Creed
Book 3: Westin's Chase
Book 4: Gambled
Book 5: Chased
Book 6: Savage Secrets
Book 7: Hart Attack
Book 7.5: Sweet One
Book 8: Black Dawn
Book 8.5: Live Wire
Book 9: Bishop's Queen
Book 10: Locke and Key
Book 11: Jax

The Delta Series:
Book 1: Delta: Retribution
Book 2: Delta: Rescue*
Book 3: Delta: Revenge
Book 4: Delta: Redemption
Book 5: Delta: Ricochet
*The Delta Novella in Liliana Hart's MacKenzie Family Collection

The Only Series:
Book 1: Only for Him
Book 2: Only for Her
Book 3: Only for Us
Book 4: Only Forever

7 Brides for 7 Soldiers:
Ryder (#1) – Barbara Freethy
Adam (#2) – Roxanne St. Claire
Zane (#3) – Christie Ridgway
Wyatt (#4) – Lynn Raye Harris
Jack (#5) – Julia London
Noah (#6) – Cristin Harber
Ford (#7) – Samantha Chase

Each Titan, Delta, and 7 Brides book can be read as a standalone (except for Sweet Girl), but readers will likely best enjoy the series in order. The Only series must be read in order.